THE
AGENT

THE
AGENT

GEORGE V. HIGGINS

HARCOURT BRACE & COMPANY
New York   San Diego   London

Requests for permission to make copies of any part
of the work should be mailed to: Permissions Department,
Harcourt Brace & Company, 6277 Sea Harbor Drive, Orlando,
Florida 32887-6777.

Library of Congress Cataloging-in-Publication Data
Higgins, George V., 1939–
The agent: a novel/George V. Higgins.—1st ed.
p.   cm.
ISBN 0-15-100357-2
I. Title.
PS3558.I356A74   1998
813'.54—dc21   98-14624

Text set in Sabon MT
Designed by Lori McThomas Buley
Printed in the United States of America
First edition
E D C B A

THE
AGENT

PART
ONE

IN THE FLEET CENTER on Causeway Street in Boston, far below the owners' skybox where Alexander Drouhin—early sixties, trim, wavy silver hair, blue blazer, white turtleneck—sat perfectly erect across the table from Joe Corwin, the bull gang in blue uniforms was pulling up the parquet floor, exposing the hockey ice beneath. Corwin—late fifties, jowly, paunchy, weary-looking, some gray hair remaining, blue denim shirtsleeves, red knitted tie pulled down—lounged in his chair. The Celtics had lost to the Phoenix Suns that afternoon, 114–96. "Caught the first'n last quarter on TV," Drouhin said. "I thought they were pathetic."

The scoreboard and clocks above center court were being tested, video images and numerals flashing across the screens and throwing white, rose, blue, and green lights on the vacant gray seats of the arena. Now and then organ music—"Tah-tah-tah, *tah,* tah-tah-tah-*tah*"—and snatches of recorded rock and roll echoed through the building.

Corwin nodded, grimacing. "Watched a little myself. Set on in my office. No one playing defense. Remember Russell, Cowens, those days? Other teams come into town, buncha run-and-gunners, they got absolutely *stuffed.* Celtics shut 'em down. Hadda turn it off."

"Well, the bright side is," Drouhin said, "at least this year they'll draft high enough to get someone, can help them. They've got the beginnings, that Walker kid, and the Williams kid has got the stuff. Assuming he doesn't report again next year looking like Namu the whale."

"I take it you don't represent him," Corwin said dryly.

"Can't fool you, can they, Joe?" Drouhin said. "But you know what *really* oughta worry them? How long'll the people wait? Reason I turned in the first wasn't to see if they'd decided to start playing again. It was to see how many were here. Only a quick guess, of course, but an educated guess—building may be new, but knowing capacities's part of my stock in trade. I'd say eleven thousand—max. I suppose as usual they announced fourteen or so, but what they had was no more'n two-thirds of the house. And when I tuned in again, I'd say half of them're gone. I realize they still sell tickets, but that's because they've got that base—the folks who still remember all the glory days when you couldn't get a ticket without mortgaging the ranch.

"Let them drift away, get out of the habit, stop buying season tickets 'fore you get the team rebuilt, you're gonna have to start all over. That could take some time. How you gonna meet the payroll while that takes its course?"

"We're not in that position, Alex," Corwin said. "That's why you came down to see me, try to peddle that lineah bullshit, you're way off the reservation. You watch our game with me tonight and look around the stands. Guarantee you, any seat you see that isn't filled, either the guy that bought the ticket for it got the flu and couldn't come, or else he had a few beers 'fore he came, one or two more here, hadda go and take a leak. We damned near fill the building every time we take the ice."

"You're not in that position *yet*," Drouhin said, his voice low, "but it's damn sure where you're *headed*. How long since you guys've won the Cup?"

Corwin scowled. "Quite a while," he said, grudgingly.

"Twenty-five years, to be precise," Drouhin said. "You're even not going to the playoffs this year, are you." It wasn't a question.

Corwin glowered at him but said nothing.

"Know offhand the last time *that* happened?" Drouhin said.

"I oughta," Corwin said. "Can't open the papers the morning, some fresh bastard doesn't remind me."

Drouhin nodded. "About thirty years ago. The Original Six. Best two played for the Stanley Cup. Bruins finished dead-last. Now how many qualify, out of *twenty*-six? Sixteen. And the Bruins're close to dead-last in the East. You know what the Rangers're going to do to you tonight and so does everyone else in the building."

"Get to the point," Corwin said. "Who're you trying to sell me?"

"Jean Methodiste," Drouhin said.

Corwin laughed. "*Jean Methodiste,*" he said. "You gotta be kidding. Why the hell would I want Methodiste? He's a proven malcontent, disruptive influence. With the press he's got a big mouth."

"*And* he's a five-time All-Star, three Vezina trophies," Drouhin said. "What he gives you's something that you really need, *right now:* credibility. Sign him and you renew it with the fans. They're starting to catch *onto* you guys, Joe—beginning to suspect you're cheaping 'em out on payroll, while you're whackin' 'em six bucks a beer.

" 'Look,' you say to the *Globe* and the *Herald,* 'we know we need to improve. This guy isn't the total answer, no—nobody is. Our defense is just okay, and we really need help on offense. But keep in mind what injuries've done.

Our first line broke down when Buck Clayton and McFeeney both went down. They'll be back next year, but in the meantime we've got kids playing on the first and second lines who we expected'd be still *learning,* on the third and fourth lines this year. But still, they're coming along. Next year they'll be gamers. And we've got some fine young talent maturing down in Providence. But in the meantime what we've got to do's find someone who can keep the *other* guys from scoring, the enemy out of our net. Hold the fort for us. Methodiste can do that. He's a proven quantity. Best career goals-against average of any goalie still active.' "

"Which's also the problem with him, of course," Corwin said. "He's also the *oldest* goalie still active. What is he now, thirty-six?"

Drouhin nodded. "Second-oldest," he said. "He's thirty-three. Thirty-four this May."

"So he's got a year left," Corwin said.

"I'd say three, maybe four," Drouhin said. "Keep in mind, all the faults you mention, guy's still always kept himself in shape. He cleans out his locker the end of the season, he weighs out at 184. He comes back, next training camp, they put him on the scale, it says 186. All summer long he's wearing pads, got juniors on Rollerblades firing pucks at him. Same as game conditions? No, not saying that, but it does keep the reflexes sharp."

"Okay, maybe two," Corwin said. "Second one as a backup. There's a couple good rookies, the draft, and this kid we've got down in Providence—erratic, but young. Talent up the yin-yang. Big investment in this kid. 'Bout time it paid off. Who knows what he does, he's twenty-two next year? Maybe turns the corner at last."

"Oh, I think there's no question he will," Drouhin said. "Fact, I think he already has. Darrell's attitude's completely different now from what it was even three months ago."

Corwin worked his tongue around the inside of his lower lip.

"Darrell Troop," he said.

"Right," Drouhin said. "That's who you're talking about, right? Read about him in the papers. 'Promising young goalie out of Junior A, Lancaster, can't seem to keep his focus.' Soldier Lucas must've told you his habits've been much better since the first of the year."

Corwin frowned. "Well, Coach Lucas said the kid's stopped doing everything in his power, every single night, to make Labatt's the best-selling beer in Providence, that's what you mean," He stopped and cleared his throat. "I thought Darrell had that guy up in Detroit for his agent— what's-his-name."

"Bob Francis," Drouhin said. "Good old what's-his-name. Bob's such a *nice, pleasant* guy, too. Can't understand why no one ever seems to remember his name. He does represent Darrell. But the end of December you sent Roger Babcock down for giving Coach Lucas some lip, and Rog, as you *know,* didn't like it. Well, while he was down there, he got to know Darrell pretty well. Took the kid under his wing, you could say. Roger's Fellowship of Christian Athletes, you may know. Had a lot to do with getting Darrell switched to ginger ale."

"And also something to say to him about who his agent should be, I take it?" Corwin said.

Drouhin shrugged. "My clients're my best salesmen, Joe," he said. "Darrell's contract with *you* runs through his second year up here. Darrell's contract with Bob Francis expires *this* year, and he told Rog he hasn't been entirely satisfied with Bob. So, one thing and another—"

Down on the floor the bull gang had finished removing the parquet and started installing the white wood and clear

Lucite dashers around the rink. The Zamboni ice machine with the Bruins "spoked-B" logos on the sides emerged from under the grandstand and began to lay down a fresh surface on the ice, steam rising behind the black rubber squeegee at the rear. Organ music blared into the empty arena, "*Boom*-boom-boom-boom. *Boom,* boom-boom-boom." Corwin and Drouhin ignored it.

"—he came to see you," Corwin said.

"No," Drouhin said, "not quite. Darrell asked me to come down and see *him,* and I did." He paused. "I believe when his agreement with Bob expires in May, he intends to sign with me."

"Which will mean that you'll be negotiating for him when he enters free agency," Corwin said.

"Most likely," Drouhin said.

Corwin nodded. "Uh *huh,*" he said. "You know, the thing I always wonder after I get through negotiating with you is where you put the hat."

" 'The hat,' " Drouhin said blankly. "I seldom wear a hat."

"That's what I mean," Corwin said. "I've never seen you wear one *in,* never seen you wear one *out,* but always after you've been in there's this humongous pile of rabbit shit on top my desk. So you must've had a big fat bunny with you that I never noticed, in the hat you didn't wear. Pulled it out while we were talking, had it shit on top my desk. Then put it away again. And as many times I've seen the results, I've never seen it happen. I still don't know how you do it."

"Thank you," Drouhin said.

"So what're we *really* talking about here?" Corwin said.

"Well," Drouhin said, "in addition to being a great acquisition for you rest of this year, PR point of view, next year Jean'd not only be your starter but a great mentor for Darrell, teach him the tricks of the trade." He paused.

"Jean very much *wants* to do this," he said. "His hope is that when his playing days're over he'll be able to move into coaching. Many goalies've done it, as you know—you had Gerry Cheevers right here, not that long ago. And Jean feels that if he can start teaching younger players now, well, it'll enhance his chances of doing it later on, in the not-too-distant future.

"And from what he knows of Darrell, well, Jean Claude thinks he's the kind of kid he'd like to work with. So *he* wants to be where the *kid's* going to be." He paused a beat. "And the kid wants to be where Jean is." He let his face show he was not allowing himself to smile.

Corwin pursed his lips.

"So what we'd have in mind for Jean," Drouhin said, "understanding his total package value to this team would be far more than just his playing skills, which are considerable, would be a two-year contract, with an option for a third year. One point five mill the first, one point three mill the second and the third, or a one-mill buyout on the third."

"Too high, Alex, way too high," Corwin said. "I'll have to think about it, talk to the head man. But tell you what I'm thinking now, what I'm going to say to him. It'd be one-one for the first, eight hundred the second, third, or a half-a-mill buyout the third."

"*Joe*," Drouhin said, "be *realistic*. Keep in mind your big investment, that what Jean wants is also what Darrell—"

His cell phone rang. "*Shit*," he said.

2

DROUHIN SAID "CALL FD" as soon as the nose of his silver Mercedes-Benz 500SL, Massachusetts registration SPR AGT, emerged from the underground garage at the Fleet Center. The voice-actuated automatic dialer on his car phone began chirping. He turned right on Causeway Street, running west, 480-watt high/low beams ("landing lights," his mechanic called them—"you could spot-weld with these things") diamond-white in the early darkness of late winter, startling the people coming into the cold and windy darkness from the subway under the Center. The lights froze those on the northerly sidewalk; the muffled, hooded figures partway across Causeway moved faster into the deeper shadows under the elevated trolley tracks toward the red, green, white, and blue neon beer signs glowing in the windows of the bars along the southerly side. He had made the left turn onto Stanhope when the phone connected.

"You have reached the Whitman residence," a woman's recorded voice said. "We can't come to the phone just now, but if—"

"Get on the phone, FD," Drouhin said. "Fire drill in progress."

Franklin Delano Roosevelt Whitman said: "What's the occasion, Alex? You get Corwin so upset he had another heart attack?"

"Nothin' like that," Drouhin said, taking the right off Stanhope onto Cambridge Street west. "Matter of fact, goddammit, I had Joe seeing things exactly our way. 'Nother forty minutes I'd've had the whole deal wrapped. Old Jean nice and comfy in his basket, tranquilized for three more years, Darrell all positioned for a primo deal two years from now. That's what *really* annoys me about this. Joe can *be* convinced, but he doesn't *stay* convinced. He talks to the GM, and you know how Phil is. Regular tower of Jell-O."

Drouhin made his voice whiny. " '*Gee,* Joe, I don't *know,* you know? That's an *awful* lot of money. I'm not interfering now. It's your job and you do it the way you think it should be done. You do what you think is right, but be sure it really *is.*'

"And old Joe thinks, 'Yeah, and if it isn't, my head's on the block.' Time I get back to him, he'll be chugalugging Maalox, having third and *fourth* thoughts. I'll have to start all over. Can't be helped, though. Buffalo Bobby's in the slammer again. We've got to go get him out."

There was a long pause. "Glenda's making turkey with oyster stuffing," Whitman said.

"Sorry," Drouhin said. "Moreno's making four point three a year plus incentives. We've got nine mill he already earned under management, and if this latest escapade doesn't get too much media attention, it's possible he still can get that three-mill shoe endorsement. Which we'll also commission, of course, and then manage when we collect it. You know our piece of that kind of action. How many turkeys you figure can you buy with your share?"

Whitman sighed, "Where is he this time?" Seeing no

cross traffic approaching at the Grove Street intersection, the lights halting jaywalkers on the traffic island in the center of Cambridge Street, Drouhin doing forty-five ran a red light at the entrance to the Massachusetts General Hospital across from the Harvard Gardens bar and grill. "Lockup out in Haymarket," he said.

THE DRIVER OF A Boston Police Department cruiser parked at the curb at the easterly side of the hospital entrance started the engine and put the car into gear, flipping on the blue and white strobe lights on the roof bar. His older partner put his left hand on the driver's right arm. "You get the plate, Donald?" he said. "Get a look at the car?"

"SPR AGT," the driver said. "Big silver Merc coupe. So?"

"Make a note of the time and the date and the place," the older cop said.

"Seven oh seven, February sixteen," the driver said. "Why do all this, 'stead of busting the guy like I should? He ran a red. He's doing fifty in a hospital zone, and those're outlaw headlights."

"What do you think 'SPR AGT' stands for?" the older cop said.

The driver frowned. " 'Spring Agitator'? I dunno."

"Try 'Super Agent,' " the older cop said. "That mean anything to you?"

"Might if I knew who it was," the driver said. "Who the hell is he, James Bond?"

"He's Alexander Drouhin, the sports agent," the older cop said.

"So the fuck difference does that make?" the driver said. "Sports agents get to run lights?"

"They do if they're careful doing it," the older cop said.

"You know what they say in the NBA: 'No harm, no foul.' *And* if they appreciate small courtesies."

"What does that mean?" the driver said.

"What's your favorite professional sport?" the older cop said.

The driver shrugged. "Patriots," he said. "Drive me nuts, but I do like the team. Got season tickets in fact. My father can't understand it. *He's* a big Red Sox fan. *I* can't understand that."

"Think he'd like box seats behind home plate, Opening Day this year?" the older cop said.

The driver turned and looked at the older cop. "Well yeah, he might," he said. "He'd kill for them, in fact. But those're hard to get."

The older cop settled himself into the seat. "Tomorrow or Tuesday, really no hurry, just make sure you're off-duty, look up Alexander Drouhin inna phone book—his office's in the Hancock. Ask to speak to his chief of security. Name's Pete Martigneau. Used to be a Statie, Norfolk DA's office, but still a moderately okay guy. Give him your name. Tell him what you just saw. Location, plate, vehicle, estimated speed, time and date. Tell him no one got hurt so you gave his boss a break, but he really should be more careful—'specially in a hospital zone, emergency vehicles, so forth—and you'd appreciate it if Pete gave him the message. He'll thank you and ask for your name, home address. Give it to him. That'll be all.

"Couple days from now a guy'll get in touch with you—he won't give his name—and ask you the same question I just asked you: what your favorite sport is. Tell him what you told me about your father. He'll tell you to go to Gate B, Opening Day, ask for your tickets. You and your dad'll be so close to the field the ump'll ask the manager how come your names aren't on the lineup card."

The driver scowled. "In other words, we let this guy do what he wants, and then he—"

"*Eeea-sy,*" the older cop said. "Remember what I said, 'No harm, no foul.' If he'd hit a meat wagon coming out of here Code Blue, creamed some poor tired intern coming back from a meatloaf dinner, I'd've been all over him like he was Jesse James. But he didn't do that, did he? And he never will. You will never see Drouhin do what he just did if there's traffic coming, or someone on foot who doesn't have the brains to wait, let him go by. You'll never catch him drunk behind the wheel. You'll never see him weaving in and out of traffic, scaring old ladies or running over dogs. Sometimes he's in kind of a hurry, but he's a better driver in a hurry'n most people are ten miles under the limit. There's enough crime around that does damage. Don't worry. We'll get our share."

" 'HAYMARKET,' " WHITMAN SAID REFLECTIVELY. "Only Haymarket I ever heard of's the fruit and vegetable push-carts down by Faneuil Hall on the weekends. Where the hell is Haymarket?"

"Worcester County," Drouhin said. "Cop Bobby had call me said it's seven, eight miles north of Fitchburg. Probably one of those jerkwater towns, makin' a buck off vice. Cities get all lathered up about some dirty movie—zone out their vices. But sin stays popular. Joints just move one town up the line. Town's got no industry, employment. What've they got to lose? Their *character* or something? No, so they say 'Okay, come right ahead, but it's gonna cost you.' Whack the joints high license fees, charge 'em all outdoors for regular inspections. Hey, it may be tawdry but it does bring in the bucks. Story of Haymarket, I gather from the cop, principal industry's gin mills, road-houses and strip joints, out along route 13. No reason why either one of us ever would've heard of it, Bobby hadn't found it."

"North of *Fitchburg?*" Whitman said. "Nobody goes to Fitchburg. Where was it the last time he got in the shit? Way the hell down in Wareham? Middleboro, some place like that?"

"I'm not sure," Drouhin said. "There've been so many. Bobby's not good at getting away with things. Bellingham once, I remember. Yeah, I think the last time was Wareham—somewhere down around the Cape, anyway."

Whitman groaned. "Why can't he ever do it somewhere around Boston? Watertown, Waltham, someplace like that, a little closer to town."

"Because he's afraid if he shows up in the red Ferrari at a strip joint around Boston, he might be conspicuous," Drouhin said. "Someone might *recognize* him. Whereas if he shows up in the red Ferrari at a gin joint in West Pisspot—"

"He'll be invisible. I get you," Whitman. "*Oh-kay,* where we meet?"

"I'm crossing Longfellow Bridge now," Drouhin said. "Taking Memorial Drive out to Fresh Pond and onto route 2. Meet me in the parking lot of the Minuteman Inn in Concord, half an hour. Know where that is, do you?"

"Yeah, right near the prison," Whitman said. "I used to go there twice a month for lunch, remember? When I went to visit Danielson, doing one to ten. For whackin' his wife around."

"Oh yeah," Drouhin said. "Well, you *were* his primary agent."

"*Hell,*" Whitman said, snickering, "I was his best *man.* They gonna have my car towed, I leave it in that lot?"

"Nah," Drouhin said. "I know the night manager. I'll give Tony a call. What's your plate again, FD?"

"Rover back," Whitman said. "RVR BCK."

"Egotist," Drouhin said. "Have three bites of turkey and see you in thirty."

"Off and clear," Whitman said. The line clicked dead.

Drouhin pulled off Fresh Pond Parkway into the parking lot of a Chevrolet dealership and dialed the number of the Minuteman Inn from memory. He asked for the night manager and told him what he wanted. "No problem, Alec," the manager said. "Can you have dinner? Excellent duckling tonight."

"I can't dammit, no," Drouhin said, putting the car into Drive and heading out of the lot. "Got an out-of-town emergency on our hands. 'Nother night with no dinner. Goes with the trade, I'm afraid."

"Ronnie was in the other day with a customer," the manager said. "Looked like she had a lot of money. They had the salmon in puff pastry. Ronnie even had a glass of wine with her. She must've bought a piece from him. He's doing well these days?"

"Very well, I'm glad to say," Drouhin said. "He said something the other night about finally unloading a Stickley dining-room set he had on consignment. 'Simply hideous,' he said. That may've been it."

"Well, it was nice to see him," the manager said, "but we *never* see you any more."

"I know it," Drouhin said, accelerating to forty-five as he entered route 2 at Fresh Pond Circle. "Come spring, I'll be back, promise you."

Once headed northwest on route 2, touching sixty, Drouhin said, "Call Julie." The phone worked and a woman answered. "Evening, boss," she said, before he spoke. "So glad you could call."

"Julie," he said, "Moreno's in the clink again, this time up in Haymarket. Get ahold of someone in Tommy

Newcombe's office out in Worcester—Tommy may be on vacation, broiling his butt in Saint Bart's, but he'll have somebody covering. Tell them I need a magistrate at the Haymarket Police Station tonight to bail Bobby out. This'll take a favor. Sunday nights they hold you for arraignment in the morning. But I do *not* want Bobby waking up in the cooler tomorrow, hungover. Neither would the cops, they know what a charmer he can be with a big head."

" 'Haymarket,' " she said.

"Right," he said. "Seven, eight miles north of Fitchburg, route 13. Newcombe's office'll know."

"Gotcha, boss," she said. "Night-night." The line clicked dead.

"Call Jean," Drouhin said. The automatic dialer went to work.

A man's voice answered hesitantly, "Yes?"

"Jean," Drouhin said. "Alex here. I said I'd get back to you."

The voice became eager: "I am moving, yes?" Methodiste said. "When will it be announced? How much did we get?"

Drouhin sighed. "You aren't moving *yet,* Jean. And I can't say for sure you will be. I still think the foundation's there for the kind of deal we want, and certainly the situation's better here in Boston for you'n it would be anywhere else. *Much* better. Here they need you. I think things're moving, the direction that we want. But there're more things still to be worked out. These things take time. There wasn't time tonight."

"They have no time," Methodiste said. "They are in the hole, deep hole. They have no defense. They have a frightened child in the goal. You have told me so yourself, that they have need of me at once. To prove that they are serious."

"*Jean,*" Drouhin said, "I didn't say 'at once.' *Because* they're in such trouble, have so many problems, *have* been playing so badly, they have the *luxury* of time, all the time in the world. They should bring you in this season, yes, to keep their fans loyal until they can rebuild the team next year. With you at the core. But it makes no difference whether they do it this week, next week, or the week after. As excellent as you are in goal, you cannot put them in the play-offs. Not this year, not by yourself. And this you also know."

"Where are you now?" Methodiste said. "As you know, I am at home. I can charter the helicopter, come and see you at your Easton place. I can be there, two hours. Pack small bag, stay over. Your house *est suffisamment.* We can talk tonight. This is most important to me, Alex, this you know. I need to talk to you."

"Jean, *Jean,*" Drouhin said, "listen to me, please. I am not at my place in Easton. I'm not even headed there. In fact I'm in my car, traveling *away* from it."

"To Boston?" Methodiste said. "I could fly to Boston. Stay in a hotel."

"Not to Boston, either, no," Drouhin said. "I am going somewhere else."

"But where?" Methodiste said. "There is no reason to go anyplace but Boston. That is where the man is who decides when I will join the team. And how much I will be paid."

"There's no reason to be anywhere but Boston when I'm dealing with *your* present business, Jean," Drouhin said. "I am not in Boston because I am going somewhere else to deal with someone *else's* business. Another client's business. An emergency has come up and I must go to deal with it."

Methodiste expelled breath loudly. "I cannot *believe*

this," he said. "You know the Islanders have not dressed me, last two games. You know they are signaling to everyone they are through with me; they will not have me back. If I do not have a new deal soon, rumors will begin, not that I am too expensive for them, which we know I am, but that there is something wrong with me. I am damaged goods. This is not so, but to have it said would be harmful, just the same. I know that you have other clients, certainly I do, but I do not see how you can believe that someone else's business is more important at this time than my business is to you. You have made much money for me, *c'est vrai,* but also have I made much for you. Surely in this extremity I should have your first concern. How—"

"Okay, Jean, I'll tell you," Drouhin said. "The emergency that's arisen is that I have a client in jail and I have to go and get him out. If I don't respond, he'll call somebody else, and that someone else will get him out. And then *they'll* have him for a client. I don't want this to happen.

"It's certainly true that you and I have prospered together over the years, and I have valued our relationship. But this man is much younger than you are now, and he's already made more money for himself, and thus for me, than you have made for both of us in your entire career."

Methodiste gasped. "You are saying *this?* To *me?* I cannot believe this."

"Believe it, Jean," Drouhin said. "I am saying it. I'm not saying it because he is a better person. He is not as *good* a person. That's why he's in jail. I'm not saying it because I like him better than I do you, or admire his character and strong sense of principle, as I do yours. I am saying it and doing it purely for business reasons.

"He has made much more money because the sport he plays, pro football, has a much higher salary scale. He makes as much in one year as you do in four, just for his play on the field. Then in addition there're all his endorsements, licenses, appearances, and so forth. It's a melancholy fact, Jean, but unless your name is Gretzky it's far more rewarding to be a great running back in football than a stickout hockey player. It's far better financially to be a wonderful baseball player or a star basketball player than it is to be a great hockey goalie because more people come to more of the games, and more people watch on TV."

He paused. "This man has one year left on his four-million-dollar contract. Five other teams today would bid *five* million dollars a year, if he were free to leave his present team, without my lifting a finger. After next year if he is healthy I will get at least twenty-four million dollars for him, six million every year.

"I can get more money for such a troublesome client, Jean, and thus more money for *me,* because there's more money to be had. Much more money than I can get for a *gentleman* like you. Five teams will bid for him. I must *persuade one* team to hire you. It's as simple as that."

Methodiste was silent. "You must be patient with me, Jean, just as I have been patient with you, many times, over the years. The trouble with Montreal, eh? Who put you with the Blackhawks? *And* got you a good deal?"

Methodiste was silent.

"Jean?" Drouhin said, "you still there?"

Methodiste sighed. "I am here," he said.

"Yes," Drouhin said. "You must allow me to work out for you carefully and well this honorable and worthy conclusion of your playing career and transition into coaching. Like Jacques Plante and Eddie Johnson, when their playing days came to an end. We grow old, Jean. This we cannot help. Let us not grow bitter, too, and forget the good things we have done together."

For a while there was no response. "Jean?" Drouhin said. "Are you still there, Jean?"

"I am saddened, Alex," Methodiste said heavily. "You will understand."

3

FD WHITMAN IN A light-gray Stetson hat, three-quarter-length brown leather car coat, green wide-wale corduroy pants, and tan cowboy boots—black; 6'1", 195; eighteen-inch neck, thirty-six-inch sleeve; thirty-six-inch waist (up two from playing days), thirty-three-inch inseam—climbed out of his dark green Range Rover when he saw Drouhin's Mercedes enter the parking lot at the Minuteman Inn. He removed the cowboy hat and locked it inside the Rover, setting the alarm. Drouhin pulled up alongside. He opened the passenger-side door and got in. "Nice night for a ride," he said. "How far you figure?"

"Thirty-five, forty," Drouhin said, swinging back out onto the roadway.

"Well, give us a chance to talk, at least," Whitman said. "Haven't been doing that often enough lately." He paused. "You've been hard to find."

"Been busy," Drouhin said, somewhat defensively.

"I know that," Whitman said. "Tonight for example. Sunday night, for God's sake. So you interrupt a meeting to travel the twenty from Boston out here. Now the forty out past Fitchburg. Then what, fifty or sixty down to Bobby's place, Natick. Then twenty more back up here to get my car, ten or fifteen home for me. Where *you* goin' to lay your head tonight, Alex? Back in Boston, I assume?"

"Can't," Drouhin said, with distaste. "Got someone coming in to Easton tomorrow, ten A.M."

"Anyone I know?" Whitman said.

"Ginny Alter," Drouhin said. "Driving up from Greenwich. Asked for an appointment. Think she's giving us the gate."

"That bothers you?" Whitman said. "I wouldn't think it would."

Drouhin sighed. "I know," he said. "She's a troublesome client. Her career hasn't followed the trajectory she or anyone else expected, won all those events eight years ago. She can't seem to come to grips with the fact that she's not sixteen anymore. *And* she's never repeated that year. She's not a draw anymore. It's just not realistic for her—or anyone else—to think we can get the kind of appearance money for her now that the newest killer teenybopper commands for the big tournaments.

"And like it or not, her coming out did *not* help her with the sponsors. Martina got away with it and so'd Billie Jean, but both of them were legends when the word got out. Ginny's never been a legend, and she's never going to be." He paused. "She's an anecdote." He paused again; he liked that.

"Very good, Alex," Whitman said, "but I don't think I'd share it with Ginny."

Drouhin snorted. "No, her ego couldn't take it. Funny isn't it, about egos—they're like boils. Infected cysts. The bigger they get, the more sensitive they become. Can't bear to have anything *touch* them. She said something to me on the phone the other day, forget now exactly what it was, but her meaning was clear enough. She suspects part of the reason she hasn't been getting the bookings she's wanted is because I'm not working hard enough for her any-more—because she's homosexual. Isn't that something?"

Whitman shifted in his seat and did not say anything for a while. Then in a slightly strangled voice he said, "Well, not too many people know about that new side of you, Alex."

The headlights swept the graceful old white, gray, and yellow houses behind the fences, scrupulously painted every five or six years, the lamps with white pleated shades centered in the six-pane windows between faultlessly furled drapes.

"And the fewer the better, right FD?" Drouhin said.

Whitman turned slightly in the passenger seat, resting his left elbow on the back of it and clasping his fingers together in front of him. "Since you bring it up, Alec, yeah. Damned *right,* the fewer the better. What you do on your own time, and who you do it with, that oughta be your business. No one else's. But over the years you've blurred the line so much between your private life and public life, it's gotten pretty hard to tell where one stops and the other one begins.

"So far you and Ronnie've been fairly discreet. At least you haven't shown up arm-in-arm at any public events yet, and nobody's seen you holding hands over veal marengo in a candlelight restaurant. But it's a *miracle*—every day I open up the papers wondering if this's the one when you and Ronnie make the gossip column. One of those wink-and-a-nod items, which the other paper then catches up with the next day, and *Boston Magazine* does a crowd-pleaser article two months from now. 'Of course *every*body *knows,* Alec and Ronnie're sweeties. Isn't it cute?'

"Day that happens, call the landlord. Tell him we're starting to issue the pink slips and we're gonna need to sublet half, two-thirds of the space by the end of the month. We'll vacate by the end of the year.

"The big dogs think being queer's catching, you know. Contagious. They find out their name-agent's gay, won't matter if Doug or McGinnis, Carl or Lionel, either the other two guys—or if *I'm* actually their main man. The name on the door's Alexander Drouhin. If he's queer then the whole agency's queer." He hesitated. "It's a real danger, Alex," he said. "A lot of people in the office think you either don't realize it, or you don't take it anywhere near serious enough. They feel threatened."

Leaving Concord, Drouhin shrugged, settling into a smooth sixty-five on the four-lane blacktop. The limit was forty-five.

"You go down, fine for you. You and Ronnie've got a big soft multimillion-dollar cushion you can land on. Spend the rest of your lives at auctions and antique shows. Having tea by the river in Florence. But the rest of us sweathogs'll be in slightly less comfortable circumstances." He let two beats go by.

"I've heard more'n one of them wonder out loud why the hell you just don't do that. '*He's* got enough, for Christ sake. If he wants to play with Ronnie, knowing what'll happen, it goes public, why the hell doesn't he just go and *play with Ronnie?* Leave his name on the door, he wants, like McDonald did when he sold the Golden Arches to Ray Kroc. Set up a buyout plan with us. But put the word out, loud and clear, *Alex Drouhin's no longer associated with Alexander Drouhin Associates. I'm taking early retirement to enjoy the fruits of my labors and the best this world has to offer.* Then beat it. Or beat Ronnie's, if that's what he wants. *Before* the shit hits the fan.' Because if it ever does, Alec, as it's bound to, sooner or later, the only hope for the serfs'll be: 'Head for the high ground.' Take as many of our clients as we can with us. Hope they don't get away, split for someone else first. Take *your* clients too, if we can."

"Oh, thanks very much," Drouhin said. "Picking over my bones, are we? You going to stab me or should I fall on my sword? You're forgetting something: Those five-year noncompete clauses all partners sign. You'll have to go on welfare."

"Alex, Alex," Whitman said. "In the first place, any decent lawyer'd chew up those clauses and spit 'em out like sunflower seeds." He did not sound convinced of this. "And in the second place, quit acting like this's news. You tell Bobby Moreno tomorrow when he sobers up that his agent's a fairy, he'll go white as a sheet and think, 'Jesus Christ. I hang around with him much more, next thing I know, I'll be goosing waiters. Blowing bellhops.' "

Drouhin laughed.

" 'S true, Alec," Whitman said, facing front again. "I can laugh at it, too, but deep down inside, it ain't funny. You got a lot of people in the office, in the know, very worried about what you and Ronnie do.

"Lionel and me, we're secure even if the agency blows up. Dougie too, to a degree. You did good things for us in our playing days. Invested our money wisely. Fact you still take half the annual profits of the firm now doesn't seem quite right—half the profits for numerically an eighth of the work—but we can live with it. Hours you put it in, you probably actually *do* about a sixth of the work. And you *are* the guy thought it all up. You laid the foundation, and dammit, you *have* made us rich. Not as rich as your-*self,* but still, rich.

"Carl and McGinnis, the junior guys—Barry and Maurice—they never were athletes. All they get's salary and share. And they work just as hard as the rest of us do.

"These're not young guys anymore, Alex. These're men either forty or crowding it, families to raise. Living beyond their means, naturally, anticipating next year's bonus, mortgaged up to their balls, tuitions staring them in the face. Depend on their jobs for their living. They lose them, they lose their *homes*.

"I said something to McGinnis the other day, how you think you got a pretty good shot at acing the Ruggles Brothers not only out of Ramon DeJesus's next Yankee contract but Humberto Manzella's next one with the Dodgers. Thought he'd be pleased, him being our top baseball guy and all. He *loves* dealing with Watson, the Yankee FO. 'Stead he got this look on his face like his doctor just told him he's got cancer of the colon. 'Fat lot of good it'll do us to get 'em, Vice Squad gets Alex and Ronnie.' "

Drouhin shifted in the driver's seat, the big two-seater rushing through the night, the bends and low hills appearing in the headlights far ahead and vanishing behind into the darkness almost at once. "Yeah," he said. "Well, tell everybody: Calm down. It's been over two years now. No one's breathed a word. It's never been that hot and heavy. We're pals more'n anything else. We've been very careful. We'll continue to be just as careful.

"I'm sorry I brought it up, actually—not that I meant to. It's just that Ginny, it struck me as funny, what she's doing. Typical of human nature. Blame *something* else, blame *someone* else, blame anything but yourself when things don't go right. It's not a matter of Ginny's lesbianism being a reason for the promoters not to invite her. They don't *care* who she goes to bed with, or what they do when they get there. It's a matter of the promoters needing a *reason* to invite her, or anybody else—and not finding one. She's just not a gate attraction anymore. Exhibitions at the Newport Casino, Tennis Hall of Fame: they're about the best she's got to hope for." He shook his head. "Jesus, sports're cruel. Twenty-four, and over the hill."

"But she's pretty well fixed, isn't she?" Whitman said.

"Oh, *yeah,*" Drouhin said. "That one year she had the hot hand, I wouldn't let her spend the money. There were times when she threatened to sue me, get at her winnings, but I'd made her parents give me guardianship powers and they backed me all the way. They had plenty of money, their own. That's how she got the coaching she did, practically from infancy. Her father was a Davis Cupper in the fifties. She's also a champion trapshooter, skeet. Had the best instruction in that, too. Her father won a silver, the Olympic biathlon—ski and shoot, ski and shoot, ski some more and shoot some more? I don't think its prospects're bright as a spectator sport, but still, a silver's a silver."

"So she was Daddy's little girl," Whitman said.

"Right," Drouhin said, "and now *she's* the daddy. Rhonda's the wife. They don't have any kids—yet, but that's the arrangement they've got."

"Ginny thinking about adopting?" Whitman said.

"*Nooo,*" Drouhin said, "Ginny's thinking about having Rhonda bear *their* child."

"Who supplies the semen?" Whitman said. "Ginny's pretty tough, I know, but I doubt she's really got balls."

"Interesting point," Drouhin said. "Rhonda's ex, apparently. Evidently a very mature fellow. No hard feelings on *his* part, his wife took off with another woman. 'That's what she wanted—hey, good for her.' He's got a new wife who likes screwing but doesn't want kids. So if Ginny's willing to—what was the word she used? 'Co-parent.' Co-parent a kid with him and Rhonda, well, he'll cooperate. His new wife's all for it, any method they prefer. The traditional method of delivering sperm, or the turkey baster, either one."

"Cheesh," Whitman said, "now *that's* broad-minded."

"It's a new and different world," Drouhin said. "You have to adapt all the time."

"How's Ginny's daddy feel about this?" Whitman said.

"Daddy's dead," Drouhin said. "So's Mommy. He was flying their Twin Beech Bonanza down to Chile—they had friends there—two or three years after Ginny's big year, and the plane just disappeared over the jungle. Guatemala, Salvador, one of those places. No explanation. Nothing ever found. Bodies, wreckage: nothing. Could've crashed, gotten shot down by the army, rebels, drug smugglers— who knows? Run out of fuel and crash-landed, gotten eaten by pygmies."

Whitman's lip curled; Drouhin, watching the road, did not see. "They do *have* pygmies down there, don't they?" he said. Whitman said nothing. "Or does anybody know?"

Whitman sighed. "Yeah, Alec, *I* know. Pygmies live in Africa. There's some in the Philippines, South Pacific. But the ones you're thinking about're in Africa. Where my people came from. Against their will. And they did not eat other people."

"*Sor-ree,*" Drouhin said. "Wasn't thinking. Again."

"Think nothing of it," Whitman said, wearily.

Drouhin frowned and thought for a moment. Then he cleared his throat. "*Anyway,*" he said, "Daddy never saw how his little girl finally turned out. But he and Claire were never after her plunder. That was always her property. Purses're nothing like they are today, of course, but with the benefits of compound interest, bless it, Ginny's got a million six or so in her management account today." He scowled. "Fee for which we can also kiss good-bye tomorrow, I suppose," he said. "Hundred and four grand a year."

"Ungrateful bitch," Whitman said.

"Oh, they all are, males included," Drouhin said.

"Although I do have to say," Whitman said, "if she's pulling her fund because she thinks our fees're too high, she's not the only one we've got to worry about. Our competitors're using it against us. And it's working. McGinnis and Lionel're very concerned. So's Barry. He said one of the Cubans he interviewed in the Dominican last year turned him down, gave him that as the reason.

"Barry said if he signed with us, we'd set up his defection, the kid said, 'Yes, and then take all the money. Six point five percent. I might as well stay in Cuba, give all my money to Fidel. *Su madre.*'

"Here's this ignorant punk, nineteen years old. He knows how to throw a fastball ninety-eight miles an hour, strut, ask a girl to fuck, and that Alexander Drouhin charges the highest management fees in the business. You tell me, we got problems or what?"

"We get the best result," Drouhin said angrily. "Our funds've had an average annual return of seventeen point five—*after* we deduct fees. Barry tell the fresh kid *that?* No one else can match that."

"Ruggles Brothers claim they deliver nineteen—after fees," Whitman said. "ProSpectors claim eighteen-seven-five. Both of them charge four percent. Bob Francis charges three."

"Yeah, and Francis's worth *two,*" Drouhin said scornfully. "Where'd the kid get this information, anyway?"

"Where do you think he got it?" Whitman said. "From our competitors. They may not be as well known as Alexander Drouhin Associates, but they *are* competing, quite effectively.

"Sometimes they eat our lunch. 'More and more often, they're doing it,' McGinnis says. 'We've got to cut the rate. Down to five, at least. Get the annual return to clients up to at least equal to the Ruggles. We don't and this keeps up, they'll eat us alive. We won't get new blood signing up. Old clients'll defect.' "

"Bullshit," Drouhin said. "Six point five is very reasonable. Used to be eight, even ten, I came in. Six-five is a moderate fee."

"*Was* a moderate fee," Whitman said. "American Express used to be *the* card. Don't forget, I did my M.B.A. thesis on this. Amex had the travel and entertainment credit-card business locked up. BankAmericard and MasterCharge were gas-credit cards with attitude, upstarts. Amex made you pay a fee to get their 'privileges.' Times changed. BankAmericard became Visa and started blowing off fees for good customers. Amex was haughty, just didn't believe what was happening. *Refused* to believe it. They had all the accounts worth having, and *their* 'members' 'd *never* defect.

"But they *did*. Credit became a commodity, just like what you bought with it. 'Member' for a price? 'Customer' for free. Product almost exactly the same? Lot of adults've got brains enough to make that choice. And in fact as economic times changed, there were a lot more worthwhile middle-class accounts out there that Amex'd never bothered to chase. And was now too lame to catch.

"That's the point McGinnis and Lionel make about us. You were able to elbow your way in twenty-seven years ago partly by taking a smaller management slice, undercutting the guys already out there. Now the field's more crowded; other guys're accepting even smaller margins, running tighter ships—and undercutting *you*. I think McGinnis and Lionel're right, Alex. That fee's got to go down. The rest of us've seen we've got to do it, to stay competitive. You don't have to come right out and *admit* it, case you're worried about saving face. Suggesting to the clients we might've been overcharging them slightly, so they then start seeking refunds. Just announce improved efficiency and long-term planning enable us to return an even greater share of historically even greater profits. Blah, blah, blah. Just as long as you do finally *do* it."

"*Ahhh,*" Drouhin said, "Ginny Alter leaving us isn't going to spook me into doing something foolish."

Whitman caught his breath. "My god," he said, "it just hit me. She wouldn't be joining that class-action suit that bastard Haggerty recruited, sue us for fraud and stuff—would she?"

Drouhin hissed his disparagement. "That pisshole in the snow?" he said. " 'Cause that's what that case is: just little Jimmy Haggerty writing his initials with his dick. No, Ginny's too smart to fall for his bullshit. Doctor Murray, Pete the Whistle, and Billy Wilderness're just sad derelicts, washed up on the shore of life. Haggerty tripped over one of them, his walk along the beach, thought he saw a way to make some easy money with a nuisance suit. At least get his name in the paper—which from his point of view's almost as good.

"It's a scut case. Doc and Sneezy and Grumpy insisted on taking all of their money out of our care when they, quote, *retired,* unquote—meaning their bodies'd been busted up in action one too many times. They were broken beyond mending, and therefore their teams were discarding them. They really had no complaints. All had good long careers, seven, eight years, two or three times the average.

"But they don't *see* facts like that, because they don't *like* 'em. Doc and Pete and Billy, these're not super-bright guys. The philosophy department at Johns Hopkins University did not lose out on three faculty comets when they opted to play pro football. So just as anyone who knew them would've expected, soon as they got their own paws on the money, they spent it foolishly. Made bad investments, drank and gambled away what was left.

"Now they're filled with remorse. Want to blame someone else. This Haggerty plays on that. He tells them, 'Well, clearly there should've been more in the funds.' Which if there had been, of course, they would've pissed away too. 'But never mind that,' Haggerty says. 'He charged you too much in management fees, making your money work so well for you you took out double what you put in. He must've misled you. Lied to you. Bamboozled you. Pulled the wool over your eyes.' This makes them feel ever so much better, and they say, 'You're *right*. Go and sue him.' "

Whitman sighed. "I hope you're right," he said. "I hope we're taking the thing seriously enough, it doesn't grow three rows of teeth and rise up out of the mist on the meadow some lovely spring morning, bite us right on the ass. A lot of us're worried."

"Bob Rhine has my complete confidence," Drouhin said. "He'll make it go away. Have no fear. It's only a matter of time." He sighed.

"What?" Whitman said. "If it's not a problem..."

"Oh, I never like getting fired," Drouhin said. "Always try to tell myself 'The client's expectations were unrealistic—nobody could've met them. Better off without him. Her.' In most cases it's true, including this one.

"But the fact of the fact is that we didn't do that good a job for Ginny. There probably *were* ways we could've capitalized more on her big year, while it was still fresh kill. But we were new then at that game and we just didn't think of them. *Carpe diem;* we didn't.

"That was not such a swell idea I had, ten years ago, I decided we should branch out into the individual competitive sports. It's a different universe, a different cosmos. We did shitty with Fred Simpson on the PGA Tour, absolutely shitty. He was right to fire us after a year. Saw we didn't really know what we were doing. We were using him to learn while his calendar ran out. He had more brains'n we did. I did. Team sports is our metier. Should've stuck with what we knew. Hubris, hubris, hubris. Just like they say in baseball about those leadoff walks, it'll get you every time."

Route 2 northwest of Concord traverses farmland bordered chiefly by deciduous trees. Their branches were bare in the moonlight. There was little traffic on Sunday evening and the outlaw headlights gave Drouhin at least 150 yards of visibility more than he would have needed to brake from sixty. But the doe in the lights didn't move; she stood stockstill and wide-eyed, left foreleg raised, beside the gray roadside farm stand on the right six miles west of Maynard. "Hey, look at that," Drouhin said.

"Good thing she wasn't already halfway across," Whitman said as they left her in the dark.

"I could've stopped," Drouhin said. "Or swerved. She wasn't very big."

"You hope," Whitman said. "That's the kind of thing I'd rather not find out."

"Hey, so would I," Drouhin said. "Hit a deer at speed, damned thing's liable not only to bend your hood all to shit but then come busting through your windshield. Have you picking glass out of your face for the next three years." He paused. "There's too many of the damned things anyway. Drive the farmers nuts. They should have doe season every year, let the farmers shoot them any time they're in the crops."

"You're so softhearted," Whitman said. "Takes my breath away."

"Reality, FD, *reality*," Drouhin said.

"Reality," Whitman said, "is that we've got a valuable property who's endangering our interest by risking the chief asset in saloon fights. Reality is that we really should be talking about what you're going to say to him tomorrow morning, afternoon, when he returns to consciousness. Or as close to it as he ever gets. How we shape him up."

"He swears the other guy started the fracas he got into down in Bellingham two years ago," Drouhin said. "That could be true. You don't have to be a pro athlete to act like an asshole when you've had a lot to drink. Other guys out there who aren't pro athletes also act like assholes when they drink. One of the things they like to do's pick fights with celebrities. Particularly celebrities best known for being *tough*."

"Meaning, then, I assume," Whitman said, "that he admits the other three brawls before tonight were his fault."

Drouhin frowned. "It was the *geography* of the phenomenon that baffled me," he said. "He covered more ground'n the Dalton Gang, in search of the very best tussles. I just couldn't figure it out. *Finally,* I got it out of him. It was the *same girl.* Well, it was a different girl every year, but he followed her around all year until he went to training camp in the summer. During the season he was on the road a lot and when he was home he didn't have all that much time to himself, get in trouble. But soon as the playoffs were over and the Bills'd lost another Super Bowl, the years they got into it, he'd come home and go out and find a girl. A new girl for the new year.

"He'd go to see her every week, at least twice, on the weekend. To protect her. Because, you see, the girl he picked for that year became *his* girl. His *property.* Then after she got through work and got her clothes on, he'd take her out on a *date.* Drinks and dinner. He'd *seduce* her. And since the only thing that interested her was the money she'd get for doing what turned the john on, not how stupid he was acting—*especially* if the john was a famous football player with a lot of money who could pay her double what she got from all the other guys she fucked and sucked after work—she'd go along with it. Hey, two hundred bucks is two hundred bucks, buys a lot of propane, heat the trailer. Especially when the chump springs for dinner and wine, and treats a girl with *respect*.

"The girls ride circuit, like judges used to. The club owners say it's because the customers like variety, but the real reason I suspect is that they're trying to discourage guys like Bobby from getting attached to specific girls, because that's when the fights begin. Guy sees *his* honey straddling some other dude, gettin' him off, and everybody *watching*, he gets *jealous*. He gets *mad*. He starts swinging."

Drouhin paused. "In lots of ways he's still a child. I wish I could do more for him. Make him see these're whores he gets in fights over, and there're hundreds of good-looking, respectable women who'd give their eyeteeth to ride him."

"Yeah," Whitman said, "well, cry me a river. Way you work for your clients, you owe nobody no apology for nothin'. You bust your ass for them. You didn't, you wouldn't have another thirty miles to go after you drop me off, 'fore you can hit the sack. You're gonna put about a hundred and twenty-five more miles on this boat, you get through tonight. I'm eleven years younger'n you are, and I wish I had your stamina."

Drouhin shrugged again, wanting more.

Whitman obliged. "You're a dedicated man, Alex, work this hard for a client, big an asshole as Bobby is," he said.

"The dedication's to the money that the asshole brings in," Drouhin said, inhaling deeply. "It isn't to the asshole. The dedication's to what pays for this boat and the other luxury accommodations. Kind of people we deal with, some of them've got certain quirks. Some of 'em're fairly unpleasant. If an agent's too finicky to deal with them, fine, go ahead and fire the player. Let someone else have the problem. And the money.

"Me, I've got a pretty strong stomach. I tell 'em they're not helping their current careers, increasing their paychecks, improving their chances of longevity, making it likely there'll be a future in the game for them when they're at the end of the line, they continue to do stuff like this. That's all I can do. They can listen or not, just as they choose.

"Bobby's usual choice is *not*. He's twenty-four. He'll be twenty-five in May. You got me thinking, on the phone, how often this's happened. This's the *fifth* time. *Five* times he's been busted for a ruckus in a pussy bar. He had a set-to down in Cranston Sunday after he got home, his rookie season. That one wasn't too bad. Little pushing, little shoving. Cops gave a kid a break. Then another one, two or three months later. Another strip joint, way the hell out in western Mass.

" 'What the hell're you doing out in Hampton Falls, for God's sake?' I asked him. He was still auditioning for Girl of the Year. He tells me he heard they got this broad out there with fifty-two-inch knockers. He didn't believe it, went out to see for himself. She did, silicone of course. He grabbed 'em and the bouncers grabbed *him*.

"That's one of the two things you're not allowed to do in those joints. You can rub yourself—*through your clothes*—under the table if you want. Or, for a small additional fee, and a gratuity's expected, the girls'll sit on your lap, grind and squirm 'til you come in your shorts. But you're not allowed to take it out and you're not allowed to touch them. He did, so the muscle moved in.

"The trouble is that when you grab Bobby, he thinks he's being tackled. Ever since he was seven years old, he's been saying, 'Gimme the ball,' and the other kids've been ganging *up* to pull him *down*. And ever since he was eight he's been steadily getting better at fighting them off 'n they've gotten at pulling him down. So when the bouncers grab

Bobby, he immediately goes into his third-and-three mode, head down, elbows out, legs pumping, forearms clubbing—just like he follows his left tackle and guard through the hole. To Bobby in that frame of mind, the world is the weak side of the defensive line, and he is coming *through*. The bouncers're big enough but they're amateurs, used to fighting with guys who're A, smaller'n they are, B, drunk, and C, usually older and outta condition. Bobby's generally fairly drunk when he gets into one of these scrapes, but otherwise he doesn't match the profile of what these guys're used to. So usually he throws off half a dozen or so 'fore the cops get there and subdue him.

"He can do that because now that he's reached what we all *hope* is his full growth—it won't be if he doesn't ease up on the chops and pizza—he is extremely *strong*. He *likes* to work out. I suspect the only reason he limits his daily sessions to four hours is that's all the *machine* can take. He weighs two-hundred-and-forty-five pounds and about four percent of it's fat."

"What percent is brain?" Whitman said. "The average male's goes a little over three pounds, which in Bobby's case'd mean a little more'n one percent his weight is brain. Way he acts, that sounds a little high to me."

Drouhin sighed. "We don't have the lab results yet. So far the tests're negative, but we've all heard him talk, so . . ."

"Parrots can talk," Whitman said reflectively. "So can cockatiels and parakeets. I've heard you can teach crows and ravens, too. To talk, I mean. I doubt they could learn math or science. And they probably couldn't play football, either. No hands."

"Shut up," Drouhin said, chuckling. "Julie swears she once heard him utter a complete sentence."

"What was it?" Whitman said. " 'See Spot run.'? 'See Fluff run.'? 'See Dick and Jane chase Spot and Fluff.'?"

"Doesn't matter," Drouhin said. "We still have hope there's some gray matter in there, and that with the proper rest and nourishment, it'll manifest itself. In time."

Whitman settled himself in the passenger seat. "Maybe, just to be on the safe side," he said, "we should think about adding a brain-transplant capability to our menu of client services."

"Only if the procedure would enable the client to do his job better," Drouhin said. "Nick Cosgrove for example. He could use an upgrade. Catchers have to handle temperamental pitchers. Most of those characters are about as smart as large bullfrogs, temperamental as divas. Nick's abilities in that department would definitely be improved if he were a little smarter.

"Bobby's? Probably not. Might even handicap him, he were somewhat smarter. An intelligent person, considering the odds, foreseeing what's going to happen to him when he takes that football from his quarterback, tucks it into his right side, and deliberately starts running *toward* five or six guys who average three hundred pounds and want to take it away from him? And *they're* doing *their* best to run toward *him* to *do* that? Well, he just wouldn't do it. Bobby does it. He accepts the ball—hell, he demands it— and he charges into the scrum, *daring* those big animals to take him down. And they have one hell of a time doing it.

"Oh, in the end they generally manage it. Not *always*— he does score eleven or so touchdowns every year—but it usually takes at least three or four of them to do it. You very seldom see Bobby brought down by a two-man tackle. I don't think I've ever seen a tape, at least since he's been in pro ball, where one man tackled him alone. And it even takes a group a while—thirteen hundred yards rushing last year, average eleven-eighty for his last three seasons? This is not a ball carrier who collapses on first or second impact. Sometimes it can even take five or six guys, his line enables him to make it through the elephants into the defensive backfield," Drouhin began to croon, badly, "where the *deer* and the *antelope* play..."

"*Careful*," Whitman said.

"Hey, just stating the facts," Drouhin said. "Defensive backs're lots faster'n the Bobbies of this world, but you're also a lot lighter. You can catch him easy, in the blinking of an eye, but then it takes six of you to bring him down. You remember that day out in Oakland last year, Bills on the Raider twenty-nine, I think it was, third quarter, Ted Minor and Reid Miller opened up a hole center left, he went through it like a locomotive? Cripes, they must've showed it fifteen times on replay before the game was over—he carried *five* guys *four* yards, then another one, *on his back,* into the end zone. Looked like Santa with his toy pack. All these guys hangin' onto him, hardly see him underneath, churning and churning along. Like he was a bus, and he was giving them a ride; on and on he went. He just wouldn't *stop.*"

Drouhin slapped the steering wheel with the palm of his left hand. *"Five guys he had on his back, and they couldn't bring him down!"* He grinned and glanced over at Whitman. "Think that play isn't going to be on the career highlights tape I send out a year from now?"

"If it isn't, I'll have you committed," Whitman said.

"Well," Drouhin said, "*that's* why we're going to Fitchburg tonight, instead of you staying home eating Glenda's turkey and me celebrating Methodiste's new Bruins contract down in Easton with some of Angela's cacciatore and a nice Chianti Riserva. Our six-million-dollar man's gotten himself in trouble again. Okay, we go and get him out. For certain kinds of people, you make allowances."

"He won't be our six-million-dollar man if he keeps fucking up like this," Whitman said. "Teams'll tolerate a lot of shit from a ball carrier like him, but unless his luck holds forever, which no luck ever does, sooner or later one of these barroom bozos's gonna decide Bobby's so big and strong he's entitled to use some kind of equalizer, stick a shiv in him. Or *shoot* him.

"That happens, even if he recovers fully, he'll never be the same. Because even if he *is* the same, teams'll look at him and wonder: 'This guy had a bullet in him. Is he now really okay? Even the *Pope* lost a step or two, after he got shot, and the Pope's got pull this guy doesn't.' They'll always have that doubt. And they'll discount his value. Remember what you always told me to remember, I was in negotiations. 'This isn't about talent. It isn't about skill. It's not about charisma, charm, or how you look. The fans may love, the fans may hate, you. The media the same. But when the One Great Scorer comes to write against your name, He'll write not if you won or lost—'" Whitman paused; they recited the last line together: "'—but how much you got paid.'"

4

DROUHIN, WHITMAN A FOOT behind him, stood at the booking desk at the front of the lockup area at the rear of the sprawling new Haymarket Police Station. The desk was a gray three-by-ten-foot Formica counter set atop a room divider four feet high, faced with gray Formica sheeting. Against the wall next to the door, within the field of vision of the officer at the booking desk, there were four dark wooden armchairs bolted to the floor. A bulletproof clear Lucite shield extended four feet above the counter to two feet below the suspended false ceiling made of white composition tiles punctured to improve sound absorption.

On the left the shield was fastened to the glade-green wall; on the right the shield and the divider made a right angle, creating an inner corridor to the left of the hallway leading back to the holding cells in the rear. The inner corridor extended back twelve feet to the entry to the area with four desks behind the booking counter. A male officer in a dark blue uniform shirt and a female cadet in a light blue shirt sat side by side at the desk in the far right corner of the room, the cadet apparently instructing the officer in computer operations, first making a series of entries on the keyboard, then moving her swivel chair away to allow him to duplicate what she had done. There were computers on the other three gray steel desks vacant behind the shield. The floor was made of Armstrong cork, quiet underfoot, and the lighting was cool and bluish, indirect fluorescent. A second male officer emerged from the corridor leading to the cell block, doubling back down the internal corridor and entering the work area through a double-hinged wooden gate that needed oiling; it groaned and squealed, the penetrating, sudden noise pointing up the hush that otherwise prevailed. Had it not been for the Lucite shield and the armed cops in uniform, the lockup area could have been the accounting office of a small independent suburban bank.

A uniformed sergeant in his early fifties with a widow's peak of sparse gray hair cut very short against his knobby skull sat behind the shield and counter on a castered, swiveled stool equipped with black fiberglass arms and a dark gray backrest. The black nameplate with white letters on the flap of his left breast pocket read: DOYLE. In front of him there was a recessed stainless-steel tray set into the counter under a foot-long cutout four inches high in the Lucite. To the right of his face at mouth level there was a small, flat black conical microphone mounted on a black gooseneck issuing from a black collar screwed down on the counter. Next to it on the right was a ten-line telephone call-director unit. To his left where the shield and the Formica partition made the right angle creating the inner corridor, a bank of three five-inch black-and-white TV monitors, each served by a closed-circuit camera that panned slowly back and forth across the two cells it covered, showing the cots, commodes, sinks, and occupants in the holding cells in the lockup. The sergeant rested his elbows on the counter and hung his hands down behind it, his forearms and biceps bulging the sleeves of his uniform shirt. Frowning, he watched intently as the bondsman, Ephraim Gold Jr., made out papers, leaving amounts blank, as though he had never before witnessed so remarkable a procedure.

"M-O-R-I-N-O?" Gold said. He was about 5'10", early forties, burly and out of shape, with receding, curly black hair. He wore a red and black lumberjack jacket and a gray leather porkpie hat. He was tanned; his nose had started to peel, mottling white.

"No *I, E*," Drouhin said. "M-O-R-E-N-O." Gold printed the letters painstakingly, mouthing each of them as he proceeded.

"*Jay*," the sergeant said loudly into the microphone. Behind the Lucite he was visible speaking the word, but since the speaker was mounted on the wall over the anteroom door, the audio boomed out behind Gold, Drouhin, and Whitman. It startled and momentarily disoriented them. Flustered, they glanced uneasily around before they realized that the man in front of them had uttered the name. Doyle smiled. In a normal tone of voice he said: "I thought it was your father was the licensed bondsman. What happened, he retire or something?"

Gold let irritation show. He looked at Drouhin, then at Whitman, shaking his head. "He always does that," he muttered. "Every time you come in, which no one does very often anymore, he pulls that trick with the microphone. They put lots of new toys in this new station when they built it, but the mike's his favorite." Then he turned and faced the Lucite.

"No, Jack." Gold said, "just like I told you last time, I came in instead of Dad. I also write them now myself. He's getting along in years; doesn't like to drive at night. No point having me drive him, having him come out at all, if I become a bondsman and take the nightwork over for him.

It's still a full-time job for him; he still does all the day-work. And I still teach business math at Chelmsford High. For me this's strictly a sideline."

Doyle's face showed he had absolutely no interest in the answer. Gold saw this. "Can I give you my card, Jack? Stick a pushpin in it, put it up above your desk like you used to do, the old days?" He reached for his wallet.

Doyle recoiled slightly and put both hands on the counter. He shook his head emphatically, waving off the notion with the same short horizontal brushing motion football referees employ to rule passes incomplete.

Gold turned to face Drouhin, so that Doyle could not read his lips through the Lucite. He lowered his voice. "Actually it isn't really a license," he murmured. "All it is is a notarized letter of appointment as an agent for a company that writes bonds for sureties. Generally they're performance bonds for building contractors: written proof that the company you claim to represent will in fact underwrite any losses incurred by construction delays or contractual defaults that're covered by a bond you've written.

"Bail reform in this state fifteen, twenty years ago? I forget how long ago. Anyway, pretty much eliminated the whole industry here. Now it's almost always a matter of posting ten percent cash-bail. Your mother's house, your father's bankbook, your wife's secret fund she's been saving up for a new washer-dryer set. You show up when you should, then when the case's over, whoever posted bond gets it back. Intact. Before, once the bondsman got his fee, it was gone. Didn't matter if your son or husband showed up every time, maybe even got acquitted; you'd had the service you paid for and didn't see your money again.

"You *do* have a clerk-magistrate coming, don't you?"

"I think so," Drouhin said. "I had my secretary call an emergency number for a lawyer we've used out here,

Tommy Newcombe. Ask him to locate a clerk for us. I do *not* want our guy held in jail overnight. That'd be in no one's best interest." He chuckled. "Mine especially."

Gold nodded. "Know Tommy well," he said. "One of my students threatened the principal with a knife last year. This was one troubled young man. Parents've got money but no sense—didn't have a clue what to do for the kid. Tommy represented him. Did exactly what was needed, best for the kid and everyone else. Got the judge to put him on probation for four years, condition being that the parents send him to this private school way the hell up in Maine, enforces strict discipline. Last report we had, he'd been designated hall monitor for his floor of the dorm, carrying a solid B average, no disciplinary problems at all. Tommy probably saved that kid's life. Tommy's a good man." Then he inclined his head and nodded again, toward the chairs. "This could be a while," he said. "Let's go over and sit down."

Seated, he resumed. "The old system was corrupt," he said thoughtfully, keeping his voice low. The sergeant behind the shield furtively removed a folded page of newspaper from a drawer below the counter and began to work on a crossword puzzle. "That's why Jack reacted the way he did when I offered him my card. Court clerks and cops like this turkey here *did* have cards above their desks, and they would put yours up, too—all you had to do was ask. But that didn't get you calls. Gratitude and a bottle of liquor at Christmas only went so far; they weren't enough to get you your fair share of business. You'd get three or four drunks a year, just enough to make it look good. But the guys who kicked back to the cops on the take were in here that many times a *week,* working day and night.

"It stood to reason. Your average citizen didn't go out expecting to get arrested, travel around with a bondsman's phone number in his wallet. He got grabbed for driving under, he's a sitting duck for a crooked cop who played sympathetic and told him who to call. Two guys Jack used to work with went to jail for being on the take from bondsmen—not from me or my dad. Other guys.

"So, this new way did cost Dad some money, but it wasn't a lot, and he'll tell you himself that now is better. Now he only writes construction bonds and says, 'But my hands've always been clean.' That's true, but I know there had to've been times when he must've been really tempted to hook up with the gravy train." He paused.

"I think that as a general rule, every system can be corrupted. Don't you find that's so in your line of work? I should think it would be. So much dough involved and all; must be a very great temptation."

"Oh, it is," Drouhin said. "At every level. And it's most pronounced right where the ability to resist it's the weakest: the point at which the young college or high-school hotshot's poised on the brink of becoming a pro. Very soon, in a matter of months or even weeks, he's going to be making big money. Everybody wants a piece of him. He can't *wait*. He's *hungry*. But the rules say we can't offer him anything to sign him up, slip him something under the table. No gifts, no loans, no use of cars; no girls and no credit cards."

"And you obey those rules," Gold said.

"You bet," Drouhin said. "Well, the people in *my* office do. Just like you and your father did. *Most* established pro sports agents do, in fact. It's not because we're virtuous; it's because we're afraid of getting caught. You interfere with a college player, coach'll bar you from the campus and access to the students. One coach ices you, all the others follow suit—and the NCAA'll back 'em up.

"That'll *kill* you. How the hell can you evaluate talent,

decide how much you think you can get for a player if he signs with you—and that's the *first* thing he's gonna ask you. When his last season's over and you can openly approach him—along with every other agent in the country, trying not to get yourself trampled—the question'll come at you while you're still shaking hands: 'How much you think I'm gonna get?' If you haven't seen him practice, watched him play, you can't answer that. Well, shouldn't, anyway.

"You can't blame the coaches. They've got a lot at stake. Once a player signs with an agent, he's de facto turned pro. Ineligible for further NCAA competition. And 'signing' isn't just writing your name on an agreement; it's any act that'd authorize someone else to bargain for the player. Any act that confers benefits and creates obligations. You sign a kid on the sly in September and his team makes the Final Four in March? If the NCAA finds out in April what happened in the fall, they'll forfeit every game the kid played in competition. Since the players we're after early're always the starters, as a practical matter that'll mean the team forfeits all its wins, and any league or regional championships they may've won. This does not go over large with coaches.

"And any established agent who did something like that *would be* caught. Just as my competitors know that I'd be delighted to turn them in, I know they'd be only too glad to do the same for me. So in a sense we're self-policing." He hesitated.

"But people still do it, give in to temptation. It's easy to corrupt hot youngbloods who can't wait for their first big score. Mostly the people who do it're the new guys, trying to break into the agenting field. Looking for an edge, that first big-name client who'll become a beacon for other hot young stars coming up the line.

"See, your first top gun is your admission card; he gets you into the Show. I know guys who've gotten their first biggie and then deliberately held him out for a month or six weeks. Not because the bad team that drafted him and desperately needed him didn't make him a good fair offer, but because by making threats and unreasonable demands the agent can create the kind of story sportswriters love. It's easy, no thought or legwork required. Do it all on the phone. TV stations use game footage to illustrate what a great player the team risks losing. It's got *conflict, suspense*. Readership and audience *guaranteed*. So it's *excellent* free advertising. The more times a new agent can get an FO— a front office—to call him a son of a bitch, the more they spread his reputation as a tough negotiator. Hotshots who'll be eligible a year later pay attention to that stuff. That's what *they* want, their very own son of a bitch.

"Not all of those beginners get caught before they get that first marquee name and come to everyone's attention. And most of them—probably not all—don't press their luck. They then stop the funny business. What it amounts to is a system in which you only play as dirty as you need to, as long as you need to. And then never do it again— unless you really have to. And unfortunately, unlike the bail bond business, there doesn't seem to be any way to reform the system we work in."

Gold nodded. "So," he said, crossing his legs, "that's how come you wanted me to be here? You didn't know the way things are now with bail?"

Whitman looked at Drouhin, eyebrows raised, a small smile on his face. Drouhin grinned. "The truth is, I didn't," he said. "It's been a long time since one of our clients had trouble with the law in Massachusetts. Florida? Yup. Texas? You bet. L.A., one or two. Had to get bondsmen for *all* of those guys. Very promising young client of ours got himself run in for statutory rape in Indiana few years ago. Valparaiso. Three days after he was drafted in the first round by the Utah Jazz. Got convicted, too. I felt for him. The girl who came on to him sure looked like she was old enough—any bartender would've served her without a second thought. We got him a good lawyer, proved she'd been putting out for at least a year, six different guys. But the judge looked at her birth certificate and found our man guilty.

"Fouled up his career pretty good before he played a single game in the NBA. While he was in jail—judge said he was showing him some mercy, only gave him three to five—the Jazz traded him to San Diego. Clippers might be able to put a rapist on the floor, and if the Jazz'd still been in New Orleans, they might've given him a shot. But if they did that in Salt Lake City the good Mormons would've burned down the building. Made no difference, he got out after doing two. Damage was done. Inmate ball in the prison gym's not enough to keep pro-level sharpness, and he couldn't get it back. Layoff ruined him.

"Another one messed up in a bar in Idaho. Baseball player, moose of a first baseman also drafted by an NFL team. Bound to happen. He was pissed off when he went *in* there—sober, but looking to get drunk. He'd spent an entire week and about eight thousand dollars on travel, equipment, guides, and lodges, hunting bighorn sheep. Sheep hadn't cooperated. He'd only seen two and missed both of 'em. He was dumb enough to say this to the barkeep. Couple of the locals started making fun of him. Said no nigger can shoot worth a damn. That's when the fun began.

"Fortunately he'd already disassembled his rifle and packed it. His fists were all he had handy. But they're as big as smoked hams and he's pretty quick with them. Time the cops got there, he had two guys napping on the floor and the guy who said 'nigger' was crawling around on it, hands and knees, nose gushing blood, looking for his teeth. Had to get him a bondsman, and a *very* good lawyer.

"Judge in that case was pretty reasonable—put him on three years' probation, condition being that he stayed out of Idaho for at least that long. 'Not to protect the sheep,' he said. 'They're safe enough from you. It's the citizens who've got something to fear. They're mouthy and at least one of them's a bigot, but they live here and you don't. So *you* stay outta town.'

"But anyway," Drouhin said, "if I *had* known Massachusetts bail law, it wouldn't've made any difference. I can't make bail for him. I'm his lawyer, among other things—civil, not criminal—and as many years as it's been since I've practiced, I do remember that much: Lawyer's not allowed to make bail for his client.

"FD here, he could, of course," Drouhin said slyly.

"But I wouldn't," Whitman said immediately. "Start mothering these guys, pledging *your* stuff when *they* get into scrapes, you do it for one you gotta do it for all of them. Pretty soon you're not gonna have any your stuff *left*. Can't repay yourself from his account, even if he tells you to; he's liable to forget or change his mind—next year sue you for embezzlement."

"Bobby's family," Drouhin said, "such as it is, all live down south. Older brother's in jail in Mississippi. One of his younger brothers died of an overdose. Sister got killed in a car crash while he was in college. Younger brother's all right, but kind of hard to reach. He's in the Navy and his present duty station's the geographical survey base at McMurdo Sound, South Pole. Mother's in a private home, which he pays for, for the alcoholically insane. Father showed up six games into his rookie season. First time

Bobby'd seen him since he's ten years old. Looking for money, of course. Got the poor kid all upset. We had a couple gentlemen go around and see him, have a conversation with him. Gave him five thousand dollars—in exchange for his solemn promise never to come back again and bother Bobby. Which he'll keep 'til he gets desperate, because he knows if he doesn't, he'll get all lamed up. But depend on it: Sooner or later he *will* get really desperate, and he *will* come back, and after that he'll be lucky he ever *walks* again.

"Friends? The reason Bobby lives in Massachusetts, the off-season, is so he'll be near us. 'Cept on nights like this, he's no trouble. Doesn't come into the office, bug us all the time. Just makes him feel a bit more secure, knowing we're around. Now and then one of us'll ask him out to dinner, have him over for a beer. He's been a lot of help to us, recruiting college kids, once they've become eligible. Sort of acting as a reference for us. He likes to do that, sit around and schmooze with the rookies, give them the inside stuff. Makes him feel *capable,* in charge, some place besides on the field.

"See, out of uniform, *and* in his right mind, Bobby's kind of shy. That's the reason why he doesn't have a girlfriend. Does this fantasy thing with strippers. He knows they won't turn him down. He likes to visit people in our office who've got kids. People who've seen just the side of him he evidently showed tonight have trouble believing this, but he's very good with kids. Does a lot of hospital visits, Boys and Girls Clubs. Big Brother stuff.

"The only other *real* friends he's got're the guys on the team. Your basic really nice guy. His teammates'd do *anything* for him. Quarterback's their meal ticket, but Bobby's their bread and butter. And they genuinely like him. Coaching staff the same: good example for the others, he works his *ass* off in practice, and he gives the staff no backtalk. Hell, if he ever got busted in Buffalo, *fans'd* pass the hat to get him out—assuming the cops ever tried to lock him up. If he ever has to leave the Bills it'll break their hearts, and his. But this being the off-season, all those people who love him're scattered far and wide."

"And knowing what kind of condition he's usually in on these occasions," Whitman said, "we kind of doubted he'd be in good enough shape to make bail for himself."

"So you were the easiest way to handle it," Drouhin said. "That was the reason I had my office call you."

The door to the public area of the station opened and a tall, heavyset, round-shouldered man with curly blond hair under a red wool watch cap stomped into the lockup area in red mukluks. He wore a neon blue snowmobiling suit with red and yellow striping down the sleeves and the sides of the body and legs. He carried an attaché case. The odor of beer hung around him. "*Whew,*" he said, slapping the case down on the counter and pulling the hat off, so that the curls flattened under it sprang out at odd angles. "Jackie," he said, as a greeting. "Jimmy," Doyle said. He did not look up from his crossword puzzle. The man turned to face Drouhin and the others. "Sorry it took me so long," he said. "Which one of you'd be Attorney Drouhin?"

"I am," Drouhin said, rising from the chair and extending his right hand. "Alex Drouhin."

"Jim Ellis," the man said, shaking Drouhin's hand.

"Jim," Drouhin said. He used his left hand to indicate Whitman and Gold. "You probably know Mister Gold," he said. Gold and Ellis nodded at each other. "This's my good right hand, FD Whitman." Ellis leaned forward and they shook hands. "Sorry to interrupt your Sunday evening."

"You didn't, really," Ellis said. "The wife and I'd been

out all day on our snow machines. We go up to New Hampshire, near Hancock. Nice set of groomed trails up there. But we were tired. We'd already put the machines back on the truck, got myself a Ford Two-fifty. Just having a beer or two, deciding what to have for dinner, my pager went off. Heading back after that anyway."

"Well, sorry to delay your dinner, then," Drouhin said.

"Ah, hell," Ellis said, unzipping the front and bending to unzip the leggings from the bottoms to the knees, so that the garment flapped around him, releasing an odor of sweat. "No harm done. As you can see, I can stand it. Wouldn't hurt me to miss a meal every day of my life. And the food at Froggy's? Where we ride? Well, put it this way: they don't *insist* you eat and drink there if you use their parking lot and trails, but they do make it pretty clear that they expect it. I doubt anyone'd eat there otherwise." He turned back to the counter and opened the attaché case. "So *Jackie*," he said, "wanna have the guy brought out?"

"I'll get the shift commander," Doyle said. "Lieutenant Pike's on tonight." He picked up the phone.

Lieutenant Pike in his late thirties was trim, 5'8", around a hundred and fifty pounds. He had a small neat black mustache and his black hair was brush-cut and wiffle-waxed. He wore a wedding ring on the third finger of his left hand and a gold U.S. Marine Corps ring—globe and fouled anchor etched in gold on a garnet stone—on the third finger of his right hand. He holstered his service pistol on his left hip.

The practiced way he furrowed his brow slightly and focused his brown eyes suggested he was about to pounce on something. During his first of two four-year hitches as a marine he had served as a guard at the U.S. embassy in Grosvenor Square in London. There he had met and "absolutely captivated"—her phrase—a 5'11" English divorcée who had come to the embassy seeking a green card that would enable her to accept a new post as pastry chef in the kitchen of Adrienne, the three-star restaurant at the Peninsula Hotel in New York. Her name was Victoria but she called herself Vicki. Her ex-husband had told her while they were courting that she was "statuesque," which made her ever afterwards very conscious of her posture, and cognizant as well of the power of words uttered to obtain desires of passion. Thirty-six and footloose, she took pains to keep her figure, and also to be captivated every time she saw an opportunity. She was very good in bed and after one particularly rewarding twilight romp—when Pike would have believed and remembered what she said if she had declared the world was a cube—she had told him that his gaze was "piercing." On another such occasion she had told him she admired his "confident bearing, just the slightest hint of swagger."

Her green card had come through before he finished his tour in London. When he visited the New York Peninsula nine years later the *saucier,* the one person remaining in the kitchen who remembered her, said she had moved on to The Peninsula in Hong Kong six years before. Then they noticed simultaneously the similarities in the way they looked at each other and carried themselves, and both of them had laughed. The *saucier* had fetched an open bottle of Vouvray from the walk-in refrigerator and they had raised a toast to "Vicki, absent friend."

"*Hullo,* Jay," Pike said to Gold. "How's your father these days?" They shook hands. "Doing great," Gold said. "All in your family well?"

"Glad to say they are," Pike said.

Doyle spoke into the mike. Pike jumped a little as the sergeant's voice boomed from the speaker. "The gentleman in the blue blazer's—"

Pike interrupted. "Goddammit, Doyle," he said, "I *wish* you wouldn't do that. Fuckin' *idiot*. Think this place is anyway, a fuckin' *bus* station?"

Doyle looked shocked. Then he lowered his eyes and pouted like a child chastised.

Drouhin, laughing, extended his hand. "Alex Drouhin," he said. "I'm Bobby Moreno's agent. And this is FD Whitman, my deputy and strong right arm."

Shaking his head, Pike shook hands first with Drouhin. "Your boy's extremely drunk," he said. "Was when they brought him in, at least.

"Whitman," he said, shaking hands with FD, "Lemme think, Seahawks?"

"Vikings," Whitman said. "Still, you've got a good memory. That was a long time ago."

"Yeah, good memory for things I don't need to remember. Things I *do* need to remember, not so good. Find I'm drawing more and more blanks. Age, I suppose." He raised his voice. "How long ago's it now, Jack, they brought Moreno in?"

"Around seven," Doyle said timidly into the microphone. "I can check the booking sheet."

"Not necessary," Pike said. "Been quiet, has he?"

"I checked him every hour, like the rules say," Doyle said. Pike frowned and said under his breath. "I wonder." Then he said: "*How'd* you check him, Jackie? Glance at the monitor or actually get off your ass and go into the block?"

"Well, he's the only one in there," Doyle said defensively. "I mean, I turned up the sound and everything. That's what those units're s'posed to be for, idnit? He was sleeping at eight, and when I checked him again just before Mister Drouhin and his friend came in, he was still at it. Snoring like a bastard."

Pike looked at his watch. "So, coming up on ten, now; he's had himself a two, two-and-a-half-hour nap. Pretty big boy. Probably burned up three, four shots of whatever that fightin' whiskey was that he was drinking."

"He drinks iced tea and vodka," Whitman said. "Not that Long Island Iced Tea, six or seven kinds of joy juice; he drinks plain old iced tea and vodka. The iced tea because it's got sugar in it and he likes sweet-tasting stuff. The vodka to loosen him up. He'll drink a beer if you haven't got iced tea, but that's what he likes best."

"Jackie," the lieutenant said, without looking at Doyle, "they make him blow up the balloon?"

"I don't think so," Doyle said. "I haven't read the report—Palmer left it in the rack, his desk. But he wasn't driving at the time of the arrest. What they've got him for's making an affray; simple assault; and A and B, DW."

"What was the dangerous weapon," Pike said, "you know?"

"Shod foot, I think," Doyle said. "Think he kicked somebody. Like I say, I didn't read the arrest report. I was doin' something else when Palmer got it printed out and put it in the rack..."

"Yeah, crossword puzzle," Pike murmured. Gold looked at Drouhin and smirked.

"...but I think Palmer said he kicked one of the other guys in the balls while two others had ahold of his arms. And then another one in the ribs."

"Know who they were?" Pike said. "The guys he beat up, I mean."

"No, I don't," Doyle said. "Like I said—"

"I know," Pike said, "you 'didn't read the report.' Look, do me a favor, all right? Go over to Palmer's desk rack and pull it. Tell us who the guys were who were injured. Besides him, I mean."

Doyle grimaced and sighed heavily. Then he pushed himself away from the counter and with difficulty climbed down from the high chair. The large paunch that the counter had concealed hung over his belt like a bedroll. Making rowing motions with his arms, he waddled toward the desk nearest the booking window. Pike looked at the others and shook his head. "Got that cowcatcher in front of him. From the back he looks like he's got a load in his pants. Would you *believe* this department's got a weight limit regulation?"

"Not enforced?" Drouhin said.

Pike laughed. "He's got a letter from his doctor. Says the patient's perfectly healthy except for this abnormal *metabolic* condition. Seems it's a *glandular* problem. All known treatments ineffective. So the chief's got a choice between putting him on hundred-percent disability, which'd amount to giving him full pay to do crossword puzzles at home, or getting at least some use out of him here, manning the desk and making people jump out of their skins with that goddamned microphone. First thing I'm going to do when I get out of here, become chief somewhere else, is make sure if there's any goddamned speaker system it's located so the guy at the desk gets just as big a blast as the people in front of it. And if it isn't, I'm gonna have it *re*located."

Doyle waddled back to the counter with a beige folder tabbed with clear plastic. He put the report on the counter. Then he put his left hand on the seat of the stool and his right on the counter, turned so that the chair was partly behind him, pressed down on the cushion and counter with his hands, and levered himself up onto the seat, his face blooming red from the exertion, his mouth gaping for air the way a freshly landed fish begs with its mouth for the water. He was panting as he opened the report and pulled the microphone closer to his mouth. "Uhhh, lessee here," he said, "the hell are they now. Oh yeah, here they are.

'Complaining witnesses: Kevin Sweeney, Matthew Swee-ney, Thomas Gaetano, David Paster.' "

"Uh *huh,*" Pike said, "thanks, Jack." To Drouhin he said: "The fighting Sweeney brothers. Paster runs with them. Gaetano's the barkeep, part owner, the Jewel Box.

"This's good news for your man. The Sweeneys're al-most always on probation for something, usually some-thing like this. Usually when they're in a fight, they started it. They're not gonna want to testify in this one because if they do they'll have to admit your client all by himself al-most beat the shit out of all four of them. This's hard to say if you're a tough guy. Your rep's important to you— that and your pickup truck's damned near all you've got in the world. You want people backing out of your way, not blocking it, laughing at you.

"And then they'll have to admit they were in another *fight,* which is a violation of probation—unless they can prove they couldn't've walked away.

"If they don't testify, Paster won't either. The Sweeneys'd call him pussy-wuss if he did, and likely as not he's got the same kind of probation problem they've got.

"Gaetano less'n a month ago testified under oath, license renewal hearing, board of selectmen, that the patrons of the Jewel Box are a peaceful bunch of happy voyeurs and dance critics to whom violence is unknown. This comes up for trial, I doubt he will've seen anything.

"No one else in those joints when trouble starts ever sees anything. Most of 'em don't want their parents or their wives or their girlfriends finding out that's where they *ac-tually* went—when they said they were going bowling, or going down the VFW, watch the game with the guys. By the time Carnes and his backup got there, parking lot was probably two-thirds empty. So, no evidence. Case dis-missed."

"Well, what about them, the cops?" Drouhin said.

"They didn't see it," Pike said. "All they saw was the aftermath. Two guys unconscious on the floor, third guy crawling around, probably in a drunken haze, looking for his missing choppers."

"Pretty obvious *someone* started it, but Palmer, Redgate, and Christopher Sweeney—not one of the fighting Sweeneys; they're cousins, and they embarrass him—didn't see who that was. Technically you could charge all five involved with making an affray, but whoever didn't start it's got a pretty good argument of self-defense."

"Well, hell, okay," Drouhin said, doubtfully. "Never look a gift horse and so forth."

"Look," Pike said, his voice conveying weariness, "nobody I work for wants this case to go anywhere but *away*. You think this town can *afford* a police station like this? The chief's got a private shower in his bathroom. Plus we've got a brand-new elementary school loaded with computers and a new wing going up at the library. New fire station's under construction, keep our brand-new aerial-ladder truck warm and dry. Where you think the money comes from?"

Drouhin and the others said nothing.

"Jay knows," Pike said. "Everybody 'round here knows. It's like I started to tell you on the phone, Mister Drouhin: Haymarket's Sin City. *We've* got no problem with tax flight. Other towns up near the border lose taxpayers to New Hampshire, no sales tax or income tax, but the only way people leave Haymarket for good's in long black cars followed by family and friends with their headlights turned on. *Our* residential tax rate's eight dollars and forty-seven cents a thousand valuation. That's the second-lowest in north central Massachusetts. Our commercial tax rate's seventeen-ten, the fourth-lowest. But our *adult entertainment district* tax rate, the strip along Thirteen where all the surrounding communities send the kind of businesses most towns want nothing to do with, that's a different story. The rate for businesses in that zone is thirty-nine fifty per thousand valuation. Next year it's going to forty-one seventy-five, and you won't hear *one peep* of complaint. They're *happy* to pay it.

"And we're happy to have them. They don't increase enrollment in our schools. They don't take books out of the library. The only municipal services they get for their tax money're the sewer system and the fire department—which so far they haven't needed. They don't add to unemployment; they reduce it. Last count a hundred and eleven local residents had full-time jobs, the joints. Not the kind of job your parents brag about—'We're just *so* proud of Oscar, he's a bouncer in a strip joint'—but steady, and entry-level slots pay nine bucks an hour. The playboys tend to be good tippers; part of their image. Barkeeps, waitresses, and dancers do well.

"Purely from the financial point of view, it's a good deal for the town, and the people in charge know it. They want no boats rocked. We charge the operators all outdoors but as long as no one actually gets killed, we let 'em operate with almost no interference. Right now there're eight of those joints out there along Thirteen, two expanding and three more in the planning stages. They've *all* got keno licenses, new game every five minutes. Man can *easily* lose a good week's pay, course of a couple or three unlucky hours, sitting at one of those screens.

"You get your choice of other kinks. The Jewel Box is one of *four* totally-nude, lap-dancing bars. There's a bar for gays who wear suits and ties who'd be mortified if someone in their families or where they work knew they went to it, even though most of those people know they're queer. Transvestite bar: Straight guys and women love the place, pack the joint on Sunday and Thursday nights for the drag shows. Not as crowded other nights, but they still do all right. There's a lesbian bar, a gay-*and*-lesbian bar, and a bikers' bar. You go out in the parking lot behind any one of those joints after dark, you're running the distinct risk of slipping on a used condom and falling on your ass.

"There're two sports bars where big TV screens continuously scroll the latest line out of Vegas, every Division One-A college and major-league professional game scheduled to be played in the U.S. and Canada every day. During football season, World Series, Final Four, you can't get *into* these joints. Another screen shows the horse and dogtrack odds. You want the info on a particular *game,* you punch in the first three letters of the names of the two teams and it gives you that game right off. Another key gets you running scores on games in progress. To get a horse race, enter first three letters of the name of track, then number of race. When there's a fight card at Atlantic City, Vegas, those odds're also available on the race monitors. But so far no elections.

"If you've listed your credit card with the offshore casinos down in the Cayman Islands, after you make your choice of team, horse, dog, or fighter, you pick up the pay phone, use your phone credit card, dial a nine-hundred number, get the automated connection, punch in your PIN number, your game or your race, the choice you're betting, dollar amount you want to bet. Visa or MasterCard. You win, they credit your MasterCard. You lose, they debit your Visa. You want to leave it there to pay your bill, end of the month, fine. You want the cash in your hot little hand? No problem. Write a check on the bank account the card was issued to."

"And you allow this," Gold said.

"In the first place, it's probably not illegal," Pike said.

"More sophisticated people do it in the privacy of their own homes, on their own computers. Feds keep *threatening* to break up the party, but so far I haven't seen them *doing* anything. It's just like the sex for sale out there; if you're not getting it privately at home, you can go out there and buy it. It may look like you're breaking the law, and technically maybe you are, but as long as everyone involved's an adult and nobody gets *too* badly hurt, we're not going to interfere—we're going to overlook it.

"Like I said, the people who tell us what to do have a different agenda from the people who run most towns. They *encourage* this stuff. Last year the fire chief pulled surprise inspections three nights of the NBA championship series. Both those sports bars were *way* over occupancy limits, all three nights.

"Know what the selectmen did? First thing was tell him privately that if he pulled that stunt again, they'd have his head on a plate. Then, sitting as the zoning appeals board, they reversed the zoning board's denial of expansion permits to double the floor space of one and *triple* the footprint of the other one. Construction started last week.

"This department's got the lowest pay scale of any police force in any community with a comparable population— eleven thousand people—in the Commonwealth. Top pay here for a patrolman's thirty-two five. Six twenty-five a week gross, eight to twelve thousand less than you'd get in any other town of similar size. And yet we've got a waiting list of almost two hundred experienced officers from other towns and departments who want to join us.

"Why? Partly because we've got a short workweek: thirty-six hours, four days a week, so the base pay works out to seventeen thirty-six an hour. But mostly because the town requires that every one of those joints out there every night from seven 'til two A.M. closing has at least one off-duty police officer directing traffic outside, and another one inside making sure that order's kept and drunks get their car keys confiscated. Your boy just went off the rails too early, 'fore the detail cops arrived. Give you odds, though, selectmen hear about this, they'll require cops on duty in the afternoons.

"The normal detail pay in other towns is twenty-five dollars an hour, *four*-hour minimum. In Haymarket the *official* hourly rate's forty-eight fifty, *ten*-hour minimum. Which means that a cop working the seven hours from seven 'til two is actually making *sixty-nine* bucks an hour. A cop on the day shift can easily work another forty official hours of details a week. Boring, but it brings him nineteen hundred and forty bucks, making his total take over twenty-five hundred a week, a *hundred and thirty-three grand a year*. People say those joints're *subsidizing* this police force? No such thing—they're *paying* for it. It's the town that's paying the chump change."

He stepped over to the counter. "Let me have the report, Jackie," he said. Doyle sullenly shoved it through the cutout in the shield. Pike stepped back and scanned the two pages. He nodded. "Looks straightforward enough," he said. He handed it to Drouhin. "See for yourself."

Drouhin accepted the papers. "*You,* Mister Whitman," Pike said, jabbing his right index finger at him. "*Now* I've got you. Long time ago, in my misspent youth, I would wager small sums on the New York Giants. I've forgotten the year now, but you once cost me a hundred bucks, big money in those days. I got the Giants over the Vikes, giving twelve points, so they gotta win by thirteen. Late in the third quarter they're up by six and on the march. They punch it in. Each team'd missed one extra point, and there's still a whole quarter to play so it makes good sense for the Giants to go for the two-point conversion. Simms fakes the hand-off; looks like he's going to run it in himself. But then he stops and throws a pass out in the flat to some receiver—name I forget, wanna say Pete Retzlaf—low snap on the extra point, and you came roaring out of nowhere and batted it away. That was it for the scoring that day and I lost my hundred bucks."

"Jeez," Whitman said, grinning, "I'm really sorry, and I'd like to help you out. But a lot of guys've told me that I cost them money when I *didn't* get to the ball and the receiver caught it. I start giving refunds I'd be bankrupt in a week. And the funny thing is, nobody's ever told me something I did *won* a bet for him, and offered me a piece."

Pike laughed. "Well," he said, "when guys bet on you, and you won, that was nothing special. That's what you were *supposed* to do, getting all that money for—win ball games for the Vikings, and bets for their loyal fans." He slipped the report through the cutout. "Lemme have the keys, Jackie," he said. Doyle opened a drawer to his right and brought out a four-inch ring of about twenty keys. He dropped it in the tray under the pass-through.

Pike took it up and said: "Come on, you two. Let's go and get your wandering boy. See if he can walk." To Ellis he said: "Jim, as far as I'm concerned, this one's personal recognizance. Chances are if he hasn't got the money on him, one of his two friends'll pay you your twenty-five."

"So I won't be needed, then?" Gold said.

"Not as far as I'm concerned," Pike said.

Gold looked exasperated. "Mister Gold," Drouhin said, "Jay, if I can call you that. We don't want you coming out here on a Sunday night and then getting stiffed for your trouble. If you'll give me your card, I'll have a check for a hundred bucks sent to you tomorrow, for your trouble."

"I'd appreciate that," Gold said, taking out his wallet. He gave a business card to Drouhin.

5

"THAT WAS CLASSY," PIKE said, jingling the keys on the ring as Whitman followed him and Drouhin down the corridor toward the door opening on the cellblock at the rear of the station, their footsteps padding on the cork floor between the glade-green walls.

"I don't care how much money a man makes or doesn't make," Drouhin said. "He puts his time in, he gets paid. If you can't use what he made or did with it, that's your problem, not his. He still gets paid." He lingered a moment over that. "Same as we do," he said.

"That's what I said," Pike said. "That's the class way to act."

"And you of course would know this," Drouhin said.

Pike, puzzled, glanced at Drouhin.

"Almost always," Drouhin said, "when we set out on one of these rescue missions, recover a client of ours from durance vile, get him into a hospital where they do detox or treat the results of steroid overdose, but're willing to call it 'exhaustion' or 'tests,' we have to run a gauntlet of TV cameramen and stupid reporters. They all seem to have this preposterous idea we're going to tell them truthfully what our client's so foolishly done. Or the nature and exact details of the horrible accident or illness that he's either caused or had happen to him or someone in his family. Even though full disclosure could permanently damage or ruin his career. Even when the client's been the *victim* of the accident, or a serious crime, they show no mercy. We still get hounded.

"Jilted girlfriend stabbed Donnie Sutter's brother in Baltimore last year, two days after Donnie's second no-hitter. The Braves were on a road trip and Donnie was in Montreal. FD had to fly up there with Pete Martigneau—he's our chief of security—to pull the wolves off Donnie. Peter's a retired State Police detective. Fortunately he thinks it's part of his job to maintain the law-enforcement connections he made in twenty years of being one, so he still had some clout with the Mounties. Donnie had to leave the team and go home to be with his mother, but they had him cornered like a rat—he couldn't leave his hotel room. Pete and FD had to go to the hotel engineering department and buy three sets of the blue coveralls the maintenance men wear and put them on over their clothes, and borrow three toolboxes, in order to sneak him out of the hotel. To get him to the airport, they hired a real hotel worker to drive them in a supply truck. The Mounties at the airport let him drive it right out on the apron to the Gulfstream we'd chartered. Got the tower to agree to put a hold on the flight plan 'til after it'd landed at Baltimore–Washington Airport at two forty in the morning.

"It didn't matter: The media scavengers had staked it out, that and the hospital, too. When Eddie died the next day, it took a special detail of Maryland State Police to get Donnie and his family out of the hospital and into seclusion. We issued a statement the funeral would be private, at a later date to be announced. After the autopsy and embalming the family had to store the body in a crypt under lock and key, hold off the funeral for six weeks. We announced it, as we'd promised, but not 'til the day after. By then some other poor famous bastard was going through *his* private hell. Donnie's grief was stale news. So the family actually did have some privacy to say good-bye to Eddie.

"That kind of harassment's the *rule,* not the exception. The lawyers and PR people we hire to do the same kind of work for our clients in other places report back the same experiences. Having to fight their way through barricades of TV-satellite-remote trucks. Doing their best to keep their dental work from being knocked out by assholes shoving mikes in their faces. Being blinded by TV lights. Tripping over cameramen crouching 'for a better angle.' And then being constantly badgered by phone all day the next day and the one after that—as long as it takes the story to die down, looking for more details. That either don't exist or no one in his right mind would divulge—in *our* offices, at least—under any circumstances. Which the reporters doing the badgering know just as well as we do. And then after you either mislead or 'no comment' them, being threatened repeatedly with the choice of denying some idiotic rumor or having it published as something you refused to deny.

"And that's just the *local* sports types. If the player's fame—for whatever reason—transcends the sport, like Pelé did soccer, Joe DiMaggio baseball, or there's a sex angle, then in addition to the local media you get the supermarket tabs. Flapping their black wings and cawing all around you every time you leave your office. Aiming super-telephoto lenses at the bathroom window. Bribing the neighbors to go through the player's trash for evidence of how much and what he drinks, snorts, and smokes. Or what his girl-friend uses for spermicide. They're the *real* horror show; compared to them, actual sportswriters and announcers're *tame*.

"And almost always," Drouhin said, "almost *invariably,* the explanation for the media stampede is either that the vultures picked the news off the police scanner or got tipped off by a venal cop, an ambulance driver, nurse, or an orderly who phoned in the news. For a price. No information about a Name is so small or so petty that someone, somewhere, won't put it on the air or print it, and once that's happened, *everybody* picks it up. Our clients get so much media exposure, denunciation, and envy for the money they make that even people cheering them resent them. And us. Nobody feels any shame about selling what they know or can find out about us to the highest bidder, and the buyers never hesitate to use it. If *your* marriage breaks up, even if it was your *fault,* your friends feel sorry for you. When our clients have marital problems, the media don't even bother hiding their glee. When they don't, the scandal sheets're not above providing some temptation, trying to provoke them. If a complete stranger sends you an invitation to a banquet fund-raiser for his favorite disease or handicap, and it says RSVP, you can throw it in the wastebasket and that's the end of it. If Bobby Moreno does the same thing, it's *news.* He 'spurned the annual event for crippled children, so Reader, you can tell he's a rotten bastard.' Ever wonder why all the pro teams and their athletes have their 'favorite charities'? To protect them from the conniving bastards who otherwise'd take advantage of them to attract gullible donors to dubious 'causes.' That's the going 'price of fame.'

"So," he said, "when FD and I drove out here tonight, we knew what to expect. Been through it before. Didn't like it a lot, but what the hell can you do? We were braced for it." He smiled at Pike. "And then it didn't happen. Nobody else was *here.* 'How could this be?' I thought, 'Someone in the bar must've recognized Buffalo Bobby

Moreno. Surely someone in the bar knows the *Enquirer*, the *Star*, and the *Midnight Globe* pay handsomely for tips.'

"Rubes and yokels galore bought themselves new customized Dodge cruising vans and bass boats with the loot they got for tailing Wade Boggs after Margot flushed him out and he confessed he's addicted to sex. Somebody who never leaves home without his camera with the built-in flash got the picture of a lifetime the night Boggs's wife whipped the SUV out of the parking lot so fast Wade got dumped onto the asphalt. When Mantle and Martin got bombed, had fights in the bars, it was all over town in the morning—though not in the papers, those days.

"But things've changed. 'What the hell's going on here?' we're asking ourselves. 'Red Ferraris're so common at the gin joints in Haymarket, no one notices one in the strip joint parking lot? Wonders who it belongs to?' "

"It's in the garage, other side of the building," Pike said laconically. "Redgate drove it back. Not the kind of vehicle you want to leave unattended in that neighborhood. Too many young wise guys, handy with tools."

With his left hand he touched Drouhin's right forearm and stopped. They were two-thirds of the way down the corridor. On the right behind Pike there were doors labeled Men and Women. "You should also know that Redgate didn't find that Colt forty-four Mag under the driver's seat," he said. "That's why it isn't mentioned in the arrest report. Which as you know is a public document. We'll have to release it tonight; tell the copy-desk kids who check the blotters for the TV stations and the papers a little after ten thirty that we busted Moreno tonight."

"He's licensed to carry," Drouhin said quickly.

"We know that," Pike said. "We have twenty-four-hour computer access to Public Safety. If he *hadn't* had the license, we *would've* found the gun. Would've had no choice. You wouldn't be in the process of getting him out, 'cause we'd be holding him. As it is, we're still giving him a break. He doesn't have a license to leave a gun unattended in his car. Nobody does—there's no such thing. So if he hadn't had the license, we definitely would've had to bring another charge against him, one not quite as easy to dispose of quietly as a charge of fighting in a strip joint." He paused.

"When you have the little talk with him I assume you'll want to have tomorrow, he's sobered up enough to understand what you say, we'd like you to mention that to him. Make sure he understands that he was lucky this time. That if cops ever officially find out he left a fully loaded firearm unattended in his car, he'll not only lose his license, he'll be in a whole other peckah shit besides. Firearms stolen from legit but careless owners're very popular with folks who're up to no good."

"I will do that," Drouhin said. "And I appreciate the *chance* to do it. We figured something like that instinct for diplomacy must be the explanation for the absence of the welcoming committee. 'Cops in Haymarket run a tight ship,' Nobody talks about nothing in public, or by means that the public can eavesdrop on."

Pike smiled. "Well," he said, "your man's not the first celebrity who's had a little trouble, one kind or another, in the fleshpots on Thirteen. And not just athletes, either. More'n one politician's sneaked out here for a professional-quality blow job—not always from a professional *lady*—or a quick-'n-dirty bum-fuck, and something's gone wrong with his plans. State senator got his picture taken, living color, at a Dress-Up Night six or seven years ago in lingerie—bra and garter belt, net stockings and spike heels. Full makeup, red wig—looked absolutely *fabulous*. Couple years ago we had a fairly prominent judge from another state very embarrassed after he had a bit too much to drink one night, got thrown out of the genteel gay bar for conduct unbecoming uptight homosexual gentlemen. Fondled a waiter who was straight—and didn't like it.

"You don't have to be queer to work in the gay bars. Equal Employment Opportunity guy actually told one of the owners that, guy who isn't queer himself. 'No discriminating on the basis of gender, sexual preference, employees, or customers. You can't tell people that they have to be gay to buy or serve a drink here.' You can be, and most of the employees are, but it's not mandatory.

"This particular waiter wasn't. He'd taken the job strictly for the money, so he could finish his training for a job in electronics. Not interested in making new friends or learning new ways. After the bouncers got him away from the judge, he called us on the phone. He wanted to file a criminal complaint. I sent Sergeant Palmer out to talk to him. Tell him that it might be in his own best interest to wait a day or so, see how sorry the judge was, what amends he might volunteer to make after his head'd cleared.

"Palmer told him his guess was his honor would be *very* sorry, and want to make things right. And sure enough, a few days later the kid pulls up out in front here with his cute little pregnant wife in their brand-new Subaru Outback. Seems he'd come into some money. Had enough more to quit the joint, go to electronics school full-time. Thanked us for our good advice. And we thanked him for helping to give the generous taxpayers who run the club another solid reason to be glad they're located where they are, sharing their profits with a town where people understand and forgive human weaknesses."

The gray steel door at the end of the corridor had a small window at eye level glazed with safety glass embedded with a wire grid. Using one of the keys on the ring, Pike unlocked the door, pulling it open with the U-shaped handle, setting off a loud buzzer. "Gentlemen," he said, bowing them through, "welcome to the animal house." Pike pulled the door shut behind them; it locked automatically.

Moreno was up. He stood at the front of the second cell, his big hands gripping two of the round ivory-painted vertical bars in the cell door above their junction with the higher of the two flat horizontal bars. At 6'3", two thirty-five, he seemed to fill the space with misery. His dark eyes were bleary and heavy-lidded, the right one swollen from sleep and the left enlarged by a glancing blow. His lips were puffy and blood had caked and dried around and below his swollen nose. His left cheek was cut. His shoulder-length curly brown hair was in disarray. An earring had been torn from his left earlobe; blood had dried on his neck. His yoked gold-embroidered ivory satin western shirt was bloody and stained with mucus, and his beige doeskin pants, sagging below his waist because his belt had been taken from him, were spattered too. The toe of the maroon cowboy boot on his left foot was badly scuffed. He bowed his head, snuffling and sobbing when he recognized Drouhin and FD.

Drouhin went up to the cell door. "Bobby, Bobby, Bobby," he said, in a soft crooning voice, "what *are* we gonna do with you? Can you tell me that?"

Moreno shook his head slowly, as though protecting something fragile that had become unfastened inside his skull.

"What happened to your face here, kid?" Drouhin said, reaching between the bars to touch Moreno's left cheek with the fingertips of his right hand.

Moreno pulled away, sobbing again. "I-uh-know," he said. "I think one of them had a ring."

"Or could've been brass knuckles," Pike said. "Glancing

blow with knuckle-dusters could've torn the skin like that. Kevin Sweeney's habit's to have something extra with him, cheap and easy to get rid of, case he finds himself outnumbered in a fight." He snickered. "Course Kevin thinks when it's just him and a friend or two against one other guy, that means it's okay to use it."

"Yeah," Drouhin said, "well, doesn't matter, I suppose. First thing we do, we get you out of here tonight, is have a doctor look at you. Make sure there's no reason you shouldn't be admitted, observation and so forth."

"I'm aw-*right*," Moreno moaned. He reared back, shaking the cell door. It rattled and banged against the frame. "I'm *okay*. Don't need no fuckin' *hospital*—just hadda fuckin' *fight*." He frowned and looked confused. "I got a little headache." He rubbed his right side with his right hand. "I think someone kicked my ribs. But I'm perfectly aw-*right*."

"You took a damned good beatin', Bobby," Drouhin said, withdrawing his hand.

"I did okay," Moreno said. "Those guys know I was there."

"That's not the point," FD said. "You could have a bad concussion, subdural hematoma. Clot breaks loose, you could lose your vision, have an aneurysm, stroke. What Alex says is right: You got to get checked out."

Moreno stepped back and lowered his head between his biceps so his torso was at an acute angle to the cell door. "Jus' wan' go home," he said. "Jus' wanna go home, go home, go *home*. Get outta here and go home."

"Mister Moreno," Pike said, "it's not just your agent's wish that you see a doctor. We in this department insist on it as a condition of release in *every* case where there's been a risk of permanent physical damage. If you were to develop some condition later on that could've been prevented by medical attention, we don't want you hiring some smart lawyer who figures the town's got more money'n a bunch of randy drunks, suing us instead of them."

"See?" Whitman said.

"Aw right," Moreno said, "I will go the doctor."

Drouhin looked at Pike. He nodded and stepped forward with the keys as Drouhin moved away from the door. Pike unlocked the cell door. "Have to ask you to let go and stand back, Mister Moreno," he said. "This door opens in." Still holding on and looking down, Moreno nodded and began to straighten up, releasing his grip on the bars and moving back in the cell. He stood in the center of it beside the bunk, his arms at his side, his head down and shoulders slumped.

"Jesus, Bobby," Whitman said solicitously, moving behind Pike into the cell as Pike opened the door, "those guys must've really kicked your ass, huh? Lieutenant here gave us the impression, you more'n held your own, but lookin' at you here like this, I guess they really rang your bell. Only *four* guys did all this? Would've thought it'd take more."

Moreno straightened up at once, throwing his shoulders back. "Three of them were on the *floor,* when the cops got there," he said. "The other one ran away. *I* was still on my feet."

"From what I heard, all this's true," Pike said. "You want to come out now?" Moreno, now erect, nodded. With Whitman at his left he moved somewhat unsteadily but at a stately pace out through the cell door into the corridor.

"If he wants," Pike said to Whitman, "you can take him into that men's room we passed on the way down and he can clean himself up a little. Wouldn't want to frighten the magistrate. Unless you think it might upset Mister Moreno to get a look at himself in a mirror."

"He's seen himself look worse'n this after regular-season

games," Whitman said. "I think he can stand it. You want to do that, Bobby? Get yourself cleaned up some?"

Moreno, walking carefully, nodded and said: "Yeah."

"Meanwhile Mister Drouhin and I'll go on out front and retrieve your belongings, get the papers ready for you to sign," Pike said.

Moreno, shambling momentarily, regained his dignified gait and nodded again solemnly. " 'Kay," he said.

Leaving Whitman and Moreno behind with the gray door closing behind them, Pike led Drouhin briskly back up the corridor. "Now," he said. "I'm sure this goes without saying, but I've been a cop in this town long enough to leave nothing to chance. When the three of you leave here tonight, I want him and you in your car and your sidekick driving the Ferrari."

"That's why I dragged FD out on Sunday night," Drouhin said. "No way do I want that car sitting around out here, drawing attention and raising questions."

"Naturally not," Pike said. "But the point I'm making is that I don't want the owner even *in* it when it leaves here. He was drunker'n a polecat before the fight started and during it he took a few pretty good shots. A lot of people saw him reeling around out there before Palmer and Chris Sweeney stuffed him in the cruiser and transported him back here. You saw for yourself just now that he's still pretty punchy. I don't want anybody seeing him in that Ferrari at a stoplight tonight, starting a false rumor that we let him drive home. He rides home with you."

"He will," Drouhin said.

"That brings us back to the gun," Pike said. "It's still in that car. Does FD have a license to carry?"

"He does," Drouhin said. "FD hates guns, wouldn't have one in the house. But in our experience with athletes this's not an isolated instance. All my associates are licensed."

"Okay," Pike said. "Now, I'll be unavailable when the

copy-desk interns start to call in. We don't allow the officer on the desk to comment beyond what's on the blotter. Sunday night, real reporters aren't on. So that'll stall off the tough interrogation 'til the deskmen roust out the varsity. That'll be after eleven, which should give you a fairly good start. Then I'll have to start taking calls and giving interviews over the phone. Otherwise they'll be out here in regimental strength.

"I want to be able to tell them truthfully that Moreno's agent requested that Mister Moreno be released tonight in order to seek prompt medical attention, and that I understand a doctor has been summoned to perform some tests tonight. But by the time they find out for sure that he's no longer here, and head for Natick, you should have him under cover there."

"You can tell them that," Drouhin said, "and it will check out. We've got a Brigham doctor who lives in Wellesley on call at all times. Now that I've had a look at him, I want him examined myself. When this news gets to Buffalo—which it will as soon as it hits the air tonight—the team'll go *apeshit*. I want to able to tell them, too, that I've had him examined and he looks to be okay. Which I think he is, but I want to be safe. I'll have her meet us at his house. Check his reflexes, look at his pupils and so forth. If she thinks there's the slightest reason why he should be hospitalized tonight, he will be."

"Good," Pike said.

"Now," Drouhin said, "If I'm in any way out of line in what I'm about to say, I don't mean to be and I want you to tell me so. My firm has small private boxes at the stadium in Foxboro, Fenway Park, and the Fleet Center. They accommodate six to ten people. Is there any reason why you and the three officers involved in this matter shouldn't have tickets to those seats sent to you?"

"Well," Pike said, "I think it would be inappropriate if

they were tickets to a night game this season, because that's the shift we're all on and we really should be here for it. But if we were to go to the Red Sox game on Patriots' Day, starts around eleven in the morning, account the Boston Marathon, we could have a hot dog and a beer or two and be back here in plenty of time to report for work on schedule."

"Done," Drouhin said. "But there won't be any hot dogs unless you insist. The usual menu's a buffet: roast beef, fried chicken, ham, and a seafood salad. Plus a choice of beverages, coffee, and several desserts."

"We can live with that," Pike said, "and if Doyle doesn't come, we'll get some of it, too."

6

DROUHIN WAS INITIALLY CONCERNED when he found
the gate open on the driveway leading to Moreno's large
and ungainly white house on the knoll overlooking the
Charles River in south Natick. There were lights on, too,
red-shaded lamps in the five Palladian windows across the
front of the house, the lanterns on each side of the portico
at the front door, and the solar-powered lights in the mush-
room fixtures on both sides of the drive. With the car window down he could hear faintly but not make out the
muffled audio of a television show noisily under way on a
set somewhere in the building.

For a moment this troubled him; the house should have
been empty. Moreno lived alone and gave his daytime cook
and housekeeper Saturdays and Sundays off. But he had a
history of giving extra keys impulsively to people he met
in joints but didn't really know very well, inviting them for
weekend stays. In October of 1995, while Moreno was
in Florida with the Bills for a game with the Dolphins,
Drouhin, without his knowledge, had had to employ some
off-duty cops to explain matters to a guest who seemed
seriously disoriented. To Moreno's distress the guest had
made it clear that after staying seven weeks he felt at home,

didn't wish to leave, and therefore didn't plan to. The cops had to help him pack his few belongings—while preventing him from packing a Minolta camera and an Apple Newton belonging to Moreno—and escort him to the Framingham line. There, they told him, the westbound hitchhiking was good, and advised him in a friendly fashion that he'd better take the first ride he was offered, never to return. Then Drouhin remembered the illumination timing system that he recommended to all his clients as a home-security measure. But he did not fully relax until he saw the Ferrari 308 GTB parked in the shadows just beyond the porte cochere.

He stopped the Mercedes in front of the two steps leading to the front door and shut the engine off. He was opening his door as Whitman emerged from the Ferrari. "I take it you enjoyed your ride," Drouhin said.

"During the day," Whitman said, hitching up his trousers, "I think driving that car the way it was meant to be driven would get you acquainted with quite a few cops. Clutch's very stiff. Now I know where Bobby gets the muscle in his left calf. And the brakes're *anchors,* man. You hit 'em and you *stop.* That gated shifter's tricky. Driving it at night, on roads you don't know, it's bit more exciting'n I'm used to. The cannon was under the driver's seat." He opened his car coat and displayed the revolver tucked into his belt.

"His door key should be in his keycase," Drouhin said. "Was the last time at least."

"Yeah, I checked it and it fits," Whitman said. "But I didn't open the door. The alarm's armed by a keypad. Last time I rode shotgun for you, he did this before? You must've had the code. I don't."

"Ninety-four, ninety-five," Drouhin said absently. "His first two really good years. He asked me when he built this place what numbers he should use, and being familiar with his habits, I said: 'Well, something *I'll* remember, knowing you.' By then I'd already brought him home a couple times. So he took the last two digits of the years when he became the star he is. Unless he's changed the number since then, and I don't know why he would, that should do the trick." They could hear dogs barking. "His dogs're glad he's home."

"Those're *dogs?*" Whitman said. "Sound like fuckin' *bears.*"

"Rottweilers," Drouhin said. "Four of them. But the kennel's in the back. Detached. They're just out in their pens."

The code worked. Whitman opened the front door, leaving it ajar, and both of them returned to the Mercedes. Drouhin opened the passenger-side door on Moreno, heaped slouching, asleep, snoring and gaping, on the passenger seat. "And this bag of crap's worth six mill a year," Whitman said. "Is this a great country or what?"

"No sneering, please," Drouhin said. "It's not Bobby's fault you were born too soon, 'fore the big money kicked in."

He took Moreno's right shoulder and shook him, first gently, then hard. Moreno awakened grudgingly, coughing and hawking. "*Oh-kay,* Bobby, come on now," Drouhin crooned. "We've got you and your car home, and the door to your house open, and you've been quite enough of a pain in the ass for other people tonight without being more of one now. So get *outta* the car, and *inna* the house, and we'll help you to get up to bed. Upsy-daisy."

Maintaining his hold on Moreno's right arm, he stepped back and pulled, and Moreno, at first passive, extricated his feet and legs from the footwell and planted them on the ground. He turned on the seat, extending and raising his left arm and hand, seeking the additional help that

Whitman provided at once. Together he and Drouhin pulled Moreno out of the car and erect. "Mwah," Moreno said, working his tongue in his mouth.

"Absolutely," Drouhin said, turning and draping Moreno's right arm over his own shoulders. "You get him on the left, FD," he said.

"Roger that," Whitman said, turning and taking Moreno's left arm over his shoulders. Together they started toward the steps.

Moreno began to sing. "No one here can love or understand *meee*. Oh what hard-luck stories they all *haaand* me."

"Yeah, we know, Bobby," Whitman said. "You've had a very hard life. Pick your left foot up and put it on the first fuckin' step."

Inside the house several phones were ringing.

Moreno unsteadily did as he was told. "Make my bed an' light the light, I'll be home late tonight.... Black...bird..." He stopped on the first step and reflected. "Where did that come from? I was just singin'? Where did that song come from? Who the hell used to sing that?"

"Blossom Dearie," Drouhin said. "Steve Lawrence and Eydie Gorme. Move your fuckin' fat ass up another step and across the goddamned entryway, and then upstairs to your bedroom, you fuckin' good-for-nothin' drunk. I'm fed up with you."

"*Alex,*" Whitman said, "you are saying this to the six-million-dollar *man?*"

"Go fuck yourself, FD," Drouhin said.

"An' *I* don't *blame* you," Moreno said, negotiating the second step and stopping once again on the flagstone floor of the entryway. "Not for one damn minute. 'S'nawful thing I do to you guys, all you done for me." He considered what he had said as he negotiated the second step. Then he nodded. "Awful, awful, thing." He shuffled across the floor of the portico and after holding his right foot extended over the doorsill for a moment at last planted it inside the house and brought his left after it, lurching to his left nearly hard enough to unbalance Whitman.

"Shit," Whitman said, using both arms to push Moreno's torso back toward upright, "getting this package up those stairs's gonna be no picnic, is it?"

The phones continued to ring.

Drouhin grunted "Stop," coming to a halt in the foyer. He was panting. "Let me catch my breath a minute," he said. "Christ, you're heavy, Bobby, you're deadweight like this."

"I'm sorry," Moreno said. "Someone oughta getta phone. Gotten it myself, 'f I was *in*side." He belched. "But I was *out*side."

"You're right," Drouhin said to Whitman.

"Course I am," Moreno said, looking at him owlishly. "I'm ah one jus' said it, *riii?* May be *drunk* but I know where I *am*."

Drouhin ignored Moreno. To Whitman he said: "He's going to be too much for us to haul up those stairs." He inhaled deeply. "Whaddaya think, Bobby? Can you make it upstairs by yourself? Or're you gonna put so much weight on the bannister you'll pull it outta the wall, fall back down here on your head?"

"Or back down on *us*," Whitman said. "I realize the guy's an asset to the company and all, and we have to protect him from harm, but I'm not prepared to put my*self* in the hospital for him. Reason I retired at thirty-five was I was sick 'n tired of having guys lots bigger'n I am knock me on the ground and fall on top of me. I say we put him on the couch, get a blanket from upstairs, and cover him with that. What do you say?"

"I uh know," Moreno said, his eyes unfocused, his head lolling as he spoke. "I can't *see* ah...*bannister* too good."

"Right," Whitman said, "and if your vote counted, that'd be another reason."

"I think so," Drouhin said, steering Moreno around so that he faced the living room and the two white leather couches flanking the fireplace and square white marble block serving as a coffee table in front of it. "In the living room you go."

"*Nooo,*" Moreno said, wrenching free of him and removing his left arm from Whitman's shoulders. "*Not* going in the living room. Know you're not s'posed to do that. Going in the *bath*room, like I always do." He staggered away from them and lumbered down the hallway to the left of the staircase, tripping over the end of the oriental runner carpeting it and banging into the imitation Windsor side table under the tall mirror on the gold-papered inner wall, but unsteadily making forward progress toward the other end and the door opening under the stairs on the right. Holding onto the door frame with his left hand, he fumbled with his right hand inside it and after pawing for about fifteen seconds, saying "fuck" three times in a puzzled tone of voice, at last found the light switch and turned it on. Then unzipping his pants with his right hand while maintaining his grip on the door with his left, he lurched out of their sight. They heard a clank.

"I hope that was him grabbing either the towel rack or the sink," Whitman said.

The phones rang on.

"Yeah," Drouhin said, starting forward, "and not his head hitting the commode." He started down the hallway. Whitman hung back. Drouhin reached the doorway and looked in. He saw Moreno with his eyes closed and his pants down on the floor, seated at a slight angle to his left on the toilet, his right hand at his crotch. Drouhin saw his face go slack and heard him start to urinate loudly into the toilet, his left hand gripping the towel bar on the wall.

"From the noise I gather he's all right," Whitman said. "Plumbing's functioning at least."

"Yeah," Drouhin called back down the hall, "but he looks like he's falling asleep again."

"Good," Whitman said, "that takes care of it, then. He's not going up to bed and he's not sleeping on the couch—he's spending the night on the pot." He looked at his watch. "It's almost midnight, for Christ sake. Those phones're driving me nuts. Guy doesn't even have an answering service, for God's sake?"

"One of the reasons he took my advice to have an unlisted number was he thought it'd mean he wouldn't get any calls—except from people he *wanted* to be able to call him," Drouhin said.

"And then he most likely gave that number to anyone who asked him for it," Whitman said.

"Well, he wanted the people at the hospital to be able to get in touch with him, his mother needed anything," Drouhin said.

"Okay," Whitman said, "so *they* give it out to anyone who asks. Look, sooner or later *he'll* finish pissing, but those *phones*'re going to ring all night—the news's hit the wires and the free press never sleeps. Let's get the hell out of here."

"No," Drouhin said. "Not 'til he's finished and we get him on the couch." The flow of urine slowed audibly. "Come on," he said, using his right hand to beckon Whitman. "We can't leave him sitting here like this. He's liable to fall asleep and bang his head on the sink." The sound of the urine stream stopped. "Come on," he said to Whitman, "he's finished." He stepped into the bathroom.

"Pull your pants up, Bobby, and see if you can stagger into the living room and lie down. Use the walls if you have to, keep yourself more or less upright."

"Jesus H. Christ," Whitman said, reaching the doorway as Moreno reached down with his right hand and pulled his pants up, gripping the towel rod with his left and pulling himself up. "He doesn't have any shorts on?"

"Never does, he goes out to have sex," Drouhin said. "He told me that once. Said he 'feels freer that way.' " Then as Moreno released his grip on the towel bar, needing both hands to buckle his belt and close his fly, he stumbled forward, nearly falling. Drouhin stepped forward. "Just put your dick away, Bobby," he said. "You can do that with one hand and hold on with the other. I'll fix your belt and help FD guide you down the hall, but you're gonna have to tuck your dick away yourself."

"Well, that's good to hear," Whitman said. "There's at least one thing you won't do to keep a client."

Drouhin laughed. "It's a fine line but I do draw it," he said. "Never mix business and pleasure." Then he snickered. "But better not try to zip your fly, Bob. Liable catch your pecker in it."

Whitman laughed but Moreno stuffed his penis into his pants, then arched his back and yawned noisily three times while Drouhin buckled his belt. "Go to *sleep*," he said. "Want to go to *sleep*."

"Not 'til you're on the couch, Bob," Drouhin said, taking his right arm and urging him toward the door, Moreno using his left hand on the wall and then the door frame to steady himself. Once clear of the bathroom, he allowed Whitman to take his left arm and steer him back down the hallway, despite the assistance nearly losing his balance as they turned the corner into the living room, shuffling his feet and drooling slightly. They brought him to a stop facing the couch furthest from the door, thus avoiding an additional dangerous turn, and wheeled him slowly and very carefully until the couch was behind him.

"Okay," Drouhin said, "now just *ease* him down there. Don't want him falling forward and cracking his head on that tombstone Marcel talked him into buying for a table. Then I'll go upstairs and fetch a blanket for him."

"Take a phone off the hook while you're up there," Whitman said. Moreno sagged onto the couch at a slight angle, but once seated felt more secure and lay down, clasping his hands on his stomach and closing his eyes. Drouhin left the room. Whitman went over to the opposite couch and removed two of the three thick seat cushions. He put one on top of the block of marble and propped the other against the side nearest the couch where Moreno lay, now starting to snore.

Drouhin climbed the stairs and, with no previous knowledge of the second-floor plan, turned right on the landing at the top. That took him into a hallway lighted by the lamps in the windows of the rooms that opened off it on the front. It was thickly carpeted. On the theory that the front rooms were for guests and show, he opened the first door on the left. It was dark; there was a phone ringing in it. Relying for guidance on Moreno's search for the light in the bathroom downstairs, Drouhin with his right hand found a switch inside the doorway on the left. It lighted a halogen floor lamp near Clan McGregor plaid patterned drapes pulled tightly open at the ends of a picture window. Through the window the light went out onto the backyard, lighting the chain-link fencing enclosing the asphalt exercise runs extending from the six white kennels. The dogs at once emerged again, jumping up against the fences and barking toward the house.

The room had been furnished as an office, but was

plainly seldom used for business. There was a desk at the wall to Drouhin's left, equipped with a Compaq computer with a seventeen-inch color monitor showing a screen-saver program of white roosters with red combs and yellow legs and feet alternately marching across and then up and down a black background, crowing softly from time to time. The keyboard, the area of the desk around it, the seat of the high-backed leather swivel chair pushed beside it, and the three-doored Moorish-style credenza were covered with unopened mail and parcels with UPS and Federal Express logos. Drouhin stepped back into the hall, but then he paused and thought a moment. Then he went forward to the desk. He leafed through the mail, without his reading glasses, recognizing his firm's buff envelopes printed and addressed in blue ink. Curious, Drouhin took his glasses from the case in his right inside-breast pocket and put them on. There were eleven envelopes from Alexander Drouhin & Associates. The one on top was postmarked October 21. The one on the bottom was dated March 2. None of them had been opened. The other envelopes cluttering the desk included several stating monthly interest rates and carrying return addresses of banks in Delaware soliciting new customers for their credit cards.

On the chair were catalogues from manufacturers of clothing and footgear for big and tall men, the Franklin Mint, Lillian Vernon, and Victoria's Secret, and pristine copies of *Sports Illustrated*, *Soldier of Fortune*, *Guns and Ammo*, *Playboy*, and *Car and Driver* magazines.

On the credenza there were six unopened boxes from the Franklin Mint and a silver wooden model of an F-16 Falcon fighter with U.S. Air Force insignia ascending from a black plastic stand. There was a fat red button in the center of the black stand. Curious, Drouhin pressed it. A speaker in the stand emitted a fifteen-second recording of the high-pitched scream and undertone rumble of a jet engine running at maximum throttle. Next to the fighter plane, atop other magazines, was a thick manila envelope imprinted with the return address "Law Offices of James R. Haggerty, PLC, 15 Court Square, Boston, MA 02108." It had not been opened.

From the first floor Whitman called, "Any luck with the blanket, Alex?"

Drouhin without hesitation removed his glasses and recased them, returning them to his pocket. Then he picked up the manila envelope, and lifting his turtleneck, inserted it between his trousers and underwear on the left side of his body, pulling the turtleneck down over it and then buttoning his jacket. The phone on the desk continued to ring. He picked up the handset and heard the caller say excitedly "Is this the Moreno residence?" Drouhin placed the handset on the letters from his office. The phones ringing elsewhere in the house went still.

He nodded and left the room, turning off the light. He crossed the hall diagonally into the second doorway on the right at the front of the house. There was an unmade king-size bed in it, a blue goose-down quilt bunched up at its center. Drouhin went to the bed and picked up the comforter, shaking it out and folding three times to make a bundle he could carry. He returned into the hall as Whitman came to the foot of the stairs, shouting, "You okay up there, Alex? Need some help or something?"

"Found it," Drouhin called back. "Located a phone and unhooked it. On my way down now. No need to come up." Elsewhere in the building, other phones began to ring.

7

IN THE FOYER DROUHIN hunched his left shoulder once and pressed his right hand against his left rib cage, in order to shift the Haggerty envelope higher up under his left armpit between his turtleneck and T-shirt, so that the bottom of the parcel rested more comfortably on his pelvis.

Whitman, standing by the open door on the passenger side of the Mercedes, noticed and stepped forward, saying: "You all right, Boss?"

"I'm fine," Drouhin said, punching in 9495 on the alarm keypad and swiftly closing the door behind him. "Oh oh," he said.

"*What?*" Whitman said.

"The doctor," Drouhin said. "I promised the cop I'd call Doctor Sheila and have her look at him. I didn't."

"Oh, *fuck* the doctor," Whitman said, opening the passenger's door of Drouhin's car and dropping down into the seat. "That cop doesn't care if you actually *did* call a doctor, had the asshole looked at, after he let him out. What the cop cared about was you *saying* you'd call a doctor, have a look at him. Now something happens, Bobby's brain wave goes even flatter'n normal, *you're* the one on the hook, not the cop. That's all the cop had in mind. Case closed. Get inna fuckin' car and drive me back to mine."

"But that was one smart cop," Drouhin said. "Until he told me tonight, I didn't know you can't leave guns in your car in this state," Drouhin said. "Have to make a note to send out a client advisory on that." He came down the two porch steps carefully, pausing on the landing to put his left foot down first, then hesitating on that step until he brought his right foot down and repeated the maneuver. He did the same thing to reach the pavement. Then he walked carefully around the front of his Mercedes, touching the sloping hood with the fingertips of his left hand as he passed in front of the car. He opened the left door and leaned on it for a moment, breathing deeply.

Whitman leaned over the transmission hump so that he could look up into Drouhin's face. "You okay, Boss?" he said. "You're not really acting right."

"Didn't sleep that well last night," Drouhin said, exhaling heavily. "Too much on my mind. Couldn't make it go away." He swung his right leg and then his body into the car, using his left hand to pull his left leg in after him. He closed the door. He clamped both hands on the steering wheel and inhaled deeply. He used his right hand to fish his keys from his right outside-jacket pocket and flopped the ignition key free of the case. "*Ahhh*," he said, starting the engine, "I'm too old to be keeping these hours."

"I've been telling you years to slow down," Whitman said, as Drouhin drove the big two-seater around the circular drive and back toward the gate. "I know why you drive yourself like you do; I understand. You think your clients're basically children. *Big*, muscular kids, physically gifted, but basically children. Think you have to take care of them. Because they can't—or won't—take care of themselves. Most of the time you're right. But it comes out of your *hide*, man. You just can't keep on doing it. To yourself."

"Shit," Drouhin said, as the car reached the gate, "I

forgot about this. How'd you open the gate, you got here?"

"I didn't," Whitman said. "It was open."

"You're sure of that," Drouhin said, his foot on the brake, staring at him.

"Alex," Whitman said, "if I knew the code for the gate, I would've known the code for the alarm. I didn't. That's why I don't know the number to close it now. Leave the damned gate open. Bobby's secure. You set the house alarm yourself. So what if he wakes up hungover in the morning, lying in his own puke on the couch; the maid tells him the yard's fulla reporters? He came by it honest. Bastard earned it. Let 'im get a little personal taste what it feels like, clean up after himself."

Drouhin eased the car through the gate and right down the street toward route 16. "I don't *know* anymore," he said. "I'm sixty-two years old and I've been in this business almost thirty years. I should *know* what's going *on* by now. But I don't. I can't make decisions the way I used to. Don't have the confidence, feeling of *assurance*, that I used to have, deciding how to deal with people."

"You don't *delegate* enough," Whitman said. "That's another thing I've been telling you for years. I'm pretty well stretched, myself, but Lionel and Dougie and McGinnis and Carl can handle much more work'n you give them. There's no reason for you to be still representing Methodiste, for God's sake. He's a lost cause. You're not making any money listening to his endless amounts of shit—he's overdue at the library, and you're paying a nickel a day to represent him. Should've shunted him to Barry or Maurice two years ago, let them get some seasoning. Darrell Troop's who you should be spending your hockey time on. Assuming hockey's worth spending *any* of our time on, of course, which I'm not totally convinced it is."

"In the first place," Drouhin said, his voice cold and flat, "when I market Jean Claude, I'm marketing Darrell Troop. That's what *I* understand about the way what's left of this business works. And what the *rest* of you, as capable as you may be, generally do not. One hand washes the other. Handled in the right way, things fit together. Because we represent Jean, we get Darrell as a client. Because we represent Darrell, we can persuade a team in trouble to make a place for Jean."

"You overrate your influence," Whitman said, his voice as hard as Drouhin's. "Your name's on the door. That's all."

"In the second place," Drouhin said, turning right on route 16 and continuing as though Whitman had not spoken, "I'm a member of the Massachusetts bar, and I can represent anyone who wants to hire me. In the third place: we're in no position these days to turn away any kind of client on any basis—the sport they play, how old they are, or how much they can command. That bastard Knight at Nike changed the rules. When a pro franchise and its game-venue lease change hands for two hundred million dollars, it's big news. People say the new buyer overpaid. Even back then, before they got Jordan and then Pippen and Phil Jackson, Nike was worth over three *billion*.

"All Knight did was put his own outfit's money to work. Signed Alonzo Mourning and Howard Miner out of college to comprehensive management contracts. Essentially he was giving them advances on their pay for promoting shoes and gear. Nike would have kept the money Knight was originally offered by the Charlotte Hornets for Mourning: eleven million a year. Mourning turned it down. Then Knight kept the money from the Miami Heat for Miner, and after that the money that he got for Mourning from the Heat. When he signed Tiger Woods out of Stanford last year, it wasn't anything brand-new; it was just the latest example of Knight seeing something he had enough money to make happen, a long time ago. If sports is the culture of this country—and it sure is now—then the way you corner markets is not by *representing* big-name people who play sports. It's by *buying* them. And then renting them out to the teams and the pro tourneys and the soft drink companies and all the other people selling stuff to people dumb enough to want to eat the same burgers and cereal as their favorite star claims he eats.

"Now Reebok's doing the same thing. We can't compete with those guys. We don't have the capital. Our selling point to the kids's always been: 'We'll run your life for you, better'n you can. You'll pay us a commission and be damned glad you did. Grateful to us.' The way we financed that offer was by getting money from the teams, the soft drink people, and the guys who make the movies and the burgers. And the guys who make the shirts and shoes. *They're* the ones with the money. Our service was getting it away from them and transferring it to our clients, taking our cut off the top.

"Unfortunately, the guys with the money figured this out. So lately what they've been doing is cutting *us* out. The reason we need old hockey players and the reason we go out Sunday nights and get drunks out of jail is because we need those guys to stay in business. We need the defensive linemen and the small forwards who can come off the bench and give the Knicks quality minutes. The guys who don't interest Nike. The utility infielders who play hurt. The pitchers carrying four-point-nine-two ERAs in the Cape Cod League getting signed to Triple-A minor-league contracts by big-league teams. Because there're thirty of those clubs now with two more on the way, and they need bodies to put out there, give them innings. The big-ticket legit marquee players get snapped up by the guys who've got the money *we* used to get from *them* for top clients so more top clients'd come to us."

"So we're doomed," Whitman said. "Dinosaurs. We're obsolete. Unless we change. I never thought the day'd come I'd hear you saying this."

"No, we're not doomed," Drouhin said. "If we recognize we're in a niche, and that that niche's changed, we'll do well for many more years. Least as long as I'm around, which's all I care about. Our job's to provide service to people who aren't good enough to have rich buyers coming to them, don't know how to leverage markets so they get the most they can for what they're worth, and don't know how to manage it after they get it."

"Welcome to the real world," Whitman said. "We've been trying to tell you that for some years now."

Drouhin grunted. In Wellesley, he took the ramp leading north on route 128/93. He accelerated to eighty-five. Whitman fidgeted in the passenger seat, then reached back to the B-pillar behind the seat and extended the safety belt, wrapping it around his chest and fastening it next to the transmission console.

"Well, you were the one concerned about the hour, back when we were at Bobby's house," Drouhin said. "Thought you wanted to get home."

"I was, and I do," Whitman said. "That's what bothers me about riding with you now—I want to make it home."

"This from the guy who pushed that Ferrari from Haymarket back to Natick in record time, well ahead of me?" Drouhin said.

"You bet," Whitman said. "I've got fourteen years on you, and I'm in much better shape. My reflexes're still good and I don't need glasses. I'm not as big a fan of the good life as you are. And I haven't been at it as long. How fast

I can drive safe at night's not the same number as how fast you can drive."

For a while Drouhin said nothing. Then he increased his speed to ninety briefly before allowing it to recede again to eighty-five.

"Just to show you can still do anything you want?" Whitman said.

Drouhin nodded. "Something like that," he said. "We all need to, now and then. It's a basic human craving. I was saying just a week or so ago to Peter that I think I'm going to have to fire Rigo and Angela. Get myself fresh help to run the place in Easton."

"But I thought you were always raving about how good a cook she is," Whitman said, his tone carrying distress. "Completely trust her with running the house. And whenever I've been there, the grounds've always looked good. So he must know what he's doing, too. And didn't you build their house on your land, give it to them?"

"I did," Drouhin said. "But the deed wouldn't have to be that big an obstacle. There're very few written agreements drawn up by lawyers that can't be undone by other lawyers. If they're well motivated."

"But why do this?" Whitman said. "And why do it now?"

"Maybe to regain—reassert—some control," Drouhin said. "Over at least one aspect of my life. As you so kindly just pointed out, I'm not as young as I used to be, and I sometimes wonder if people aren't trying to take advantage. Just as concerned as I am about the future of our end of the business, how much downsizing has to be done, it's still to remain a going concern. A viable firm. A valuable asset. This's something I have to think about."

"Of course," Whitman said.

"Yes," Drouhin said, after a while. Then he reduced the

car's speed to eighty. "Know why dogs lick their balls?" he said, as though he had just thought of it.

"Can't say it ever concerned me," Whitman said.

"Because they can," Drouhin said.

"Oh," Whitman said.

"Keep it in mind," Drouhin said.

PART
TWO

8

ALEXANDER DROUHIN'S twenty-two-room house was invisible from the road, route 123 in Easton, but Frank Clay was prepared for that. Seeing the name on the Missing Person report, he'd recalled reading a long feature article about Drouhin in the paper some years before. Stuck in his mind was the oddity he'd found in the fact that the ten-foot chain-link fence surrounding Drouhin's acreage "for security purposes" had been carefully concealed, "to preserve the scenery," set back from the roadway and hidden behind tall, tangled, bushy, reddish-brownish vinelike crown vetch Drouhin had had planted for the purpose. Wondering again why a sports agent would feel threatened, and whether his concern recorded then might hold some clue to his disappearance now, Clay, before leaving the office, had called up NEXIS on his personal laptop and read the article again. His memory had been accurate. Passersby saw only the plain white two-board fence along the road that Clay was seeing now on his left. He'd forgotten that same question—why a sports agent would need tight security—had occurred to the feature writer.

"Many of my clients are nationally famous—the Olympians even internationally—long before they turn pro. These are *young* people, remember, magnificent athletes, but they've always been sheltered. Their families, their coaches, shield them from the world, so they can concentrate on developing their abilities—which was generally pretty much all they were interested in doing anyway. So they tend to be one-dimensional. When they first come to me, what they are is what they do. I don't mean that they're stupid, not by any means—the boneheaded athlete's the exception now, not the rule, I'm glad to say. They're intelligent enough, but socially inexperienced. So when all the hard work finally pays off and they first turn pro, they have a lot of catching up to do. They don't know what to expect when they first go out into the world without that protection around them.

"Just from the privacy angle, it's impossible for them to stay in hotels, eat in a restaurant, have a drink in a bar, whatever, and have any hope of being left alone. 'Autograph seekers': you say that and people think of some eager ten-year-old kid with freckles on his face, waiting outside the gate to get a foul ball signed by his hero. But that's Norman Rockwell stuff, a thing of the past now. Today it's a major year-round business for those hounds—those signatures're worth big bucks to the collectors at the card shows. So the people who go after them, they don't care where the guy is, what he's doing—they'll stop at nothing. That's why the players stopped signing for free—they should take time out of *their* lives and give it away, to create stuff people then *sell?* Players found out *that* was going on, that's when they said, 'Forget about that crap. You're going to make money off our signatures, baby, we're going to make money too.'

"That's what they're griping about when they say the teams should stop being cheap and lease their own planes for road trips, fly general aviation. When teams fly commercial, even if it's a private charter, got the whole plane to themselves, they still have to run the gauntlet at the commercial terminals, going in and going out. Either sign and look like suckers, or refuse, and look like stinkers.

"Memorabilia's even worse. To the *rich* jock-sniffing collectors, personal gear *is* holy relics. The guys with the big private collections compete with each other more'n the players do on the field. Money's no object. They'll pay almost anything to one-up other collectors. Guarantee it. Create a savagely competitive market like that, people will compete just as savagely for product to sell in it. They'll stop at nothing. If a player has to set his equipment bag down to use the men's room in an airport, he'd better take it in the stall with him, plant his foot on it, and keep it there, even when he's reaching for the paper. Because unless he does that, someone'll stick a tire iron or a nine-iron in under the door, snag the duffel by the straps, and snake it out of there. Before the player can pull his pants up, open the door, and go after him, the thief is long gone with the goodies.

"That's what the Red Sox players were talking about when they complain about the team making them carry their own luggage on road trips. Not that the players're too proud or too feeble to schlep it themselves; without equipment managers whose job is to handle it and watch it on the road, they couldn't relax for a minute, let their stuff out of their clutches. You got any idea how much money you could get for a mitt? A cap? An actual warm-up jacket that an actual player really sweated into—him*self*? Cal Ripken Junior's uniform shirt? Rickey Henderson's shoes? The bat Junior Griffey used to hit his hundredth home run?

"Thousands of dollars. So these people're extremely aggressive. What some're willing to pay incredible amounts of money for, others will therefore go to incredible lengths to steal. Give them half a chance—they will. You and I may think they're sick, but nothing can stop them.

"And as you and I also know—these young athletes often do not—this is also a *dangerous* world. There are lunatics out there who'll do anything, *anything*. Think of Monica Seles, all right? Stabbed in the back—not after stupidly allowing herself to be lured into a dark alley at night; sitting at courtside, in broad daylight. During a tournament, in front of thousands of people. The end of her ranking as Number One in the world, if not the end of her career. Star ballplayers in every sport have to use aliases when they're on the road, stay at different hotels from the rest of their teams. Not because they're too good for their teammates—for their own safety. So that the nuts, possibly armed, won't find them when they lie in wait with weapons at the official team hotels.

"You should see the letters they get. People they've never met're either determined to have sex with them or else they're haters, determined to kill them. Sometimes it's the same handwriting. The same person wrote both letters, the mash note and the death threat, a month or six weeks apart. The death threat after the next road trip when the athlete didn't show up to have sex. 'I can't have you then nobody can.' That's when you really begin to get worried, small beads of sweat—if not blood—pop out on your face. This can be a frightening world.

"I take a holistic view of this business. I think of it as a profession, in fact, a legal specialty. Just as some of my friends in the bar specialize in corporate law, real estate law, tax law, litigation, I specialize in sports law. To me that means I should do everything I can to improve the total welfare of my clients. So I think it's part of my job to *protect* them, physically, and do as much as I can to see to it that nothing bad happens to them out in the world as

I do to protect their interests during contract talks, getting the best possible deals and endorsements, and advising them financially.

"Not all agents feel this way. They say it's too paternalistic. I'm aware of that, but I wouldn't feel right otherwise. So when my clients come to Boston to see me, I put them up at my place. And if they're going to play for a team in Boston—until we can get them settled in their own places. The elaborate security's not for me—it's for them."

Clay looked for the fence and the mailbox, numbered 1100, and found it on the left, about six miles west of route 27. He drove the black Corvette through the white wooden gates—"always open," the article had said, "strictly for show"—and then past the keypad on the post on the left at the heavy iron gate fifty yards further in, following the curving driveway southwest through the empty meadow on either side, beige in the mid-morning light of the third Monday in February of an open winter. The country looked open too, all the way to the tree lines several hundred yards away. "Twenty-eight acres" the article said. "Enough for the subdivision of more than twenty house lots originally laid out for it." *Worth how much now, with the Boston commuter trains coming back?*

The meadow was a plateau. When Clay reached the edge about a quarter mile from the road he found himself looking down at an enormous building set into the southerly side of a long gentle slope leading down to a three- or four-acre pond. The main house was three-storied, with great bay windows on both sides of a black double door under the columned portico. The brass fittings on the front door gleamed in the sunlight. The second-floor window above the door was a Palladian arch about fifteen feet tall, flanked by two more, about ten feet tall, on either side. Five third-floor windows were set into gables in the gray slate roof.

There was a large chimney in the center of the house and another at each end.

The two-story wings extending like embracing arms at thirty-degree angles on each side of the main building were white stucco, with white columned walkways. There were four doors in the wing on the left. The wing on the left had one door at each end. There were four smaller chimneys on the roof of the easterly wing, one above each door, and one at each end of the westerly wing. Another chimney rose behind the house, suggesting a third wing at the rear. Off to the left at the tree line behind the easterly wing at the front there was another house; a low brick ranch with white trim. Next to it on the southerly side was a long garage with ten doors. The asphalt apron in front extended fifty feet to the south; there was a thirty-foot white circle painted on it. "Mercy," Clay said.

The drive divided in front of the westerly wing, the right leading down toward the rear of the house and the left the entrance to the circular front drive. Clay entered the left at the five-o'clock-point and drove the Corvette past the two State Police cruisers parked behind the Crime Scene truck in front of the door. Beyond that were two Easton Police Department cruisers, the second marked "Chief" above the badge painted on the door, parked behind Dr. Myrna Roscommon's black cruiser, gold-lettered "Bristol County Medical Examiner" on the door. Clay pulled in at the eight o'clock position in front of her car. He left his trench coat on the passenger seat.

There was yellow Crime Scene tape around the pillars of the portico. The tape snapped in the wind. He climbed the two steps of the flagstone portico and ducked under it. A black hexagonal wrought-iron lantern hung from the ceiling. Mourning doves grieved in the meadows. A steady cold wind blew from the northeast. He rang the bell. After about forty seconds that seemed longer and made him wish he had worn the trench coat, a young female uniformed trooper whom he did not recognize opened the door. He hesitated in mid-stride, imperceptibly, he hoped; even after several years of exposure, he was still not quite used to the sight of well-built young women in State Police uniform, their neckties held several inches out from their bulging shirtfronts, the ends two buttons above the black belts needed only for convenient carriage of sidearm, cuffs, radio, and other gear, the uniform pants being quite tight enough over the buttocks and thighs to stay up by themselves. This one had short dark hair and brown eyes in a fresh, open face.

"Clay," he said, starting forward again, thinking: *Oh my dear, twenty years ago, what I could have done with you. Tried to do, at least.*

She put up her hand. "Sir," she said, "this's a crime scene. No one admitted without ID."

He stopped and sighed, remaining in the wind, and reached into the left inside pocket of his gray tweed jacket, producing his State Police ID and badge. "Lieutenant," she said, stepping back, "sorry to be so picky, sir." The black tag with the white lettering on the slope of the pocket flap over her left breast said: "Gagnon."

"No," he said, stepping in gratefully out of the wind. She shut the door firmly behind him. "You did the right thing, Gagnon. Never apologize for following procedure. No one can gig you for that. Two bluebirds out front; who else've we got here?"

"Trooper Ernst, sir," she said. "He's in the kitchen with the couple who take care of the place. They're the only ones who were here all last night, so he's making sure they don't talk to anyone else 'til after they've talked to you."

"Well done," Clay said.

The foyer was circular. Directly ahead there was a broad mahogany staircase carpeted in a predominantly pale blue Aubusson held flat against the risers by brass rods. Beyond the stairs there was a closed door on each side. The floor of the foyer was pink marble, bordered in deep maroon stone. In the morning it was lighted by a skylight; for the hours of darkness there was a broad gold and crystal chandelier suspended in the stairwell. In the center of the floor the five interlocked Olympic rings were inset in gold. Behind the rings was a round mahogany table with a large bouquet of two dozen white and yellow football chrysanthemums, brilliant in the sunlight. To the left behind the inset of the rings there was a curved mahogany table displaying replicas of the trophies awarded to the winners of the French, U.S., and Australian Tennis Opens. There was a white card with black script between the French and U.S. trophies. To the right behind the inset of the rings there was an identical table. It held replicas of the trophies awarded to the winners of the British Open and the U.S. Open. Between them there were two white cards with black lettering.

The paneling was dark mahogany with fluted entablature. There was a double door with fluted columns and an intricate cornice on each side. Lighted shadow boxes flanked the doors. The one closest to the front doors on the left contained a replica of the Vince Lombardi Trophy, a silver football on a silver pylon. The one further away contained a half-size replica of the Stanley Cup. The one closest to the front door on the right displayed a replica of the World Series Trophy, a miniature silver stadium topped with the flags of the major league clubs. The further box on the right contained a replica of the National Basketball Association Trophy.

"They're all in the library," the trooper said. "It's through those doors on the left."

"I like to acclimate myself in the surroundings where the crime occurred, get myself oriented, before I try to investigate it," Clay said. "Quirk of mine." He went over to the table on the left, putting his glasses on, and read the card: "Reserved for Wimbledon." The cards on the table on the right read: "Reserved for the Masters" and "Reserved for the PGA." He straightened up and looked at Trooper Gagnon again. "That door?" he said. She nodded. "Thanks," he said. "I'm, ah, I'm expecting Trooper Nicholson and Corporal Bateman. I may not hear them come in. If I don't come right out, please have one of them track me down and let me know they're here."

"I will, sir," she said, and she smiled. *Christ, someone's daughter in this job. What the hell is this world coming to?*

He entered a sitting room forty feet long by thirty feet wide. It too was mahogany paneled and fitted with a large gold and crystal chandelier. Three Oriental rugs spread horizontally across the floor. There were two conversational clusters of brown leather couches at the enormous bay window, its ledge cushioned with thick pillows. At the center of the room under the chandelier there was a circular table ten feet across. A mixed bouquet of snapdragons, stock, and daylilies stood at the center. To the right were six red leather barrel chairs on brass casters haphazardly arranged around a fireplace with a raised hearth six feet wide. The hearth was clean.

Over the mantelpiece there was a six-by-three-foot oil painting freezing Curt Flood at the instant when his bat met the ball; he was in the home uniform of the St. Louis Cardinals. On the mantelpiece there were two baseball bats, two replicas of the Heisman Trophy, and two more prizes Clay could not identify on sight. He went closer and read the legends; the first was the Outland Trophy, awarded to the college football defensive player of the year in 1986. Clay did not recognize the player's name engraved on it: "Dominic Vantresca. Oregon State." The second was a copy of the Vezina Trophy; it carried a plaque stating it had been awarded to Jean Claude Methodiste as the NHL goalie allowing the fewest goals in the 1993 regular season. Leaning against the left corner of the fireplace there were two putters illegibly signed on the blades. Three hockey sticks stood against the right corner. One of them was a goalie's, expansively signed "Jean Claude Methodiste" across the broad blade.

In the panels around the room there were large drawings and paintings—several by LeRoy Nieman that Clay recalled having seen in *Sports Illustrated*—and photographs of other athletes in action. At the far end of the room, two shadowed tables flanking open double doors filled with light were crowded with Revere bowls of various sizes, five or six on the left and four on the right.

A man in a suit appeared at the doors, silhouetted against the light. Peering into the shadows of the darker room, he said, uncertainly, "That you, Frankie?"

Clay at the mantel turned toward the voice, squinting against the light. "Yeah?" he said.

"We're in here," the man in the light said.

"All right," Clay said, turning back to the articles on the mantel.

"Think you might join us, some time today?" the man said.

Clay shrugged and stepped away from the fireplace, making his way among the barrel chairs to get to the doors. The man in the light waited for him. Closer, and squinting, Clay said: "Chick, Chick Bertinelli. All right. Sound of your voice, thought it might be you, but against the light like that, couldn't tell for sure. Might've been someone important. Haven't seen you in a long time."

"Yeah," Bertinelli said. "Took you long enough to get here."

"I was in the office," Clay said. "I was going over some things. That ugly case with the priest. Barely got the stuff out when the MP call came in. Well, the evidence to back up the kind of charges Father Jimmy's got pending's not the kind of stuff you just want to leave out on your desk, just lying around, before the case's been proven. Someone might just take a look at it. So I had to put it all away again. Took some time."

"Still," Bertinelli said. He came up very close to Clay, as though seeking a better view.

"I know, I know," Clay said. "I've been telling them and telling them, saying it for years, Fall River's too far from Easton. Must be twenty miles or so. We gotta find some way, move those two places closer together. Because mark my words, some day there's gonna be a homicide up there and we're gonna be doing something else. Quite naturally. We're always busy when some other damned thing else happens. Don't sit around like a buncha small-town cops, nothing better to do'n enforce the leash law, we're waiting for something worthwhile to happen. So by the time we do show up, Chick Bertinelli'll be *pissed*. Wait and see if I'm not right."

Bertinelli came up even closer, within a foot, making a point of inspecting him. "You're sure you're going to be all right for this, Frankie?"

Clay held his ground. "I'm never all right for *anything* when I've got someone in my face, Chick," he said. "After all of these years we've disliked each other, this by now's something you oughta know."

Bertinelli shook his head. He stepped back. "I don't know," he said. "I've never been sure about you." He used his right hand as though presenting the library as a vaudeville act. "Anyway, body's in here, Lieutenant, case you'd like to take a look at it this week."

The library was thirty by fifteen. A pink and beige

oriental rug twenty-eight by fourteen covered the floor. There were three sets of French doors in the southerly wall overlooking the pond, one near each end of the room and the center set, letting in the light that had framed Bertinelli in the doorway. Mahogany valances and heavy pink and beige tapestried drapes framed the doors. Light from the set at the easterly end of the room illuminated the area behind the desk where Myrna Roscommon in a long white lab coat, and two uniformed men appeared to be doing something with something in the chair behind the desk. Light also came from the sixteen-paned window behind the desk.

To the left of the desk there was a chrome gurney fitted with a white sheet and something black and shiny folded thickly at the foot. There was a large black toolbox open at the other end. Two men wearing short white lab coats and latex gloves bent and crouched as they moved around the desk and the two high-backed leather chairs at odd angles in front of it—there was another in each corner behind the desk—pausing now and then to dust and lift a print, or to use a soft brush to transfer substances, or tweezers to collect small objects from the surfaces to small plastic bags.

" 'Lo Myrna," Clay said.

"Hi Frank," she said, without turning. "Right with you."

"No hurry," he said. There were photographs and pen-and-ink drawings of athletes arranged in vertical rows from ceiling to floor between each of the three windows. Each of them appeared to have been signed by its subject. At the westerly end of the room there was a four-foot fireplace with a raised hearth. The hearth was clean. Over the mantelpiece there was an eight-by-four-foot oil portrait of a man in his early fifties, his right buttock perched on what appeared to be the left-hand front corner of the massive desk at the easterly end of the room, his left foot on the floor, his hands, left over right, resting loosely clasped on his right thigh. He wore a medium gray suit, dark stockings visible between the cuffs of his trousers and his tasseled black loafers, a jacket unbuttoned over a claret-colored, white-collared shirt and wine-red tie, a hexagonal gold link on the white French cuffs visible below the sleeves of the jacket, along with part of the bezel of a gold Breitling multi-dialed watch. The face, neck, and hands were deeply tanned. The curly silver-gray hair had been cut full. The man had blue eyes and he had put a sparkle in them when he posed, his lips slightly parted to evince delight, and anticipation. He looked poised and coiled, ready to spring.

Behind his right shoulder a ghostly halfback in a Chicago Bears helmet and number 17 home jersey plunged forward, his left arm extended, a football cradled in the crook of his right. In the center above the subject's head a slim left-handed black man in a Red Sox cap and home uniform shirt extended his arms in a home-run swing. Above the subject's left shoulder a smaller figure in a Bruins helmet and home uniform followed through on a slapshot. Just below him, a muscular black man in a Los Angeles Lakers number 44 shirt lofted a jump shot. In the lower left-hand corner, next to the subject's left calf, a man in a white cap, white cardigan, and checked trousers lined up a putt. In the lower right, next to the subject's right calf, a woman in a tennis dress arched her body to serve. Clay went up to the picture and read the brass plaque at the center of the lower edge of the frame. "Alexander Drouhin. 1994. "THE ONLY WAY TO PLAY THE GAME, NO MATTER WHAT THE GAME."

Bertinelli, still near the doorway, cleared his throat and said, "The body's over *there*."

"And I am over here," Clay said. "Myrna'll let me know when she's ready for me. He's not going anywhere. When she says so, I'll be right along."

The walls on each side of the door were occupied with bookcases, tightly packed with leather-bound volumes in sets alphabetically arranged by author. *Books by the foot,* he thought. He pulled down Nathaniel Hawthorne's *Tanglewood Tales.* It took some effort. There was a bit of excelsior on the top of the gilt binding. It resisted when he opened it, making a cracking sound. With some effort he restored it to its place on the shelf.

"I think we're ready for you now, Frank," Roscommon said, straightening up but not turning around.

"Goody, goody," he said, turning toward the desk.

9

THE DOCTOR STEPPED AWAY from the desk chair to the left and the uniformed officers peeled off to the right. The two technicians in white lab coats interrupted their work and straightened up. The corpse sat slumped in the chair, the bloody mass below the silver grey mane where the handsome, smiling face had been lolling off to the right. Clay was wildly tempted to laugh, but managed to restrain himself.

"Jesus Christ," he told Nicholson and Bateman later, "all I could think of was what we did when Tessa first got diagnosed, no question anymore what it was, and no question how it was going to turn out either—just when. So now expense really is no object; it's *time* we're running short of, so what would she really like to do? And she said she knew it would be a silly waste of money, which was why she'd never mentioned it, but secretly she always wanted to take one of those Caribbean cruises. The ones they had Lauren Bacall advertising on TV: Royal Caribbean Lines. 'The others, they look sort of tacky to me. But hers, they sound like class.' Tessa was always a great admirer of Lauren Bacall. She didn't think any woman with a tobacco-smoke-and-whiskey voice like her own'd ever steer you wrong.

"So then, that settled it. That's what we'd do, while she could still get around. I got the tickets, first class, top drawer, and they cost me a bundle, I can tell you. Time I got through, airfare and hotels, also first class, it was almost eight thousand dollars. But this time it really was: 'You only live once,' and not much longer, either; just enough for some horrible pain. We both tried not to think about that.

"So now there we are, we're on the boat, and it's not what she expected. 'I don't know,' she said afterwards, 'it was kind of *embarrassing,* you know? People falling all over you, kissing your ass? All that showy deference, like you're some kind of nobility, much higher-class'n the riff-raff in economy class, or on Carnival Lines. When all you really are is fatter pigeons, let themselves get plucked for more money. Made me uncomfortable, kind of.'

"She was right. Everything was too much, overdone. Everybody making this big *production* of everything—and you're a part of it, *in it.* It gets on your nerves. But you're on a boat; can't get off and go home. Have to play along, no matter how you feel now, the money you spent. Like chicken pox: Once you've got it there's nothing you can do but let it run its course—but God, it sure does make you itch.

"I felt the same way she did, from the very first day on board, six more to go. But naturally neither one of us's going to give it away to the other one. We've been married a long time. We love each other. We got a tough road ahead of us when we do get home, ending in the cemetery. I don't want her to think her dream's a disaster; she can't let me think she's not having fun after I spent all that dough, like I still let her down. You do that kind of thing when you've got a good marriage; protect each other. Don't always tell all you know. Keep things to yourself, for each other's sake. If you make yourself miserable enough for two, maybe that'll mean your partner can be happy.

"Besides, we really did like each other. So with great effort we made it through almost three days of this charade without giving each other away. Then it's the third night. We're 'seated at dinner,' these other three couples, the men in their tuxes—you picture me in the ruffled shirt, the black tie, the white jacket? I looked like a bargain-price bandleader, counterfeit Guy Lombardo, live from the Roosevelt Grille. And the other three couples: Two of them're from New York, Westchester County, in their seventies. This's become a tradition with them. Been doing it now every winter for seven years. Third couple's from Evanston, Illinois. He just retired from Northwestern, American history. This's his retirement bash, gift from his wife, which he seems to be working pretty hard to enjoy. Very nice guy. Since history's mostly what I read, I had fun talking to him. Tessa and his wife also hit it off, spent most of the day at the pool. 'One thing at least about what I've got: I now can get as much sun as I like. No more worries about melanoma.' I spent the days with him. Walking off the food around the boat, talking.

"He's worried about how he's going to stay occupied, now that he'll have no more classes to teach. No meetings he's got to be seen at and sit through, or someone'll make a pass at his parking place next to the building. No reports to write. Really nothing he's got to get done. And no worries about making sure the money keeps coming in. So, how's he make sure he actually *does* the writing he always said he'd do if only he had the time, now that he's got it—*and* stays away from the sauce? Which I can now relate to myself, as they say.

"And then there is us, Tessa and I. We're the youngest people at the table. You get to our age, this's not the kind of situation that you're used to. Most occasions we go to, we're among the older parties. May've made us a little giddy.

"Well, this third night they did nothing—the dining-room staff—they hadn't done the first two nights. It's just the third night it got to us. It's time for the main courses, they wheel up the carts and surround us. Circling the wagons, you know? That's all I could think of, every time they did it. 'Good God, must be an Indian attack.' The four waiters, the white cotton gloves, white Eisenhower jackets, brass buttons, black pants, one behind each cart, parade rest. Two big silver covers over the dinners on the carts. Then their captain, grand marshal, whatever he is, nods his head. The waiters all snap to attention. Put their hands on the handles of the big silver covers. The captain nods again. *Whoosh,* off come the covers, in unison, right? Like a fuckin' drill team. All that's missin' is the drums 'n bugles. Military precision. For a *dinner*.

"I couldn't help myself. I look at Tessa. 'Well,' I say, 'where the hell's the U.S. Marine Band?' We both start laughing our asses off. No one else does. The professor and his wife look like they might like to, but they don't. This is because the other two couples don't like it at all, us making fun of the ritual. They've been taking all this hoo-hah very seriously. Solemn, respectful; you'd think they're at a funeral Mass for some really important dead person.

"But tough for 'em. That dinner broke the tension between me and Tessa. After that we stopped pretending. After that when we were by ourselves we made fun of everything we felt like making fun of, all the ridiculous fanfare. Since there was a lot of it, this didn't give us much time to rest, but we had a lot better time.

"That's the thing I miss so much now. Not having her

around. We always had so much damned *fun* together. Now there's no fun anymore."

He cleared his throat. "Anyway, that's exactly the feeling I had today when Myrna and the rest of them went away from the corpse. It was as though they'd all collaborated in the preparation and presentation of some marvelous spectacle, solely for my viewing pleasure. Synchronized undertakers: the next Olympic sport. I thought it was weird. Something must've showed on my face." Bateman and Nicholson looked respectful and said nothing.

"YOU OKAY?" THE DOCTOR SAID.

"Sure, I'm okay," Clay said, trying not to sound irritated, but failing. "If that used to be the same guy in the picture behind me, *he's* not okay, but *I'm* fine." He approached the desk. He did not touch it or either of the chairs. He looked down at the cushions. "You guys," he said, looking up at the technicians, two average-looking, average-sized men, one in his forties, the other in his early twenties, both with receding dark hair and nervous brown eyes—they could have been father and son—standing near the bookcase on the inner wall, "you get pictures of those cushions?"

TALKING TO BATEMAN ON the way to the kitchen after the body had been taken away, Clay said, "You know something? After years and years of looking at them and not seeing them, I guess, I finally figured out today what it is about technicians, makes me want to give them lots of orders and then get away, real fast."

He had sent Nicholson away to "take pictures of everything, everything. Every room in the house. Every view from outside it. Film's cheap. Any indication makes you think there may be something in what you see that might turn out to be important, take a picture of it. I trust your judgment, Al, like I have for years. Never let me down before. I'm sure you won't start now."

Two months into his first plainclothes training assignment as Clay's assistant at crime scenes, Corporal Gary Bateman remained vaguely uneasy in his company. He had tried to explain his initial edginess to his wife. "It's like I'm on the Bomb Squad and he's some device that might go *off*, you know? You jiggle him or something, he'll explode." Gradually he had begun to relax. Not yet sure enough of his ground to bandy snide remarks about other people with Clay, especially the dead ones—Clay called them "our best and favorite witnesses: they never lie to you"—he was now able to feed straight lines to Clay at gory venues.

"What did you discover about techs?" Bateman said obediently.

"I discovered I'm afraid of them," Clay said. "I have a small phobia about them. They all look to me like the kind of people . . . if you hang around too long, 'til after they finish their work, they'll start trying to sell you more insurance. The thing to do with technicians is give them lots of orders and then beat it."

"Does this apply to Al?" Bateman said, keeping his face expressionless.

"*No,* it doesn't, wise guy," Clay said. "Al's a detective like us, only his chief tool is the camera. Al's working *with* us, not *for* us."

"You," Bateman said. "Working with *you*. I'm just learning the ropes here."

Clay looked at him quickly. "No," he said. "Us. If I fuck this up, you know, I'm gonna share the blame generously. Don't think I'll take a fall all by myself—forget it, not after all these years. In fact if I can think of a way to do it, I may put *all* the blame on you. 'Of *course* I screwed up,' I will say. 'What'd you expect, send a rookie to work with me on it?' "

THE TECHNICIANS LOOKED AT each other and then both of them shrugged. "We can take some more," the younger one said.

"Good, do it," Clay said. "I don't know how old those chairs are, or the last time they were reupholstered, but whoever sat in them last was heavy, two very heavy people, great big behinds. I want pictures of the way the leather bunched up out from under their butts."

"Uh, Lieutenant," the older tech said, "the chair on the right there was tipped over, we came in. On its back. We stood it back up to work on it.

"You took a picture of it first, though, before you picked it up," Clay said, "and you dusted it for prints. Took several pictures of the entire grisly scene here from ten feet away, before you touched a thing."

"Of course," the older tech said.

"Good," Clay said, "I hope so. I suppose you didn't find any brass. Empty shells?"

"No, Lieutenant," the older tech said. "What appear to be powder burns and residue on the edge and surface of the desk at the right corner as you're looking at it there, but no casings. We micro-vacced the rug all around the desk, bagged and initialed the yield, which was small—this room has been frequently cleaned. There was nothing obviously helpful grossly visible."

"Revolver then," Clay said. He hunkered down between the chairs and sighted across the desk at the body in the chair. Curly silver-gray hair remained above and behind the mess of bloody meat, gray matter, and shattered white bone that lolled down over the collar of the white turtleneck and the blood-soaked, fringed blue paisley shawl over the shoulders.

Now that it had been so badly damaged, Clay observed—as he had not, looking at the portrait—that Alexander Drouhin had had an abnormally large head. The mass was deeply concaved in the upper left quadrant. The headrest of the black leather chair was splashed with blood, gray matter, and bits of gray bone on the left side. Judging from the painting, when Drouhin had been alive the head had looked to be in good proportion to the rest of him, but in death it looked like something that should be removed and discarded, so that the large, well-kept body, still apparently in perfectly good condition, could be cleaned up and, after being fitted with a good prosthesis, restored to service.

Without looking at them, Clay said to the technicians: "After the guest of honor's out of here, I want you guys to test that window and the curtains, all the area behind the left side of that chair, for any evidence there is of what happened as a result of however many traumas were inflicted on this guy, okay?"

"Yes," the technicians said together.

"Because I want the DA who ends up trying this case to be able to give the jury who hears it the most vivid picture possible of what someone did to this fine, famous, handsome, rich, successful guy. You follow me?"

"In other words, like always," the older technician muttered.

Clay turned his head and looked at him at the instant when the younger technician was beginning to present his older colleague with a small smile of congratulations for his boldness. The smile disappeared and both of them stood silent. For a few moments Clay did not say anything, just studied them and worked his tongue against the inner surfaces of his lower front teeth. Then standing up he said in a low pleasant voice: "No, not 'just like always.' That's my point. I haven't talked to anybody so I don't know exactly what devices he'd deployed yet, but I do know this man—if he wasn't obsessed, he was acutely concerned about security and had an extensive system in and around this property. I also know, although I don't have any actual evidence of it yet, that the system wasn't armed last night or early this morning when his killer or killers came in. Someone *admitted* them, probably the victim himself.

"This means the killer was someone he knew. And because we already know both that *he* was famous and handsome, and rich and successful, and how he *got to be* famous and rich and successful, we already have a pretty good idea that whoever he let in was rich, famous, and successful. Not knowing of course that his guest or someone with him had it in mind to kill him. Even though he or she was maybe *even more* famous, even richer, and more successful in his or her own right. Because that's the kind of people that Alexander Drouhin ran with, knew and hung around with, and would've gladly let into his house late at night. Because representing that kind of people was what made Alexander Drouhin what he said he was, one of the best-known sports agents in the world.

"Which means we also know for sure that whoever did it's going to have the best defense lawyers and forensics experts available anywhere in the world. You two're going to have to testify in front of them about what you did and found at the scene, and when the defense team gets you on cross, and a *team* is what it'll be, they're going to hold your feet to the fire. Probably longer, to a hotter one than you've ever had them held to before. You'd better be ready for that. You'd better start getting ready, *today,* or you're gonna have serious blisters.

"Because *think* about that. This case is going to run us up against the iron. It's the kind of case that makes this game exciting. There's at least a strong possibility whoever did it's a goddamned celebrity. A household name. A *hero*, idolized by young and old alike. Have you guys got any idea how hard it is to convict a celebrity these days? Or did you sleep through the Simpson trial? People don't like to convict their heroes. Goes against their grain.

"The jury that tries this case'll be made up of people just as susceptible to misdirection and emotional appeals as the Simpson jurors were. No matter who we wind up nailing for this, and how good our evidence is, even if it's *far* beyond a reasonable doubt, this case has the potential to be one tough bastard."

He paused. "Do we understand each other now?"

Both of the technicians nodded. "Good," Clay said. "My burden's already lighter.

"Now Myrna, my darling," he said, turning away from them and hunkering down again, "could you bring yourself to go behind the chair, take that ruined head by the hair, and pull it up and back for a minute, so I can get the angle?"

"Sure," she said. She went behind the chair and did as he asked, gripping a latex-gloved handful of the curly silver-gray hair remaining at the rear of the upper right quadrant and gently pulling the head upright. The lower jaw appeared to have escaped structural damage. Much of the meatus of the left ear remained.

"The chair was pretty much straightaway when you first saw it?" he said.

"It was turned slightly to his right," she said. "As though he'd been looking at the spot about where the foot of the gurney is now."

"Turn it for me, please," he said.

"About this far," she said, swiveling the chair five degrees to the right. "Very slightly, as I said."

"Yeah," Clay said, squinting. "So he was probably either dead center or turned five or ten degrees to his left when the first slug hit him." Still crouching, Clay scrambled sideways to his right between the chairs and the front of the desk, moving awkwardly like a horseshoe crab stiff on the joints and somewhat out of practice, using his knuckles and toes to propel and brace himself, touching nothing but the carpet. There was a brushed-aluminum wastebasket beside the desk. "That would've tended to drive him back to the right. Same with the second; had to be at least two."

"I agree," she said. "At least two."

"So he was probably talking to whoever was sitting in the chair behind me, the one that was turned over," Clay said. "And the guy—if it was a guy, of course—put the muzzle of the weapon on the edge of the desk and pointed it at his head. Used Zen marksmanship, 'when it feels right, light 'er off'—didn't aim, just let 'er rip.... Was he pleading for his life, you think, when the shooter fired? Did he see the gun come up from under the desk and just go nuts, and start begging?"

"I don't think so," the doctor said. "Then he would've been standing, or trying to stand—I *think* that would've been his first instinct—when the first slug hit him. And most likely he would've fallen out of the chair, or away from it. He was firmly planted, sitting down, at the time of first impact. I doubt he ever saw the gun. I think the shooter brought it up just above the edge of the desk while Drouhin had the floor, was talking, eye-to-eye with the person in the other chair, trying to convince someone of something, and *boom,* the shooter let him have it. Then *boom* at least once again.

"It was a powerful load. As you see, the slug blew out the top left-hand part of his head on entry, pasted what was left of it to the back of the chair. The blood from the exit wound coagulating in his hair. After that, maybe a spasm or two, if he had time for that before the redundant second bullet, he wasn't going anywhere. He was a sitting duck."

She peered over the top of the chair and looked down at the ruined head. Her short blond hair was dark at the roots. "You have to wonder why the shooter thought a second round was necessary, seeing what that first one must've done. Much less a third, if there was one."

Clay stood up, saying, "Ahh." To her inquiring look he said, "Old legs don't stay bent quite as long as they used to without complaining. You can let him doze off again. Second shot? My guess is the shooter fired it double-action before the explosion of tissue in the head from the first one was over. He'd made up his mind before he came in to make sure, fire the second one in case the first one only nicked him."

The doctor released the head, allowing it to loll forward and to the right. "Or the shooter was enjoying it," she said.

Clay stared at her. "*Uh huh*," he said softly, "you're John's daughter, all right."

She nodded to the two men in uniform. "You can bag him, boys," she said. She came around and stood beside Clay at the front of the desk.

Clay looked down into the wastebasket. In it there was a large manila envelope folded in half. To the technicians he said: "Use the forcep when you pull out that envelope and bag it." There was a thick letter-sized, buff-colored stapled document facedown in the center of the blotter on the desk. "Same with whatever he was reading and turned over before he let his guest in so the visitor couldn't read it."

The men in uniforms aligned the desk chair and the gurney and unrolled the shiny black body bag, unfolding and unzipping it. Then they kicked the release lowering the gurney to knee height and one on each side lifted the body out of the chair, the legs in gray trousers flopping slowly apart. The men shifted the corpse into the open bag. Then one pushed the chair away and both of them lifted the gurney to waist-height again, locking it. They stuffed the feet, legs, hands, and arms inside the bag, carefully pulling the top of it up and over the ravaged head. The man at the foot pulled the zipper closed, fast.

"Guess time of death," Clay said to the doctor.

"Sometime well after midnight," she said, frowning. "As early as two, late as four. I don't want to be more specific than that 'til I look at the stomach contents and so forth, you find out for me when and what he had for dinner. If he did."

"At least we can be pretty sure the cause of death wasn't poison," Clay said.

"There's that," the doctor said, laughing. "And we also know he wasn't fresh kill when we got here. He'd been dead in that chair for a while."

"So the trail's been cold for at least six hours, and no one's heard nothin', of course," Clay said. He looked morose.

"Apparently not," the doctor said. "Do they ever?"

Clay looked rueful and shook his head once.

The older technician cleared his throat and, using forceps, held up the buff document that had been on the desk. "First page's a letter," he said. "Law Offices of James R. Haggerty, PLC, Fifteen Court Square, Boston, Mass., oh-two-one-oh-eight. Addressed to Mister Robert Moreno, Forty-three Riverwood Drive, Natick."

"Same's the return address on the envelope," the younger technician said, holding it up.

"Okay," Clay said, "bag 'em both. When you've worked

'em over for everything on them, make me three sets of photocopies, would you?"

"On your desk this after," the older technician said.

The doctor led Clay several steps away from the desk, cleared her throat and said: "Look, what I said back there, about whether you're up to this. Whatever I said. Of course I know you are. You and my father go back a long way. He was just talking about you the other day, that time the two of you picked up the fugitive in Florida, and Northeast Airlines wouldn't let him on because he had the measles. You two had to rent a car from Hertz and drive him back. 'Four days on the road with the spotted son of a bitch,' my dad said. 'Running a fever, pissin' and moanin', cryin' like a little kid; he wanted *pity,* and *peppermint stick ice cream.* And this is a guy killed three people. Frank couldn't remember he ever had measles, and neither could I. We both thought we were gonna get sick.' "

Clay grinned and nodded. "That was some trip," he said.

"Well, that's what I mean," she said. "I don't want you, of all people, mad at me. If you're mad at me then my father will be, and I don't want that to happen. I really didn't mean anything."

He patted her arm. "I'm not mad at you, Myrna, and it's not just you. I'm oversensitive, I know. But it just seems like it's everybody lately, looking at me funny, then asking me if I'm all right. It's making me nervous. What is it, I'm showing symptoms or something? Of what? What is it about me lately that's making people think I've got something wrong with me? Tell me what it is; I'll change what's causing it the minute I find out. Go to a doctor and have it removed, that's what it takes. Just tell me the Christ what it is."

"It's...you've got a lot of friends, Frank," she said. "You had a hard time. They worry about you. They can't help it, they're concerned. Maybe they let it show too much, but basically what they're saying is they care about you."

"The hard time was a while ago," Clay said. "I went through it and I got over it. I'm all right again now. Have been for some time. I promise you, with what I know about it after all these years, I wouldn't be back at it again if I didn't feel up to it, doing it, I wouldn't even be trying. But I really am," he hesitated one beat, "absolutely, all right."

"Well," she said, "if you say so, you are. I know you don't make up stories. But you seem kind of, I don't know, *down,* that's all. I don't know, dejected or something. Gloomy."

The uniformed officers began to wheel the gurney out, one pulling at the foot, one steering at the head. Bertinelli stood back from the doorway, arms folded, looking disgusted.

Clay turned his back on Bertinelli and lowered his voice. "Myrna," he said, "that's a different matter. Look at what we've been looking at while we've been talking to each other. The guy who's leaving the room for the last time, man with his face blown away. In the morgue you're going to find when you sift through what's left of his scrambled brains that whoever killed him not only used a much heavier weapon than the job needed, but hollow-point bullets the *Geneva* Convention forbids in wartime. And *dum-dummed* the damned things to boot. So they'd tumble, end-over-end, instead of flying straight. The purpose wasn't only kill him—it was to mess him up to the maximum, too.

"Now what kind of a person feels the need to do a thing like that? What kind of person're we dealing with here, that thinks death's insufficient, killing the guy's not enough? You heard what I said to the techs. More'n likely the man who did this—I don't think it was a woman—is a famous athlete, admired throughout the country, if not throughout the world. Probably visits little kids in cancer wards—Dana Farber Institute, and orphanages. He's an idol of millions. But we—although we don't know yet who he is, we already know he's depraved, a violent degenerate. Don't you find that a little depressing, we live in that kind of world?"

She nodded and bit her lip, but did not say anything.

"*I* do," he said. "I know *I* do. So I *am* dejected. Of course I'm dejected. What was it you said? 'Gloomy' too. It's the right way to feel in this job. That's what I mean, I wouldn't be trying to do this job now if I didn't feel right with myself. This's the kind of job that *makes* you dejected. If you don't get that way from seeing what we see, hearing what we hear, doing what we do, then there's something wrong with *you*. As Ann Landers says, you should seek counseling. Or have a couple stiff drinks and reconsider maybe taking that evening adult-ed course in oil-burner repair—you may be in the wrong line of work."

"Yeah," the doctor said, "I know. I really do."

"For example," he said, "about eighteen years ago, I'm an eager young corporal—well, older'n Bateman but still fairly young, in my thirties—down here, working detective first time. Seeing how I like being out of the uniform into the suit, how the guys I work for liked me that way. Very exciting time of my life. If this works out I'm taking a whole new direction, my career with the State Police. If this works out my ambition's no longer going to be the colonel in full pack and attitude; I'm going to be a Detective Lieutenant Inspector, wear a regular tie, and sneer at the Uniform jerks. *Much* higher calling. You could say I was somewhat gung ho.

"We'd been having this series of armored-car holdups, trucks getting intercepted making cash deliveries and pick-

ing up checks and worn-out currency for the Federal
Reserve from small banks and branches. Not too many,
maybe six or seven in about a year, nobody'd been hurt,
but of course that was always a threat. These robbers were
serious people on serious business—they wore masks—
and they were not in any mood for interference. If some
wanna-be hero who'd seen too many Westerns decided to
try something stupid, then there was going to be gunplay.
And the hero'd lose. So these guys were getting to be a real
pain in the ass, a hazardous nuisance, you know? As John
said, they hadda be abated.

"He came down from Boston. He wasn't happy about
it. I think he was running a major fraud investigation and
as you know, he never liked distractions. My boss, the guy
in charge of the Bristol office, Lieutenant Andrew Lioy, had
to give way to your father. Andrew was also unhappy. Not
at John, at who called him in, which of course was the DA,
up for reelection and taking no chances on Andrew. They
never did get along. Andrew retired on high blood pressure,
year later. I always suspected he faked it. Did something
to make it go up. DA did, too. But he wasn't kicking. He
was grateful."

The doctor smiled but said nothing.

"Anyway, make a long story short, two or three days
after he got there, John knew who was behind the stickups.
How did he know? Old-fashioned detective work? Some
kind of inspired hunch? Neither one. Back in the late fifties,
John'd been down there, had the same kind of problem.
Took a lot of shoe-leather and three or four generous plea
bargains, but finally they developed a couple informants.
When the robbers struck next, cops were waiting.

"Fast forward. John studied reports for a couple of days,
went out to a couple of scenes. Came back to the office
and made a phone call: MCI Walpole, as it was then

known. 'Is Jimmy Blades still in there, working hard in the furniture shop? He isn't? He finished his term? When did you check him out? Less'n a year ago, huh?'

"Then your father makes another phone call, this time to the parole office. 'What's the current address for James Cicerone?' He gets it. Now he's in business. He does a chronology of the recent robberies. These guys're treating 'em like regular paychecks. An annuity. Every six or eight weeks they go and do another one. John figures one's coming the following week. Puts a very loose tail on Jimmy Cicerone, sits back, and waits for him to move. On the following Thursday he does, along with three other guys. By the end of the week Jimmy Blades is back in the furniture shop, which is now his job for life. He'll retire from it to a prison hospital or else some day he'll die in it, but he's not going outside again.

"The driver of the getaway car for Jimmy and his sidekick, another experienced hard case named Delaney, was a kid named Kevin Hulse. Talented wheelman, did some stock-car racing at the old Seekonk Speedway. Didn't have much of a record, which in his kind of case usually meant up 'til then he'd been smart enough not to do things he'd get caught at. Not many hoods're that talented. That's why they have long records young. So this made him a guy who could make it legit, and therefore worth some effort to salvage. But the odds were against it. Even picking his spots, he was only twenty-four and he'd been moving up in grade pretty steadily. From using a motor vehicle without authority to grand larceny, motor vehicle. From assault and battery to assault with a deadly weapon. From unarmed robbery to robbery while armed. For which he'd gotten five years and done three.

"Now it's robbery while armed and *masked*, and not just once but seven, eight times. He's got to trade someone else.

He would not. He'd give up *nobody*. Knows nothin' from nothin'; he's Mickey the Dunce. Okay, he was making a choice. Your father talked to him, the DA talked to him. 'The rest of your *life;* you'll be an old *man;* blah-blah-*blah;* blah-blah-*blah,* blah-blah-blah-*blah.*'

"Nothin', he's stoic. It's like talkin' to a rock. Now it's MCI Cedar Junction, they changed the address, but it's the same building it always was, and back in goes our Kevin, a long lease but not life.

"Last week, you may've read about it, we had a botched money-car robbery, freestanding BayBank ATM in a mini-mall, Myricks. Just two guys in a car—everything's down-sized now, even robbery crews—outside the paint store, but they arouse someone's attention. Who this was we do not know. Person did not wish to give her name. We could probably find out if we wanted; there's a beauty parlor in that mall, and that's the only establishment in there where a sharp-eyed female customer'd have any reason to hang out for almost three hours, right?"

"The full treatment," the doctor said, "which I'm due to have pretty soon. I told Steve if we're going to that benefit dinner, it's back to the tinfoil and tint for this girl, or people'll think I am *old.*"

"Can't have that, can we?" Clay said.

"Absolutely not," the doctor said. "You *guys* maybe can, but we can't. Anyway, if you find out who had an appointment for color and so forth, around that time, you'll have a fairly good idea who your witness is—she ought to look pretty good, too."

Clay chuckled. "I don't like to do that," he said. "Word gets out we're doing that, it'll discourage people from using those cell phones to help us, God bless 'em, and we certainly don't want to do that. This public-spirited lady got back to her car and called Star SP. She said where she was, and that when she'd arrived, she'd seen two men in a car at the paint store. Just sitting there, not buying paint. Two and a half hours later she comes out and they're still there. Still no sign they've bought any paint."

"Or had their hair done either, most likely," the doctor said.

"Looked pretty scruffy, in fact," Clay said. "This lady in addition to being smart has good eyesight. When our operator—not the brightest light in the chandelier, fortunately these calls are taped—asks her if she can speak up a bit, the lady says she's using the speakerphone, doesn't have the phone to her ear; doesn't want to move her lips any more'n she absolutely has to. 'Because they're parked facing out, you see. They're not looking at me right now, but they could at any minute, so I'm pretending to look for something in my purse while I talk to you.'

"She gave us their descriptions, two white males, one mid-thirties, other early forties, gray sweatshirts. She thought she saw they had Levi's on when she passed their car going in and coming out of the beauty parlor but only could get quick looks. She gives us make, color, registration plate number, bent antenna, left front hubcap missing, and dented rear deck on their car. In other words, everything but their Social Security numbers and their mothers' maiden names. And our dazzlingly bright operator says to her, *very* patiently, 'Now madame, just *exactly* what is it that makes you think this is something that should interest the State Police?'

"There's this pause, you can hear the woman catching her breath, and then she says, 'I think they're waiting here to rob someone.'

" 'Like who?' says our Einstein on the switchboard.

" 'Maybe the men in the station wagon who take care of the bank machine, you think?' the caller says. There may be just a touch of sarcasm.

"And of course it's quite justified. The reason the two guys have to go on stakeout, park themselves in plain sight in front of the paint store for three hours, is that the people who service those cash machines're quite aware they're tempting targets, so they vary their comings and goings. They never come twice to the same place at the same time. They never drive the same color Taurus wagon that they drove to that one the last time. Of course they almost always drive a Taurus wagon, so if the robber's got the brain of a golden retriever, that dodge isn't going to throw him too long. But still, you do the best you can.

"Which, at this point in the conversation between the lady and our genius, is exactly what the lady sees pull into the parking lot: a metallic green Taurus wagon. Which she notices because the robbers, noticeably, notice it too. One of them jabs the other one: 'Finally, our prayers've been answered. We can knock off this job in a minute or two, take a leak, and go have some lunch.' Not that she hears them say this, but that's the way they're acting. The passenger starts putting on a mask. The driver raises, cocks, and puts down what looks to her like a big pistol, and after she reports these developments to us, she sensibly signs off. 'I'm outta here,' she says. The line goes dead.

"Luckily the genius has finally gotten the idea. The dispatcher calls, 'Robbery in progress—all units respond,' and the sergeant calls BayBank and tells them to heads-up their ATM service guys on the cell phone and tell them to keep right on moving—but nice and slow, please, freeze those robbers 'til we get there—through that parking lot and then go right out the other end of it.

"Units converge. By the time our larcenous fellows realize that Taurus isn't stopping, they've got much too much company around them with guns drawn to even think about making a break for it. Without a shot being fired, we get the masks, we get the guns, we get the robbers."

"Now that should've cheered you up," the doctor said.

"Oh, it did," Clay said. "But that's the thing about this trade: The job giveth and the job taketh away. Even when it goes right, and makes you feel good, it also makes you feel bad. The guy in the passenger seat was Kevin Hulse, the guy I helped your father put in jail seventeen years ago. He's been out of Cedar Junction seven weeks. Now we're going to put him back in the furniture shop again. For the rest of his life. And rehabilitation, no doubt.

"I get great satisfaction from doing my job. I can't say it gives me great joy."

They heard the door shut at the front of the house. "Mister Drouhin leaves home for the last time," she said.

"Or else Nicholson and Bateman finally got here," Clay said.

"Either way," she said, looking at her watch, "I gotta run. I already had three customers waiting in the icebox before this even happened."

"But you'll do me a kindness," Clay said. "Move Mister Drouhin to the top of your list."

"Of course," she said. "By the time I get there he'll be naked on the table. I'll call you this afternoon. You'll have the report tomorrow."

"Say hello to John for me," Clay said. "Tell him I liked it better when he was in charge. I wish he had this one to wrassle."

"I'll tell him that," she said, patting his arm, "but I won't believe it and neither will he. Take care of yourself, won't you, Frank?"

"I will, Myrna," he said. "That I will." She was near the door of the library when he called after her. "Say," he said, "when're you gonna make an honest man outta Steve?" She stopped, laughter shaking her shoulders. "I'll talk to you, Frank," she said. Then she went on toward the door where Bertinelli still stood, disapproving.

10

CLAY STOPPED IN THE doorway, taking the same position in the light that Bertinelli had taken when he hailed Clay at the living-room fireplace. He could hear Nicholson in the foyer, talking to Gagnon. He raised his voice. "Al," he said, "you and Gary wait there. I'll be right with you." He put his hands in his pockets. "So, Chick," he said, "still wasting the taxpayers' valuable time, hanging around here, watching an investigation you didn't even start? Must be peaceful in Easton these days."

Bertinelli's voice sounded like a partially clogged drain. "I already told you, Frankie, made no secret of it. I don't know about you. Never really was that sure about you, either. Going back to when I was with the Attleboro department in eighty-three, saw how you handled that Mafia murder."

"The Campbell case?" Clay said. "In the first place I was still a sergeant then; didn't make lieutenant 'til the next year, eighty-four. I wasn't in charge of that case. John Roscommon was, the AG's office. We had three grand juries sitting at once, Essex, Bristol, and Norfolk, so you didn't see John around much. He was the man in charge of the show. But I was reporting to him.

"In the second place, there was nothing wrong with the

way we handled it. What was out of kilter was a young and excitable *AAG* getting overheated, derailed by hunger for his first scalp into thinking that what he *knew* happened was also something he could *prove* happened. So he jumped the tracks, got an indictment we all knew he couldn't prove, and when the time came to prove it, sure enough, he couldn't prove it.

"Billy Raymond. He's aged well, calmed down a lot, since he was Assistant AG. The Honorable William J. Raymond, associate justice, Superior Court. Everyone speaks very highly of him, praises his patience and careful intellect. But back then he was a ball of fire, out of control. Inspirational in front of the grand jury, which can be a dangerous gift. Made the blind to see, the deaf to hear, the lame to walk—and then preached the gospel to them. It went to his head. Got the idea he could not only indict, but *convict,* the legendary ham sandwich.

"I told him and told him, and so did Roscommon, 'Billy, don't do this, it's not gonna come out like you want. There's no judge in the grand jury room. If the villain's present he doesn't have his lawyer. But when you try the case in court, those other guys'll be there. They won't *let* you dance your dance and sing your song and do your magic tricks, no matter how good you are. They'll make you produce *evidence,* and if you don't the judge'll be delighted to blow you out of the water. There're two basic things you need for a good murder case: the guy who did it and the evidence to prove it. You've got the right guy, no question about it. The evidence you don't.' He wouldn't listen."

"And then what happened year before last?" Bertinelli spoke as though Clay instead of defending himself had acknowledged the justice of Bertinelli's distrust. "That demolished what little confidence I ever did have in you."

Clay did not say anything.

"Your friend the hockey player intimidated my officer," Bertinelli said.

"The hockey player was *Wayne* Cashman," Clay said. "As far as I know he was never a state cop. My friend was *Roger* Cashman, unfortunately dead now. Embolism dropped him in mid-sentence on the stand in Taunton Superior year ago May. Fifty-two years old. What a shame. Far as I know, he never played hockey. And Roger intimidated nobody. Unknown to me, he and Jimmy Smith also left the Newton Marriott, Trigger Early's retirement party, early, right behind me. The nerve of the bastards, call themselves friends of mine. They didn't believe my statements that I hadn't had too much to drink, and since both of them lived down near where I do in Somerset, they decided to follow me home. Since I did know for sure that I'd had *enough* to drink, I stayed away from route twenty-four, motored down one-thirty-eight. When your officer found me just before midnight I was in my car next to the K8 light tower in the parking lot where the theater is. Roger and Jimmy were one traffic light behind me. My stop was perfectly innocent. Safe driving above all requires that you stay awake, so, feeling somewhat fatigued, I'd decided to take a refreshing short nap before resuming my journey."

"You were *lucky*," Bertinelli said, scornfully. "You'd driven there *drunk*. You were sleeping it off."

"Care-*ful*," Clay said. "There was no evidence of that. The engine wasn't running. No key in the ignition. When Roger and Jimmy caught up to me less'n a minute after your officer rapped on my window and woke me up, they pointed those matters out to him. He's a bright lad. He listened. He called the station and conferred with your night-shift commander, believe it was a captain. He agreed that everyone's best interests'd be served if I let Jimmy drive my car home, with me in it, Roger following to collect Jimmy there and take him home. And so that was what was done."

"My officer was young," Bertinelli said. "Only two years on the job. It wasn't very hard for your pals to buffalo him. And when he called in to clear it with the duty officer, Captain Walsh, Ned just made a mistake. Not like him. He's always been levelheaded. But not that night. State cops or no state cops, he should've told the kid to slap the cuffs on you and run you."

"On what charge?" Clay said. "Open and gross public napping?"

Bertinelli shook his head. "You may think I'm tooting my own horn here," he said mournfully, "which I don't like to do, but I've been a good chief in this town. Run a clean operation. Seventeen years now. *One* civilian complaint of harassment. The court threw it out. I run the kind of force that operates so smoothly the townspeople never have to think about it, so they never give us any credit, take us for granted. I call that 'success.' I took an oath to see to it that the laws're faithfully enforced and I intended to keep it. Far as humanly possible, I always have.

"The only time I've gotten the swerve, it was State Police that did it to me. Protecting one of their own. That'd ever come out, we would've been pilloried, getting sucked in like that. Time I found out about it, reamed Walsh out good; told the kid what'd happen if he pulled that stunt again— after that there was nothing I could do but make a stink, go to the press. That's not my style, never has been. So I didn't.

"Since then I've thought now and then 'Maybe I should've.' Like today, for example. Seeing you back on the job, full of beans. Maybe allowing SP to get away with faking my men out where you were involved by itself *wasn't* my biggest mistake. Maybe I made it the big one by keeping quiet about it. Letting *you* all get away with it. But it doesn't matter now. Hell, it didn't even matter the next *day*. You weren't *sick,* injured, or disabled after all, so you weren't fit to be driving. You were *drunk*. Your normal bodily functions were all right. So no test is done, nothing gets written down, nature takes its normal course. Few hours's sleep and the proof disappears, overnight. All water over the dam now. Nothing I can go back and change.

"So, you're right. You supersede me at the scene of a homicide. But I know you cut corners, and nothing else I know about says that I don't have some kind of concurrent jurisdiction, murder happens in my town. So I can stay around and keep you under observation. Make sure what you're doing is what you're supposed to do, and that you actually do it. So afterwards I'll know for sure that you didn't do something else, or nothing at all. I've got a right, I think, to do that, and an obligation, too. I'm going to carry it out."

"You a friend of the dead guy?" Clay said.

"No, no," Bertinelli said. "I met him once. The secretary of the planning board called me when he filed the plans for this place. That east wing's two-bedroom condos. One and a half baths, small kitchens, full basement with screening room, hot tub, and pool tables. It was pretty obvious he was planning having guests here, short-term residents, lots of company. So, then, knowing the kind of work he did, and having common knowledge from the papers and TV the kind of weird things pro athletes tend to do for entertainment, I called him at his office in Boston and I said to him, 'Mister Drouhin. I'm the chief of police in this town you want to build in, and I think it might be helpful if you and I had a chat before you get too deep into things here. The next time you're coming down here, I'd appreciate it if you'd give me a call ahead, so we can arrange a time for you to drop by.'

"And he did. He made an appointment, and he came into the station, and I said what was on my mind and he listened to it. I said, 'Mister Drouhin, I'm not gonna mince any words with you. I'm gonna lay it on you like a big thick rug. We're glad to have you here and we want you to be happy here. But more than that we've got a quiet peaceful town here, and God willing I'm gonna keep it that way.

" 'I don't go to many games anymore. When I was down in Attleboro I used to go to Fenway a couple times a year. The Legion down there'd charter a bus and thirty or forty of us went as a group. We all had a very good time. But when I became chief here, I got out of that pattern, and the only time I went was when I would take my son. But then it got too complicated. The chief's job's unpredictable. You have to buy tickets way in advance; then something happens the day you're s'posed to go, some kid gets lost or there's a drowning, you're dragging the ponds. You can't leave your post. So you wind up not using the tickets. That's a waste of money, which's one thing that I hate. But that's the only way to be sure you'll get good seats.

" 'But I still watch sports. On TV. All the sports except boxing, which I'd say should be banned if I didn't realize they'd do it anyway, undercover, on the sly, no legal oversight at all. Like with those illegal cockfights and pit bull fights they still hold just over the border down there in Rhode Island. That'd be worse.

" 'Anyway, because I watch sports on TV and read about them in the paper, I know famous ballplayers often get in major trouble. Not necessarily any of your clients, but a lot of the players who get paid millions of dollars've gotten very bad reputations, for doing bad things off the field. I'm talking about rapes and taking drugs, fighting in bars and driving so drunk that everyone on the road at the same time gets the hell scared out of them—or worse yet, badly hurt.

" 'I don't want them doing those things around here, and I want us to be clear on that. If they do, I'll have my officers arrest them and put them in the lockup, and I will not let up on them in the morning when they see the error of their ways, tell me how sorry they are and now they want to go home. No matter how famous they may be, they'll be prosecuted to the fullest extent of the law. I will put their butts in the Faunce Street jail down in New Bedford, and I will make sure they stay in it a long time. You understand me on this?'

"He said, 'I understand you.' That's the first and last time I talked to the man, and that would have been about, well, over ten years ago. We never had any trouble."

Clay regarded him for a few moments. "So it's media then you're worried about. TV and newspaper dogs'll be outside the door when I go out, and SP'll get all the publicity. Your picture won't be in the papers, on TV. People in Easton'll start thinking, 'When something big happens, first time in years, where's Chief Bertinelli? Down at Dunkin' Donuts probably, havin' coffee. Whadda we pay this guy for?' "

Bertinelli did not say anything. Clay chuckled. He took a step toward him. Bertinelli stepped back. "Okay," Clay said, "just seeing if I could accommodate you. Thought maybe when I told you to get out of my face back there. 'Maybe I was unfair. Maybe the guy wasn't smelling my breath, he's just gotten nearsighted.' I guess I was wrong, thinking that.

"But regardless, I want to set your mind at ease. The reason Trooper Gagnon and Trooper Ernst got here and sealed the building before you or anyone in your department had a whiff of something going on is because Drouhin's chief of security, Pete Martigneau, used to be a detective lieutenant in the Norfolk DA's office. Peter's boss doesn't answer, seven thirty this morning, his secretary calls to tell him the general manager of the Tampa Bay Buccaneers's finally agreed to a teleconference about one of Drouhin's prize clients. His secretary gets worried. This is not *like* Alex. Alex's devoted to his clients. Alex's meticulous. Alex is dedicated. Alex'd mush naked in that thousand-mile Alaskan sled dog race if it'd mean a better contract for his client from the Bucs. Or the Steelers or the White Sox, or the Maplewood Roller Derby Queens. Julie buzzes Peter, gives him the first heads-up. 'Alex's outta-pocket. Something must be wrong.'

"Old habits die hard, Chick. Pete calls us, not you, because Peter *was* us, not you. And besides, calling us means he can stay in his office in the Hancock building, drinking coffee and reading his papers, while SP saddles up and checks out not only Easton but also Alex's town house on Beacon Hill and his summer place on Nantucket. More bang for the buck, you know, Chick? That's still the name of the game. Peter doesn't think that Alec chartered a Gulfstream and pulled a scoot to his place in the Bahamas last night. He's been known to do that, but not without warning, and *never* when he's trying to schedule negotiations.

"That means wherever Alex is, incommunicado, it's probably somewhere in Massachusetts. Peter makes one call to SP and he's covered all of Alec's billets stateside. Taking nothing away from Easton PD, but good as you say you are, that's a capability you just don't have."

Bertinelli said nothing.

"As for the press, we co-opted them. There's a voluntary

lid on until noon. As soon as Trooper Gagnon called in—
on a landline, smart lady—that she'd found him, he was
here and he was dead, we tipped the locals and the wires
that there's something going on out here but we weren't at
that point sure enough to tell them what it was. We promised the DA'll hold a press conference in Fall River at eleven
forty-five and tell them everything he can, so the broadcast
media can go with it on the noon news and the afternoon
papers can start going through their files for background
and photos, if they haven't already. In exchange for their
agreement not to come out here and bother us or go with
it 'til then.

"So, Chick, if that's why you're standing around here,
shifting from foot to foot, get your name and face on the
air at lunchtime, I'm afraid you're wasting your time. Ain't
gonna be no media here until at least early afternoon. By
then I am sure they'll be swarming around here like locusts.
Because when they've made a person famous covering his
every word and deed, when he dies, by definition, that is
big news too.

"As soon as the DA's given his briefing, we'll fax a copy
of it to you. So if you want to go back to your office, maybe
have a bite to eat, go over last night's blotter, do any other
small chores you might have, and then come back out here
around one fifteen, you'll have a pretty good chance of
having your picture taken and lots of people asking you
stupid questions. Of course the only truthful answer you'll
have for them'll be that all you know they already know,
because the DA and the State Police're running things here.
I'd think that'd make you feel pretty silly, but you can do
it if you want. I certainly won't stand in your way.

"And likewise I certainly have no objection if you want
to stand around in here all morning watching me. But after I send Sergeant Nicholson about his business and tell

Corporal Bateman what our plans are today, I think about all you're going to get to see between now and eleven thirty, when I use the phone to brief the DA, will be the door to the kitchen wing closing behind my rear end when I go in there to debrief the caretakers of this place.

"This's likely to take a while. When I was a sergeant, long ago, I had a defendant that I interviewed piously tell her lawyer from the stand on direct that the reason that she hadn't mentioned having been on the medication that made her very dizzy was because I'd just assumed that she'd been drunk and never asked her. My small oversight meant she beat a flagrant DUI–second-degree-manslaughter case that we should have had won on the stairs.

"Since then my approach to interviewing witnesses's been to hoover them. If I don't ask you how many times a week you masturbated when you were fourteen years old, it's not because I'm afraid to, too delicate to say it. It's because I can't see how that information could possibly enable the eventual defendant to get an acquittal, and therefore I don't need to have it.

"You're not getting anywhere near me and someone I'm interviewing. Until I get the story, you can go pound sand. I never let anyone but the people who work with me or under me sit in on witness interviews, and my guess is that's what I'm going to be doing in the kitchen for what's left of the morning.

"Your call."

Bertinelli stared at him. "I still don't know about you," he said.

Clay clapped him with his left hand on his right shoulder. "Chick," he said, "You need more fiber in your diet."

11

IN THE KITCHEN, TROOPER Ernst, 6'3", about two hundred muscled pounds in tight medium-blue twill uniform shirt, black Sam Browne belt bristling with armaments and tools, medium-blue riding breeches and black puttees, looked out of place at the sinks under the sixteen-paned windows with the southwesterly view. He was rinsing a glass coffeepot. He turned when he heard Clay and Bateman enter the room, Bateman shifting a two-inch brown leather attaché case from his left hand to his right and pulling the door closed behind them.

"Lieutenant Clay," Ernst said. Then he nodded toward two people seated at the middle of the long dark green table at the southerly end of the room. There was a pewter cream and sugar set at the center of the table. There were ten other black ladder-back wooden chairs with beige seats made of varnished woven rush pushed in at the table. The floor was made of two-and-a-quarter-inch teak boards. There were beige runners made of woven hemp between the wall cupboards and appliances built in on both sides of the room and the preparation island in the center.

"This would be Mister Arigo Catania and Mrs. Angela Catania. They run the place for Mister Drouhin. We didn't know how long you might be in the other room. We'd just decided to make a third pot of coffee, and since Mrs. Catania made the first two, I volunteered to make this one."

He filled the coffeepot with water, poured it into the brewer, put the pot on the heated plate underneath the filter bail, and turned the unit on, somehow squaring off the motions in military fashion, as though he had studied coffee preparation in a small arms manual. "I can assure you they haven't talked to anyone else since I got here a little after nine this morning, in the middle of their breakfast at their house over there across the lawn." He nodded toward the corner of the house at the tree line next to the vast garage, visible through the picture window in the southeasterly wall.

"At that time I then escorted them here. Using the key kept in their custody. The security system at that time was disarmed. Mrs. Catania then admitted us through the back door. At that time I employed my radio to communicate with Trooper Gagnon in her official vehicle. When she arrived at the scene she communicated this to me by means of my radio. I then went to the front door and admitted her. I then returned to this room. Since then Mister and Mrs. Catania have not left this room. Trooper Gagnon conducted a search of the premises, during which I believe she informed you by telephone that she had found what appeared to be the body of the person reported missing."

"Well, except for the bathroom," Angela said.

"You're right, ma'am," Trooper Ernst said. To Clay he said: "I had been advised of your strict rule that if at all possible witnesses be isolated until you have debriefed them, but I did allow them to use one of the bathrooms next to the elevator behind the staircase in the front hall. All that coffee, you know. I inspected it first and was able to ascertain that it has no second exit and there is no telephone extension in it, and I stood in this doorway when each of them was in it, so I was able to see whether either of them went anywhere else while they were out of this room. Neither one of them did. Only one at a time left my sight, and only to go to the bathroom."

"Good work, Trooper Ernst," Clay said gravely. The Catanias looked to be in their mid-fifties, and to share the opinion that life was generally severe. Seated, Arigo Catania looked to Clay to be just under six feet tall, a barrel-chested man, about 180 pounds, with wiry iron-gray hair cut short. His face was weathered. He wore a blue-plaid flannel shirt, jeans, and brown boots with raw-hide laces and black lug soles. He appeared apprehensive, wearily resigned to the random occurrence of disappoint-ments he would never be able to anticipate, prevent, or understand.

She was a sturdy woman, 5'6" or so, around 160 pounds, in a dark blue Adidas sweatsuit and white running shoes. She wore her gray hair skinned back over her ears and gathered at the back of her head with a rubber band. She looked apprehensive too, but resentful and defiant, seeking someone to blame for what she clearly believed to be an unwarranted disruption of her plans for the day, the restriction of her movements, and the considerable personal inconvenience caused her by the person who had killed her employer. Clay again suppressed an urge to laugh.

The kitchen was large, about five hundred square feet, and very bright. Beyond the table where the Catanias sat the southerly end opened onto a Plexiglas sunroom, the curved roof supported by interior buttresses made of dark brown aluminum. It was shelved and filled with plants with shiny broad green leaves. The interior wall sheltered two stainless steel Zero King refrigerators and a butcher block counter fifteen feet long with cherry wood cupboards above and below it. Against the wall on the counters under the upper cupboards were two Cuisinarts, two Waring blenders, a salad spinner two feet across, a large pasta machine, an espresso machine, two stainless steel coffee percolating towers, and a coffee grinder two feet tall, the clear Lucite canister atop it filled with beans. At the far end of the counter there were two Thermidor double ovens built into the wall. There were eighteen white cylindrical lighting fixtures partially recessed in the ceiling thirty inches apart. In the center of the kitchen there were two four-burner Jenn-Air gas ranges built in back to back into the preparation island, also cherry wood, under stainless steel ventilating hoods mounted back to back. Under the two sixteen-paned windows over two large stainless steel sinks there was a commercial-size stainless steel dishwasher recessed under the counters next to each of the sinks.

"There'll be coffee for you and the corporal in a few minutes," Ernst said.

"Thank you, Trooper," Clay said. "You've done a good job here. You needn't stay any longer. Get yourself back out there on the road and keep your eyes peeled. If you see the pretty young woman with long reddish hair and a tan shearling jacket driving the blue and tan Ford Bronco Two who cut me off on twenty-four coming up here this morning, one-thirty-one ZEK, throw the book at her. If she isn't weaving in and out when you see her, make up something plausible and I'll back you to the hilt. For her I want life plus twenty on-and-after." Trooper Ernst looked startled.

"Just kidding," Clay said. "You did a good job, and I'll mention it in the dispatches, but we don't allow spectators when we interview witnesses. So, off you go. Many thanks."

Trooper Ernst looked relieved. "Thank you, sir," Ernst

said. He took his black-billed medium-blue uniform campaign hat from the counter next to the doorway and put it under his arm. "Trooper Gagnon, sir?" he said.

"I want her to stay and keep charge of the door and the phones until I dismiss her," Clay said. "I also want her to make sure nobody intrudes on the interview Corporal Bateman and I will be conducting with Mister and Mrs. Catania, while we're enjoying your coffee."

"Very good, sir," Ernst said, opening the doorway to the foyer, "I'll tell her that."

"Mister and Mrs. Catania," Clay said, approaching the table as the kitchen door closed behind Ernst, Bateman with his attaché case behind him, "my name is Frank Clay. I'm a detective lieutenant in the Massachusetts State Police. This is Corporal Gary Bateman, also State Police. Our badges and credentials," he said, he and Bateman taking the black leather wallets from the pockets inside their jackets and flopping them open to display their shields and photo-ID cards. The Catanias glanced incuriously but politely at the credentials and nodded, unknowingly reconfirming Clay's experience that the only people who actually read, compare, and verify means of official professional identification are people who themselves carry official identification, take their work seriously, and are actually engaged in their official duties when shown someone else's ID. Clay and Bateman put the wallets back in their pockets.

"Corporal Bateman knows shorthand, a rare and wonderful thing in a young detective." Bateman had fair skin and blond hair, so that when he blushed, as he did every time Clay said that, introducing him to a new witness, his face became very red. Both Catanias surprised themselves by smiling, relaxing a little, as nervous and apprehensive witnesses usually did when Clay made Bateman blush. That was Clay's motive for doing it.

"As you see, Corporal Bateman is also a *modest* detective, an even rarer and more wonderful strain that we seldom encounter among our young investigators. He's going to take written notes of what you people tell me. In addition, unless you object, he's going to record this interview on tape."

Bateman put the attaché case on the table, opened it, and took out a brown folio containing a 14" × 10" pad of lined yellow paper and a Realistic mini-cassette recorder. "Do you have any objections to that?"

The Catanias looked at each other, seeming to resolve doubt, and then shook their heads.

"Okay," Clay said, "I'm going to ask Corporal Bateman to sit at this end of the table so he can see both of your faces while we're talking and the machine will receive clearly what's being said. And now that he's turned it on I'm going to repeat for the record what I just said to you, and again ask to you to indicate for the record, this time by saying it aloud, that you have no objection to the tape machine being used to record my questions and the answers you give." The Catanias nodded again, remaining silent. "Do you have any objection to being recorded, Mister Catania?"

"Oh," Catania said. He was flustered. "See? Already I forgot. No, I don't have no objection."

"Mrs. Catania?" Clay said.

"No," she said primly, "no objection."

"Very well, then," Clay said, "we can get started. Now, from watching television you're probably both quite familiar with the formalities that I have to go through next, which is to advise both of you of your constitutional rights.

"I don't want this procedure to alarm you unnecessarily. Usually when the cops on TV do this, they're pretty sure the person they're advising is the person who committed the criminal act. I can tell you that is not the case in the present instance, where you are concerned. It's just policy; when I do a formal interview with a witness, even though it isn't sworn, I always give them their rights. That way I know I'm less liable to forget to do that some day when I *am* interviewing a suspect, and destroy my case against him. You understand?"

They both nodded.

"You have to say it aloud, please," Clay said.

"I understand," the Catanias said together.

"Good," Clay said. "Under the Constitution of the United States as interpreted by the courts, each of you has a right to remain silent. You don't have to talk to me or Corporal Bateman. Do you understand that right?"

They both nodded. Clay sighed. "Mister Catania, Mrs. Catania: I realize you're both new to this and that it probably doesn't make any more sense to you than it would to any other sane, hardworking man or woman who's never had any personal experience before with the hoops that we policemen have to jump through, the hurdles we have to climb over, how squarely we have to turn the corners we run into, in order to have a perfectly ordinary conversation about some dreadful event. So that maybe we can find out who did it. And do our best to see that that person is punished.

"Of course you communicate with each other, and with the other people that you know and come in contact each day, by means of shrugs and winks and nods. We all do. But when I ask you questions in this kind of, well, *formal* conversation, you have to answer aloud, so that your answers will be recorded on the tape and Corporal Bateman will be able to write them down. So later on when we catch the person or persons who came in here and killed Mister Drouhin last night or early this morning—and we *will* catch them—and the prosecutors prepare the case to go into court, there won't be any doubt about what you meant to say to us here today. What will be on the paper and the tape will not be what Corporal Bateman and I *think* you must've meant, or *understood* you to mean, when you nodded, but what you actually *said*."

The Catanias looked sheepish and nodded.

"So, do you both understand that you have a right to remain silent?"

"Yes," they said, she a beat behind her husband.

"Good," Clay said. He spoke more rapidly: "Anything-you-do-say-may-be-used-against-you-at-a-trial-in-a-court-of-law. Do you understand that?"

The Catanias looked at each other. "I guess so," he said. "Okay," she said.

"If you do decide to answer any questions, you retain the right to stop answering at any time. All you have to do is say so, and the interview will be terminated. I will stop asking you questions. Do you understand that?"

Mrs. Catania looked at Mister Catania somewhat anxiously, but he nodded and made a brushing motion with his left hand over the table. "Yes," they both said, she hesitantly, this time two beats behind. Then she nodded, put both hands on the table, and pushed herself out and around from it in her chair so that she faced Bateman at the end and Clay standing to his left. She pursed her lips and clasped her hands together in her lap. She nodded again. She felt better.

"You both have the right to have attorneys and to each have an attorney present while we talk to you," Clay said. "Do you understand that?"

"Yes," they both said firmly, almost happily, gaining confidence now, getting the hang of the thing.

"If you can't afford attorneys, the court will appoint attorneys to represent you, at no cost to yourselves. Do you understand that?"

"Yes," they both said, after glancing at each other, almost cheerful now, pleased with themselves.

"Good," Clay said. "Now, with that out of the way: Mister Catania, the big iron gate at the entrance to the property was open when I arrived here today, as I gather it was when the uniformed officers arrived earlier."

"Yeah," Catania said.

"Had you already opened it this morning or was it ever closed last night?"

"It was shut when we locked up and went to bed last night," Catania said. "I know it was because there's a bank of monitors in the room just off the kitchen in our house, just like the one downstairs in the basement here. I check them every night before I turn in, part of my normal routine. The front gate was in what the people who built it told me's the night-default mode. Unless you disarm it— like you would if you're expecting company; if Mister Drouhin was having one of his big dinner parties or a meeting in the west wing screening room—it's open in the daytime even when there's nothing going through it, nothing breaking the infrared beam. Between the posts. It closes automatically at seven thirty every night.

"At six thirty in the morning it goes into day-default mode. If you don't disarm it, it opens and it stays that way 'til it goes back into night-default at seven thirty."

"What if there's a big snowstorm overnight?" Clay said.

"I do the plowing, sir," Rigo said. "On nights when we have a lot of snow, I get up in the morning and plow out the driveway, so that the gate can then swing back. Then after supper, plow again if there's been more snow. Push it right out on the road. Across the street. So the gate can close.

"It wasn't like that when we first moved in here. It didn't have the day-default mode. Unless you overrode it in the morning, it stayed in night-default all day. But it was driving us nuts, set up like that. All day letting people in do things around the property. Deliver things: the mail, the food, the liquor. And then letting them out again when they were finished. After a couple of months we finally went to Mister Drouhin, and—"

She interrupted him impatiently, making a brushing motion in the air with her right hand. "Oh, that was the *first* time we went to Mister Drouhin, the time about the gate," she said. "The *second* time, *that* was the important one, the one that *mattered*. When we finally faced him down and he agreed with us we couldn't live in this house, sleep in it, with him while he was here or had any of his people here, either. We couldn't do it no more."

She spoke fiercely; the words rushed out of her, driven by indignation long suppressed from anyone except her husband and Drouhin. She glanced at Arigo and nodded once, emphatically. He shook his head twice, casting his eyes down at the table and slumping in his chair, folding his arms on the table and sighing, defeat and sorrow on his face. She scowled. Then she looked back at Clay and Bateman. "And that he'd either have to find us some other place else to live or else we'd have to leave and he would have to find somebody else to come in here and live in this *cesspool* with him. And do his dirty work."

Clay pulled out the second chair to Bateman's right, angling it so that when he sat down there were two chairs between him and Angela on the same side of the table and he had an unobstructed view of Arigo sitting at the other side.

"Were you also present at the time of that confrontation with Mister Drouhin that your wife just described, Mister Catania?" Clay said.

Catania sighed again and nodded, his head still lowered. His eyes were closed.

"Aloud, please, sir," Clay said.

"I was..." He had to stop and clear his throat. "I was there. I didn't want to be, and I wouldn't've been if I'd've known she's going to do it. But she sprung it on me. Just as much as she did on him."

She broke in. "It *had* to be said," she said, slapping the table. "You wouldn't, so *I* had to say it."

"I wouldn't," he said. "I told her not to do it. Said I *wished* she wouldn't do it. She'd get mad at him again, when he wasn't around, and start saying if I wouldn't get us out of here, she would leave by herself, she had to. Leave *me,* to get away from this house." He shook his head. "I never been able to control her. I told her, lots of times. I knew he wouldn't take it from her, take that kind of talk from her. Anyone else, either. I was sure. We'd be out on the street.

"I was afraid," he said. "She said I was afraid and I admitted it. Jobs like this're hard to find. The wealthy people who hand them out almost always're hard to work for. You have to put up with a certain amount of, I don't know, stuff, you want to hang onto them. I didn't want us to lose these jobs. Where could we get new ones as good?" Temporizing, he avoided her gaze by looking at Bateman and Clay. "Mister Drouhin's a proud man. He don't take any guff from anyone. He tells how people call the owners of the teams 'the lords of baseball,' and how puffed up they are. Brags how he can 'bring them to their knees.' Same with the football and the hockey and the basketball owners. When he's on the phone with them, say he calls you to the room to fix a drink for him, get him a glass of beer, some wine, or get the fireplace going, he's buddies with them. Jokes and sweetness. Saying nice things to them.

"But when he's got a *client* here or on the phone, talking

about the owners, and he calls you in the room, *then* he can't say enough bad things about them, calling them 'bad, mean bastards.' " Angela frowned and Arigo knew it. "And, well, you would know, cheapskates and liars, con men, thieves, and bull artists. No respect at all for them then.

"He knew Angela didn't like cursing and swearing, and he didn't do it around her. See, nights and weekends when he was here with just Ronnie, between the basketball and football drafts and the big contract-signing seasons? No boarders in the east wing, no big dinner party on? Angela cooked all his meals here. He used to tell people she's the best cook he'd ever lived in the same house with, including his grandmother, his mother, and both his ex-wives. He was right. I never ate no food they cooked, but I've eaten lots of Angela's and I don't have no trouble believing it was true. If I'd've gone to him and said me and Angela'd stopped getting along, he would've asked her to stay and told me to get out. So, no bad language around her.

"But he was still a proud man and he had a bad temper. I was afraid if she lit into him like that, he'd fire the both of us and order us off his property. I seen him lots of times when he was really mad—not at me, at someone else he'd thought'd rooked him. He was a scary man."

"And an *evil* one," she said forcefully. "We worked for a wicked, evil man, and so was a good many of the people that he brought here, had stay here. Wicked, evil men. And *women,* too," she said scornfully. "Women without self-respect. Who'd do anything those men wanted, any time of day or night. No matter who was in the same house with them. Listening. Trying their best not to, just wanting to go to sleep but you didn't have no choice—couldn't help but hear, those *animals,* in their wickedness. And *sin.*

"Butter wouldn't melt in Mister Drouhin's mouth when

he was asking me to cook something, chicken cacciatore maybe, but Satan was in this house when Mister Drouhin had those men here. With their whores and pretty boys, swilling liquor, taking drugs. Having sex. And always, *always* making noise. Couldn't help but hear them, what was going on.

"Put your head between two pillows, try and block your ears? Forget it, didn't do no good. Mister *Drouhin* didn't care; he had *cork* on his bedroom walls. If he wasn't with them, he couldn't hear a thing. But we didn't have that, on the third floor. When his clients cut loose down here on the first floor, we *heard* them, way up there. Or in the west wing, in the hot tub and the sauna, the pool. Swimming with no clothes on. All the racket going on. And the music that they played just as high as it would go? 'Music' was what they called it, but if you asked me what it was just filthy talk, people hollering dirty words, loud as they could, at the top of their lungs, about killin' and rapin' and hurtin' each other.

"One night while we were still livin' here, the east suite on the third floor, bangin' and crashin' got so bad, two A.M. or so, I give Rigo good poke inna ribs—I knew he wasn't sleepin' 'cause no one could sleep through that. I told him, 'I don't care whose house this is. We live in it too, and we got to get our rest.' East wing was full. Four athletes staying in it. Big black men. Mister Drouhin's working on their contracts with the teams. All had women with them. None of them's married. Came right out and told me they're their girlfriends. One of them had *two* girlfriends with him. All of them had babies, somewhere else of course—other people taking care the chillen while their mommas party here—players would tell you that. No disgrace in doin' that, women neglectin' their babies while they're out with other men—they all thought it was funny.

Half a dozen other players with their women here for dinner that night. Way most of them're dressed they might as well've been naked, falling out of their clothes, *naked*. At the dinner table. That's no way to act. Wasn't very hard imagine what comes after that.

"Mister Drouhin liked to do that. He enjoyed it. Bring his old clients down to talk to the young ones. Tell them a great man he was, what great things he'd do for them. So they would all admire him.

" 'You go down there,' I said to Rigo, 'and you tell those noisy bums to turn it down there, and *behave*.'

"So, he didn't want to, but he put his bathrobe on, over his pajamas, and went out the hall. I heard the elevator come, door open, him get in. By now I'm all awake myself. Hadn't been to sleep yet anyway. So I sit up in bed in my pajamas and turn on the light, wait for the noise to stop, Rigo to come back up, tell me what they'd been doing down there.

"The noise *didn't* stop, didn't even let up. Pretty soon I hear the elevator come back up. Then I hear the door close on the third floor, and Rigo open up the door to our apartment, and when he came into the bedroom his face was white. Looked like he seen a ghost.

"I said: 'Rigo, what happened? They're still making all the noise down there. Didn't you tell those animals we got to get some sleep?'

"He took his bathrobe off and come over and sat on the bed. He shook his head, like he didn't believe what he saw. He said: 'They're in the living room. They've got a big fire in the fireplace and all the chairs pushed back against the walls. They've got two of the chairs from the kitchen in the middle of the room and there's this young black woman sitting in one looking at the fireplace, with no clothes on. Her hands're tied to the chair behind her, and her legs're tied the chair legs. And behind her in the other chair there's a naked young white woman, and she is tied up, too, same way. Both of them're laughing their heads off, like they're crazy, or they're drunk. I didn't see them before. They must've come here after dinner. The people who were at the dinner're all dancing in a circle around them and touching them all over, men and women both, touching them, and those two naked women, laughing, squealing—like this is all the best thing in the world.

" 'I didn't say nothing to them. Wouldn't've done any good. I went back to the elevator and I came back up here.'

"I was mad at him. *'Rigo,'* I said, 'you should've said something. You should've told them that if Mister Drouhin ever wakes up and finds out about this, he will call the police and throw them all out.'

" 'Mister Drouhin wouldn't've done no good,' Rigo said. 'He was dancing with them. He had his pants on but he didn't have no shirt or shoes. Looked to me like he was drunk.'

"It went on most the night. Sun was coming up when they all started leaving, doors slamming, horns blowing like it's New Year's Eve. We got no sleep at all.

"That was the day I told him off. I couldn't live with that stuff anymore," she said. "It just wasn't right, and I reached the point where we're out here, noon, twelve thirty, feeling awful. No sleep. I'm giving my husband his lunch, and Mister Drouhin's finally up. *He* feels just *fine,* naturally—*he* went to bed and got a nice night's rest for himself this morning, after his company left. He comes out here, gets himself a cup of coffee, he's *humming* to himself, just as happy as can be. He starts in telling us about all the big plans he's got for the weekend, caterers coming and so forth, a band. Just like last night, only bigger, more people.

"You know what that tells me. 'Another big all-night

party, only this one'll be for *two* nights. Two more nights of no sleep.'

"I look at Rigo. Maybe this'll do it. After what we've just been through last night, maybe he'll say something. Tell Mister Drouhin he's got to stop treating us this way. Or else we will leave. But Rigo *isn't* saying anything to him. Rigo isn't saying boo."

She paused and looked at her husband again, this time somewhat hesitantly. He was staring down at the table, but when she stopped talking he felt her eyes on him and shook his head again.

Gradually her expression softened into pity and regret. She turned in her chair so that she faced him, and extended her right arm across the table, touching his right hand with her fingertips.

"Oh honey," she said, "I know it makes you feel bad now, hearing me say, tell these things. It hurt you that day, when I told him off. But I've got a temper. You don't. One of us had to get *mad*. And you know I was right that day, when it all sort of boiled over in me. That day when he come out here and just started talking, another gang coming in, well, that day I finally knew I just couldn't stand it, we just couldn't stand it, one single more day. And I said it. We couldn't live the way we live, the way we want to live, try to live, at least, decent, God-fearing lives, and do it in this house. Our souls're in danger. One way or the other we had to get ourself out of here." She patted his hand. "Honey, you *know* that," she said, begging.

At last he took a deep breath and nodded.

"Look up at me, honey, please, will you? Look up at me and say it to me, that we couldn't stay here and live in this house while the stuff was going on, and live the way we want to live. You know what Father Malachy told us, and Father Hanratty too. 'As we strive to keep our bodies temples of the Holy Spirit, every house that we inhabit must become a House of God. Unless the Holy Spirit be welcome in the dwelling place, and the Evil One be kept out when he batters at the door; be cast out if he enters in, then the Children of the Light must remove themselves away from there and dwell no more therein. Lest their lives in Christ be snuffed out, and their very souls condemned.' "

It took him a while, but at last he mumbled "I know" and lifted his gaze as though asking forgiveness.

She patted his hand again. "I'm just trying to do what's right here, honey," she said. "These men're policemen, and Mister Drouhin's dead. They're trying to find out who did it, and they need to know all these things. What kind of a man he was. You know I love you and I need your help on this, like I do on everything we do to love and serve the Lord. I depend on you. I depend on you all the time."

"Yes," Arigo said, "I know that." He began to brighten.

"Yes," Clay said. "Well, let's just catch our breath here, give the corporal a chance to relax and stretch the fingers of his writing hand a little, 'fore he starts getting cramped. This's strenuous work. May not look like it, but it is. Little break'll do us all good." He rose from the chair. "How about some of that coffee, Corporal? Mister and Mrs. Catania?"

She started to rise. "No, no," Clay said, "you two just sit back and relax a bit too, give your vocal cords a rest. Just tell me where the mugs are—I'll fetch."

12

"THIS'S EXCELLENT COFFEE," Bateman said.

"That's a compliment to treasure, Mrs. Catania," Clay said. "We cops're coffee *gourmets,* the best in the business. We're also certified in doughnut studies, bagel assessment, and pastry evaluation. Spend a lot of time on duty studying these subjects."

Bateman blushed again. Angela looked slightly troubled. "Well, I'm sorry," she said, "ordinarily I'd be able to offer you a sweet roll, but Mister Drouhin's been trying to lose some weight the past few weeks. He said it'd help him if I didn't keep any of that stuff around."

Clay laughed. "I didn't mean what I said as a hint, Mrs. Catania," he said, thinking *Jesus*. "That's an old joke about us cops. Our weakness for doughnuts and coffee. But the corporal's right about the coffee—it's very good."

"That was Mister Drouhin's department," she said. "He had a service. Delivered every week. More often, we needed it. All I had to do was call them a list what I needed. Didn't need to say what kind, what brand. Just how much to bring. He told them what kind he wanted delivered— say I was to order a roast. They would bring prime rib. I thought he paid too much for what he bought—always the premium kind. Didn't care about price. *Told* people that. First time they came here, so much for this, so much for that, so much more for this. All premium, *deluxe*. I had to check what they brought in and then sign on the line.

"The next time he came down, I showed the receipts to him. I said, 'They're overcharging you. We don't need to pay this much.'

"I know what I'm talking about. I was in charge of ordering what I needed to make good meals where I ran kitchens before. And I said to him, 'Mister Drouhin, the people at Campbell House were old and, you know, feeble, small appetites, but they were well-off. They had plenty of money—didn't mind spending it to spoil themselves. They were always perfectly satisfied with the meats I got from Fletcher's. And the house doctor told me choice was better for them anyway, not as much fat as in prime. And before that, the members and the guests at the Hillhouse Club never had a word of complaint about the food I ordered for them, never the high-priced fancy grades. People don't know what grade they're eating. It's whether the food's cooked right.'

"Mister Drouhin paid no attention at all. Put the delivery receipts in his briefcase—kept all his accounts there. Looked at me like he's trying not to laugh and said, 'Never cut a corner here. Always get the best.' So when he wanted me to cook some new thing we never had before, the service that come reg'lar didn't carry it so I had to special order—venison or buffalo, he liked to try new things he'd heard about someplace—I always said, 'The best you've got.' "

She giggled. "Sometimes even *that* wasn't good enough. He didn't like bear much. But I agree with you, what he buys makes real good coffee. I just think he pays too much for it."

She reached and patted Arigo's hand again. Then she pulled her arm back, shifting her gaze to Clay and Bateman. "I will say Mister Drouhin may not've *meant* to be an evil man. I wish to be fair and just to him, especially now he's dead and can't do any more harm. May God forgive him for his sins and be merciful to his immortal soul. And the angels bring him into paradise."

"Amen," Arigo said absently. Then he became embarrassed and tried to cover it by blinking several times.

"Ronnie had his own room next to Mister Drouhin's in the master-bedroom wing," she said, "and I know he did sleep there. When I changed the bed it'd always been slept in. So'd Mister Drouhin's. I know from the Apostle Paul that without charity I am as sounding brass, so I try to believe it was just friendship between them. Not unnatural. But it's hard. I know Mister Drouhin was of the flesh. He allowed the evil and the wickedness that went on here. The spirit of darkness was upon the house when he used it for sin, and that spirit was in *him*—he embodied it.

"When he wasn't here, the dark spirit wasn't here. Light was in this place. It was nice. I *liked* it. Felt it was my home. And when he had godly people here. Some of the men and women who came to stay, or visited people in the east wing. Some of them were good. Many of them, in fact. Godly men and women, living right and trying to do good in their lives. In the holy name of Christ.

"The Fellowship of Christian Athletes. Some of them belonged to that. They were not of our faith, but they were devout. Some of them had been ordained, ordained ministers of the gospel, the holy word of God. Just as we have, they had dedicated their *lives* to Him. When they would do something in a game that was especially good, they would take the time to thank Jesus for helping them to do it. Praise His holy name. Right then and there with all the people looking at them. Cheering them. Calling out their name—and they would give thanks to God. That was powerful witness.

"They were sincere. Mister Drouhin told me once he had to go to the football commissioner and tell him that if they put in some new rule they were thinking about, stopping the players from showing they know they owe everything to Jesus, giving public witness that all their strength and skill comes from *Him,* almighty *God,* seventeen of their very best players that Mister Drouhin represented told him they'd stop playing. They would *quit.* Wouldn't play no more, no matter how much money they was making. If somebody told them that they couldn't let the people see them having fellowship in Christ."

"Yes," Clay said, "so, what happened? After you braced Mister Drouhin with the hell-raising going on here? You're both still here. Did he build you that house over there?"

"That's what he did," Arigo said. "He acted like he was...I dunno, like somebody hit him. After Angela got through with him. Telling him what bothered her. *Nothin'* like what I thought he'd do to us if she ever talked to him like that. And then he said: 'Well, lemme think about this. I certainly don't want that to happen.' And then he went out of the kitchen, and Angela sat down and we had our lunch. And I felt pretty good. I like to eat. I thought: 'Well, if he was going to fire us, we'd be already fired. But we're not, so it must be he isn't.' "

"Rigo works hard here all day," Angela said. "One big meal at night: not enough for him. Needs a good breakfast, lunch."

"That day, I remember, I was pruning trees," Rigo said. "It was spring. Lots of old trees on this property. Taking down limbs that broke loaded with snow. Cut 'em up into firewood. Out in the air all morning, you know? Really get hungry. Look forward to lunch.

"Anyway, I just finished saying to Angela here, 'Geez,

maybe your idea was right. Maybe he didn't know, he just never thought of it, what went on here'd upset you.' And back inna the kitchen he comes.

" 'Look,' he says, 'here's what I'm gonna do for you, all right? Gonna build you a house of your own, over there by the tree line, next the storage garage. I want you to stay here, rest of your lives. Never want you to leave. I can't stop the things go on here. People see these athletes on the field, and they admire them. Then they read in the papers, hear rumors, TV, things some of them did. And they're shocked. I don't blame them. But all by myself, no matter how *I* might feel about it, I can't ever hope to stop it.

" 'But I understand you, and I do agree with you. You've gotta feel right about it, feel comfortable working and living around here. So this new house will be *your* house, not mine. I'll build a house on it and deed it over to you. Give it to you free and clear. 'Quipped and furnished way you want it. When the tax and water bills come, you just give them to me and I'll take care of them. And your supplies. What you want or need. The weekly orders. Figure four bedrooms, your kids come visit. Though you may not want them during draft and signing seasons, when I've got the players here. Two and a half baths, *all* that kind of thing.

" 'Otherwise things stay the same. You take care of this place. Keep an eye on things. Do what you've been doing. Manage the plant. And of course keep on making those wonderful meals.'

"And that's what he did," Arigo said. "The builder talked to us. Did we like the plans. 'No, put this here and then that there.' All like that. Did it all just like we wanted. It was like on television. Those two guys in the van come and ring your doorbell and say 'You just won the big jackpot. All your dreams come true.' Mister Drouhin gave us our dream. We never would've had it, except what he did for us." He stopped for a moment. "The town says it's worth over two-hundred-thousand dollars. I know. I seen the tax bills."

"How much did he pay you?" Clay said.

The Catanias looked at each other and then back at him, hesitating. "Well," she said.

"I know," Clay said. "In this country you can ask people about their religion. Their politics. Their children and private lives. They'll tell you the most personal things. Heck, they'll do it on TV, give them half a chance. But if you ask them how much they *make*, well, that's a *sensitive question*. Forgive me, I have to ask it. Money's often a motive in murder cases. How much did Drouhin pay you?"

"Four thousand dollars a month," Angela said. "Plus our food, of course. We don't drink very much, but any wine and liquor that we wanted. We like a CC-ginger now and then. Glass of wine with dinner. I felt kind of funny taking it, 'specially the liquor, but that was what he said. He insisted. 'Don't wait around for me to offer,' he would say to Rigo. 'I assume you're taking it and I want you to. Wait for an offer, you'll go thirsty.' So we would.

"When he hired us originally it was three thousand, and he said two thousand was for Rigo's hard work on the grounds. Keeping everything working. And a thousand was mine. For running the house and making the kitchen work right. But then when he raised us to four thousand, he said we're each getting a five-hundred-dollar raise, Rigo's for the cost of living and mine for veal marsala."

"And our *cars*," Arigo said. "He got our cars for us— my Jeep and her Regal. Traded every five years. I told him he didn't need to. Weren't all that worn out. But he said taxes, something. Meant he had to pay less. Health insurance and some kind of pension. Top of Social Security. I was never clear on just how that worked. He said if we worked 'til we turn sixty-five, or got sick and had to stop before that, it guarantees two thousand a month, plus what we get from the government, Social Security. Make sure we had enough to eat." He frowned, considering. "Said it all came out of the agency. Our jobs and the property here. We was all part his business. I don't know how he did that."

"And we just don't spend a lot of money," she said, "go out much, or travel. Carlotta and Celia and their husbands, they come here in the summer. Mister Drouhin's not around much in the summertime. Says that's just about the only time he can relax at all, while his clients're either playing, on vacation themselves. Or in camp gettin' ready to play."

"He goes Nantucket," Arigo said.

"So we've got the place all to ourselves. Nice days the kids can swim in the pond. It rains they can swim in the pool. Picnics on the lawn. Show movies in the theater in the basement. Thanksgiving too, he's up in Boston; they come. Have dinner with us. It's like it's *our* estate."

She smiled. "Maybe that's why we don't go away. We're just not the traveling kind. And: Where could we go that'd be better'n this? Last time we took a trip ourselves, Mister Drouhin let us use his place in Grand Bahama. Three years ago. It was nice. But we really didn't like it. Wasn't really anything to do. We don't like to gamble. And the only show we went to, half-naked women, men telling dirty jokes. We don't like that kind of thing."

Rigo's face showed he did not entirely agree with that claim, but he nodded. He had reached a judgment. He cleared his throat. "Mister Drouhin had some bad habits. And he could be hard on people, but he was a good man to work for."

"If you could stand him," Angela said. "*And* keep your distance."

Clay looked at Bateman. "No motive for these folks, I'd say, Gary—you think?"

Bateman smiled. "I don't see one, Lieutenant."

"Okay," Clay said to the Catanias, "before we got side-tracked a while back there, we were talking about the front gate. I'm going to ask Corporal Bateman to go back in his notes and take us to where we were when that happened."

Bateman went back through the pages of the legal pad. "Mister Catania'd just said: 'At six thirty in the morning it goes into day-default mode. If you don't disarm it, it opens and it stays that way 'til it goes back into night-default at seven thirty. It wasn't like that when we first moved in here. It didn't have the day-default.' "

"Okay," Clay said, "how was it different when you first came here? Other than of course that you were living in this house then, not in the one Drouhin built for you over by the trees."

"There was only default mode. The daytime was the same as it was at night," Arigo said. "Anyone who wanted to come in but didn't have a keypad number or a card had to buzz us, and we would have to go to the intercom and find out who it was. Then we were supposed to look at the monitor and see what they were driving, to see if they were who they said they were, mailman, UPS, Federal Express. And if they were okay, then let them in. But they always *were* okay—most of them came so often, we got so we recognized their voices. So after a while we stop checking the monitor. Took their word for it. Let them in. Then the gate'd close after they came in, and when they went to leave we'd have to buzz them out.

"We couldn't get anything *done*. You know. Finish a job. You never notice how many people come to a house like this every day, 'thout ever having to come *inside*, until you have to let every last one of them in and out of the *yard*. The rubbish man. Meter readers from the gas. Electric.

Cable repairman. The oil man and the man with the fire-wood. The drivers from the car dealers—Mister Drouhin'd forget to tell us they're going to come. Bringing one car back from service. Taking the other one out."

"And then all the people who *do* have to come inside the house, fancy place like this," she said. "The kid from the florist—Mister Drouhin wanted fresh flowers in the front hall, the living room, and the dining room every Friday. Cleaning service, also Fridays. Food-service people with the order for the week. He's throwing a party, delivery people from the caterers with the tablecloths, the morning. The spring, the fall, if it was going to be out on the lawn, that nice view the pond, then the people with the tent and the tables and chairs. The man who laid the fog down, kill mosquitoes. Platform for the band. 'Thank you,' he'd say, when his guests said how nice it all was. 'I fell in love with it at first sight. It's such a beautiful setting,' But that setting-up was a lot of *work,* and he was never here for that. I don't think he realized—"

"And the house being new then," Arigo said, "people're still coming to put in more things. Fix things'd been put in. Didn't work right. The water-meter man comes twice a year, but he always has to get into the basement. The man who took care of the pool and the landscapers for a week at a time taking care of the shrubbery twice a year. In the morning. Out to get the lunch orders. In bringing lunch back. Out to get something they'd forgot. In bringing it back, and then out at four thirty: 'See you folks tomorrow.' I got so I hated those guys.

"It seemed like we're running back and forth, the inter-com and buzzer all day long. So after a while we went to Mister Drouhin and told him, and he agreed to have the gate company come and add a new default code for day-time." He paused expectantly.

"So now how does it work?" Clay said, leaning forward.

The cadence and inflection of Arigo Catania's voice changed. Now he was reciting. He lowered his eyelids to concentrate. "Now it's open all day. Unless you defeat the code and close it. And it closes for the night at seven thirty; stays closed unless you override the mode and open it. Then it shuts again.

"If someone goes out after that, they have to open it before they can leave. There's a keypad next to the front door. There're pads in the four stalls under this house and in the ten in the garage next to our house. A person with a sender—that is, a transmitter—can open it from their car. It stays open until something passes through it. Closes after. Soon's the car's passed through the beam. A person with a sender when they come back has to open it again. If they want to come back in.

"A person living here for just a while gets a keypad number. I make it up for them personal. They pick four numbers, like, say, eight-nine-six-seven, and I put them in the machine. They can open or close the gate by putting their keycard number on the keypad at the gate. After the person has his own place, Mister Drouhin tells me. I erase the access code. Won't ever work again.

"Regular visitors—Ronnie, and people who work in the agency, Angie and me—we all have our own keycards. Open the gate by sticking the keycard in the keypad slot."

Finished, Catania opened his eyes and beamed. "And so that's how the gate works now."

His voice returned to normal cadence and inflection. "When the office called this morning and told me when Mister Drouhin didn't answer at the big house, and they'd called you, the police, they asked me, open the gate. And told me not to go to the house. But when I looked at the monitor in our house, gate's already open. Somebody disarmed default mode last night. Now, it wasn't me or Angela that did that, because, like I say, it was closed when we went to bed."

"What time would that have been?"

"Ten thirty," they said together. "We watch the first half of the late news on Channel Fifty-six," she said. "Then we go to bed. Used to stay up and watch the late news on Five at eleven, and we miss Chet and Natalie, but getting up early way we do, five thirty, six, depending on how many's here—got to be too late for us."

"Who do you think opened it?" Clay said.

"Well, Mister Drouhin," Arigo said. "When he came in after midnight. But then it would've closed again behind him. Someone opened it after that and left it in day-default mode. "When Mister Drouhin came in last night . . . I know it was way after midnight. He called in the afternoon and said he had a meeting, Boston, and he'd have dinner there. He'd be down here around nine thirty, ten. Said he had someone driving up to see him here, tomorrow morning around ten. Which now'd be today. Needed time, to get ready."

"Did he say who the appointment was with?" Clay said.

"Nope," Arigo said. "That was something you weren't supposed to, well, you know, *ask* him. Who was coming here. If he didn't tell you, he didn't tell you."

"Ten o'clock," Clay said to Bateman. "Ernst and Gagnon were here before that. If someone'd come in that drive to keep that appointment at ten, they would've seen the cruisers and the meat wagon in the yard. Gathered there must be some kind of trouble. Turned tail and run. Gagnon didn't say anything to me about that happening. If it had she would've."

"So either whoever had the appointment called up and cancelled it without knowing what'd happened," Bateman said, "or else the person with the appointment arrived several hours earlier, ready for trouble, got let in by Drouhin, had some kind of a fight with him, killed him, then got the hell out."

"Okay, Corporal," Clay said, "the first thing we do's find out who it was, and whether that meeting got cancelled, and when. We get through bothering these good people here, I want everything there is to know about Alexander Drouhin's phone habits. Especially whether incoming calls here were logged by caller-ID and if conversations were recorded, who has got the taped or digital records."

To the Catanias, he said: "Do you know anything along that line? Who took his calls when he was out, all that sort of thing?"

"His phone didn't ring when he wasn't here," Angela said. "Our phone that rings in this house also rings in his house, so that if we were over there, we would get our calls. And also those from the people who sold things to him and did work around his house."

"Call forwarding, then," Bateman said. "Most likely to his office." Clay nodded. "Make a note to call the DA's office soon's we finish this conversation and tell them we need subpoenas *duces tecum* on every telephone company known to man, served this afternoon."

"Did either of you wake up again during the night, before you got up this morning?" Clay said.

"No," she said.

"I did," Arigo said. "I've been having some trouble with my prostate."

"I heard there's been a lot of that going around," Clay said. "Did you hear any loud noises during the night?"

"No," they said together. "But we're both pretty sound sleepers," she said. "Mister Drouhin laughed at us. He said nights when he came in after we'd gone to bed, it took him ten-twelve rings to wake us up. And both the houses being brick . . ."

"Does that mean he was shot, that was how they killed him?" Arigo said. "You asking if we heard a loud noise?"

Clay disregarded the question. "I'm sure while you were sitting here with Trooper Ernst, you must've formed some theory who got in and did it. Once you'd found out Mister Drouhin was dead, I mean."

"I think someone must've called him and said they wanted to see him," Arigo said. "So he disarmed default. Opened the gate. Mister Drouhin would've had to let him into the house. The cards and codes that open the gate don't work on the house alarm. That works on a key. We always arm it when we leave. When he comes home late and turns it off, comes in, he always rearms it right off. Mister Drouhin let the killer in the house.

"The doorkeys are coded and numbered. Locksmiths won't copy 'em. Only the company that made them. Lose one, you have to get a whole new set of keys. Re-key all the locks. Have to write to the company, serial number of your system. Have to have a witness to your signature. Company sends a man out from Dayton, in Ohio. The new keys. And you have to show him ID. He gives you the same number of keys that you had in the old set. Re-keys all the locks. New key set costs seven hundred and fifty dollars. Plus the locksmith's travel expenses."

"Have you ever lost one?" Clay said.

"*No*," Arigo said, horror on his face.

"Sorry," Clay said. "I just thought from your detailed knowledge of what happens when you do, maybe it'd happened to you."

"No," Angela said, smiling with her husband. "After they put the alarm system in, they get everyone who's going to have a key together in one room. And they tell you that you'd better never lose that key, because if you do it's going to cost you or the people who you work for an awful lot of money. To get the security back. And it makes a big impression. Fourteen years ago now, and to this day I still remember how that alarm man scared us."

"How many of them are there?" Clay said. "The keys, I mean."

Arigo looked at Angela. She nodded for him to answer. "The only people that we know about who have them except us are Mister Drouhin and Ronnie, and Mister Martigneau in Mister Drouhin's office. So it seems like Mister Drouhin had to've let the murderers in. But that would've been after we were in bed."

"And anyway," Angela said, "even if we'd been up and around, watching TV or something, all we could've seen would've been the headlights. The east wing's between us and the front door."

"I assume," Clay said, "there're all-weather video-cams around the perimeter. So that anyone at the panel'd be able to see virtually everything going on outdoors."

"There are, sir," Arigo said.

"Are there recorders on the monitors to tape the pictures the cameras transmit?" Clay said.

"Yeah," Arigo said. "If something moves in the sector that they cover. The cameras pan all the time. You can always see what they're seeing. There're motion detectors in them. The tape for the camera doesn't start unless someone either overrides default and starts it or something at least as big as a good-sized dog, German shepherd, comes in their field of vision. A year or so ago we had wild turkeys. Mating season, I guess. They were big enough. The cameras were going on and off all the time. Then the turkeys went away. Couldn't tell you why."

"Maybe they were modest," Clay said. "Didn't like having their pictures taken while they were making out."

Angela's face showed she did not think that was funny and Arigo saw that he'd better not, either.

"Once a recorder starts," Arigo said, "it will then tape everything that camera sees in that sector for the next twenty-four hours. Even if nothing moves after that, the tape for that one runs.

"If you don't take the tape out of the magazine in the console before the end of those twenty-four hours, it rewinds. The next time the motion detector fires it'll tape over what it saw the last time."

"Is there a camera that sees who comes and goes through the gate?" Clay said.

"Yeah," Arigo said. "It's on a post just below the top of the knoll. There's all that bush stuff behind it so you wouldn't notice it 'less you knew where to look. Can't see it from the road."

"So the tape deck in the monitor for that camera'd show who came in here and went out of here late last night," Clay said.

"I doubt it," Catania said. "Mister Drouhin's habit was to shut off that camera when he was expecting guests here at night. Disarm default and open the gate."

"Why?" Clay said. "Why have this kind of system if you're going to shut it off, defeat it?"

"He told us the people he had coming here're spooky about privacy," Angela said. "I didn't believe it. Near as I could see, they spent most of their time trying to get their names in the paper and their mugs on television. And he spent most of his time trying to help them do it—and also getting his own on. Taking the credit.

"I think it was because after we had that big scene with him about the people he was bringing here, and what they were doing here, he didn't want me and Rigo to find out who came in here after dark. After we went home. Or what time they left and what they looked like, leaving. He was a terrible liar. He really did lie all the time."

"Now Angie," Arigo said, "you know that isn't true. He paid us good, and made us comfortable, and he didn't lie all of the time."

"Well, he sure kept in practice," she said.

"Yes," Clay said. "Well, be that as it may, is there a surveillance system inside the house as well?"

"Not as far as I know, sir," Catania said. "I know it's possible to do that, watch what people do in rooms where they don't know or think they're being watched. I've seen it done on television, tiny little peepholes you'd never notice if you were right in the room, and behind them there are cameras seeing everything.

"That heavy black guy that's the mayor again of Washington, D.C.?" Arigo said. "That Barry guy, the junkie, went to jail? That's how they got him, using cocaine in a hotel room with a woman. She was in her underwear. When he finished having crack they were going to do it—you could tell." Angela frowned but Arigo plowed ahead. "But then the FBI came in and arrested him. So they didn't. It was all a setup, and he never even noticed. They shown it on TV. We seen it in our house one Sunday night. He had no idea what the heck was going on."

"He was too busy misbehavin', notice what was goin' on," Angela said with satisfaction. "Wife divorced him right after that, I b'lieve. Served the sinner right. But then after he got out of jail, why he just turned right around and got himself another wife. No problem." She sniffed. "It's no wonder some men act like dogs. They know there's some tramp somewhere that'll let 'em get away with it, anything they want to do. Long as they've got money and a famous name."

Arigo waited out her speech with practiced deference.

When she had finished, he resumed. "So that stuff could be in here. But I've been all over this place, and I never found anything'd make me think that. And Mister Drouhin told me about all the other surveillance and security devices. And showed me the screens where the pictures come up, so we wouldn't set it off. By accident, you know? And so that we could run it when he wasn't here. He never showed me any kind of inside surveillance.

"Now, that don't rule it out. As good as he was to us, he would do almost anything, Mister Drouhin would. But generally he made no bones about it. Anything he did. I don't think he cared what we might've thought. What he said or did. What he wanted from us, what he paid us for, was the work we did for him. He believed he owned us. And I guess he did."

"He owned *everybody*," Angela said. "Thought he did, anyway. The caterers Rigo said? All the people who came here, drove us crazy, 'fore they came and changed the gate? Bartenders. Maids. Parking kids? Summertime, his tent parties down the pond? Cars as far as you could see out there in the front, rows and rows and rows of them—six, eight kids or so to valet park them. Same thing with all the people who came here and put on his shows. He invested in their businesses. Gave them the money to start. Catch was that they're always ready, beck and call, to take care of him. Didn't care how they did it. Long as it was 'Chop-chop,' when we called them, said he was coming. He used to say that."

She frowned. "Sometimes he said it to us. Rigo always made himself laugh, but I didn't. Mister Drouhin didn't like it, but I didn't care. He was paying us good money, but not enough to laugh when he lorded it over us."

"Except that time when Angela told him we'd leave," Arigo said, "I never thought he cared what we thought.

But I don't agree with her on that. I don't think he turned off the gate camera when he had people coming in because he didn't want *us* to spy on them. I think he turned it off because he didn't want anybody, ever, to be able to find out who'd been here any night.

"People came here at night that shouldn't've been here. People who worked for other agents. Players who had other agents. Undercover cops. Private detectives. He'd see me working, around the property, when someone famous left. That he thought I might've recognized, TV or something. Picture in the paper. And he'd come up to me and say, 'Now Rigo, no one's ever to know that gentleman was here.' And I'd look at him and say, 'What gentleman, sir? I haven't seen anyone today. I never see anyone here.' He'd grin at me, and the next time I happened to be in the house at the same time he was, working on something, he'd yell at me to be sure to take a bottle of Canadian Club out of the cellar, he knew we liked it, and enjoy it on the lawn, watching sunsets on the pond.

"See, Angela and I sometimes like to take a couple lawn chairs out and have a CC-ginger around twilight in the summer, watch the sky get dark and the stars come out. Fireflies. And lots of bats live in the pines behind the house. They come out at dusk to catch bugs, mosquitoes, over the pond. They're like warplanes in the movies, swooping, diving, everything—just going all over the place. Having a wonderful time. People're afraid of bats, but they won't bother you. Sometimes they come close enough so you can hear the air, their wings, but they've got that sonar thing they use and they'll never hit you.

"Anyway, we're out there one night, us and the bats. It's twilight and we're sitting back up there in the shadows. And I seen this big green Cadillac El Dorado come down the drive behind the house and stop right at the back door, the garage inna cellar. I never seen it before, but whoever was in it'd been here before. I forget about the bats. I could see what color it was and what the guy looked like because there're three double halogen floodlights with motion detectors on them up under the eaves inna back. Those buggers came on. The guy in the car never saw us.

"Wasn't looking at nothing but the back door anyway. He was a white guy, had blue pants and a white shirt on, necktie pulled down from his collar, gray hair which he's losing. His head was shiny. He was kind of fat. Pudgy. Hadn't been taking care of himself. He was maybe forty years old.

"He's holding a package, gray box, in his lap. My eyesight's good, a man of my age. I had my binoculars, I could've told you how long ago he'd shaved, but I didn't. We're out watching bats, not looking at stars. The box is about big enough to hold a loaf of scali bread, all right? A foot by six inches. Pretty soon the light comes on over the inside stairs to the door, and it opens. It's Mister Drouhin. In his shirtsleeves. Man hands him the box and he takes it. Gives the man an envelope and shuts the door. Man gets back in the Cadillac, turns around and leaves.

"I think that's why he shut off the system, the cameras. He had people come here that he shouldn't've had coming here or doing what they did."

"Supplying drugs?" Clay said.

"Some kind of drugs," Arigo said. "I found a box that looked a lot like the one the man gave him that night all mashed up in the basement trash compactor, following week. Someone'd put bottles in the chute, probably one of the bartenders. Caterers. Not supposed to do that—s'posed to recycle glass. But when I pulled the bag out it was partly cut open. Didn't spill, but it was gonna. I set it down on the floor while I figured out what to do. Didn't want to have to clean up all that garbage off the basement floor. Which I've had to do before—talk about your dirty jobs. Decided the best thing was to get one of the big trash barrels, fifty-five-gallon drum, top cut off. Put it on its side next to the bag. Then slide the bag in—bottom was all right, cuts're at the top—and then when it's in, stand the barrel back up.

"I do it. Get the bag in and then put one foot on the barrel and pulled it 'til it stood up. But when the bag crashed down to the bottom of the barrel, the bottom split too, and there was that gray box. Took it out and read the label, white label, black print. Never forget it. Return address was Cajun Laboratories, Four Mile, Colorado."

"Never heard the place," Clay said. "Who was it addressed to?"

"That part'd been blacked out," Catania said. "Looked like Magic Marker."

"We've got equipment now that could read through it," Clay said. "Tell me that you saved the box."

Arigo shook his head sadly. "I didn't," he said. "I thought about doing that, but then I thought, Mister Drouhin wants this thrown away. I work for him. I threw the box back in the barrel. Rubbish man took it away."

"Well, not unexpected, but still too bad." Clay said. "Okay, what I would like you to do for me now, Mister and Mrs. Catania, is state your date and place of birth, and tell Corporal Bateman, if you wouldn't mind, your Social Security numbers. Most of us still have them on our driver's licenses."

"I don't remember my Social Security," Angela said. "I was born in Winthrop Hospital, May fifteen."

"And the year, ma'am?" Clay said, suppressing a smile.

She grimaced. Then she said: "Oh, I guess if I have to. Nineteen forty-nine."

"Thank you, ma'am," Clay said, ignoring Arigo's surprised glance at her.

Angela did not ignore it. "You just never mind," she said to her husband.

"And you, Mister Catania?"

"Fourteenth of August, nineteen forty-four," he said. He was proud of his memory. "Providence, Rhode Island, Roger Williams Hospital. He then recited his Social Security number."

"Thank you," Clay said. "Now what I would like you to do, Mister Catania, is take me down to the control room and check the tape decks with me. Just on the outside chance Mister Drouhin might've forgotten to turn off the system when his visitor came to kill him last night. Corporal Bateman'll will keep your wife company while we're gone. Then when we finish that, I'd like both you and your wife to give us a quick tour of the inside of this house and the garage across the way. Can you do those things for me?"

"Yes sir," Catania said.

Nicholson appeared outside the window, his Nikon at eye level, taking a picture just as Catania and Clay stood up. Angela saw the motion from the corner of her eye. "Hey," she said, "who's he?"

"State Police photographer, ma'am," Clay said. "He's working for me. Nothing to be alarmed about. He may come in here for interior shots while your husband and I're downstairs."

"Do I have to be in them?" she said. Despite his assurances, she was alarmed.

"Not unless you want to be," Clay said.

"Well I don't," she said firmly. "I don't like having my picture taken."

"Then if he comes in before we're back from the basement," Clay said, "Corporal Bateman will accompany you to another room while the photographer works in this one."

She nodded, satisfied.

Catania led Clay back out through the doorway into the foyer to the door under and behind the broad staircase, down into the basement. An air piston closed the door behind them. The walls, steps, and risers of the staircase were covered with beige carpeting and the basement floor was made of beige asphalt tile. The monitoring station at the foot of the stairs consisted of a console with three keyboards and three television screens set into a gray metal console at the center and two ancillary stations flanking it at forty-five-degree angles. There were three black upholstered high-back swivel-castered armchairs, one in front of each panel.

"More complicated'n it needs to be," Catania said, contempt in his voice, lumbering down the stairs, his heavy footsteps muffled by the insulation. "It's the kind of security system you'd have in a fucking *prison* or something— not a big house in the country like this."

"Did you tell him that?" Clay said.

"Mister Drouhin?" Catania said, "No. He wasn't the kind of man you gave opinions to, you get what I mean. He wanted you to do what he wanted you to do, and if you worked for him your job was to do it, not ask a lot of questions.

"Or find fault, all the time, like Angie," he said. "He was always very nice about it. Tried not to let it seem like he was throwing his weight around. Mentioned many times how his parents didn't have much money and he went to Brown on scholarship. 'Never could've gone there otherwise,' he'd say.

"He'd tell you about how he saw the West Coast while

he was in college. The Northwest and Alaska, while he was in law school. Delivered cars. Answered ads in papers from people who were moving west, wanted their cars waiting, they got out there. 'Then when the summer ended, I'd answer another ad. Drive a car back to the east, some rich guy moving here.'

"One of the people he drove a car for ended up owning a hockey team. Forgotten now which one he said. 'It's a small world, Rigo. We go around a few times and then we come around again. In nineteen sixty-six I drove his Austin Healey from Corvallis, Oregon, to Bethesda, Maryland, in three days, redline all the way. Three speeding tickets, Montana, Minnesota, and Wisconsin. Tore 'em up and threw the pieces in the wind.

" 'Twenty-three years later I took him to the cleaners on a contract for a player he wanted so bad it didn't matter to him, guy was at the end of the road. There's nothing I like better 'n dealing with an owner who got rich enough to buy the team he bled for as a kid, never got over worshipping. His hometown heroes. Babies'll give you a tougher fight to keep their candy. Sat there with this big shit-eating grin on his face while I took his money away from him. Had no idea I was also the guy who wore out his crappy car almost thirty years ago. Maybe my wild-ass clients're right: "Live fast, leave a good-lookin' corpse." ' "

"He didn't," Clay said. "Not the last part, I mean."

"That's sort of what the young lady trooper told us when Officer Ernst brought us over here," Catania said. "We asked to see him—after all, we'd both *worked* for the guy a long time, never mind what we thought of him, or why—and she said she didn't think that'd be a good idea. He was hurt pretty bad?"

"I've seen a lot of corpses in my time," Clay said. "I'm sort of hardened. None of them've been what I'd call 'attractive.' Death by homicide doesn't usually offer that option. Even death by poisoning leaves you an awful shade of gray. But the way he got it was *very* messy—he wasn't even in the running for Best Dressed. Okay, where's the camera on the gate?"

"First one on the left," Catania said. "They read left to right. You see something that you want to see more of, you can hit the toggle under it, aim and hold the camera on it, zoom in if you like."

"Remarkable," Clay said.

"He said he used to like to come down here at night when no one else was here. Sit in the middle chair. 'Surveying my domain.' He told me that. I never actually saw him do it, but I had no trouble believing it. It was the kind of thing he'd do. It was all just a big dream he had. 'They say every man's home is his castle—mine really is. I think I'll put in a moat.' I kind of pitied him.

"You may've noticed I don't say these things about him around Angela. It only gets her going. You saw how she is where he's concerned. But I try to keep in mind that we've worked for him ever since he built this place, over fourteen years, and I have to say the man did pay us well, even if he did make us lose some sleep 'til he built our house. I'm sorry he's dead now. Sorry he died the way I guess he did. But Mister Drouhin was kind of an asshole."

OUTSIDE IN THE CIRCULAR drive, after they had toured the house, garages, and grounds with the Catanias, and Clay had briefed the DA on the phone, Clay said to Bateman, "I'm hungry. The next place we have to go to today is Drouhin's office, Boston. Fairly long drive. Know Edgerly's Steak House?"

"Up one thirty-eight there in Canton?" Bateman said. "Yeah, I know where that is."

"Buy you lunch," Clay said, "*if* you can tell me what the hell was in that gray box. Otherwise you buy your own. LSD, you think?" he said. "Maybe Ecstasy?"

Bateman shook his head. "I don't think pro athletes'd take that stuff," he said. "Fashion models and stupid kids're market for those killers. My guess'd be steroids, sir, anabolic steroids. Summertime? Football training camps a month away? Players trying to bulk up, fast, 'fore the season starts?"

Clay looked at him and pursed his lips. "You know, kid," he said, "you've got real promise. I don't watch my step with you, pretty soon I'm going to be the one with the pad and the tape recorder. You'll be the man in charge."

Bateman reddened, but grinned.

13

PETE MARTIGNEAU WAS AT ease in his northwest-corner office at the headquarters of Alexander Drouhin & Associates in the new Hancock building. The door leading to the reception area was closed. He tilted back in his brown leather chair and put his feet on his desk, the black tasseled slip-ons gleaming. He crossed his legs at the ankles and clasped his hands behind his head. He smiled. *He's had something done,* Clay thought. *Something's different. Changed. What the hell is it?*

"Frangie, hey," Martigneau said reproachfully, "of *course* we're upset. How else would we be? But this's a pressure business. We can't just say today, 'Okay, close it down, Alec's dead. Everyone go home and weep.'"

Martigneau chuckled. "We did that, he wouldn't be. Dead, I mean. He'd come back from the Beyond and ream us out good. A hundred and thirty-three other people work on this floor. Every one of them had a full calendar ahead of them today when they came in. They do their jobs right, when they leave tonight—top guns after seven, on their way to meetings—their daybooks for tomorrow'll be jammed. If they weren't already. That's how you get to the fifty-first floor, and that's what you do to stay there.

"Alec may've died, but that does *not* mean we can just stop dead in *our* tracks, ignore the interests of the clients that his name attracted. Certainly we'll be closed the day of the funeral. Soon as someone tells us when it is. But in the meantime we've got our clients' *business* to look after. People all the world're expecting to hear from us. *Today.* They will. That's the way Alex would've wanted it."

Martigneau unclasped his hands to use the right to make an encompassing wave. *Okay, monogrammed cuffs. New, but that isn't it.* "Alec *built* this place, and this's how he wanted it to operate. This's his *vision,* come true. You maybe think we don't *know* this? Aren't sorry he's *dead?* Angry at the person who did it?

"Look at me, you think that. Without Alex, I'm retired on a cop's pension. FD Whitman's doing card shows, signing autographs for three bucks a pop. Should've majored Broadcasting, he's in school. We know who built what we've got here. And we're sorry that he's gone. But we deal in reality. You guys got any idea, scope of the things we do here?"

"Educate us," Clay said, keeping the tone of his voice as neutral as he could.

"It's not jock sniffing, star fucking," Martigneau said. "Which most people, I think, think it is. We're a full-service agency. Don't just negotiate contracts and endorsements for our clients. We offer a whole spectrum of services. Handle financial and estate planning. Manage money. Investment advice. Tax preparation. We broker and lawyer real estate transactions. Hey, since free agency, client living Kansas City today's liable to be house hunting in Anaheim next week.

"Our job's to simplify life for them. So they can concentrate on doing what they do best. Playing ball and keeping their commitments. Hey, that's what we get paid for. If a client's got a problem of any kind, he knows he can come to us in absolute confidentiality. We don't *have* the solution? We'll *find* it.

"Mental problems? Hey, they happen. Athletes're people, have human feelings. Failings. Pro sports onna major-league level? Not your stress-free environment. We've got two board-certified psychiatrists and three clinical psychologists affiliated with us, on call at any time.

"Substance abuse? No secret. Too many top athletes decide because they're young and strong and fearless, they can fight the booze or drugs, and win. Isn't so, but they believe it. Naturally they crash and burn, and when they do, we've got help ready. Privacy to get detoxed in.

"They get in the shit, get involved with the police, 'fore they admit they've got a problem? Headline-hunting DA— hey, you and I both know, Frank, there're hundreds of 'em out there—thinking 'National TV, when I hook this guy'? At Drouhin we're prepared for that—we are *ready* for 'em. In every major-league city where we've got a client playing, home or on the road, we've got the top criminal lawyer on annual retainer. Standing by to help him, day or night, that should ever happen.

"Our client doesn't feel right? What the team physician tells him? Diagnosis isn't panning out? Something happens off the field or outside the playing season, client winds up injured? Family member with some problem, needs treatment? He don't know which way to turn? Which doctor to go to? Hey, that's all right—*we* do. Instant access to the top hospitals and doctors in this city. Any injury, condition that you'd care to name. We fly him in. His parents. His kid or his wife, whatever—get them the proper attention.

"It's an attractive mix. An excellent package, and the players know it. That's why we've got more work almost 'n we can take care of. We're the premier *national* sports agency in the United States. Satellite offices in Atlanta, L.A. and Chicago. International client roster—Canadian, Russian, *Swedish* hockey players. Dozens of *primo* baseball players from the Caribbean. Basketball players from Greece. Italy. Africa. Countries used to be behind the Iron Curtain. Our clients defected, it's still *there*. Came right to us, all right? Like the Neil Diamond song about people comin' to America? Best athletes're *here*. In *this* office. In Boston.

"Now this's confidential, but I know I can tell you. We're going global. Had scouts all over the world for years, sure, but in April we open our first overseas branch, in London, staffed full time. In August—Tokyo. First of next year, looking for space in Germany. Maybe in Greece. End of next year, *Moscow*. Hey, I'm telling you, this thing is *big*.

"Only last week Alex copied divisional directors his memo, Myron Stone. Prof in charge BU's Far East operation? One of our consultants. Asked him to keep his eye peeled, bright kids, either came from China and Japan themselves or their families did. Speak the languages and're also interested in American pro sports. We've already got people *working* for us in those countries, but not enough of them to run the kind of full-time operations Alec thought we'll need, the fairly near future.

"I'm telling you, the *vision* this man had. Alex Drouhin created this in nineteen sixty-nine. 'Six years before Messersmith,' he used to say. Back in the Dark Ages of pro team sports, baseball reserve clause tied the player to the first club that signed him. For life. Peonage was what it was, indentured servitude. Player was property, a chattel. Only way he could get away was retire or the club traded him. All the other pro sports took their lead from baseball. Same clauses their agreements.

"Agent was pretty much handcuffed. The team that

drafted a player had exclusive rights, a year. You couldn't shop the kid. Either he signed with the outfit that drafted him or he sat out until the next draft. The only threat the agent had was his client'd dump a year.

"Teams had the gun hand. They knew it. Players don't like to even *think* about sitting out. It's more'n just lost income, which to a talented kid who's never had much looks like even more than it is. It's a year off a career that isn't gonna last that long—no matter what he does. Guys like us who make their livings with their heads, we get *better* with the years. Slow down physically, but do better work. You learn things, all right? Those years of experience count.

"Athletes, as time goes by, best they can do's adjust. To a *degree,* they can substitute smart and cute for the *power,* strength, and speed they gradually lose. But only to a degree; nowhere near enough to compensate entirely. Flexibility, stamina—sooner or later those things're gone. Recover from injuries slower. George Blanda kicking field goals in his fifties. Gordie Howe playing hockey with his boys, the Whalers in *his* fifties. They were *freaks.* Nolan Ryan, still pitching in the majors, he was forty. Fitness nut. Carl Yastrzemski retired the Red Sox, eighty-three—almost that old himself. Forty-two. But except for the cigarettes he also stayed in shape. Still, main thing kept him going was the Designated Hitter Rule. Don't have to play the field anymore.

"The general rule in every sport is when the legs go, it's the end of the road. Most guys, every birthday's one number closer, the end of their career. Big-buck, long-term contracts're gonna *end.*

"They learn this, they're still kids. Athletes're very conscious of time passing. High school, college—the reason that they got to be the varsity quarterback, the power forward, the starting pitcher, wasn't necessarily because they're better, or even as good, 'n the seniors and juniors who were playing, they were freshmen. Guys they replaced couldn't play anymore. Their age was against them. Used up their eligibility. So even then it's very clear: calendar's the enemy. Makes 'em anxious to get started.

"So, back when Alec opened up, only threat he really had was, 'Well then, I'll sit him out.' Only time it truly scared a general manager or an owner's when he's desperate. And the kid Alex had was a franchise player, could fill the building for him.

"Six years after Alex opened, three rooms on the third floor, down on Tremont Street, reserve clause got knocked out. That changed all the other rules—whole industry, in fact. And Alex was there on the ground, ready for it. Scooped up the ball and ran with it. Alex was a one-man machine.

"Things've kept on changing, too. More gradually, but still changing. Salary caps for example. The old days an owner, general manager, they'd *never* dare to tell a Mickey Mantle, a Duke Snider, time'd come to retire. Club couldn't afford three more years for diminished skills. Needed the money and the roster spot for some twenty-two-year-old? Hey, the owner would've gotten lynched.

"Nowadays it's the *rule,* in all professional sports. So the agent has to be a fuckin' *priest,* all right? Prepare his client spiritually for the inevitable. Get him ready for the end. Tell his thirty-two-year-old All-Pro linebacker with a shot at the all-time sack record, going into option year, that even though he's still happy playing for the Forty-niners, say, they're not going to extend him four more years. Guarantee the kind of money that he's used to. *Two* more years, with a buyout option, that they may do. But if he expects to be a full-time player gettin' top wages when he's thirty-

six, he's going to have to resign himself to moving—
Philadelphia Eagles or the fuckin' Jets. Some rebuilding
team in the toilet. Needs a gate attraction, jump-start
season-ticket sales.

"That's a hard thing to do, lay the truth on clients. Inna
first place the *agent* doesn't want to face the fact, any
more'n the client does. Can't blame either one of them.
Been together for some years in Fat City. Making each
other lots of money. Trusting each other. Usually by now
they're buddies. Friends. Not only *know* each other's secrets, but've *kept* them.

"No one wants to give bad news their friends. Or lose
them—particularly over *money,* which both of them've
now got enough of. If dough was all that was involved,
there wouldn't *be* a problem. The player'd say the agent,
'Hey, you're short? Take a hundred K out of my account
this year. Pay me back when you're healthy again.' Or the
agent'd say: 'Jesus Christ, man, you're a shooting guard,
not a Masters champion. Quit playing Nassau with PGA
pros. I'll advance you three hundred.' Grand. 'Pay the
sharks, back alimony. Pay *me* back next year, your signing
bonus.'

"But the problem *isn't* money, even though that's what
it looks like. It isn't status, either, although it also looks
like that. Because how much money a man makes playing
sports is how he thinks the world measures his dick, and
therefore how *he* measures it, too. Which is *another* problem, one that never goes away. But *hey,* not one you can
do much about. The real problem with the early-thirties
client is that when you tell him what he has to face, you're
talking about *time,* and what does to all of us. No matter
how good a person you've been, how spectacular a player,
sooner or later it's all gonna come to an end.

"Nobody likes to hear that. Sometimes when the player

hears it, he may not believe it. He may think 'This guy's not on my side anymore. He's washed up and so he's telling me I'm finished. I *know* I'm not finished. Six or seven years left. So what he's *really* telling me's that *he's* over the hill. Can't do the job for me anymore, get me what I know I'm worth. I don't need a new team; I need a new agent.' And out the door he goes. And he gets a new one, *easy*. These're shark-infested waters for the agents, too.

"So, there've been *good* changes, and there've been *bad* ones, and that is one of the bad ones. You have to give your clients regular reality checks. And I won't deny that some around here—I haven't been one of them. I'm director of security, not an agent, and security's all I do. But for some of the agents here, senior division people, well, I do know that the past two or three years there's been the definite feeling building up that Alec hasn't always kept up with that kind of change as well as he might've, as well as he used to. 'Lost a step or two,' as they say about players getting older. 'Yard or two off his fastball.'

"I've overheard them saying he was getting slower to catch onto things, missing opportunities that he would've just glommed *on to* years ago. *Capitalized* on. Things've gotten away from him a little."

"Yeah," Clay said. "Well, one of the things I was planning on asking you for, of course, is the chart of your corporate setup here."

"Sure," Martigneau said. He unclasped his hands and languidly extended his left hand to pick up the phone. He pushed the red button. "Alice," he said, "would you have Lisette make three or four copies of the organizational chart? For Lieutenant Clay. Yes, thanks." He hung up.

"But while that's being done," Clay said, "was any one of these people who thought the boss might be slipping a little bothered by it enough to want to kill him?"

"Well, it's *possible,* of course," Martigneau said, first turning the corners of his mouth down to show disapproval, then looking up at the ceiling, "but *anything*'s possible, isn't it? First thing I used to do, I was still doing the job you're doing now, was try to separate the *possibilities* from the *probabilities.*"

Clay snickered. Martigneau lowered his gaze and stared at him. "Well, I *did,*" he said. "That *was* my procedure."

"Oh, I'm sure it was," Clay said. "It's everybody's, in this line of work. Always has been, ever since I can remember. I learned it from John Roscommon. Reason I laughed was because up 'til now I didn't know you're taking the credit for inventing it."

Martigneau swung his feet off the desk and spun the chair around to sit up straight behind it, resting his forearms on the blotter. "No matter what else anyone ever said, no one ever said you didn't have a mouth on you."

"Thank you," Clay said. "Tessa used to say it was only a part of my natural charm, but still, an important one."

"Well, Tessa misled you," Martigneau said. "But never mind that. I wasn't suggesting I invented the procedure. Only that I was always careful to follow it. In every case. And I wasn't sure you were doing so in this one.

"*Really,*" Clay said, interrupting, "you *always* followed procedure? In the Crayton case, too? If you followed it in that case, I'd say it let you down pretty bad."

Martigneau furrowed his eyebrows and said nothing.

"Because by the time Amabile got the deathbed confession from the *real* killer," Clay said, pretending to reflect, "unless I'm very much mistaken here, the *probable* killer you'd gotten convicted, using your method, had done about, what? Ten, eleven years? All in a good cause, of course; gave the opponents the death penalty the best argument against it they could ever hope to have. *'Elinor*

Miller was *innocent*. Suppose some *other* cop makes a mistake, and we kill an innocent person?'

"But even though she'd done good, for a high-priced call girl, Ellie still was rather pissed off, I recall. Hired herself a lawyer with two rows of teeth, up and down, got herself, what? How much *did* the state settle it for? Four point three, was it? Not that the AG had much choice—case'd gone to trial, jury would've given her the gold off the State House dome, tunnel tolls the next twenty years.

"But still not bad, either. Four hundred and thirty grand a year for rusticating in MCI Framingham, ass out of service, her prime earning years. I'm sure she would've done well. But I doubt she could've made *that* kind of money, hawkin' her wares on the open market. Which's what she'd been doing the night Hobart Crayton seized out on the hotshot, and you sent her to jail for selling him the white powder."

"That was a long time ago," Martigneau said.

"I *know* it was," Clay said. "Eight years ago, about, the truth started to come out. Less'n a month after you took early retirement. Landed this job you got now. They let Elinor out, three weeks or so after your farewell dinner, I thought to myself: 'Jesus Christ, that's good timing. Pete should've been playing the stock market all these years. He was wasting his time in this job.' "

Martigneau tightened his lips. His face reddened and he narrowed his eyes. He was about to say something to Clay when Alice Meladie called him on the intercom. "Yes?" he said into the phone, managing to keep his voice mild. He looked up from the phone at Clay. "I don't know," he said into it, "let me ask him."

"When do you think the DA'll announce cause of death?" he said.

"Well," Clay said, "I know he's already said the preliminary finding's homicide, and we don't expect it to change.

I asked him not to get specific about the cause, so I doubt he will. Why do you need to know?"

"The media," Martigneau said. "Three or four of our clients've been in trouble involving firearms. One or two've used hunting knives for purposes other than hunting. Several've used their hands on other people who were smaller than they were. You may recall one rather troubled athlete—not one of ours, I'm glad to say—threw a man through the window of a bar in Toronto a few years ago."

"And the bar was on the thirtieth floor of a high-rise like this," Clay said, "so by the time the EMTs arrived at the place where he hit the sidewalk, the annoying guy was rather dead."

"You can see why the case'd interest them," Martigneau said.

Clay nodded. "I can," he said, "and I also suspect that they're driving your PR guy absolutely nuts, asking him what it is."

Martigneau nodded. "Drew Houser," he said. "He could use a break."

"Tell him to tell the media that State Police sources've told this office that the cause of death was gunshot, and the DA'll hold a press conference in Fall River at four thirty. No suspects've been named, if there appears to be more than one, and no suspects *will* be named, until someone has been charged and taken into custody."

Martigneau repeated that into the phone. He said, "Read it back to me." He paused, then said, "That's it," and hung up the phone. He shook his head. "Reporters," he said. "Can't live with 'em, but also, unfortunately, can't live without them. Where were we?"

"You were about to say 'Thank you,' " Clay said.

Martigneau reddened. "Yeah," he said. "Should've said thanks."

"You're welcome," Clay said cordially. "Before the

phone call, we were having a pleasant conversation about possibilities and probabilities."

Martigneau frowned and nodded. "Right," he said. "Okay. I don't think it's *probable,* or at least very likely, that anyone in here—as concerned as I know some of them were that Alec might be losing it a little—that any one of them would've wanted him dead.

"In the first place, he was still the Meal Ticket. The Rainmaker. The Founding Father. The Man who had The Idea. To us it's incredible that he's dead. So, if you still think it's odd more of us aren't weeping and moaning around here, that's another explanation. We're dry-eyed partly because we haven't gotten it *assimilated* yet. It hasn't registered. He was a monument, like Trinity Church down there." He flipped his left thumb back over his shoulder. "Monuments don't disappear. Tears'll come later, I'm sure."

14

"BUT YOU DON'T FIND it hard to believe someone killed him," Clay said.

"Hey *Frank*," Martigneau said, "at one time or another everyone in this place was *sure* that someone'd try to kill him. He thought so, too. His limo driver, Oliver, he travels heeled at all times. Supposedly protecting Alec. But Alec didn't *like* being driven in the limo. Only time he used it was when he was taking somebody around, playing perfect host. Showing a client the town or taking a party to a dinner or a game. Other members the firm used it more. He much preferred to drive himself. *By* himself. Very fast. He was a very good driver. 'I do like my fine motorcars,' he'd say. Never had less'n a dozen."

"I counted nine this morning," Clay said. "Two Jags, the big silver Mercedes two-seater—"

"The five hundred SL," Martigneau said, nodding. "Twelve cylinders, five liters. In recent months that was his favorite."

"Anyway," Clay said, "I wrote them all down. Also had their pictures taken. Not including the plow and the tractor, or the Catanias' two cars, the Buick and the Jeep, it came to a total of nine."

"That'd be right," Martigneau said. "The little Beemer roadster he left in the garage under the house on the Hill. To sport around in when he was there. And for Ronnie to tool around in when he wasn't. Alex didn't always *want* Ronnie with him. 'I'm *fond* of Ronnie, but he's *frivolous*. When I'm doing business I can't have him flouncing around. Always interrupting. "Oh *excuse* me, Alex. Didn't realize you were on the phone." When am I *not* on the phone? When I have someone with me. Anyway, that means I can't concentrate. Maintain my *focus*. Well I simply can't have that. Fortunately Ronnie understands. So unless I specifically invite him to Easton, or Nantucket, or Bahama, he stays on the Hill.'

"Had a GEO Tracker, pink, at the house in Grand Bahama. Called it his 'toy car.' Eddie Bauer Jeep at the house at Tom Nevers. So, with the nine at Easton, that would make the dozen.

"Anyway, Alec was aware that this world's full of nuts, some of whom're armed. He was licensed to carry. Not that that meant he had any idea how to *use* what the permit let him carry. Alex had lots of cop friends who liked getting hard tickets to big games, and'd overlook speeding and other infractions if the tickets came their way. Someone would've given him a permit. *Did* he know how to handle a gun? Probably not, but that's a guess. I'm not really sure. I don't think he was sure himself. He swore he'd been around guns since he was a kid, could use one if he had to, but he swore to lots of things that weren't completely true.

"He wanted me to think he had an arsenal. But the only firearm I ever actually saw him with was a Model One American Derringer. Two-shot, hinged-action, double-barreled. Over-under. Chrome, rosewood grips. When he carried it, which wasn't very often, he had it either in the

left outside pocket of his jacket or his pants. I doubt he
ever fired it.

"For what he told me he paid, couple hundred or so, it
was a nice little gun. Well made. But even so, the only real
use you could've made of it was as an offensive weapon.
Sneak pistol. To shoot someone at real close range—who
had no idea at all what you planned to do. As a *defensive*
weapon, shooting *back* at someone, the only use for it *he*
ever would've had, it would've been next door to useless."

"Well, but still," Clay said, "I've always thought it'd be
helpful if you had a forceful way to let someone who shot
at you know you didn't like it. Even if you didn't hit him,
Bullet coming back *his* way might cause him second
thoughts. I doubt hunting'd be anywhere near as popular
as it is, the ducks and the deer returned fire."

"No question about it," Martigneau said. "But that's my
point. They make the thing in your choice of calibers. Alec
picked three-fifty-seven Mag. 'Packs a wallop,' he said.
That's why I doubt he'd ever fired it. If he had he would've
known the person firing it took almost as much of a wallop
as the guy taking the slug. Way too much bullet for that
frame. Slug wouldn't go where you wanted. Desperate situation, he'd've taken a round or two himself, long before
he got close enough to use it. Which would not've improved his aim.

"But I didn't tell him. Wouldn't've been any point. If it
made him feel safer to carry it, what harm was there? Alec
made a lot of noise and threats. That as part of his negotiating strategy. But he was not a violent man. He wasn't
going to lose his head some day or night, yank it out and
shoot someone, client too demanding, GM frustrating him.
And when he *did* have some reason to think there was a
chance he might be harmed—he got anonymous death
threats, fucking cranks blaming him when a star client

refused to re-sign with the home team, went to the biggest rival—we took them seriously. Threatening call, letter in red crayon on a brown paper, words out of magazines pasted to a page; recent years, a piece of e-mail, one of the talk shows called in and some crazy was after him: If he got it 'fore I picked it up, he did the sensible thing. He'd come into my office and say to me, 'Pete, another nut's out there. Probably nothing to it, as usual, but still, can't be too careful. Better clear your calendar.' And then I'd saddle up.

"That was the drill. Strap on the piece and guard the body. Pick him up in the morning, whichever residence he'd spent the night. Accompany him here to the office. Sit in on any meetings, conferences he might have here with people we didn't know. Ride shotgun with him if he left here during the day. Take him home at night and tuck him in.

"I don't think he packed the popgun on those occasions, but I never asked him. Also whether that was the only gun he had. Never asked him that either. Or where he might've kept them if it wasn't. He probably would've lied to me if I had. Alex *loved* secrets, mystery, and if there wasn't anything to keep a secret, he'd lie and say there was. One of course that he couldn't tell you.

"But regardless of what he claimed, obviously he didn't think he was good enough to defend himself with whatever guns he had. Otherwise there would've been no need for those details. Wore me out. Pain in the *ass*. Cut into my love life, too."

"How many were there?" Clay said.

"Most years, two or three," Martigneau said. "Probably a couple dozen, maybe twenty-five or twenty-six, since I've been here, eight years. Not many, considering how high his profile was. Way he lived. Number of people he pissed off?

Not many death threats at all. His trademark tantrums during negotiations? He thought a GM was trying to blow smoke up his ass, his first instinct was to drop a dime, get one of the columnists to gore the guy in the next morning paper.

" 'Always keep your opponent on the defensive. He won't do what you want, ruin his bagel. He sits down to eat his fucking shredded wheat, opens to the sports page, what he sees's a great big headline what a lying prick he is. Doesn't care about the fans, lets his best players get away. So he dreads to go to the office. Knows the phones aren't gonna stop.'

"That didn't work, he'd go up a step, and whack the owner. Probably worried us more'n it did them. Good many of the guys who own pro teams're self-made men. Tend to be hard cases who met even tougher guys on the way up. Made friends with some of them. Did favors for each other, sometimes involving muscle. Reading what Alex'd said about one of them could give you a shudder in the morning.

"Like Tip O'Neill said about politics, sports agenting ain't beanbag. It's hardball, every day, and no one played harder. Mickey Sloane, Detroit catcher, 'member him?"

"No," Clay said.

"You should," Martigneau said. "Mickey was an All-Star catcher in the seventies, early eighties. Your type of guy. People weren't convinced he had the physical equipment, play major-league ball. Much less hang on thirteen years. Couldn't run much, but you expect that. Not many catchers can. Bodies aren't built for speed. Arm just okay. His pitcher wasn't good, holding runners close, good ones could steal on him. They did, close to fifty a year.

"Era he played in, 'fore expansion watered the milk, his offense was good. But nothing spectacular. *Now* someone with his numbers'd make two point five, maybe three mill a year, easy. Back then, lifetime two ninety-eight? Eighteen or nineteen homers? Not bad. But far from outstanding. Lots of guys had those numbers then.

"The intangibles were what kept him in the majors. Pure determination. Not as good as Carlton Fisk or Johnny Bench, no—Thurman Munson, either. Didn't have their natural ability. But the same *kind* of lunchbox, work-boots, hard-hat player. All out, all the time—balls to the *wall*. The same *fire*. People compared him to them.

"He'd do anything to beat you, *anything*. Find a way to win. Ninety or so RBI a year, nothing special, right? 'Til you looked at when he *got* those ribbies. Late innings. Close games. Extra innings. Invaluable. One of those spark plugs you can't put a price on. 'We win by ten, he drives in one. We win by one, he drives in two.'

"Motivational speaker now. Goes around the country giving inspirational talks. Bankers' conventions. People who sell automobiles. Life insurance. Computers. Managers in brokerage houses. He was here a month or so ago. Hospital administrators. How do they deal with staff morale under managed care? This's a big issue. Hey, sure it's all bullshit, and don't think he doesn't know that. But eighteen grand a pop? That's a good price for bullshit. He's making more wearin' a suit and slingin' it now'n he ever did blockin' the plate. But he loved those days—foul tips in the balls, knucklers off *his* knuckles—just the same. Always stops in to see Alex, any time that he's in town. Have a drink and a meal with him, cut up a few the old touches. One reason or other, I'd never met him. Alex brought him in here, introduced us.

" 'Alex is the *man*,' Mickey tells me. 'I always loved going into contract talks with Alex representing me. It was *exciting*. I used to tell people those were the only times the Tigers played the tiger.'

"He was that," Martigneau said. "Alex was silky and Alex was quiet, but Alex had very big teeth and sharp claws. He was a fighter, just like Mickey was, and he'd use anything he could get his hands on to win. He did not back down and he didn't *kowtow*. And a lot of times the people that he dealt with didn't like that. General managers, owners, TV honchos, sportswriters who've forgotten why people read the sports section, think the reason is they want to read about the writer, not the game? He wouldn't genuflect to them. He'd come right out and tell them: 'What my clients think of me matters to me. What you think of me doesn't.'

"Alex was no respecter of persons. One time or another, course of twenty-eight years, he must've pissed off hundreds of people. *Proud* people who expect to get their way. Network sports producers for example—always very jumpy about ratings points. Low Nielsens, their heads come off. They'd get on Alex, one of his stars's holding out. Alex'd say he didn't give a shit about their Nielsens, or what New York paid to show the game. 'Til his star got a contract that reflected his value to the team, he was going to sit out. 'And *fuck* what it does to the ratings.' They'd get *bullshit* at him.

"Alex wasn't stupid. He knew they hated him. He accepted it. The reason he did things the way he did was because it worked. But he was under no illusions doing it his way made him friends. He knew the consequences. 'Most of the GMs and owners'll cool down after the struggle's over, month or so, maybe two. Sooner, later they're going to want—or have—to talk to me again. Come on too strong, or piss me off, I won't take their calls 'til they beg. But some of course never do get over it. Tough. I know mine and mine know me. Rest can go fuck themselves.' "

"So, if you were still back in your old suit—" Clay said.

Martigneau, snorting, interrupted. "Yeah," he said, "right. I'd really like that. Ninety-dollar job from Filene's Basement. Making sixty grand a year." He paused. "Things've changed, I'm glad to say. Shirts're Turnbull Asser. The suit's Joseph Abboud. Shoes're Gucci. Tie's a Ferragamo." He shot his right cuff. "Watch IWC. Car in the garage is a Jag."

"—who would be your principal suspects?" Clay finished. Bateman nodded.

"They've got a new product now for computers," Martigneau said. "I don't know if NESPAC or SP's got access to it yet—we've had it here for years. Computer CDs that give you every listed phone number in the world, also the address. Coded so you can break the subscribers down by occupation and location?"

"Northeast State Police Compact has it," Clay said. "Also had it for years. Twelve-year-old kids and Avon Ladies've got it, too. Buy it from Egghead for a hundred-thirty bucks. Get to the point."

"Key the enhanced version to pro sports," Martigneau said. "Put up Alec's name and ask for every other name in that index who owned, managed, coached, or played pro sports in North America since nineteen sixty-nine. That's your list of suspects."

"Narrow it down for us," Clay said.

"Frangie, I *can't* narrow it down," Martigneau said. "You're asking the impossible. When I was doing what you're doing now, victim like Alex, I'd go in thinking the motive was either money or revenge. People in his bracket don't kill, or get killed, for love. Spurned lovers get paid off in cash. Well, Evelyn Nesbit, the Girl in the Red Velvet Swing, but she was a long time ago, and that skier Claudia Longet picked off with the rifle on the slope in Colorado, years ago—whatever the hell his name was."

"Spider Sabich," Clay said. "And the lady's name's 'Claudine.'"

"Thank you," Martigneau said. "I don't really have any use for that information, but I'm always eager to learn. Tonight I'll be able to say to my dinner companion, 'I bet you don't know who Claudine Longet shot.' At which point she'll stand up and say, 'No, and I don't give a shit. I'm going to the ladies' room. Try to get real while I'm gone.'"

"You're making a lot of dough now," Clay said mildly.

"Frangie," Martigneau said, "I put my pension check into my tax-free muni bond fund. I shelter the max from my salary here and do whatever I want, the Dom Perignon with the salmon and caviar—and got money left over the endah the month." He leaned forward and grinned. "My guess is I pay more in *taxes* now'n both of you guys *make*, put together."

"Is this a great country or what?" Clay said.

Martigneau sat back, his wrists on the desk, his palms open and fingered spread. "Hey, like I said, it's a whole new world now. All about money. People own the pro clubs, some years ago they begin to finally figure out what they'd actually been selling, networks and local stations. Since TV became such an important part of our lives. Forty years ago the package was 'ah thrill-ah vict'ry annie agony-ah defeat.' Direct to the people in their living rooms at home. *In order to sell tickets at the stadium.* Just enough TV games to keep the customers eager for trips to the ballpark. Peanuts and Crackerjack. Hot dogs and beer.

"Twenty years later, it'd gone way beyond that. Gone so far it's not the same thing anymore. Mid-seventies, it dawns on the owners: Now, what they're selling is *spectacle. Entertainment. Product.* Only better. From the financial point of view, which is the only view there is, this's a *way better* thing. Rule of thumb: Today you can now figure sixty percent of any pro team's revenue's from TV. And why? Because sports *draw*.

"You make a movie, TV series, you're never sure people'll come to see it. Say you spend a hundred mill on a flick. Critics say it's a stinker, kids don't like it either? You die. Spend three-quarters of a mill on a two-hour backdoor TV pilot. Critics can love it, but if the net puts it up against *ER,* chances are no one watches. That option to make thirteen episodes for a new series in the fall? Now worth a Big Mac and fries. Once again, you die.

"When you're selling sports, there's almost always a hungry audience guaranteed. Fans. Sports fans're people with a mission. They'll tune in if they possibly can. At no charge to you, newspapers and talk shows remind them. Day after day, they deliver your message, 'The Redskins game Sunday's a big one, crucial to Patriot postseason hopes.' 'Less they take two out of three from the Yankees at the Stadium this weekend, Sox're out of the play-offs.'

"Think about it. Sports is the only business that almost never pays to advertise itself. *Other* businesses pay sports—first the TV people for the broadcast rights, and then to advertise the sports they bought, in order to resell them at a profit to the hungry sponsors.

"What the broadcasters're buying's that guaranteed audience. What they use to buy it is the money they get from the power to cut the games bite-sized. Lots of two- and three-minute interruptions they can dice up some more and sell to the sponsors. Baseball came pretty well equipped: breaks between innings. All the broadcasters had to do was make sure the teams took three or four minutes switching between defense and offense—plus at least a long weekend to change pitchers.

"Football already had halftime, the breaks between the

quarters, and the two-minute warning. The broadcasters got the leagues to double time outs per team from three a game to three each half. Then they got brazen. In exchange for more money, they got TV time-outs. No pretenses: 'We're stopping the damned game to sell cheese snacks and burgers. Fred'll tell the people, "It's time to make the doughnuts." ' Pizza Hut'll sell you two pies, any two toppings. Fourteen ninety-five. Delivered to your home before the fourth quarter. Don't go to the bathroom. Sit there like a good boy and watch the Army recruiting commercials.'

"Hockey face-offs, longer and longer. Tire makers. Brewers. People who make cars and trucks. Computers. Deodorants. Airlines. People who say their package delivery service's better'n the U.S. Postal Service. Postal Service coming back, 'But we're cheaper, work Saturdays.' *All* of 'em pounced on those minutes, like the pups onna kibbles.

" 'Ah-*hah,*' said the league owners, 'there's no limit to how rich we can both get if we not only let you TV guys show big events, but *create* more big events. The World Series is big? Split the leagues into three divisions each. First we make the top division winners and the fourth team with the next best record play two series for the right to play for the league championship. After which the league champs'll play the World Series.

" 'Super Bowl's a cash machine? Do the same thing with football. Split the National and American conferences into three divisions each. Make the top four teams play for the right to compete for the conference titles, and those two play the biggest event since Moses parted the Red Sea.

" 'Same thing with the NBA and the NFL. So now in baseball, instead of just one jackpot at the end of every season, you'll get *at least twelve* jackpots a year. Maybe as many as *twenty-one* nail-biters. In football *six* must-sees before the Super Bowl. Eight teams in each NHL conference'll play four series to become one of four teams playing two series, see which two teams play Stanley Cup. Same thing in the NBA, end of the regular season, only twice as much of it. Sixteen teams out of twenty-nine play until two're left to fight for the championship. It's enough to make your head spin.'

"Why you think the people at Andersen Windows buy time, the Final Four, and brag their glass doors're so tight they can keep a hurricane flood tide out the family room? Because they think the guys 'n gals at Hooters're gonna drop their Bud Lights? Jump into their Jeep Wranglers, and go buy a setta French doors? I seriously doubt it. I think they're teaching the parents what to tell the builders, now that the mortgage and tuition loans're paid off and they can finally swing that winter place, the Gulf Coast of Florida.

"That age spread's what makes sports programming unique. Network programmer can look at a pilot of sitcom or a cop show, soap or a newsmag, pretty well tell you what kind of an audience it'll get—if it gets any audience at all. Not the size of it, but who'll be in it. Kids, young adults, young parents, thirty-five-to-fifty-fivers, senior citizens. Mattel don't buy time to sell Barbie Doll action figures during *NYPD Blue*. The computer game makers don't push their stuff during the evening news. Most programs are audience specific. Any entertainment program that attracts two viewership segments's a success. One that appeals to three's a major winner.

"Team sports appeal to *all* of 'em. The parents install team loyalties like software in their kids. Train 'em to watch just like the grandparents trained them. Young adults always watched, can't remember when they didn't. Started when they're kids, and then when they were in high school. Sports were how the girls decided which guys to have sex with. The guys knew this, so they played sports if they could.

"This dynamic does not change after high school, which is why they're all in Hooter's in their tight Wrangler jeans and cutoffs, watchin' the ball games. Planning get laid afterwards.

"The empty nesters watch because they've still got the habit. Their parents trained them to, and then they trained their kids, so it must be important. And besides, this's what they're gonna talk about tomorrow at the office. The seniors tune in because they've been doing it so long they wouldn't feel right if they didn't. Think they'd started losing it.

"You hear what I'm *saying? Sports is now the American popular culture.* Bigger'n movies ever were. Bigger'n rock 'n roll ever was. You've got the rights to televise a big game, you've got a positive lock on all market segments when the game begins. Later on it turns into a blowout—fourth inning, second quarter? You'll lose share in media markets outside the regions the teams represent. But hey, whadda *you* care? The advertisers've already paid for the time. They know life involves risk. Nothing you or they can do about that.

"Alec called it 'the *second* quantum jump in pro sports.' He said most people thought the big change came when Curt Flood went into court asking for free agency, trying to knock out the reserve clause. There's a big picture of Flood over his fireplace in Easton. You probably saw it."

"I did," Clay said.

"That painting's an indication of Alec's basic contempt for the people that he represented," Martigneau said.

" '*Contempt*'?" Clay said. "How 'contempt'? The Catanias said he completely subordinated himself to his clients' wishes. Degraded himself, even, when necessary."

"I *told* you," Martigneau said, "Alex'd do anything for money. If getting money meant bringing in a bunch of two-hundred-dollar call girls to throw an orgy for his clients, he'd call the escort service and the orgy would go on. Always had me make sure it was a 'reputable' service, though, meaning good-lookin', honest whores. No undercover cops, or scandal-sheet reporters who'd stop at nothing, including star fucking, in order to get a ripe story.

"Though Alec was funny about that. I don't think Alec ever had any strong moral reservations about taking part in orgies, but if holding them'd been purely a matter of his personal taste, he never would've done it. Sex was relatively unimportant to Alec, except as a way to get money. He didn't *mind* it, but he didn't *require* it, either.

"I think when his second wife, his *trophy wife,* Martine, came to Nantucket a day early and found him in bed with Ronnie in the house he then had in town, she was probably as much relieved as embarrassed. Mad, of course, too, sexpot like Martine, aced out by a *man.* But she kept her perspective: That discovery gave her the filleting knife to skin him. After that the pre-nup was history.

"See, if it'd ever gotten out that Alex had a sweetie and his name was Ronald, those macho-macho men we represent would've dumped us like burning white phosphorus. FD and the other partners've been the horses in this outfit for the past several years, gotten most of the business and done most of the work—but Alec's the name on the door. If it'd gotten out he was a sissy, whole shop would've gone in the toilet."

"You must've been a little nervous," Clay said.

"We were scared *shitless,*" Martigneau said. "So was he. Sent me around to see her. 'Talk some sense to her. If she goes public with this, I won't have any money to give her a settlement.'

"I met her at the house he'd bought for them, Louisburg Square. She had her lawyer there, Al Fortunato, seemed like a reasonable guy. Capable. She kept that house, full of French furniture. Appraisal said three point one mill. Along with the house on Coffin Street and the condo in Boca Grande. She was cool, as our clients say. Understood Alec completely. No desire to ruin his business. She might even have been glad it was over. I got the distinct impression Alex hadn't called on her very often for the conjugal act, and that she would've preferred much more action.

"What Al said Martine wanted was exactly what she got: Every place they ever lived in, and enough money to live in them by herself for the rest of her life. I did not for one minute believe she had any intention of doing that. She didn't look to me like a woman of thirty-eight who was swearing off sex forever. She looked like she was just getting back into harness."

"Ever test that theory out?" Clay said.

"You know I wouldn't tell you if I did, Frank," Martigneau said. "So why'd you even ask? But the answer is no, I didn't. Martine would've laughed in my face. Last I heard she was flying down to Washington on Wednesdays to screw the secretary of commerce. Or maybe it was transportation. I forget. Martine was out of my league.

"Alec's too. Along with Beverly, his first wife, that he dumped and paid off when this business really took off. They did have the two daughters, but the only time I ever met Bev, without Alex, was at a Jimmy Fund dinner, she was with her second husband. Local TV exec, well known studhorse in his younger days. She looked very contented. Didn't seem to miss Alex at all.

"I doubt he works Ronnie very hard, either. My guess is that all Alec ever really wanted to do with anyone, of either sex, was cuddle. I think that's what Ronnie likes to do, too. Run the money-losing antique shop Alex subsidizes for him on the sunny side of Charles Street and at night hold hands with him by the fire. Damned expensive snuggling, you ask me." He frowned.

"Curt Flood," Clay prompted.

"Oh yeah," Martigneau said. "Alec had the Curt Flood portrait because he thought his *clients,* the ones who'd even *heard* of Flood, knew there was a time when ballplayers weren't gods, thought Flood was *the* symbol. 'And he was one. But not for the reason the kids think. He wasn't the Messiah, he was John the Baptist, the trailblazer. He showed the way, but that's all. People forget: In the U.S. Supreme Court, Curt Flood *lost.*'

"Alec said if he thought anyone he represented would've known who Peter Seitz was, 'I'd have *his* picture over the fireplace. *He's* the man who belongs there.' I can't tell you how many times I heard him give that speech. Bar association banquets, fund-raising dinners, God knows how many of those things I went to with him. Alex showing off. Chauffeur and a bodyguard. I told him once if he ever got the flu and couldn't make it to Chicago, if no one there knew what he looked like, I could make the speech for him."

"*I* don't know who Peter Seitz is," Clay said.

"Of course you don't," Martigneau said. "That was Alex's point. Exactly what Alex was saying. In seventy-three the Baseball Players Association got the owners to agree to binding arbitration in salary disputes. The owners submitted their figures, players submitted theirs. The arbitrator had to pick one of them. Not allowed to split differences.

"Charlie Finley got *hammered.* All the Oakland A's stars—Reggie Jackson, Rollie Fingers, Sal Bando, four, five more—went to arbitration. Joe Rudi lost and Gene Tenace lost, but most of the bigger dogs won. Owners didn't like this—fired the arbitrator.

"Very next year, seventy-four, Finley didn't pay all the money that he owed to Catfish Hunter. Catfish claimed that made him a free agent. Seitz was now the arbitrator. New York lawyer. Yankee fan? Nobody knows. He agreed with Hunter, and Hunter signed with the Yankees. Five years, three million bucks. Chicken feed now, six hundred K a year, but in those days a staggering fortune.

"Seventy-five, Andy Messersmith, pitched for the Dodgers, and Dave McNally, spent his glory years with Baltimore but with Montreal by then, got Seitz to agree that if the team and the player couldn't come to terms, the team could renew the player's contract for one year at the old price. But at the end of it the player became a free agent.

"The sun should've started coming up in the west and going down in the east. That knocked out the reserve clause. Owners fired Seitz and brought suit, but the courts wouldn't overturn him. The damage was done.

"Big uproar: 'Players'll become footloose mercenaries, destroy baseball as we know it!' And in fact that's exactly what happened. Then it happened in the other sports: the *beginning* of the world of pro sports as we now know it.'

"Remember what I said," Martigneau said. "Alec's great insight—his *vision*. I think Alex was a genius. I know *he* certainly did. He had this ability—well, he had it then—to see the industry so *clearly*. 'Whole' was the word he used. Recognize not only what it *had* become, but that it was still in flux and changing, and see what it was *going* to become, five or six years down the road. Everyone's aware that what you learned to do when you got started may not work forever, any line of work. Things always change. *Alec's* ability was to see what things would *become*.

"Here's an example. Free agency's a wonderful thing, but knowing when and how to use it makes it lots more wonderful. The ability to look down the road when your client's twenty-two and you're negotiating his first big, long-term contract—after his three-year rookie agreement that's governed by the collective bargaining agreements. How many years it covers and what options it includes make a hell of a lot of difference in how happy he's going to be with you when you're going in to negotiate his third agreement.

"It depends on the sport he plays and how much of a physical beating he's taken playing it, but, as a general rule, if the client's thirty and coming off a productive year— you'd be surprised how many athletes'll tend to coast in the option year, no matter how much you tell 'em it's going to cost 'em—going into that third-contract year, still going strong, you're probably going to be able to keep him fat and happy until he's over thirty-five.

"If he's thirty-*two,* it'll be a different story, and he won't like the way it turns out anywhere near as well. If he's healthy, you'll still be able to get him mega-dollars, but only for half as long. The chances are the team won't guarantee more than two or three years, and when he turns thirty-five they'll cut him loose, use his salary to pay three new young guys who're already seventy percent as good as he is now, one of whom might turn out to be a late bloomer.

"Salary caps, the luxury tax on teams that exceed them? *Big* tremor, seven-point-fiver on the Richter scale of pro sports. If you're a GM who expects to keep your team competitive next year and the year after that—and every one of them tries to, because that's what puts the meat in the seats and what turns on the lights on the cameras— you can't fall in love with your veterans. You *have* to stay competitive. To do that and stay under the cap, you've either got to trade your over-thirty stars for young talent, top prospects or draft choices, or else resign yourself to letting the warhorses play out their options and then sign on with someone else, getting nothing for you in return.

"With, Mister GM, very few exceptions, you do *not* give five- and six-year contracts to players who're more'n a month or so over thirty, no matter how popular they are. You can't. Cal Ripken Junior was an exception, not the rule. The rule of thumb is that within a year or so the player over thirty-five is either going to break down or decide that since he's made enough money so he doesn't *have* to do the work anymore—exercise, diet, make the road trips, miss the golf season, push himself all the time—he's not going to. He may not *tell* you he's packing it in, may not realize it himself. But that's what he'll do: phone it in.

"*Everybody* in the business knows this, *now—Alex* knew it eight years ago. So when he negotiated his twenty-two-year-old star's first long-term agreement, he never asked for more than four years. Same thing with the second agreement, when the kid was twenty-six. Sometimes he didn't have any choice. If his client was a journeyman, he had to take what he could get. But when he had a proven talent, a Type A player, Alec's policy was that he wouldn't take any deal for five or six years for any client under thirty unless the GM was offering drilling rights in the Gulf of Mexico. And he wouldn't take *less'n* five or six for one who *had* turned thirty.

"What Alex did for this business was catch up to and pass the people who now own and run the pro teams. Sports is entertainment. All over the world. Which country has the biggest entertainment industry? Which one exports the music, styles in clothing; the *movies?* This one. American entertainment rules the world.

"If Britain produces the Beatles, the Rolling Stones; if Germany produces Steffi Graf; and Martina Navratilova and Ivan Lendl come out of Czechoslovakia; if Greg Norman becomes a world-glass golfer, growing up in Australia, where do they come to compete? They come here for most of the year. By definition, in the world of entertainment, the USA's the Big League. And now it's the sports sector's going global.

"Alex saw that coming, long ago. No question about it. He built this operation on that dream, up from the ground. No one who's here today would be here without him. He envisioned the future, then made it come true. Now we're sitting here in the middle of it." Martigneau brought his hands down on the desk. "We scarcely believe our own eyes."

Clay's narrowed. *Okay, he's having his barber trim the eyebrows these days. Used to leave them all bushy. And he's been south for a couple of weeks. That'd account for the tan. But what the hell is it? There's still something more. I got it: Where are the jowls?*

"You used to wear glasses," Clay said.

"Oh *yeah*," Martigneau said, "years ago, sure, I wore glasses. But as the old joke goes, only to see." He laughed. "I started to get nearsighted when I was in my thirties. Reacted in the usual way, of course, went into total denial. But after a couple close calls out on the road, driving at night, knowing why it *really* was I'm missing signs at turnoffs—couldn't read the fuckin' things—I decided my life was more important than my pride. So I got glasses. Wore 'em until a year or so after I came here. I was comfortable. Didn't look thirty anymore, but what the hell, huh? I wasn't. Never even considered contacts. But then Alex one day said glasses made me look old, and that made the clients uncomfortable. Said I should get contacts instead, and I did. Do *not* want the cash cows disturbed."

Okay, little plastic surgery on the face, a nip and a tuck. Contacts. The tan. There's still something else more going on. What the hell's he done to himself? "It's more'n the contacts," Clay said. "You been working out since I saw you last? Lose some weight? You look different."

"Oh, the *weight*," Martigneau said, "lots of people've said that. No, as a matter of fact, I weigh five pounds *more* now'n I did when I retired. What it is, I'm in much better shape. Way less body fat, more muscle. Hang around with these athletes all the time, you start *thinkin'* a little like they do. Used to be, end of the week, I'd cut out a little 'fore five, have a few beers with the guys. Then go home. That *will* tend to give you a gut.

"Now since being here, if I'm through before five, I still leave my desk. Some things never change, matter how old we get—and I still do like my beer. But what I do first is go into the gym we got here, other side of the building. Work out for an hour or so. Then, around six, still go out for the beers, but these days, no more'n two. I've been takin' better care of myself." He looked down and patted his stomach. "Got to: you get into the fifties, expect to see seventy-five."

Hair transplants: that's it. Transplants or a very good hairpiece. The last time I saw you, you son of a bitch, the top of your hut needed thatch.

"Geez," Clay said, "that must get you home pretty late nights, you're still living in Medfield. How's Joycie feel about that?"

Martigneau was amused. "You jerkin' my chain, Frangie, havin' some fun? Or're you just out of touch? Joyce and I've been history over six years. Lasted two years after I started here."

"Sorry to hear it," Clay said.

"Hey, it happens," Martigneau said. "What can I say? I've got a different life here'n I used to have, my cop days.

Out of town, on the road a lot. Movin' in fast company, man gets opportunities. Hard to turn 'em down. Hell, *you* know how it is, Frank. You had a small whiff of the quiff, you're working the AG that time. That babe from the FDIC, up from Washington? Women aren't the same these days as they were when we're growin' up." He smirked.

"Plus I also see, you must've gotten a new barber," Clay said.

"Well, ah, yeah," Martigneau said, patting the top of his head. "There's a good salon on Newbury Street. Dougie showed me where it was, year after I got here. They're not exactly *cheap,* but I've got to admit they do good work."

"*I'll* say," Clay said. "They also do checking accounts, maybe?"

Martigneau looked puzzled. "Checking accounts? These're hairstylists," he said. "Buncha fags who know how to do hair. Why'd you think they do checking accounts?"

"I dunno," Clay said, "I was just kind of hoping. Every checking account I've ever had, there's less in it today 'n the last time that I looked. So looking at you now, how much more hair you've got now'n the last time I saw you, I wondered they also do checks."

Martigneau looked stern. "Frank," he said, "along with the women the world's changed, too, since I was a cop. It isn't just the athletes, getting bigger and stronger. Everyone's become much more concerned with nutrition and fitness. Appearances matter more now. If you don't look as though you take care of yourself, this new generation won't work with you. They'll go and find somebody else, looks like he can relate to them. Who can understand where they're coming from, right? Knows what their needs and their aims're now, what kind of things matter to them?

"I go into a room with ten twentysomethings we'll be

representing this year, soon as the Final Four's over, give them the lecture on gambling and drugs, and I look like I'm sixty years old, those kids're not gonna hear one word that I got to say. What do I know about drugs? What can I tell them they don't already know, about people who want the inside information, because they're betting on it? I'm an old fogey. They tune me out. Result is, they then get in trouble."

"I thought if college players committed to an agent before the NC-double-A championships," Bateman said, frowning a little, "they lost their amateur status, got disqualified. Couldn't play in the tournament. If they did anyway, their teams'd forfeit their games. Tournament doesn't start 'til the week after next. They haven't even announced the teams yet."

"Well," Martigneau said, "that's true, that is the rule. But you can still have *conversations* with them, and if you've been around as long as we have, got the experience we have, you can pretty well tell who'll be signing up. Alec started this business a long time ago, more'n twenty-five years ago. This is a reason to trust us, but we have to *explain* it to them. If we look our age, the kids'll take it as a reason to *mis*trust us.

" 'There's a *reason* we've been around as long as we have,' he'd say. 'We've got experience, staying power. We already *know* all the people you'll ever work for. No matter which team drafts you, chances are that we've done deals with them in the past. Know what their payroll actually is; how much money it *looks* like they've got to deal with, under the salary cap; how much they *really* can get to work with, if they do some creative things with their payroll structure. Know what it is that makes them tick, and how much they really need and want you, no matter how cool they try to play it.

" 'And after we get it for you, then we also know how to make sure you hang onto it. In-house investment and money management; tax advisors, keeping an eye on what comes in, goes out, at no extra charge to you. So that when you retire, the end of your career, you don't retire into pension dependency—you retire as a rich guy.

" '*That's* how you last twenty-five years in this cutthroat business, representing more players each year. Always dealing on the level. Knowing what you're doing. Never forgetting who you work for. Working for them day and night.'

"When Alec's clients gave him his portrait, which *they* paid for, at the black-tie anniversary banquet at the Westin a couple years ago, thousand bucks a plate, benefit the Jimmy Fund at Dana Farber Institute, cancer little children, Kermit Nickerson—All-Pro six years for the Bears, Hall of Fame, Canton, Ohio—read the plaque to the people: 'Alexander Drouhin, 1994. The only way to play the game, no matter what the game.' Then he leaned into the microphone and said, 'We all know I don't need to say anymore. That really says it all.' Brought the house down—standing O."

"Yeah," Clay said. "And sometime this morning somebody brought *Alec* down. Maybe someone at that dinner, you think?"

15

"HEY, COULD'VE BEEN," MARTIGNEAU said. "Could've been someone who was there. Over four hundred people came. Quite an assortment. *Multo* politicians: two ex-governors, congressman who *wants* to be governor, seems to think he's going to be. Hardly anybody else does. Read a telegram of congratulations from President Clinton. Had some trouble doing it. *Awful* time pronouncing 'felicitations.' Later I saw Alec burn the telegram in the men's room, drop the ashes in the toilet. Nothing but contempt for Clinton. Alex was a right-winger. Flat-taxer. Would've been a Steve Forbes man, 'cept he thought seventeen percent was way too high: 'What was the name of that TV show the girls used to love so much? About raising two bunches of kids in one house? *Eight is Enough*. Should apply to the income tax too.'

"*Hated* government. *Never* voted—said there was no point in it. Special-interest groups'd never stand for the kind of change he wanted, and the pols'd always do what the interest groups want. 'Need their votes to win.' But even though he meant it, he didn't talk about it—publicly, I mean. He said he kept quiet because if his opinions ever got out it'd cost him business. Always put business first. 'People'd call me a racist.' I think he was right.

"Anyway, Speaker of the Massachusetts House was there. Entertainers—Mel Tormé was in town for a gig at the Regattabar, Cambridge. He came. Made a little change in the lyrics of the song Paul Anka wrote for Frank Sinatra, substituted Alex as the guy who did it *his* way. Some guy who ran for vice president once, a few years back. Forget his name, he didn't win. Pete Rozelle. Eight university presidents—they'd found they could not only hit Alec up personally from time to time but also depend on him to advise his clients to donate to 'the great institutions that'd done so much for them' and who'd made millions in return, filling the stadium, going to bowls."

"Four or five bishops from various faiths, two black Muslim preachers, three or four rabbis. Not one but *two* Catholic cardinals—the one who gave the invocation said he was pinch-hitting for the pope. Said John Paul the Second wanted all of Alec's friends to know he'd really tried to rearrange his schedule, but it just couldn't be done. *I* laughed—thought the cardinal was joking. Lots of people didn't. Just sat there and nodded. They could understand. 'Pope's a busy guy.' "

"Drouhin was a Catholic?" Clay said. "I didn't see any evidence of that around the house in Easton."

"I assumed he didn't have a religion," Martigneau said. "If he did, he sure didn't let it interfere with anything he wanted to do. And he kept it a secret from me, everybody else I know. The clergymen were at the dinner because Alec could do favors for them. Have his clients show up at their big charity events. Visit their hospitals. Talk to kids' groups. People on the circuit've got very clean hands. One's always washing the other's.

"Not many personal friends. Maybe four or five couples, people he'd known in college, law school, plus the people they'd married. But that wasn't surprising. Alex didn't *have* many personal friends, people he just *hung around with,* kept in touch with, just because they liked each other. Few he did have he didn't see much.

"His daughters were there with their husbands. Brenda, Alexandra. Didn't look like they were enjoying themselves. Not surprising either. Alex admitted to me he'd never been much of a father. After he and Bev got divorced he didn't see much of the girls. He told me once Bev used to ride him about it, tell him just because he'd decided to leave her didn't mean he'd divorced the kids too. Didn't make any difference; he didn't change. Hell, he missed Alexandra's wedding, summer of ninety-four. Her step-father gave her away. Alex did have the decency to be *kind* of embarrassed about it.

" 'Well, *Jesus,*' he said, '*she* set the date, two years ahead, I had no way of knowing when it came around there'd be a *players'* strike in progress. How much choice'd I have? Negotiations going on around the *clock,* for Christ's sake—I had to be in *New York,* on *top* of things. *Paid* for the goddamned party, didn't I? Three hundred–plus free-loaders, two bands, *plus a DJ?* Honeymoon on the fucking *Nile?* Time the whole shindig's over, I'm lighter by eighty-three thousand *dollars?* I mean, Jesus H. Christ, shouldn't that count for *something?* And anyway, how the hell does Zandra think I *got* the money, *do* that for her, anyway? Not by neglecting *business.*'

"Julie had to keep track of his daughters' birthdays and anniversaries for him; pick out the presents and buy 'em. Make sure he at least saw and personally signed the cards. Thanksgivings and Christmases he made it a practice to be out of town. He bought a nice house for each daughter when she got married, one in Lincoln, one in Wayland. And the big beach house they share on the Cape. Down in Eastham. But I don't think he's ever visited any of them more than once, if that.

"He told me once his youngest was especially 'probably

permanently' mad at him because he 'wouldn't take her little peckerhead husband into the agency. Which I'm sure's the reason he married her. She's nowhere near as good-looking as her sister. Or her mother, either. Poor child's got no tits at all. Ben figured if he married her, I'd give him a job. If I could've without damaging the operation, I would've. Somebody's got to make the coffee. Take care of the copying machines. But he'd be worse 'n worthless in here. Overestimates his own intelligence—*couldn't* under-estimate it. His family's got some bucks so Penn gave him a degree. And then some cash-hungry B-school gave him an MBA. But that doesn't make him smart. Wouldn't *take* the kind of job he's fit for—mailroom attendant, gofer. He'd expect to be an actual *agent*. Like *me*.

" 'He couldn't do it. He'd fuck up. He's weak and he's a jock-sniffer. 'Stead of thinking about how to get the best possible deal for a client, making sure the guy's staying out of trouble, isn't throwing his money away, little shit'd be getting his picture taken with him, asking for his auto-graph.'

"Well, maybe so," Martigneau said, "but the older sister apparently agrees with the younger one. Both couples left the dinner early. Said they had to get home and relieve the baby-sitters. I assumed that meant Alex now's got grand-children. Never heard him mention any.

"Most of the people there were from the world of sports, major league or college. My guess is that if your suspect was at that party, he would've been one of that group. The dignitaries were there basically to suck up. Alex could give them things so they had to pay tribute. But if you were one of his athletes, still active, an owner or a GM he'd done business with in the past and most likely'd hoped he do business with in the future, you were there because you *had* to be. And that would've been why you would've known him well enough to have a reason, want him dead.

"Play-by-play guys, color men, top sports columnists, and talk-show people: one time or another he'd either fed something good to most of them or saved them from making a mistake that would've really humiliated them. The emcee was Frank Gifford, all right? Howard Cosell sent regrets; he was sick. Alec always publicly denied it, and the media people all deny it, but they used each other all the time. Alex fed them inside information in order to increase pressure on club management. They used it to prove they were in the know. They knew he was using them, but what he gave them was useful to them, even valuable. Helped to make them the brand names of sports media. And they knew he was vindictive. If they didn't flatter him by showing up, he'd take his goodies to their competition.

"So a fair number of the people who ate the surf 'n turf that night were not there because the menu appealed to them or they liked Smart Alec—which they knew better'n to ever call him to his face. Some of the ones I saw there had every reason to hate him—and keep in mind I've only been in this place the last eight years. God knows how many other enemies he'd already made, the nineteen years before I got here. Add in the ones who may *not*'ve had a really good reason, but hated him anyway, on general principles? Could've been a majority.

"I'll bet every player he represented at one time or another wondered if Alex'd dixied his deal. Tanked it. Talked him into accepting less money than maybe was available— so that the owner'd give a fatter contract to another Alex client who was younger, and'd still be producing agent fees for him after the older guy retired. Most of them probably decided, 'Nah, Alex'd never do that. Alex is my *friend*.' But some of them may not've, may've always had that doubt."

"Would any of them've been right?" Clay said.

"Alex always made it a point to tell his clients, when they first came to him, he'd never gain one client an advantage at another one's disadvantage. That in addition to being an agent he was an attorney, a member of the Massachusetts bar, and that he always negotiated each contract as the client's lawyer, acting in his best interest, strictly on the merits of the player's individual case. What the guy's experience, his record, his age and condition would indicate he should expect to get from a team that needed someone with his skills and probable professional longevity."

"Where'd he get that law degree?" Clay said. "The Catanias said he went to Brown on scholarship. They didn't mention where he went to law school."

"He was as vague about that as you'd let him be," Martigneau said. "And as I'm sure you noticed, the Catanias're not the brightest lights along the Great White Way. He probably never told them.

"My guess is the reason he was vague because Central New England Law School in Bolton didn't get accreditation from the ABA—causing much to-do—until the year before Alec graduated. And lost it two years later. Something to do with the fact that despite many big promises, the law school still didn't have very many law books. No law *library,* in fact—they told the students to use the county law libraries in the superior courthouses. Worcester or Fitchburg, whichever was closer. Both of which of course closed at five and generally weren't open weekends or holidays. Few years later CNE went out of business."

"Was he a member of the bar?" Clay said.

"Yeah, he was," Martigneau said. "That was the truth. But he wasn't eager for you to find out when he was sworn in—the November of the year *after* the June when he graduated from Central New England, which meant he'd probably flunked it a couple of times, once in the summer and again in the winter, before he passed it on his third try the following summer.

"Alec was very sensitive on the subject of taking tests. He was very *smart,* and a *fiend* for preparation, so I have to think he was a choker. Took the collar on exams.

"He'd take heat whenever FD said a new client was a dull blade. See, in addition to having been one hell of a ballplayer, FD's a very bright guy, and every now and then he's been known to make fun of one of our recruits after the kid's left the office. 'Wonder who reminds Ezekiel every morning that the zipper's at the front of the pants, so he doesn't get 'em on backwards, then panic 'someone's sewn me in,' when he has to take a leak?'

"Alex'd get on FD for making that kind of crack; they got him really hot. Which of course is why FD made them: to get Alex going. 'That kid knows how to do what he needs to do to get it done, and he's got the size and equipment to do it. Hundred-and-thirty-pound nerd with a *six-*pound brain and an MIT pocket-protector couldn't fend off a six-seven, three-fifty lineman. And then deck him.'

"And FD, he'd just *smile,* knowing why it was Alex took the heat, someone even *suggested* one of his new customers might not be extremely smart. He took it as alleging that if the client had any brains to spare, he would never've signed on with Alex."

"Was FD right?" Clay said.

"About the *actual* brains the kid had?" Martigneau said. "Who knows? Some of them after they're through find they've got brains they never had to use before, and therefore never bothered. Once that's all the talent they had left, they turned out to be fairly smart. About how smart the kid *seemed* when he first came through the door? Pretty often, FD was right. As an ordinary rule, rooks except at skill positions don't light up the evening sky. About that being *why* the kid signed with Alex? Nah. If signing with Alex proved anything, it was the opposite: Alex was *good*.

"And what FD said that set him off, you could say that about most of the pro athletes every agent represents. When I was at public gatherings with Alex—the drafts, the breakup dinners, the banquets, milling around the hospitality suites at the hotels, the luxury boxes before the big games—I met a lot of players signed with other agents. They walked the walk and talked the talk. They had the jewelry. But they were *young,* and they'd spent most of their days in high school and college working on the bump-and-run, their vertical leap. In the weight room. Learning the strike zone. Trying to get their time in the forty-yard dash under five seconds. Mentally they were underdeveloped. *Raw*.

"Give you an extreme example. Six or seven years ago, one of our younger players got arrested for loafing out at a beauty contest in Oklahoma City. Someone remembered Billy Wilderness'd played a lot of football for Oklahoma State before he declared in ninety-three and Alec got him signed with the Houston Oilers. Didn't update their research 'fore they invited him to judge the contest. Didn't know he was out on bail in a date-rape case in Broward County. Later got convicted, too, sent to jail for seven years. Which took care of *his* career. But at the time of the beauty contest, terms of his bail allowed him to travel freely. After all, he's a professional ballplayer. Has to travel with his team. Can't deprive a man his right to make a living—just 'cause he's *charged* with something.

"So the night of the contest, local TV, Billy's taken aboard about a bottle of champagne at the reception and a ringside seat with four other guys in tuxes, right at the edge of the runway. By the time the sixth or seventh contestant in the swimsuit competition swiveled down it in high heels, boobs spilling out of her top, Billy'd seen all he could take. Stood up and climbed onto his chair, which put him on eye level with her crotch, unzipped and whipped out his whanger, hard as a *rock*. 'Oh, *baby*,' he says, loud enough for the TV mikes to pick up, 'look what *I* got for *you*.'

"Miss Enid fainted. I've never actually seen it, but they tell me Billy's Johnson bar *is* pretty impressive—TV had no trouble picking it up. But that's to be expected. Billy's a pretty big kid. It took three security people and half a can of Mace to get him quieted down enough to cart him away. This was also good TV, although I guess most of the good folks at home weren't allowed to see it.

"Billy couldn't understand it. Why Miss Enid or whoever she was'd been so upset. Why the cops'd acted that way. He told them, and then the lawyer we got for him, that when he was in *high* school, he'd started doing that. Showing his tool to women that he hadn't even been properly introduced to. And a lot of them'd invited him to put it into one of their openings. He thought if he saw a woman dressed and acting in an obviously sexy way, then it was okay to expose *his* best feature in return. That that was what she wanted. The fact that the other times he'd done it he'd generally been in whorehouses didn't seem important to him.

"And nowadays they may not *be* any smarter'n they were traditionally, have any more social skills, but by the time they reach pro level, almost all of them can *talk*. As FD says: 'Now they're glib enough to get by.' Division One colleges and universities realized a while ago that if they expect to attract top high-school talent—which they have to have if they expect to get their games on national TV, where the money is—they have to be able to point to pros who've developed their skills in their programs. The more pros they can claim to've developed in the past, the better their recruiters do in the present, and therefore even better in the future.

"Dean Smith's won more basketball games coaching at North Carolina than any other college coach in history, playing a very tough schedule. It's news when the Tarheels *don't* make at least the round of eight in the NC-double-A tournament. He does this by getting a kid like Michael Jordan and developing his great natural skills, so when the once-in-a-generation player leaves for the NBA, Smith'll have someone to replace him. Not as good as Jordan, no, but good enough to keep UNC playing deep into March. On national TV. Which in turn recruits *this* year's graduating high-school seniors for Dean Smith's program, where they'll get TV exposure and develop into pros.

"The way you increase the pool of people who've made the pros coming out of your program is by facing up to the fact that you're never going to have twelve stars on your roster for basketball, fifty-plus on your football team. Most years if even five percent of your players have pro-level ability, you'll be doing very well. Most of your players're going to be good enough to play on the college level, maybe take your teams to the NC-double-A play-offs or the bowl games, but relatively few of them're likely to be great or even play many years with the pros.

"The Number One pitcher who takes your team to the College World Series at Omaha will probably make the majors. But the chances are he'll be the fourth or fifth starter on the Rockies' roster. He probably won't have a long career, six or seven years. Before it's over he will've played for three or four clubs, and every year there'll be some coach who tries to see if maybe he'd be more valuable as a setup man for their best reliever, tinkers with his motion and most likely ends up screwing up his mechanics, so he hurts his arm.

"Not a great ride, but he should be grateful. When he came in, the major-league minimum salary was a hundred and fifteen thousand dollars a year. By the time his last team released him, no longer worth his salary, he was probably making at least six or seven hundred thousand dollars a year. If it hadn't been for expansion, he never woulda *seen* a major-league game unless he bought a ticket.

"There *are* ways for a kid with just a little better than mid-level pro skills to get a higher-end pro contract. One of them is by looking like he's going to be a gate attraction. Face it—if you project to hit fifty homers a season, and you can defend yourself well enough in the field so you aren't risking serious injury out there every time a ball comes your way, you're going to make some good money. You can fart in church, spit on the umps, and kick photographers in the nuts, but if you can perform in any sport at the superstar level, you *will* make the millions.

"*But,* if you're a middle infielder who bats two sixty-eight, maybe with the potential to win a Golden Glove in any given year but no hope whatever of driving in more than fifty-eight or sixty runs a season, you're going to have to sell yourself as a guy who gets it done. A Mickey Sloane. The guy with the intangibles who can turn eight other guys on the field or four other guys on the court at the same time into a championship-caliber team.

"Example: When Doug Flutie was at BC he threw the Hail Mary touchdown pass that beat Miami back in eighty-four, and since he graduated he's had a successful pro career. Most of it's been in Canadian Football, but his teams've won the Grey Cup and he's been MVP several times.

"Gerard Phelan *caught* that Flutie pass and actually *scored* the touchdown. You could make a pretty good argument that what he did was harder'n what Flutie did. He played a few pro years, mostly as a sub, and then his career was over. He didn't have star-quality skills. Without 'em you have to develop a personal image as Local Hero. He didn't. But if you want to play a long time, and can pull it off, then the media may convince your GM or your owner for a few years that he can't afford to do without you.

"Mike Greenwell's last contract with the Red Sox—ten million for three years? Ridiculous. The guy was a defensive liability, a train wreck in the outfield. He'd hit three hundred most years, sure, but he wasn't a slugger, and his run production wasn't what you need from the middle of your lineup, fourth or fifth hitter. But the GM was new and the Boston reporters still believed in Red Sox tradition: The left-field job belonged to the incumbent. *He* decides when he can't do it anymore. Ted Williams played his whole career in Boston. Yaz succeeded Williams. He did the same damn thing: retired in place. When Yaz stopped playing in the field, Jim Rice was the best the Sox had to put out there. He could be surly with the media, but he was durable and he also put up the numbers—forty-six homers in seventy-eight, three sixty-four his career; lifetime batting average three-oh-two. When his eyesight went, overnight it seemed like, Greenwell was the best the Sox had available. Nowhere near as good, but still, indispensable.

"To bulletproof yourself like he did when you're really not that good, you gotta romance the media. The mandatory pre- and post-game interviews—'Whadja hit, Spike?' 'I think it was a hangin' slider, Brian.'—aren't going to do it. What you're gonna need is *charm*. The time to learn how to do it's while you're in the minors or playing in college. So once the competitive schools became aware of how important this is, not only to their players but to their own future recruitment prospects, they added a feature to their athlete support system. When they got a kid whose high-school coaches and teachers hadn't taught him how to get through an interview without making a total fool of himself, they *trained* him. When the kid'd already had some grooming—which most good athletes coming out of high school these days do have—they made him practice it with speech teachers. Gave him elocution and vocabulary lessons if he needed them. Used their media labs to improve his on-camera technique. Polish him, make him better. Not so incidentally get him ready *now* for the day down the line when his pro career's over and he wouldn't mind a job as a game announcer, color man. Doing some commercials. And *tell* him you're doing that, looking out for his long-range interests. Making sure he'll still have a bright future when his playing days're over.

"Now they say O. J. Simpson's TV career'd started slipping before the night the first jury said he didn't kill his wife and her friend. But his alibi for that night wasn't that he'd come home dog tired from a full day at the muffler shop and gone straight to bed. His playing career'd ended ten, twelve years before that, but he was still turning a good buck hustling rental cars, doing sideline commentary on TV games. Later on the night they died he flew to Chicago for a fee-paid personal appearance the next day. O.J. can barely *talk.* But he can *smile,* and he'd been an NFL *star,* made it into the Hall of Fame. That's worth money.

"Guys like Frank Gifford, great career with the football Giants, *many years ago;* the people who watched him play're either dead or well into their fifties now, and he's well into his sixties. But he's an articulate guy, still making a very good paycheck, doing NFL games on TV. Bob Trumpy was an okay football player, he's just fine as a TV announcer. List just goes on and on.

"Now it's generally recognized that unless the player just got here from another country where they don't speak

English, a stick-out athlete needs to be reasonably articulate. Most of them are. Are they actually smart? Most of them probably aren't."

He folded his hands on the desk. "Look," he said, "it's no insult to say that. You can go a long way in this world and do pretty well without being especially smart. I'm proof of that. I'm probably not very smart. Probably neither're you."

"I'd say you're half right," Clay said.

"Okay, so I left out 'conceited,' yeah, but still, I doubt you're terribly smart," Martigneau said. "I try to be more realistic. I was lucky. I'd found a job where the amount of intelligence I had was enough, as long as I worked very hard and used every bit of it. Frank, I don't try to kid myself: I'm a workhorse, a plodder. Like you are, like it or not. But *I* knew I was at a dead end in the DA's office. Fifty years old and going nowhere but retirement. And boredom. Then death. Probably a chief's job in some jerkwater town where the pressing problem for law enforcement's whether the convenience store's keeping *Playboy* sealed in plastic behind the counter. Selling cigarettes to minors.

"Joyce and I're fed up with each other. I'm banging a forty-two-year-old Mass. Defender. Nice enough lady, but we're going nowhere. We were just clinging to each other, exchanging complaints and bodily fluids. She knew it just as well as I did. She'd put on a few pounds since her husband'd left her, *said* she oughta lose some weight but didn't seem to have much interest in doing anything about it. And then after the few drinks, the tender moments, the few *more* drinks, she'd tell me she wished they'd at least had some kids, her and her ex-husband, so when she got old she'd have someone around who cared about what the hell happened to her.

"Few nights I did go straight home from work, Joyce wouldn't be there. Her story was she's taking night classes for her MBA at Bentley. In Waltham. She did get the degree, so I dunno, maybe she *was* in class all those nights and the classes *did* run until midnight or after, long after I'd gone to bed. But there was no question our next stop was the divorce court. We couldn't *stand* each other anymore.

"Eight years ago November, Emmett Beavers got home one Tuesday morning from a Monday Night Football game the Patriots lost to the Seahawks. Out there in Seattle. He went to his condo in Harbor Towers and slept for six or seven hours. Got up around four in the afternoon and had something to eat. Did some errands. Went back home and watched TV for a while, but he was lonesome and unhappy. His girlfriend'd recently left him, moved back to Alabama. Around the cocktail hour he went to Louie's Lounge in Brookline, see if he could treat his bruises by applying alcohol internally. Drown his sorrows. Also see if he could maybe scare up some stray pussy, like he had in there before. Ladies who like the athletic type tended to hang out in Louie's.

"The place was full of marathon runners, as it generally was, and since it was November and the Boston Marathon's in April, the runners may've been working out but they're not in serious training. So *they'd* been enjoying refreshments. Also present were some members of one or two of the local rugby clubs, had some experience raising a glass.

"I was never really sure who said what to who, or how the fight began. Emmett said the other people in the bar made some insulting remarks about his performance in Seattle and all he'd done was defend his self-respect. The people Emmett sent to the hospital said he came in with a *mammoth* chip on his shoulder, spoiling for a fight before the door shut behind him. Announced to the room at large, 'All road runners're *pussy*. Ain't athletes at all. Afraid of fuckin' *contact*.'

"Emmett's voice carries, or at least it did then. It was like the old joke about O'Reilly going to Burke's apartment on the third floor to ask him what the doctor meant when he gave him the bottle and said he needed a specimen to do a urinalysis.

" 'What is that?' says O'Reilly. 'Piss inna bottle,' says Burke. 'Oh?' says O'Reilly, 'Shit in yer hat.' And that's when the fight began."

"For some reason or other," Clay said, "I've never been that fond of Irish jokes. Especially the really old ones."

"No," Martigneau said. "Well, I can understand that."

"I've always much preferred the ones about Canucks," Clay said. " 'All the facts you need to know if a Canuck girl's a virgin: Was she ever alone with her father?' "

Martigneau licked his upper lip. Bateman kept his gaze focused on his pad. After a while Martigneau nodded and leaned forward over the desk. "Yup," he said. "*Oh*-kay, we both know the rules. You have to talk to me and I have to talk to you."

"So far, so good," Clay said.

"Regardless of whoever started the fight, Emmett gave a much better account of himself beating the living shit out of the marathoners and the rugby players 'n he had in the Seahawk game. I think in the game he gained about seventy yards on the ground in over twenty carries, caught one pass for six more, but in the lounge he sent three guys to the hospital for stitches.

"They held another one overnight at the Brigham for observation. One of the ruggers. The bartender who'd called the cops told the EMTs that Emmett'd given the guy a very nice forearm shiver that knocked him off his feet headfirst into the bar, and the doctors were concerned the concussion might be serious. Emmett himself required an ice pack for a badly bruised right eye and six stitches for a split lip. X-rays at the Oy Vay Memorial showed fresh cracks in his seventh, ninth, and twelfth ribs on the right, the eighth rib on the left, but it wasn't clear whether he'd gotten those in the football game or the tussle in the bar. So all in all I would say whoever'd started the fight, Emmett'd won it."

"Oy Vay Memorial?" Bateman said.

"The Beth Israel," Clay said. To Martigneau he said: "Go on."

"Emmett *certainly* came out of it a lot better'n the rugby player. The Brigham doctors were right. The concussion victim lost consciousness. Never regained it. He died four days later."

"Bringing you into the case," Clay said.

"Bringing me into the case," Martigneau said. "Alec called to say he was Emmett's lawyer and ask if he could see me."

"Naturally you saw nothing wrong with this," Clay said.

"No, I didn't," Martigneau said, "and neither would you've. Over the course of the years I've met with many lawyers whose clients looked to be in the shit, before they'd been arrested or charged, and heard their side of the story. As, I'm sure, you have too."

"No question about it," Clay said. "But I never got a high-paying job with one of those lawyers right after I told the DA on his client's case that the evidence just wasn't there."

Martigneau made fists with both hands and pounded the desktop with them. "The evidence *wasn't* there," he said. "I went over that case with a *micro*scope. There were the conflicting statements on the issue of whether Emmett'd started the affray. People who frequent bars've often been known to decide they'd like to take a piece out of a handy celebrity. Emmett may very well've been telling the truth. There was clear and convincing evidence that the man who died of the concussion'd plowed into the fracas when it was still at the stage of a shoving match, tried to jump Beavers, and Emmett reacted in self-defense.

"Depending on who you believed, maybe Emmett'd provoked the attack. And maybe he didn't. If he didn't, once someone else did, maybe he overreacted. But as we know, fighting words don't make it okay to fight the guy who says them. He was heavily outnumbered, and in my judgment fully within his rights to defend himself as he saw fit at the time."

He pounded the desk again. "And *that's* what I told the DA. 'He's a celebrity in this town. If he gets indicted, his agent'll get him a lawyer who could get a charge of buggery reduced to following too close. He's black, and in this county the chances are a good part of the jury will be liberals. Those that aren't'll be Patriots fans. They'll never convict him. I don't like bringing cases that I think we're going to lose.' He reviewed the evidence. He agreed with me."

"And then you came to work here," Clay said.

"Like I said," Martigneau said, "at that point in time my life was in the toilet. I really needed to make a change. Alex told me that the weak link in his chain of organization was at the exact spot where Emmett'd gotten into the grease, and gotten me involved with him. Security.

" 'In the past nineteen years I've had three different guys I've depended on to do it,' he said. 'They've known what I wanted done. Keep an eye on our clients. Phone's not enough. Go around and *see* them every so often, see if

there's *any* indication they haven't been behaving themselves. Drinking too much, using drugs, hangin' out with
the wrong type of people. Maybe bettin' on games. If you
hear anything, rumors, gossip, that they're getting out of
line, check 'em out. If there's any reason to think they are,
tell me so I can get hold of them, bring them in here, talk
to them, get them some help, *before* the stuff hits the fan.
Remind them that I insist on this openness. Part of our
contracts with them.'

" 'These guys're far more vulnerable'n they *dream*.
People know who they are, what they look like. They're
famous. When they get in the shit, it makes all the papers.
The bigmouthed assholes on the talk shows drag their
names and their teams' names through the mud. Then the
next time one of them plays out his option year and I have
to go in to make a new deal for him, the GM or the director
of player personnel starts off by telling me my guy's a well-
known menace who beats up women and throws cherry
bombs into crowds of little kids. A liability to the team,
public relations point of view. GM'll be on the offensive,
which's where *I* want to be.

" 'GM will say, "Your boy's made himself radioactive.
If we play him the sportswriters're all over us. I've put out
trade feelers and I can't get a thing. People don't even call
back. Nobody wants him, even though they agree he can
still play. I sign him, even half he's been getting, I'll be doin'
you a favor. You telling me your guy'll walk? Good, I believe you. Solves a big PR problem for me, *and* gives me
some room under the salary cap. Walk him. Know what
you'll be doing? Putting an end to his career. Making sure
he never comes back." '

"And Drouhin says, 'Where do you think that leaves me,
the agent? Ever hear of Shit's Creek? See a paddle in my
hand? Yes, you have, and no, you don't. Incidents like

Emmett's have to get headed off, and, I'm convinced, at least ninety percent of them *can* be before they happen. They're money out of *my* pocket. None of the people I've hired so far've managed to do that. It seems like I'm forever getting calls in the middle of the night from some dingbat of a client that he's gotten himself busted in a roadhouse in Nogales and I have to call a bondsman, make his bail.

" 'It's always a surprise,' Drouhin'd say, 'another fucking fire drill, and it shouldn't be. The clients who get in the shit don't fall into it on their way home from church. The sewer beds're never in the center—they're way out on the outskirts of town. When the client dives into the sludge he's been off course for a while. If I'd've known about it, maybe I could've done something. Gotten him some help, found somebody to beat some sense into him. *Before* he destroyed my bargaining power *and* ruined his whole career. *But every time it's happened, I haven't seen it coming*—and therefore I haven't been able to do anything to fend it off. Emmett's just the latest example. I need a man like you, Pete, who can take charge of security for my entire operation, *and do that fucking job for me.* I'll hire as many assistants as you think you need to do it, and pay you a hundred thousand dollars a year to start. And if you do it right, I'll double it the next year and include you in profit sharing. You want the job, yes or no?'

"So I said yes," Martigneau said.

"I would have too," Clay said. "Wish Emmett'd picked my county to get in the shit, and Alec had said that to me first."

16

"LIKE YOU SAID, FRANK, timing's everything," Martigneau said, too smugly. Seeing Clay smirk, he tried at once to compensate, raising his eyebrows and looking rueful. "Not that it's all beer and skittles. The salary's nice, sure, but there's a wicked catch: The government seems to think you're just the middleman and it's entitled to most of it. Trying to hang onto some of it for yourself, I tell you. Since Clinton threw the curve on taxes—ninety-two, 'I'm gonna cut 'em,' ninety-three, when he's elected, 'Fooled you folks, they're going *up*'—it's been a real challenge. You make any kind real money, 'less you're careful, you're gonna hand over damned near half of it to the government. Top bracket, thirty-nine point six goes the feds, six percent the state, you live here; a good chunk of what's left to the locals, and then more tax on whatever you buy. Once you knew those numbers, you had no trouble understanding why Alec didn't like government.

"There's only so much you can shelter. What you've got to do to keep a lot is *defer* as much you can, and still live pretty good. Like the millions players get. Alex's always insisted they take a lot of it in tax-deferred annuities. We sell them here, agents for insurance companies. Then down the line as the annuities start paying, we collect the money and manage it for the clients.

"If they wouldn't agree to that, *coming in,* Alec would explain: 'Then I'm not sure I want to represent you. You must like paying taxes. This means you're not rational. For most people this's a serious handicap, but you've got an unusual talent. The public and management allow highly talented people a certain degree of derangement. Almost require it, it seems like. So for a while you can probably get away with it—as long as you still perform and don't become violent. For you right now it's not a problem.

" 'For me it is. Your condition's a problem right now. I don't deal with it now, it guarantees trouble down the line. You won't listen to me now, you won't listen later on. When you're in your early thirties, and the best deal we can get for you isn't what you want—that's when the sand'll hit the gears. Since even now you're not in full command of your wits, you won't be able to accept reality when that day comes either. You'll decide to fire me and go find another agent. And *that'll* mean I will've done a lot of work for you—for which *I'm* not gonna get *paid.*

" 'If I were dumb enough to put myself in that position very often, I'd be too dumb to've ever gotten anywhere in this business. Word would've gotten around *Drouhin's kinda stupid.* You wouldn't've come to see me, and neither would anyone else. So my policy is, You reject my advice, you get somebody else. We've got no future together.

" 'Always remember the reason you came to me. It's a good one. You know you need reliable advice on contractual negotiations. Then a reliable representative to conduct them. Also someone who's equipped to explore—and exploit—the ancillary possibilities. The picture cards. The product endorsements, personal appearances, that sort of thing. Then someone to manage and look after the major assets you acquire under the terms of those contracts and agreements.

" 'You came to me because people you respect and trust told you I'm the best in the business. They were right. I am. No agency takes better care of their clients than Alexander Drouhin and Associates take of ours. *Nobody*. But *we* can't do it, *I* can't do it, if you won't accept my advice. So let's save us both the heartache. If we're not going to get off on the right foot, from the beginning, I don't want to represent you.' "

"And they would *take* this guff from him?" Clay said.

"Bet your life," Martigneau said. "So would you, if you'd been an athlete. First place, you want the guy who represents you to be *tough*. So before you hire someone, no matter what you may've heard, you find out for yourself if he is. You do it the same way you succeeded in sports— it's the only way you know. You attempt intimidation. If the agent doesn't demonstrate toughness to *you*, how much toughness is he going to show a general manager who doesn't want to pay you what you're worth?

"Athletes come in here *looking* for that treatment—*testing* him. If they get in his face, will he wimp out or slap them down? No, and yes.

"In the second place, say you weren't a first- or even a second-round pick two years ago, but now you've matured. Still no stick-out but shown you can play some. Your team wants to keep you. You agree on, oh, two million. (Except in hockey, two mill's no longer real big money, pro sports, but in the real world it's considerable dough.) You *sort of* still realize this. Sure, you've got a shitload of *attitude*, other guys in the league may know you're only a journeyman, take no shit from you whatsoever. But to ordinary people outside, in the ordinary world, you're a real *major leaguer*, a guy who actually made it, and that makes you some kind of some kind of a hero. People've been kissing up to you for *years*. But you know the only reason was because they're looking to buy a piece of your career—a personal appearance at the grand opening their store, four rounds of golf in their celebrity pro-am charity tournament, a speech at their school's athletic banquet—as cheap as possible.

"You know most of the coaches, managers, and GMs never played worth shit. Those who could, can't anymore. They give you a lot of noise about the way you do things, you just tune them out. Most agents and investment advisors never played much ball either. We've got a few exceptions like FD in here, most agencies have, but most advisors are klutzes. But they're not telling you how to play second, post up or break free, the thing you know how to do. They're telling you how to hang onto your *money,* and you know that while you've been working on the catching the outlet pass or killing off penalty minutes, they've been negotiating deals and taking care of *money.*

"You'd never admit it to anyone else, but even you vaguely know you haven't got a lot of *sense.* You're a twenty-four-year-old *kid,* for Christ sake. You like your cars, your boats, the clothes, nice place to live, hot babes to bring to it and no trouble finding 'em. 'Two million a year?' you say. '*Wow.* Even after taxes, over a million for me.'

Alex knew you'd say that. " 'Not so fast,' he'd say to you. 'You don't sound like a man who wants to listen, but I think you're ready to. Let me tell you about the real world. Compound interest. The Rule of Seventy-two.

" 'How much dissipation you figure you need? Or figure you can stand, before you break down? Look at Mickey Mantle. Played eighteen years, sure, but he came up when he was only twenty. Time his liver gave out, even he

admitted chasing the broads and fighting the booze probably cost him two or three more active years.

" 'You gross five hundred grand a year, you can get the
Range Rover. The speedboat. The nice place to live. Get
laid in it six times a day. Grossing five hundred you can
ruin your health, entertain all your pals, and score the best
bimbos in town. The only thing five hundred grand's probably not enough for's a lot of gambling. The house always
wins. And anyway, even if you could beat the odds, bettin'
a buck against ninety-four cents, it just isn't a good idea.
Gambling players make owners nervous. Figure their field-
goal man gets short with the sharks, he might shank a
three-pointer or two.

"So that you don't need. Five hundred after taxes leaves
almost two-eighty-four large for playtime. Need more'n
that, you got something wrong with you.

" 'It's the only way to go,' he would say. 'If we tell the
team to put the other one point five mill into a tax-deferred
annuity, real estate investment trust—only return eight percent, but they're nice and safe—in nine years it'll be worth
three million dollars. Eight into seventy-two is *nine*. *Nine
years*. Tenth year that mill and a half'll generate two hundred and forty K. Something happens, you're thirty-two,
not playing ball anymore, you'll still be set for life. Never
have to work another day, unless you want to. Fund'll pay
you twenty thousand bucks a month, rest of your natural
life.

" '*Think* about that, willya? Those're the alternatives.
Take the whole wad now, pay almost a million in taxes
this year, blow the rest on fun and games—nine years from
now if you're not playin' you got nothin'. If you can't find
a job announcing somewhere, doing color for the box,
you'll be working construction weekdays, card shows on
Sundays. Looking for a greeter's job in Vegas, keep yourself

alive 'til the Pension Fund kicks in. Pathetic. *But,* if you control your appetites *now,* sock a buck and a half away *this* year, nine years from now you'll be secure for the rest of your *life.*

" 'Then, if you *are* still playing, making four mill a year and don't need that much money, putting most of it away, you let the interest accumulate in the original fund. In the eleventh year it'll generate almost two hundred *sixty* grand income. Fourteenth year, the mill and a half you put away this year'll be worth over four million dollars.

" 'You don't start paying taxes 'til you start collecting. The trust we draw up for you'll skip a generation. *Your* kids won't get the principal, but they'll get the same income, and your grandkids'll get the principal. *They'll* get clobbered by the tax man, 'less the law gets changed or they can find a lawyer even smarter'n I am. But they'll tell anyone who asks if they're related to you, 'Yes, indeed, Granddaddy,' and then they will *smile* and say that you might not've been the best middle infielder who ever lived but you were a *Hall-of-Fame-grade* grandpa.

" 'Now,' Alec would say, 'which makes better sense? You follow the sound advice you came to me to get, or do you turn it down? You do, I throw you out, and you then go and get fucked up. One way or the other.' He would put it right to them. And after one of those performances, the kid would almost always say, 'I think we do it your way.'

"He did the same kind of thing for his employees. You've got forty-thousand-dollar-a-year clerical people in here laying off three hundred bucks a month from their pay into four-oh-one-K plans. To which Alex was adding three point seven five percent of the agency's profits every year, bonus incentive. And he's given division directors guaranteed consulting contracts that'll pay us six-figure salaries long after we've retired."

Martigneau hesitated. "That's what I can't figure out, the fact that Alex's dead. Wondering: Could it've been someone in here? Haven't had enough time yet to really sort it out, but it seems to me like you could read it either way. The fact that Alex was not only *sharing* profits but was also the principal reason there *were* profits to *be* shared means that no one in here'd ever want to kill him, the Golden Goose. Or the profit-sharing plan made someone in here *want* to do it—because they thought they could *increase* profits, once he was out of here."

"Excuse me," Bateman said. "Was it 'three point seven five percent you said back there? The annual profit distributions Mister Drouhin made to the employee four-oh-one-K's?" Clay glanced at him, raising an eyebrow, but said nothing.

"Yeah," Martigneau said, frowning. "Every year we ended with at least a seven-and-a-half percent profit— which we did, *every* year—Alec distributed three-and-three-quarters percent of the employee's salary to his four-oh-one-K. In addition to the regular contribution, based on their regular salary."

"So then that would mean," Bateman said. Then he glanced at Clay.

Clay frowned and shook his head. "No, no," he said, "go right ahead."

"I got my bachelor's in accounting," Bateman said to Martigneau. "People thought I was weird—I actually *enjoyed* the course work. So sometimes I get hung up on numbers. But if I've got it right, this firm routinely made a profit of seven-and-a-half percent. After what looks to me like pretty heavy overhead. Rent this first-class space—has to be expensive. Equip it. Pay employees, their health insurance, unemployment compensation, cover worker's comp, all the rest of it plus executive compensation—pay all that and still net a profit of seven point five? The gross must've been a *lot.*"

"Oh, I can tell you, it *was,*" Martigneau said.

"Mister Drouhin then distributed half of net profits to the employees," Bateman said.

"Right," Martigneau said.

"In an average recent year," Bateman said, "how much would a seven point five percent profit here amount to?"

"Well, geez, just *offhand?*" Martigneau said, widening his eyes and arching his eyebrows.

Clay cleared his throat. "Ballpark," he said. "We're going to see the books, of course, so then we'll know definitely. But for the moment, your best guess."

"I'm really not sure," Martigneau said, "so I don't want you to hold me to this. But my best recollection would be, oh, around thirteen."

"Million," Bateman said.

"Yeah," Martigneau said, "thirteen mill. I think last year I heard Alec say if we kept on doing as well as we have been, we'd gross two hundred million within a year."

"Which would mean then," Bateman said, "that one way or the other last year Mister Drouhin distributed six and a half million dollars in incentive bonuses to the other hundred and thirty-four people who work in this office. While keeping six and a half million for himself."

"Well, ah, yeah," Martigneau said.

Clay looked at Bateman again. "Okay," he said, "that's probably your motive. Guy was not a slave to love; this we know. Unless we find someone who really hated him enough to knock him off *and* that he trusted enough to let into his house late at night—which a smart boy like Alex, suspecting the hatred, probably wouldn't've done—the motive was money. Someone in here wasn't satisfied with his piece of the office's half. Wanted a piece of Alec's half,

too. Nice going, kid. I may hafta take early retirement."
Bateman blushed.

Clay looked back at Martigneau. "In addition to his six
point five last year," he said, "did Alex take a salary?"

"One point three, I believe," Martigneau said.

Clay whistled. *"Mercy,"* he said, "one point three plus
six point five. Seven million, eight hundred thousand dollars. Did the one point three come out of gross?"

"I assume so," Martigneau said. "Like I said, my job's
running security, not accounting. But I know my salary and
the other directors' pay were considered overhead. Profits
were figured on what was left after all the bills'd been paid
and everybody'd gotten what they'd earned."

"Well, I don't know about you, Gary," Clay said to
Bateman "but I would call that *extremely* good pay."
To Martigneau he said: "Who paid for the plantation in
Easton?"

Martigneau exhaled. "The firm did," he said. "He had
it built before I got here, but I know there was opposition
to the idea. Alex overrode it. 'We need this retreat.' To
seclude his new clients, keep them out of trouble,
circulation—distractions—'til he could get them signed.
I'm pretty sure he paid for his other places, the town house
on Beacon Hill, the houses on Grand Bahama and
Nantucket."

"Decent of him," Clay said. "The cars."

"The agency leases twenty-two cars," Martigneau said.
"The Lincoln limo that Oliver drives. The directors get to
choose the kind they want, in my case the Jag. Alec's
Five hundred SLC and his BMW Seven fifty sedan. The
Catanias's two cars. Ronnie's Z-Three.

"Alec's Rolls convertible, his Ferrari, his classic Jags, the
XKE and XK One forty, the Range Rover, the GEO
Tracker in Grand Bahama, they were his. Bought with his

own money. He'd point that out whenever someone said he sure knew how to spend the money. 'I do,' he would say. 'When it's for business purposes, to increase profits, the company pays. When it's for my own pleasure, *I* pay.' "

"There's a helipad at that estate," Clay said. "Old Alex have his own chopper?"

"No," Martigneau said. "He wanted one. He also wanted a corporate jet, a Gulfstream Two. But as he said, 'Now and then I have to give myself the same kind of talking-to I give the rookies. 'Ownership's *expensive*. Not only does it divert money away from your investment in your future, but except for real estate, what you own doesn't *last*. No matter how much you spend on maintenance, *things* wear out. So they depreciate. Lesson here's never buy what you can lease, never lease what you can rent, never rent what you can borrow. Unless it's essential, you need it to live and do your job, and you'll use it every damn day—*then* you can buy it.'

"The helipad he did use, not every day but often enough to justify the expense of putting it in—which wasn't very much, just asphalt. He'd charter a Jet Ranger, four-seater, to meet clients who flew into Logan, sometimes T. F. Green Airport, down in Warwick, on the other side of Providence, coming to Easton to see him. Flew them in over the traffic. It was expensive, five, six hundred bucks an hour, but worth it. Clients really ate it up."

He paused. "Alec himself only used it once. There was one night about five years ago when he got back to Boston real late, day later'n expected. He'd been in San Diego for a no-hassle contract extension session with the Chargers, three more years for Marshal Pray.

"Strictly routine. Marshal'd had a good year. Been the kind of workhorse the Chargers'd thought he would be when they signed him. Eleven hundred yards rushing, 'nother couple hundred or so passing. In the pros he was a running back, and a damned good one, too, but a big reason for that was he was deadly on the halfback option. Good enough so whoever had him knew if all three of his quarterbacks got hurt, Marshal could fill in for a while. He played quarterback at West Virginia, and he still knew how to pass. So when Marshal took a pitchout, the opposition never knew what to expect. They dropped back—he ran. They blitzed or they covered the run—then he passed.

"Marshal was twenty-eight and healthy, happy with the Chargers. Chargers were happy with Marshal. Alex figured it for a bang-it-in, bang-it-out trip. Leave in the morning, get it done that afternoon. Have a decent dinner on the ground with his happy client. Grab the red-eye, and he's back at his desk here the next day.

"One of Alec's strengths, as opposed to normal human beings, was that he could sleep on airplanes. I mean actually *sleep*. He'd get on the plane at ten forty-five, on the coast. First thing he'd do'd be tell the stew he already had drinks and dinner. Now all he wanted was sleep. Second thing he'd grab the pillow and blanket out of the overhead. Then he'd sit down, cover himself up, put the pillow back his head. Tilt the seat all the way back soon's the plane was airborne. Asleep before it got to cruising altitude.

"It was incredible. I was on some of those trips with him and it was like I was coming back alone. No one to talk to. Thank God for the cocktails and movies. Sometimes the food wasn't *that* bad. Once or twice flight wasn't crowded, stew was friendly. Little action, Mile High Club. So it wasn't *always* lonely.

"Course when we landed in the morning I'd be wrecked. *He'd* come off at Logan, seven fifteen, fresh as a daisy. And *hungry*. Oliver's first stop was Au Bon Pain, coffee and bran muffins. Next stop was here. Shower and change, and by the time FD or Dougie or I wandered in around nine or ten, whoever hadn't been with him, he'd've been at his desk for an hour or two. Making calls, catching up on stuff in Europe.

"He was right about the San Diego deal. But when he got back the Harbor Island Sheraton, he had a call. Trouble in Chicago. Client in a contract jam with the Blackhawks. Dougie Morris was handling. Same guy Alec was trying to peddle to the Bruins yesterday afternoon, our *former* All-Star goalie Jean Claude Methodiste. Problem client, always has been. Talked himself out of the starting job with Canadiens—*les bleu-blanc-rouge*—five, six years ago, squawking about his defensemen not blocking shots. 'Les *bay-tards* do not *impede*. I am *sans day-founse.*'

"He was right, but stupid. It's a lot easier to trade a disgruntled, *expensive* goalie 'n it is to trade two of your three defensive lines. And besides, *les Canadiens* had a kid in the minors about ready for Saint Catherine Street. Jean Claude had a million-three contract, *very* big back then for hockey. His big mouth made him expendable.

"He hasn't improved with the years. Twenty-nine then, approaching the tail end, what was sure to be his last big contract. With the Blackhawks or anyone else. After that if any team'd sign him it'd be as a backup. Would've thought he had to know it. Dougie went in assuming he did. But if Jean did, he wouldn't admit it. Got all bent out of shape over how Dougie was going at it.

"A big part of it was that Dougie, not Alex, was the guy handling it. Jean thought that meant Alex was writing him down. He thought it meant that because he was getting older, he wasn't first-tier anymore.

"He was also right about that. It's *amazing* how often people who hired Alex ten or fifteen years ago, precisely because they saw he was ruthless, get astonished when the years've passed and he starts being ruthless with *them*. It's about *business*, not friendship. Fact Alec's always *cordial*, concerned about their health, looking after their best interests, of *course*; but that didn't mean they were *friends*. What the *hell* did they expect?

"Anyway, finally *Dougie* lost it. That can happen too. Agents're people, they also get frustrated. Dougie called in and said Jean was outta control. Could Alex stop in Chicago, calm everybody down before the whole thing went up in smoke. So Alex now has to have Julie remake his travel plans. He gets back to Boston—I dunno, Wednesday morning 'stead of Tuesday, Thursday 'stead of Wednesday—and he's got a client driving up from East Greenwich. Ginny Alter. He's meeting her for lunch at the house in Easton, noon. Going to try to talk her out of going public with the fact that she's a lesbian. No way he can drive there from Logan in time. He tells Julie have a chopper waiting, he lands at Logan, eleven.

" 'Scared the *hell* out of me,' he said. 'I'm up there in this thing with no wings on it, pilot's chattering away, happy as a lark: "Look at all the *cars* down there—isn't this *terrific?*" And the whole time I'm thinking, *Jeez-sus Christ, I'm gonna die.* I swear to God, as long's I live, I am never gettin' onto another one of those things again.' "

Bateman looked inquiringly at Clay. "Go ahead," Clay said.

"What you said back there about the firm managing clients' money," Bateman said to Martigneau. "That interested me. When you were reciting the pitch you give to college prospects, I seem to recall you saying that you don't charge a fee for managing their money."

"*Whoa,*" Martigneau said, "No-no, no-no, *nooo.* That I *never* said. What I said, and what in fact I do tell them, is that there's no extra fee for tax and investment advice, that sort of thing. For *management,* there is."

"Ah," Bateman said. "So, what exactly did that entail?"

"It depended on what they wanted us to do," Martigneau said. "A lot of our clients—most of them, in fact— want us to not only *advise* them about investments, but then *handle* the actual money placement. Oversee their accounts. Make such trades as we think necessary and prudent. To lock in profits and minimize losses. Instead of them taking the time and having the worry of doing it themselves. Good many of them also have their bills and so forth sent directly to us. Saves them the bother of writing checks, keeping accounts straight. Our clerks do the scut work. And in addition to getting our *advice* on taxes, most of them, again, want us to prepare the *returns* and see to it that the checks are made out in the proper amounts. So all they have to do is sign." He smiled. "Some don't want to do *that* much. They've given us powers of attorney to sign their names for them—never go near their accounts.

"So: *Advice* we give them for no extra charge; when we do additional *work* for them, we charge."

"But you invite the kids to think it's all included," Clay said.

"If they think that, they think it," Martigneau said. "When it comes time for them to decide whether they want to do the work themselves or have us do it for them, then they're made plainly aware that we charge."

"And how much *do* you charge?" Clay said.

"Only a nominal fee," Martigneau said. "Plus normal brokerage commissions, of course—we have two licensed traders in-house, three Registered Investment Advisors and three CPAs at last count. Plus two other lawyers besides Alec. For their work we charge our clients what they'd pay at Merrill Lynch, Coopers Lybrand, or Grabbem and Skinnem, P.C., Law Firm and All-Night Car Wash. I'm not really sure what it is."

"Take a guess," Clay said. "You know we're going to find out anyway, when we subpoena the books." He paused. "Which subpoena is about to be prepared. Gary, take out that cell phone and call the DA. Tell him we want a paper, Alexander Drouhin Associates. Two hundred Clarendon, Boston. *Duces tecum.* Forthwith. Right off, this afternoon."

Bateman brought the phone out of his briefcase and placed the call, repeating Clay's instructions into it. Martigneau sat at his desk glaring. "That's hardly necessary," he said.

"It's *very* necessary, Peter," Clay said. "I don't want anything to disappear. Anything does, it's your night in the barrel. Now answer the question. What's the firm fee for the financial services? I know you've got some idea."

"Well, *yeah,*" Martigneau said, "I realize that. But then I don't want you coming back here and saying to me 'You told us four and it turns out it's four point two five. Were you trying to deliberately mislead us?' "

"Heaven forbid I should do such a thing," Clay said. "Badger a poor witness like that. But you're *not* a *poor* witness. You're a very *good* witness—you've had *years* of experience testifying. All three of us know you've got a pretty good idea what the service charge is, if not to the penny. So why not quit horsing us around, huh? *Answer the question,* best of your knowledge. What was the fee for the service?"

"I think it was six point five," Martigneau said. "But that's just the last number I heard. And I don't know when that was, I heard it. May've changed since. I don't want you to hold me to that."

"Well, *if* it's changed," Clay said, "we can be pretty sure it's like everything else—it hasn't come down."

"Probably not," Martigneau said.

"How much does the firm have under management?" Bateman said.

"Now that one I *really* don't know," Martigneau said. "I really have no idea."

"Hundred and fifty million?" Bateman said. "*Two* hundred million?"

"I honestly have no idea," Martigneau said.

Clay pondered for a while, squinting. "But almost certainly well over a hundred million," he said.

"Yeah, probably," Martigneau said.

"I saw a piece in the paper some time ago," Clay said. "Your man Alex was quoted as saying he represented his clients as a lawyer. An *attorney*. Didn't take a percentage of the contracts he negotiated for them. Charged them only for his *time,* by the hour."

"Well, that was true," Martigneau said. "His rate was high—and portal-to-portal. But if he charged you forty thousand bucks for the eighty hours that it took him to get you a four-year, ten-mill contract, how unhappy would that make you?"

"Five hundred *an hour?*" Bateman and Clay said together.

"I think it was that," Martigneau said. "Plus expenses. Alex used to say that the reason first class costs so much more'n coach's because first class's so much better. 'You want Alex Drouhin to negotiate your contract because he's the best? You pay Alex Drouhin's fee.' When he first came in, most agents were taking ten percent or so of what the contract was. His fees were a bargain."

"Until you figured in the six or seven percent that he creamed off every dollar that came in, and then went out, under those bargain contracts," Clay said.

"Well," Martigneau said, "like I said, this is a business. Alex had to pay to run it. So our clients have to pay to use it."

"In other words," Clay said, "when he talked to his new clients, and when he gave that interview to the newspaper, he misled people into thinking he was charging strictly by the hour—not a percentage of the take. Lots less than he actually was."

"Look," Martigneau said, "one of the surest ways to find out whether Alex was doing something was to see if he'd ever said in public that he wasn't, and never would. Alex and the truth were friendly enough, but at a distance. They didn't always see quite as much of each other as some might've liked—even some of us in *here,* sometimes.

"Alec always concealed the truth until it was absolutely clear that revealing it would be to his advantage. Until then he assumed it wouldn't be. He had absolutely no compunction about lying if he thought it'd improve his negotiating position. He assumed everyone else did the same thing. Any time a GM or a coach told a reporter what his first pick in the next draft'd be, and it turned out to be *true,* Alex was astounded. '*Why* would he do that? Now if he can't get him signed, he's gonna look like *dogmeat.* Always practice misdirection 'til you have to show your hand.' "

"And so it'd follow," Clay said, "that when the rest of you were out in the world by yourselves, acting for the agency, you had to shade the truth too. Because you certainly didn't want to say something that'd contradict what Alex'd already said. Give away the fact that he'd been lying, if he had."

Martigneau shifted in his chair. "Well," he said, "you know. A few years ago during the presidential campaign, the media figured out the candidates weren't even *pretending* to answer questions anymore. No matter what anyone asked them, they kept saying the same thing, over and over. They called it 'staying on message.' And at the time I thought, 'The hell, that's nothing new. We do that all the time.' Of course we do—you want to be consistent with what the boss's said."

"You said Drouhin brought you in here because security'd been lax," Clay said.

"It was," Martigneau said. "Extremely slack. Give you an example: None of the guys who'd run security before me'd done anything beyond routine background checks on people who work here. If they didn't have a criminal record in Massachusetts and there was nothing in their credit record to suggest it might not be a good idea to let them handle money, and if there was no confidential information that suggested drug use, they 'must be clean.' They'd be approved. No check to see whether they might at some time've lived another *place,* under another *name,* or what their reason might've been for changing it.

"People do that, you know, and not just because they're women and got married. Sometimes it's because they think they'd do better in the future if no one they met in it knew about their past. For all Alec'd known, he'd been hiring people who were on the run, looking for a place to hide, get access, and steal again."

"Had he been?" Clay said.

"Nobody violent," Martigneau said. "He'd been lucky— nobody with a history of fraud or embezzlement, either. But a number of people had minor records Alec didn't know about. Kind of stuff that wouldn't necessarily make you stop and say, 'Uh-uh, this guy's a wrong number,' but might make you hesitate a little before you took him on, make sure you had enough liability insurance.

"Arigo Catania, for example. Thirty years or so ago, 'fore driving under became the huge big deal it is today,

Rigo got busted a few times. Had a real drinking problem. When Alex hired him and Angela, Rigo didn't see any need to mention it. Probably because Angela told him she'd beat the shit out of him if he did.

"Only peculiarity Alex knew they had was that every Sunday, Catholic holy day, they'd travel fifty miles or so to some farm outside of Worcester, hear the Mass in Latin. When I asked Alex how much he knew about them, he said just about the only things were how old they were, that they're both citizens, and that they told him they had to have Sunday and holy-day mornings off because they had to drive so far to church. Told me they said they were 'Old Catholics. Don't believe in the pope.' My guess is that Rigo didn't buy much of it but he was scared of Angela. That was a way she had of keeping him in line. You see the tractors?"

"Yeah," Clay said. "Big one with a cab and a plow on it. Smaller one with a gang mower."

"Right," Martigneau said. " 'Bout ten years ago, Rigo's using the little one to mow the slope in the back, leading down to the pond? Rolled over on him. Shouldn't've. That's a compound slope. It declines and it's tilted, too— falls off to the west.

"The way you mow a slope like that is you *minimize* the grade. This you do by extending the grade, making it longer. Do it on the diagonal. Say you start off at the northeast corner going down to the pond. You take it nice and gentle down to the southwest corner. Then you mow around the edge of the pond. Then you take it nice and gentle up another row to the northeast corner. Then nice and gentle back down to the southwest corner. Do another strip, around the edge the pond. Then up the slope again, to the northwest corner.

"Not Rigo. Rigo started at the *north*east corner and

264

mowed down to the *south*east corner. Then he mowed back up again, *maximizing* the grade, and down again and up again, until he got to the middle of the lawn down by the pond, turned around and started back up, the steepest part. And even with the weight of the mowers it was towing, the tractor tipped over on him. Dumped him and flipped on its side, partly on him. Broke his back.

"This happened at four in the afternoon. He was in a lot of pain, of course, but not as much as he might've been—he was partially sedated when it happened. He was also incoherent, smelled of Canadian Club. There wasn't any question he was drunk. The question was whether his spinal cord was severed and he'd be paralyzed for life. As you've seen, he wasn't. Eight, ten weeks in traction and he was almost as good as new. But if he hadn't been, Alec would've wound up supporting him and Angela forever. And if he'd done it out on the road in the car that Alec leases for him, doing an errand for Alec, and'd hit a stopped school bus, say, Alec would've wound up in bankruptcy.

"Dishonesty, violent tendencies, problems with addictions, now racial and sexual harassment: You take a big chance when you hire someone to work for you. If he gets hurt, then either *can't* work, or doesn't *want* to. If he isn't getting the job done and knows it, knows damned well you're going to fire him. Well, he also knows you've got deep pockets—he may decide to strike first. Blame you for causing his problem and then sue you for harming him, causing him pain and suffering, emotional distress.

"That kind of crap isn't funny, not if it happens to you. These days a lying lazy bastard like that is very likely to *win*. The Equal Employment Opportunity Commission said a year or so ago that if your employee's nuts, you have to modify his schedule or his working conditions so that he can keep his job. Otherwise you're violating the federal Americans with Disabilities Act. Discriminating—the psycho can sue you. Postmasters're gonna have to set aside space where their disgruntled workers can clean and oil their assault weapons."

Clay laughed. Bateman said, "Is that true?"

"About the EEOC? Yeah, it's the truth," Martigneau said, grinning. "About the postmasters, I haven't seen a compliance announcement. But it wouldn't surprise me.

"Anyway, Rigo and Angela were satisfied with the care he got, as well they should have been. Alec's employee policy took care of the medical bills and he paid them salary as usual while Rigo was laid up. And fortunately for Alex, no tin-pot lawyer'd been around to see Rigo flip the mower, and nobody else got hurt, so no one got talked into suing.

"But still, the fact Alec'd dodged disaster once when Rigo's thirst got the better of him didn't mean Rigo's problem wouldn't cause another one. Alec might not be so lucky again. So when I found out about the problem I drove down one day when I knew Alex wouldn't be there, and I had a little heart-to-heart with them in the kitchen. Angela promised me she'd hold all the keys and never let Rigo drive anything bigger'n a nail—and wear a thimble doing that—after he'd been into the Canadian Club. Seeing them together, I thought she could do it. Since there haven't been any more incidents—I've heard about at least—I'm inclined to think she's done it."

"How about in here, in the firm?" Clay said. "Find any security risks in here, people that had to be fired?"

"Yeah, a few," Martigneau said. "We had one guy, Luther Broadaxe, we had to let go a year ago. Former second baseman with the Cincinnati Reds. No matter where he was, what he was doing, everyone always loved Luther.

So everyone, including Alex, felt bad about brooming Luther. Talented guy, good people skills, but Alex had no choice: Luther hadn't changed from the charmer he was when he was playing baseball, but working for Alex his outgoing ways amounted to talking too much—to too many people who could make money off what he learned from working here.

"Soon's I found out he was doing it, couple years ago, I had a talk with him. Explained it all again, very carefully. Reminded him why every dugout and locker room he was ever in has a sign in it that says everyone but members of the team has to be out of it forty-five minutes before game time. What we find out about our clients and the people that they work for is proprietary information. The competition'd like to have it and so would the gamblers.

"Hypothetical: We don't have one, but if we did, the fact our twenty-six-year-old twenty-game Cy Young winner's going to jump from Team A to Team B this winter when his contract expires'd be worth all kinds of money to all kinds of people. Since he's still under contract, Team A could allege tampering, maybe get a high draft pick from Team B in compensation. Teams C, D, and E wouldn't bother making offers, meaning that we've now got no chance to start a bidding war to hike his Team B price, which we always try to do. And to make it a real horror show, if this gets out before the season's over, it raises the question of whether our young pitcher's giving all his heart and soul for Team A every game he starts, or saving his arm for next year. Word like that changes gambling odds.

"So there're people who'll pay big money for that kind of inside dope. The fact that Luther was *giving* it away, because he's friendly, liked to talk big, show he is an insider, that changed nothing. I reminded him, 'You keep your mouth shut about what you learn here. You could get us all in the shit.' Luther said he understood, but he didn't stop, so Alex had to fire him."

"Put him on the list," Clay said to Bateman.

"You may have trouble interviewing him," Martigneau said. "In addition to being a sociable fellow, Luther was a motorcycle freak. Had an Easy Rider, big chopped-hawg Harley. Got creamed by a semi Friday before last Labor Day, rotary this side the Cape Cod Canal, at the Sagamore Bridge."

"Take him off the list," Clay said to Bateman. To Martigneau he said, "You know where Drouhin was last night?"

"He was in Haymarket," Martigneau said, "which I'd never heard of before and I've lived in this state all my life. He hadn't expected to be there, but that's where he was. Getting Buffalo Bobby Moreno bailed out of jail."

"Anyone else with him?" Clay said.

"Ordinarily, I would've been," Martigneau said. "Standard operating procedure when one of our people gets in the gravy after business hours in a town within driving distance—or where we don't have legal coverage—is for Alex to call me. I go with him to collect the guy's wheels. But I was in New York last night, retirement dinner for Spec Fuller."

"I don't know who that is," Clay said.

"Former FBI, Southern District," Martigneau said. "NFL Security office. Just a small do, but a friend. Nice party. Caught the last American out of JFK. Got home little after midnight.

"Alex was meeting with Joe Corwin, the Bruins. Owner's box. Fleet Center. Pitching Methodiste to them. They need a proven goalie. Jean Claude needs a job. He's in the option year of his contract with the Islanders. They're not gonna exercise it. They'll unload him and his salary for a draft pick. Bruins have picks, need a goalie, gate attraction. So it's a nice fit, looking good.

"Middle of it, Alec gets a call. Moreno's in the pokey, Haymarket. Your standard emergency drill. Alex cuts the meeting short, starts calling for backup. Since I'm outta town, he calls FD. FD meets him, Minuteman Inn up in Concord. They head for Haymarket. Get Moreno out of custody. Alex drives him home to Natick. FD follows in Moreno's car. Alex drives FD back to Concord. FD goes home. Alex goes home to Easton."

"We should talk to FD," Clay said.

"He's waiting for you," Martigneau said.

PART
THREE

17

FD WHITMAN, 49, 6'1", had gained weight since his playing days in the NFL. "About twenty pounds," he conceded cheerfully enough, shaking hands as Martigneau put the question to him while introducing Clay and Bateman. Whitman's office adjoined Drouhin's northeast-corner suite. The interior door between them was open.

Whitman's head was shaved. He wore a white shirt with a gold collar pin and a red paisley tie. His cuff links were block letters in gold: RVR on the right cuff, BCK on the left. His trousers were slate gray cavalry twill, sharply creased. His shoes were highly polished oxfords. He wore a heavy gold NFL championship ring with a purple stone surrounded by diamonds and etched with the ram's horns logo of the Minnesota Vikings. There were several trophies and framed team pictures on the light birch credenza behind his matching desk. There were four certificates in gold frames on the credenza as well. "Tend to get heavier, you get older." He grinned. "I'm comfortable with it."

There were three chairs in front of Whitman's desk. A door to his left opened into it. "Not with the reason that brings you here, though," he said. "I'm not comfortable with that at all." He gestured toward the door to his left.

"Who's going to sit in that office now. *How* do we replace Alex. Whether we *can* replace Alex. Those're very big questions." He shook his head. "But anyway, how can I help you guys?"

As Martigneau went to the chair at the left of Whitman's desk, Clay said, "Ah, Peter, you're not going to be part of this."

Martigneau stopped behind the chair. "Beg your pardon?" he said. "I'm chief of security here. Part of everything goes on in here that I think I need to be a part of."

"And that was perfectly all right," Clay said, "as long as what went on in here wasn't under criminal investigation. Which everything that goes on in here now is, and will be until we find out who killed Alexander Drouhin. And since as you've told us you're now a rich guy, not a cop anymore, you've got no jurisdiction. I want you out of here now. Door closed behind you. And I want that door closed over there, too. Furthermore, case you've forgotten, taping conversations is against the law in Massachusetts, unless you have a valid warrant or all parties thereto consent. You don't have a warrant and Corporal Bateman and I don't consent, so if you do it you'll be committing a felony. And in this instance that could also amount to obstruction of justice. Should it turn out that the reason you did it was to coordinate stories when we leave."

Martigneau clenched his teeth. "What the *hell*'re you suggesting?"

"I'm not *suggesting* anything," Clay said. "I'm *telling* you. You're not going to sit in on this interview, and I don't want you to record it—or eavesdrop on it—either. If you do, and I find out about it, I'll recommend to the DA that you be prosecuted."

"You son of a bitch," Martigneau said.

"Thank you," Clay said. "My compliments to *your*

mother as well. Now if you'd be good enough to leave?"

Martigneau left loudly, closing the door behind him. Whitman stood up behind the desk, went to the door connecting the offices and closed it. He went back to his chair and sat down. "Gentlemen," he said.

"Okay to tape?" Bateman said, loading a new cassette into the recorder.

Whitman shrugged. "Fine by me," he said.

Bateman turned on the recorder, identified those present, and had Whitman repeat his consent.

"Peter tells us he was in New York and you took a ride with Mister Drouhin last night," Clay said.

"Uh huh," Whitman said. "I came in after lunch for a couple or three hours. Often do that Sundays. Find I think better when the phone's not ringing. Habit I picked up from Alex. The two of us used to ad-lib a lot of valuable conferencing time those Sunday afternoons, too. Kept each other up to date on things. Nothing formal, no agenda, just whoever's leaving first poking his head in the other guy's office 'fore he pulled out. Ending up sitting down for a while. Spitballing ideas. Free-associating matters one of us'd noticed that ought to concern us. Not recently, though. Past couple of years, hasn't happened that often. Alec seemed to've broken the habit."

He pondered that for a moment, frowning. "Because he wanted to, I'm sure. He knew I'd be likely to be in here, any given Sunday. And that before I left I'd look in to see if he was. Start a conversation if I saw him. In recent years he didn't want that to happen, so he stopped coming in. Alex was deliberate, very controlling. Seldom did things accidentally. When something happened, or *didn't* happen, matters that he was involved in, the reason generally was because he wanted it that way.

"Of course yesterday I wouldn't really've expected to see

him. I knew he had an afternoon meet-at-the-Fleet, trying to get some steady work for Jean Claude Methodiste—*that* trophy-class pain in the ass. Anyway, I did get some work done. Can't say I actually solved any problems, but I got 'em focused better. That might not seem like much, but *I* was pleased; it was more progress'n I'd made during the week. Left about four thirty, went home."

"Where might home be?" Clay said.

"Andover," Whitman said.

"Fair hike every day," Clay said.

"Little over twenty miles each way," Whitman said. "The kids go to Phillips. It's a good school. When they were in the lower school, the wife and I agreed they were too young to leave home. So I made the commute. Now they're upperclassmen, but all of us like the arrangement the way it is. We're used to it. They can leave home when they go to college.

"Got home around five fifteen. Worked out on the tread-mill forty-five minutes. That's a compromise: fifteen minutes less'n I probably should stay on it, fifteen more'n I really want to. Do it to keep my weight down, but of course it makes me thirsty, so when I get off I always have a glass of beer—which keeps my weight *up*."

"What kind of beer?" Clay said.

"Sam Adams," Whitman said. "Would've had two, but Glenda was making a turkey, so I know I'm going to over-eat because I always do, that's on the menu. She was on her phone while I was on the treadmill. That made me nervous. She was talking to my younger sister Martha. Marty will *not* shut up. This was dangerous for the turkey. If Glenda got too distracted, it'd get kiln-dried, become ply-wood, but there was nothing I could do. Glenda likes to talk herself; that's why they like each other. Sometimes I think Glenda married me because Martha asked her to, to get me out of her hair, keep me out of trouble, and leave her in sole possession of the telephone.

"I went in the study, turned on the TV, see if that'd get my mind off beer and turkey. Spurs and Blazers, not much of a game, they weren't working and that meant the game didn't do the job for me. When Glenda cooks a turkey there is no place in the house where you can go and not smell it roasting. So I'm sitting there trying not to drool, make myself think about *anything* but food, wondering if the satellite service this place buys for all us agents—choice of *several* lousy games every night—is worth anywhere near what we pay for it. And my phone rings. I let it. I don't want to pick it up. I don't know who it is, but Sunday night at dinnertime it can't be anything but trouble. I figure 'Let the machine handle it. After dinner I'll deal with it.'

"It's Alex. He's calling from his car and it's like he can not only see me sitting there in the same room with the machine but knows exactly what I'm thinking. He tells me through the speaker to pick up the phone. I do it. He's left the Fleet, heading toward Cambridge. Now that I know it's him, only thing I've got left to find out is exactly what *kind* of trouble he's not letting me put off 'til after dinner.

"Alex's very good about not bothering his people at home. Only time he ever calls one of us at home at night is when something bad's happened. But I've been spoiled. Since Pete joined the outfit he's been the man who answers the fire bell. Trouble is, last night Pete's out of town, just like he was the *last* time Bobby Moreno got in the shit, and I had to go down practically all the way to the Cape. I think Pete's got some kind of sixth sense or something, tells him when Bobby's gonna blow and be a problem, so he books himself an out-of-town gig and takes off. I don't know it's Bobby this time until Alex tells me, but before he gets beyond 'Get on the phone, FD,' I know the first real shot I'm going to get at that turkey's fading away into the cold future.

"But what can you do? Bobby's big bucks to us, one of our few real big-money clients."

"Really," Clay said. "Pete just gave us to understand this outfit's *coining* money."

"Oh, we're *doing* all right," Whitman said. "But we're doing it the same way the major-league clubs're doing all right—by emphasizing volume and forgetting quality. We've got a lot of playing clients, well over four hundred, last count, but the vast majority of them're either journeymen or top-level performers at positions that lack glamour, don't get that much notice. Right fielders. Defensive linemen. Small forwards who can come off the bench and shoot some treys for you, if they're having a good night. Second-line defensemen in hockey. They make decent money now, anywhere from half a mill to three mill a year, because when expansion became an epidemic, they became essential. But they're underappreciated.

"You could say we now specialize in guys like that. It wasn't wise to say it around Alex. He didn't like the idea that we'd become that—a Ford dealership, not Rolls—without his consent.

"Not that anyone ever mentioned it. The rest of us about five years ago just began responding to the market. No deep, dark conspiracy or anything, we just came one-by-one to the awareness that the market'd changed, and Alec hadn't. He'd fallen behind. So for the agency to survive, we had to do something, and we did it. Sort of like common knowledge a deprived spouse's committing adultery. Go ahead do it, but don't *say* you're doing it. We started aggressively going after the second- and third-tier talent.

"It was a marketing necessity. More often'n not now, guys with ordinary talent who would've been reliable subs twenty years ago're playing every night. Salary caps—and luxury taxes for exceeding them—mean very few teams in any sport can afford to field All-Stars at every position. Even if there were enough of them to go around, which there aren't. So what the personnel people look for's the right mix, the two or three stars who can team up with the just okay, run-of-the-mill guys to win sixty percent of their games. And since that's what every team's doing— fielding two or three household names fronting for a good bench—on paper, any given team can do that. *If* they get reasonably lucky and nobody really gets hurt.

"And anything over sixty percent's gravy, in any pro sport. The only time you can *expect* to win more than ninety-eight games in a baseball season, fifty games in an NBA year, ten games in the NFL, is during an expansion year—maybe the year after that—when you'll have new, weak teams to feast on. So the attitude is get what you can afford and hope for the best.

"With that mind-set in the front offices, it stands to reason that the agents with the biggest inventory of fungible players are the agents who will do the most business. So we went after those players.

"Alex hated the idea. He's too competitive. During his glory years he corraled the stars. It grated on him now that we don't represent Junior Griffey, Roberto Alomar. That Brett Favre and Jerry Rice and the other superstars today have other agents. To Alex that was a gross miscarriage of justice—'Those guys belong with us.' He really believed it. Rest of us therefore did everything we could to ease the pain for him. So, when Alex calls and says that one of our few guys with six-mill potential's deep in the shit, whoever's got the duty postpones the turkey, gets the coat back on, and goes to meet Alec at the Minuteman Inn.

"I do it, go to Concord, leave my car there. We're on the road in his big Merc. 'What's going on?' I say.

" 'Usual thing,' he says. 'You remember the drill. We're

going up to the lockup in Haymarket to rescue Bobby Moreno. I'll get him bailed and drive him home. You bring his car back.'

" 'How'd it go at Fleet Center?' I say. 'Cut a new deal for Jean?'

" 'Well, I was getting there,' he says. 'Corwin was pretending not to buy my theory that he's got to start rebuilding now, but he was having a hard time doing it. I told him: "Joe, you've got a bad team here. *That's* the reason why the building's half empty every night; the reason why you have to lie about attendance. Next year you're going to have even *more* trouble selling season's tickets and luxe boxes'n you had *this* year. The reason's because your team is *bad*. Nobody even watches when they're on *free* TV. Remember the old days, Orr was here, hottest ticket in town? Now people can't *give* the things away." '

" 'And that's when my phone rang,' Alec said." Whitman paused. "So he had to break it off with Corwin. Riding with Alec was always exciting, but never more so'n when he was frustrated. Pumped. By now we're flying. Speedometer needle so far over on the right, all I could see was the base of it high up the left. I don't know how fast he was going. I've been with him when he's doing a hundred and ten—not that I liked it. Route Two's a good road. Last night was dry and clear and there wasn't any traffic to speak of, but it's farm country, lots of animals. Came up on this boarded-up farmstand, and there's a deer standing next to it. Luckily she knew the deer rule that says 'Freeze,' so she didn't bolt out in front of us—and even luckier, she wasn't already in the middle of the road when she went rigid. I said to him, 'Alex, for Christ sake, I know you're excited, but that doesn't make you Roger Penske. You're not an Indy driver. Slow the hell down, for God's sake.' So he did. I doubt we were more'n twenty or thirty miles an hour over the limit after that."

"You still had some time between Concord and Haymarket," Clay said. "What'd you talk about?"

"What we used to talk about on Sundays in the office," Whitman said. "The only thing we really ever had in common—the business. He'd called Jean Claude after he'd called me and Jean Claude hadn't been happy with what he'd had to say. Jean's unreasonable, always has been, but if Alex talked to me the way he talked to him, I'd be hard to handle too. He told Jean he'd had to break off the talk with Corwin because the call from Haymarket came in. He said he was going to get back to Corwin this afternoon, see if he could wrap the deal, and if he couldn't then he'd drop a dime on him for tomorrow's papers. Let the riffraff know how shortsighted Joe's being about getting an established, available, *star*. Alec said that didn't satisfy Jean. 'He swore at me,' he said.

" 'I don't know's I blame him,' I said.

"Then we talked about some other things going on in the office that I'd like to've taken up with him long before last night—except, like I said, for the past year or so it's seemed as though he's never been around."

"Like what, for example?" Clay said.

"Look," Whitman said, "I'm sure Pete's already told you something about what's been on everybody's mind here— all the senior agents, anyway. Barry and Maurice're still young enough to land on their feet somewhere else, haven't really built up any equity of years in this operation. And Lionel and I've got those cushions we built up when we were playing—we both had good long careers, and we listened to Alex. When it started coming in, we started socking it away." He hesitated.

Then he spread his hands, palms up and open. "Look," he said, "I understand you have to conduct your investigation, and I don't want to get in the way of it. Want to help you any way I can. But I hope you'll keep in mind that if any of this stuff Pete's probably told you, or that I tell you myself—if any of it ever leaks, what we've all been worried about, it'd wreck the business. Whole shebang could go in the toilet."

"But if that's going to happen," Clay said, "isn't it pretty likely to happen anyway? If it hasn't already begun, just as a result of news going out that the founder of the company's been *murdered?* Regardless of anything we may do or may not do, I wouldn't think the founding father's violent death'd inspire confidence on the part of the clients you've got—much less attract the ones you'd hoped to get.

"And not only is he dead, whoever did it almost has to've been someone connected in some way with the firm, either in it or buying its services—which if so means there's a second scandal brewing. Gary and I've only been on this case since this morning, a matter of hours, but already we know that except for this agency, the guy had no *life*. This was *it*. So whoever ended that life had to've been tied up in some way with this operation."

"That's not what I mean," Whitman said. He got up and stood beside his chair, scratching the back of his head with his left hand while looking at the floor as though he thought he might have dropped what he meant to say on the pale blue carpet, and with a little time would find it. He put his left hand in his pocket and used his right hand to scratch the back of his head. He took two paces to his right and then three paces back, stopping behind the chair and putting his hands on the headrest. He exhaled heavily. "What I mean is that I hope you can limit your investigation, and what comes out in public about it, to what made someone want to kill Alex Drouhin and who it was that did it. That's all I mean."

"Well, what else is there?" Clay said.

"A lot," Whitman said. He pressed down on the headrest

so that the chair tilted back to its limit, the coil spring in the base groaning. He let go of the headrest and as it snapped upright took three paces to his left, searching the carpet again. "I said Alex didn't do things by accident," he said. "That wasn't quite right. He got into this business by accident."

He raised his head and studied Bateman and Clay. "Look," he said, massaging the back of his neck with his right hand, "Alex felt he could confide in me, and believed I confided in him. To a certain extent I did. In recent years not as much's he thought, he'd gotten much more sensitive, developed kind of a persecution complex. Things didn't go the way he wanted, he'd overreact, start talking about some conspiracy. I got more cautious about what I said to him, how much I told him.

"I probably *knew* him better 'n anyone else in the firm, all right? Not as *long* as some of them—his secretary, Julie, she's been with him since Day One. Given him her *life,* really. And naturally she knows a lot more facts, details of his adventures, history before I met him and so forth, than I do. And our PR guy, Drew Houser, he also met close to the beginning. Drew was a sportswriter for the old *Record-American.* Had the Celtics beat when Alex was negotiating his first-ever contract—for Rusty Reynolds. Either you guys remember Rusty? What a character."

Bateman and Clay shook their heads. "Okay," Whitman said, retracing his steps to the chair. "Reginald Reynolds the Third was the nephew by marriage of one of Alec's few actual law clients, classmate of his at Brown. The client's family ran a string of about thirty hardware stores, all over northern New England. The client's in-laws, Rusty's family, lived on the West Coast, so when Rusty came east to go to college, this guy took him under his wing.

"Rusty didn't look like he'd need that much protection.

He was a big red-headed guy, freckles, all arms and legs, six-seven, eight, two-forty or so—*big* for a player in those days. Big anywhere, but especially in the Ivy League.

"Rusty was a great guy, and he could play some hoops. For a white boy at an Ivy League school, Rusty could play a *lot* of hoops. When he graduated—from everything I heard or saw, if it'd been anybody but the son of Reynolds Paint they probably would've flunked him out, first semester freshman year; it isn't just the athletes who get free passes—it didn't seem all that far-fetched for him to try out with the Celtics. He couldn't do many other things as well as he played ball, as he'd tell you himself—'except fuck Eileen.' They had seven kids. Pro basketball didn't pay much in those days. A star might get a hundred thousand, and by no stretch of the imagination was Rusty any star. But his family was so rich he didn't *have* do *anything*. He could play ball as long as he wanted.

"Either the year he graduated or the year before, Brown made the semifinals of the NIT. The National Invitational was still the big tournament in those days. So the big gawky kid from the Ivy League'd gotten some attention. NBA teams still had territorial rights then. If the kid was in your territory, if you wanted him, you owned him. Naturally if you'd heard about him, you tried him out. Celtics decided he wouldn't do too much damage if they used him to give Bill Russell breathers, so Rusty stuck. Averaged maybe eight minutes a game, maybe got as many rebounds as he collected fouls, two or three. Sometimes scored a point or two.

"One night Johnny Most called him The Doofus on the radio. This was back in the days of transistors. The Garden crowd picked it up. Whenever the Celts got way ahead, they'd start chanting: '*Doo*-fuss, *Doo*-fuss.' Big cheer when the coach put him in, garbage time. Crowd gave him standing O's when he got a basket. He was a good-natured kid, had some ham in him. He played into it, grinning like a bastard, shaking hands with himself over his head—big local favorite.

"That's why everyone was so surprised when the big goof refused to sign a contract for what I guess would've been his sixth season, sixty-nine. Wasn't money. He didn't like his roommate. Said he snored and kept him awake. Wanted a room by himself on the road. Why the hell he just didn't ask for one and pay the difference himself, I don't know, but he was *adamant*. He wouldn't do it. *Record* ran a back-page headline, 'Doofus Won't Budge.'

"Anyone with half a brain of course could see that this was not the best strategy for a guy who liked playing basketball better'n anything except fucking Eileen. By then you're starting to see more and more big men coming along, and a six-eight, clumsy, heavy, slow guy was not in a good position to make nonnegotiable demands. People were beginning to ask if maybe he'd inhaled too much thinner, summers in the paint factory. So Alec's client-classmate got in touch with Alec, asked him to step in and see what he could do to calm Rusty down—and then smooth things over with the Celtics, before the big dope talked himself right out of the NBA.

"Alec did anything and everything the hardware guy asked him to. 'And *promptly*, too,' he said, 'because when the guy's not only your *biggest* client, that's what you do.' And he had the *time* to be obliging, because up to that point Alec had not been a big rousing success at the practice of law. So he called Rusty and got his side of it, and then he called Red Auerbach and made an appointment.

"See, in those days you didn't have the player associations that you've got today. You didn't have to be certified to represent a guy in a contract stalemate with an NBA club or negotiate for one with an NFL club—there wasn't anyone to certify you. There weren't any so-called 'contract advisors' then—what our formal title is now in the NFL—because there wasn't any governing body, any union, to say who was one and who wasn't and make rules so you could tell the difference.

"If there had been, there wasn't anyone then to enforce them. Punish you by forbidding clubs to deal with you if you broke them. If you did something you shouldn't've done, the only people who could get you for it were the cops or the bar association.

"Now it's all very complicated. The unions make you pay fees and go to seminars, jump through hoops and do the limbo, and if you get out of line in one sport your ass gets kicked in all the others. But then it was just 'You can pick up a phone—you're in business.'

"What Alec did for Rusty was simple enough. Auerbach'd been going to give him an extra grand anyway—he'd taken one of Rick Barry's elbows in the teeth, cost him a couple incisors—so what Alec had him do was make it five hundred and use the other half to rent single rooms for him on the road. That way everybody saved face in the newspapers—lots of times the most important thing—so everyone was happy.

"Thing of it is, in this world when you *publicly* succeed at doing something widely known that was actually fairly simple, what people notice and remember's that you did it, not how easy it was. All of a sudden this struggling young lawyer who could mediate between a pro athlete and his team became a very hot item. And that was another thing. Alex was thirty-four, not really that young anymore, but in this country how you look—he always did look young—and how long it's been since people first recognized your name, those're the things they look at to decide how old you are. Since Alec and what he'd done were more or less novelties back then, it stood to reason he must be young, and so he was.

"After that the business came to him. There were other lawyers and advisors doing the same thing of course—hell, the gladiators probably had some kind of agents to negotiate who got how much for going out with the net and the trident and how much for the guy with the short sword and shield—but Alex came in just as the people who owned the pro teams and the people who broadcast pro games were beginning to glimpse what they had the means to do, right in their hot little hands. *Before* the people who *played* the pro games figured out how to get some control over how they were run.

"The kind of opportunity he just stumbled into doesn't exist anymore. Nowadays a kid with pro potential doesn't have to go looking for someone to represent him. Before he's out of high school he knows who does that kind of work because *they*'ve come to *him,* pitched what they can do. There isn't any rule against it—except that you can't pay an amateur under the table or bribe anybody, the kid's family and friends, managers and coaches, to steer him to you. You're not supposed to lie about your competition, but there's no rule that says you have to tell the truth. Otherwise it's open season, strictly buyers' market.

"Alex could not seem to understand that, that business doesn't automatically come to you any more just because you've been in business the longest and your name's so well known. He knew the lyrics to the song and he would sing it to you, but basically he thought he'd become the Alex Drouhin all the players used to flock to *because he was Alex Drouhin—unique* in all the world.

"It was like John Fremont believing he found gold at

Sutter's Mill because he had talent, a gift. In his heart of hearts, Alex simply could not see the steady stream of new clients, a fair number of them All-Stars, that came to him twenty-five, twenty, even fifteen years ago, had arrived in his office because there really weren't that many other places they could go to.

"So he refused to come to terms with the fact that we now have to *recruit* the less-talented athletes who're now the backbone of the business. And he absolutely would *not* accept the fact that when most of your clients are making just over the minimum wage, when the best of them're getting maybe twice, two and a half times that, and there're very few in your stable in the headline-making brackets, then the ceiling on fees that the unions allow—four percent in the NFL—means you can't realistically expect your profits to remain at seven-and-a-half percent a year. Year. After year. After year."

"But according to Pete, he did it," Clay said.

Whitman, looking mournful, nodded.

"How?" Clay said.

Whitman shrugged. "Basically by ignoring the union regulations that establish the maximum fees. Prohibit you from circumventing them by packing, charging the client for services besides negotiating player contracts, endorsement and appearance agreements."

"Which you do," Clay said.

"Which we do," Whitman said. "But when you pointed that out to Alex, he said the six point five included legal advice and protection, tax advice, estate planning, investment counseling and brokerage services, medical protection—the whole ball of wax. And when you argued with him that the fee for those services to football clients *still* wasn't supposed to exceed four percent of the client's contract with the team—or reduce the baseball client's take below the annual minimum wage—*and* that by systematically charging two point five more than that, we were *clearly* in violation of association rules, he just said 'Oh pooh' and dismissed it.

"He wanted to charge Tornado Ryan two hundred and ninety thousand dollars, his sacred six point five, for reviewing the purchase-and-sale agreement and searching the title on a three-point-seven-million-dollar house 'Nado bought in Pacific Palisades. 'Nado won the Heisman Trophy, senior year Ohio State, unknown for a defensive player. OSU's where he got his nickname, worth about a million bucks. Some sportswriter said he got into backfields the same way a tornado gets into a trailer park, with about the same results. But he more'n measured up to it. Went to the Pro Bowl six times. Having him at linebacker was a major reason why the Raiders had one of the lowest points-scored-against averages in the NFL. The old rule again, 'Scoring gets the headlines—defense wins the games.' But off the field, 'Nado had a big weakness. He couldn't believe anyone he trusted'd ever try to con him, and consequently he could be conned.

" '*Alec*,' I said to him, 'you can't do this.'

" 'Why?' Alec said. 'He'll pay it.'

" 'Because it's unconscionable,' I said. Know some lawyer talk myself now, I've spent so much time around the bastards. 'If that wouldn't be conduct that shocks the conscience, I don't know what the hell would be. And what you just said—that if you charge it, he'll pay it—that's *why* it's unconscionable. Tornado's gullible enough so that if you tell him that's the going rate for that amount of work, he'll believe you and pay it.

" 'Even if you're lucky, the Players Association doesn't find out and discipline you, maybe suspend you, the bar association might get after you. Cheap opportunity for them to score some good PR points for a change—demonstrate there're some outrages even *lawyers* disapprove of. Fucking newspapers'll *crucify* us. And to *Tornado,* of all people. 'Nado thinks of you as practically his *father,* for Christ sake.' "

"So," Clay said, "did he do it?"

"No," Whitman said. " 'FD,' he said, like he was my mother, caught me stealing from her purse, 'you wouldn't turn me in, would you?' And because I figured that'd be the only way I'd get him to drop the whole idea, I lied and said, 'I don't know—I might.' "

"*Would* you have?" Clay said.

Whitman considered that. "I'm not sure," he said after a while. "I've thought about it now and then since— Tornado bought the house three, four years ago—*Would* I have reported him? Maybe when I told him that, I really didn't know. Maybe it wasn't a lie.'

"It's a complicated question in this business. When you know or have good reason to believe someone in your outfit's deliberately doing something that's against the rules— and doing it all the time—what the hell *do* you do? The union rules don't recognize partnerships or corporations as contract advisors. Only individuals. So if someone in your office were to get suspended, say, even decertified—as he would if it came out he owned an interest in a team—in theory it'd be like a player getting banned for life, for betting against his own club. *He'd* be history, but the team'd stay in business. And so if your colleague got disciplined it'd have no effect on you.

"But that's only in theory. In an operation like this, one man's name on the door, if he were to get suspended, decertified, it would inevitably have considerable effect. Probably, in the long term, catastrophic. I would've expected to be able to keep *my* clients with me if Alex'd ever gotten crossways with the authorities, and I'd think Dougie, McGinnis, Carl, and Lionel'd probably've been able to hold onto theirs. Whether we all would've stayed together under one umbrella, new name, or split up and go off on our own? Those'd've been other questions.

"But for Barry and Maurice, still turning a toehold into a foothold in the business, a development like that'd be disastrous. The people who know us senior people, they'd have a certain personal loyalty that'd probably keep them in the fold. But not enough people know Barry and Maurice, 've been their clients, to keep them going for long. And new clients, I think, would become few and far between. There'd be a taint. It'd make a rookie think, 'Well, why go to an agency where there's been a big, smelly scandal, when there're so many others that're clean?'

"Hey look, if a players' association'd scragged Alex, no way would it've been *good* for the rest of us. The only thing we could've done if that'd happened would've been damage control. 'Man the pumps. Shut up and bail.' "

Clay's voice was soft. "Would the long term effect on the agency've been worse, you think, than the long term of his death is likely to be?"

Whitman pulled at his left cheek with the thumb and forefinger of his left hand. He used his bottom front teeth to gnaw his upper lip against his top teeth. He scratched his nose with the nail of his left forefinger. He exhaled. "I don't know," he said. "I'll never know that, whether his dying'll be worse for us'n if he'd been caught and disgraced."

"You've thought about it, though, haven't you," Clay said, not asking.

Whitman gaped. He inhaled through his mouth. "Jesus Christ," he said, "once we heard today the man was dead, of course the first thing we thought about was what it'd do to the firm. That's the way survivors always think. But not *until* he was dead, not *before* we'd heard what'd happened down in Easton. Whether we'd be better off if he died instead of staying alive but getting in big trouble—we *never* thought about that until today."

18

"WHAT YOU SAID ABOUT it seeming like Drouhin was avoiding you in recent years," Clay said. "Not coming in on Sundays anymore, like he'd done before—that kind of thing. You must still've had concerns about the business, things you needed to talk over with someone else—someone who knew the trade, understood the firm's place in it. Like for example how you said that you and the other senior agents—what were their names again?"

"Dougie Morris," Whitman said. "Roger McGinnis. Carl Isabelle and Lionel Padgett. The juniors—or associates, as we call them—are Barry Regis and Maury, Maurice, Vincent."

"Where does Pete Martigneau fit into this?" Clay said. "He gave us the chart of the organization but we haven't had a chance to study it yet. How would you rank him in this?"

"On a par with McGinnis and Carl," Whitman said. "Look, almost from the very beginning, Alex's been busy. That's why he brought me in. And then as the years went by, workload got heavier and heavier, brought the other guys on board. But the understanding between me and Alec always was that if he wanted something done by any one of us, all he had to do was tell me. And I'd see that it got done.

"Alex *loved* the road. He *thrived* on it, glad-handing his way across the country. I've been convinced for a long time that he did much more of it than he needed to. I called him the Road Warrior one day at one of our monthly conferences—he was attending by speakerphone from his hotel room in Denver—and it stuck.

"Now all that hands-on stuff was good for the business, no doubt about it, but as he spent more and more time on planes and less and less time here, he lost sight of the larger picture. Dropping in between commitments romancing individual clients elsewhere doesn't give you the overall perspective you need to spot new trends. So he didn't have much choice but to cede daily authority to someone else. He had to have a foreman on the ground in here, to carry out his directions. Even if he hadn't actually given them, or realized that something needed to be done.

"That's what I became, his foreman. Either I'd personally take care of what he wanted done, or else I'd see to it that the guy who should be taking care of it was instructed to do it—and then that he got it done. I was the conduit between Alec and the other guys. That's why he called me his deputy, his right-hand man. That's why my office's next to his. The other guys he called 'my crack team of associates.'

"Until two or three years ago I was back and forth between this desk and his six or seven times a day. Several times a year he was out of town for fairly long periods of time. His annual safari to the West Coast, for example. Every year he'd spend two or three weeks doing a bunch of deals out there. Always in the winter. He bundled them, to justify two or three weeks in the sun—which of course he didn't really need to justify at all. During stretches like that, I'd spend as much time behind *his* desk as I did behind my own, working by phone with him on files that he was working on out in Palm Desert. And when he was on the ground here, as I say, we were back and forth through that door six, eight times a day. If I didn't have something I needed to discuss with him, he'd have something to talk over with me.

"Then one day I realized we weren't doing that much anymore. And it wasn't because I'd reached the point where I knew all the answers, or because he was on the road more. It was that when he *was* home, he was working out of Easton. I called him on it. He claimed to be surprised I'd taken it that way. Said all he was looking for was efficiency. Saving time. 'The traffic's a time-wasting bitch.' Since we worked so well together when he was away, why not do the same thing at short range, worked so well at long? Said *he* certainly hadn't meant to make any change in our working relationship. Hadn't noticed any, either. 'Maybe when they get the new commuter train running through here next year, I'll start coming in more again.' "

Whitman shrugged again. "I dunno," he said. "Alex loved secrets. This could've been one he was keeping from me. Something'd happened, I'd done something wrong, but he wasn't going to tell me—going to let me find out for myself. All I can tell you is my perception, and that was that things were different. Maybe as far as he was concerned, things were still the same."

"He still considered you first among equals," Clay said.

"Well, *yeah,*" Whitman said. "There was a big difference between my status vis-à-vis Alec and the status Lionel, Carl, and McGinnis had. There was a personal aspect in mine, and there never was in theirs. He and I went back much further. I was on a different footing. According to Alex, that hadn't changed."

"What was different?" Clay said.

"I was his first real hire, after Julie," Whitman said. "When I first signed with him, coming out of Michigan in seventy-one, he was running the show alone. Back then it was still small enough so he could do it. 'Me and Julie, two desks, four chairs, two phones, and a file cabinet. That's the entire operation.' It wasn't, exactly. Drew sat at Julie's desk and did the press releases by moonlight, evenings and weekends. When Alex was involved in a breaking story, Drew ignored the obvious conflict of interest and wrote Alec's statement for the press. Then he wrote *about* it for the *Record* as soon as he'd finished dictating it to the *Globe* and the *Herald*. 'What the hell, man's gotta eat, right?'

"Alex liked it that way. Power and prosperity were both new to him. He was very reluctant to share them. He covered it up well, but I always thought he was highly insecure. He thought if he let you use anything he might never get it back—you'd try to take it away from him, permanently.

"I think now that hesitation to relinquish any part of his control was a big reason why he took *me* on as an employee in seventy-six. Not that it was the *only* one, by any means—the Vikes looked good to go somewhere pretty soon, as we did in seventy-seven, Tarkenton fully aboard—and my name was getting known. Alec does like having the stars around. But that was only part of it. The only kind of person he could've brought himself to hire would have to've been someone in my kind of situation. Someone with another demanding commitment elsewhere who therefore couldn't possibly compete with him for top dog in the office.

"I fitted the bill. As long as I was still playing, the most I could devote to this business was five months a year. The NFL schedule was shorter and there weren't as many pre-season games, but there was still training camp, and the regular season lasted into the winter, which, in Minnesota, where I played and therefore had to live part of the year, is from Labor Day to the Fourth of July. I had to have some time off. Unlike Alec, I wanted a life outside my job, and I've always had one. Not only that, but after a season of pro football you've got some healing to do. So that left me about twenty weeks a year to spend on this.

"That suited him fine. As long as I was still playing, I had my own form of celebrity. I wouldn't be getting in his footlights as the ascending star in the sports-agent biz. I think that was the only way he ever could've brought himself to let anybody share *his* work, *his* glory, and *his* profits. And he really *needed* backup, in the spring, the first half of the summer—just like these days, those were his busiest months. I couldn't get involved in any negotiations involving pro football as long as I was with the Vikings. This was before owners had more than one team in one sport. But I could work on baseball and basketball contracts with him, and I did.

"I did that for eight years, 'til I retired in eighty-four. Learning the ropes of negotiating. First with the client. Neophytes're always surprised to discover they have to do that. That it's as least as tough to bargain with your client as it is to negotiate with management. But boy, is it essential. The college kids and minor leaguers come in here with stars in their eyes, heading for the *Big* Time. Goin' to the *Show.* And expecting you'll get them the moon. You have to bring their expectations *down,* get 'em so that they'll accept something you've got a shot at getting for them—in the real world. *Without* convincing them you're chicken. And brother, that work is *hard.* But if you don't make their expectations realistic, going in, they'll *never* be satisfied with any deal you can make. Alec didn't let me sit in on actual deals 'til after I'd learned that.

"Every August I left to get ready for the season. And

every February, I came back. *After* Glenda and I had some vacation—we had a little place in the Dominican Republic, pre-satellite days, nobody knew *nothin'* 'bout football. I really could kick back. So my introduction to the business was gradual, didn't make him feel threatened, paved the way for further expansion. Alec was very impatient with anyone who didn't seem to know exactly what he was doing at all times. But he resented it when he felt challenged. Seeing I could not only come in and work with him but buy a piece of the business, *without* trying to upstage him: that allowed him to relax and learn something, too—to delegate a little.

"I'm not saying that the first few years were always pleasant, every day a picnic. As a trainee—and younger'n he was—I may've posed no threat. But by definition I didn't know what I was doing. Therefore he could look down on me. Try to boss me around now and then, like he did Julie. Not that he was as hard on me. I wasn't a woman, and as a client I brought in enough to offset my apprentice agent's pay. 'Sotch a *deal*,' as he'd say when he was feeling anti-Semitic. Which was a good deal of the time."

"He was an anti-Semite?" Clay said.

Whitman sighed. "He was an anti-Semite in an occupation that attracts many Jews. Doing business with many clubs owned or run by Jews. He contributed heavily to the United Jewish Appeal and he collected dozens of awards from temples and synagogues. 'Goy of the Year plaques,' he called them, but I never heard a Jew speak of him in anything but the most cordial and respectful—even affectionate—terms. When we have the memorial service—as of course we will, though we don't know where or when yet—there'll be yarmulkes all over the place.

"Slightly over half of his clients were blacks. More than

fifteen percent Hispanics. 'Spics 'n Spades A.C.' He laughed when he said it, but he was a racist. A racist with three black men among his six lieutenants. A racist with a lifetime membership in the NAACP. A major contributor to the United Negro College Fund. He made the final decision on every hiring, firing, and compensation issue in the firm. He hired thirty-seven African-American or Hispanic men and women as highly paid employees. Those he didn't appoint directly to managerial positions had just as clean a shot at promotion into them as any white boy did. He was hiring minorities *long* before quotas, proactive commissions against discrimination.

"He had a reputation as a philanthropist and a *peerless* host, because he thought giving and spending money on the grand scale was good for business. He begrudged every dime he gave to charity and every dollar he spent entertaining the people who hired him, or whose goodwill might be useful to him. The only personal pleasure he took was from the fact that it was all deductible, ten cents or a dollar less the government'd get.

"The man who hated government and held politicians in contempt maxed out on donations to about a dozen political committees, every election cycle. Without regard to party. The only question was, Can he hurt me if I don't? Will he help me if I do? Meaning anything that might affect how much money pro sports made, and how much he got to keep. 'You can't *fight* city hall, but you can fuckin' well sure *rent* it.'

"He was a male chauvinist pig. He made it a policy to try to charm every woman he met. He sneered at every male homosexual he ever knew or suspected, behind their backs, of course. Until he became one himself. He called Ginny Alter a 'stupid dyke,' and the night he died he was truly depressed because she was going to sever her connection with us. He fawned over people whose vices disgusted him, and invited them into his home to practice their debauchery. With prostitutes that *he* procured.

"He publicly cultivated clergymen—*large* contributor to the Cardinal's Annual Appeal, Catholic Charities. In private he called them a bunch of swindlers fleecing old people out of their pensions, shielding middle-aged child molesters.

"Long ago we lost count of how many people he'd saved from destroying their lives with drugs, booze, or gambling, getting them into treatment, and if they couldn't afford it, paying for it himself. At least twenty. But he saw their illnesses as weaknesses of character, and despised them for it.

"He wasn't particularly well educated, despite those four years at Brown. He told me he spent most of his college days politicking. Class treasurer. Student senate. 'Wasn't much time left for learning.' He bought the books in his study in Easton in one lot. 'I don't know which ones I bought—enough to fill the shelves.' Only book I ever saw him reading was a paperback of *Valley of the Dolls,* on a plane to California. He was diddling the idea of representing authors. Nothing came of it. Someone asked him once if we represent movie stars, he said met enough crazy people in sports. 'No need to go hunting for more.' His idea of literature was *The Sporting News, Sports Illustrated,* our balance sheets, and the monthly statements from banks and brokerage houses.

"He believed sports'd become the American culture, and he made everybody else in here believe it with him. The Gospel according to Alec. Far as he was concerned, 'The Star-Spangled Banner' is the national anthem because it's played before the games start—not the other way around." Clay and Bateman laughed.

"Rimshot," Whitman said. "Only other music he knew'd

come out of the jukeboxes in the bars where he went drinking with his buddies in college. His wives made him take them to Europe and go to museums with them. They got him to take them to the theater and to concerts, and he hated every minute of it. But he made them pay. He was bored, and when Alex was bored, you knew it. But when there were no clients within earshot, for those he thought were ignorant, dumb, or lacked taste or were phonies, there was no limit to his scorn." He paused again.

" 'Phonies,' he'd say, in private. 'Big talkers, blowhards, and fakers.' Sneered at 'em: 'Jerks.' But you could make a pretty strong argument that he was the biggest phony of them all. You saw the vulgar display in the entrance foyer down at Easton, all those replicas of trophies?"

"Uh huh," Clay said, "very impressive."

"You probably took it to mean clients of his'd either won them themselves or been on teams that did, and that the Olympic emblem in the floor was here because his clients'd been in the Games," Whitman said.

"Not exactly," Clay said, "I took the collection—and the white cards reserving space for trophies missing from it—to mean that he wanted people to think he represented top athletes in every major sport."

"Well, you being a detective, and all," Whitman said amiably, "you had an advantage his gullible visitors usually didn't. Alec made sure everybody noticed he never bragged on his client roster. That way he hoped you'd deduce the boasting that he *could've* done, from the display. Mislead *yourself*.

"The fact was he never had a client who won even one Grand Slam championship in golf or tennis, or any realistic hope of signing a client like that. He never had one who was a member of a team that won the NBA championship or the Lombardi trophy.

"I could go on if you want, but the gist of it is that I

weight down my hand with this big millstone of a ring because Alex made me. He thought if prospects saw it they'd think the guy riding shotgun for him played for a Super Bowl winner. And that'd make them likelier to sign with us. I think he was probably right.

"But I never actually told anyone I was on a team that did that because when we played Raiders in the Rose Bowl the ninth of July of seventy-seven, they ate our lunches for us. Thirty-two–fourteen. If Alex hadn't asked me, said it'd be good for business, I never would've even *worn* the damned thing—flaunting *second* prize? 'Look at *me,* I'm a loser?'

"But he did it and he got away with it. Alex could be and do all those things because he had this razzle-dazzle, magical ability to make people believe lies he'd never had to utter, overlook remarks and behavior they would have found obnoxious in anybody else, and talk them into doing things they really didn't want to do. Knew were not their best interests. It was uncanny. Very often a client or a GM regretted an agreement from the instant he signed it. And then when it expired, Alex could talk him into signing a new one. It was extraordinary how he could manipulate people.

"Julie's a nice Quaker girl who's devoted to him. For all practical purposes she's dedicated her life to him. As far as I know she's never had a boyfriend. Or a girlfriend. Her family lives a half-day's comfortable drive from here, out in Westfield. She almost never sees them. But Julie isn't stupid. She'll tell you this man she's treated like a king for thirty years is one of the most unprincipled people she's ever met. 'Anyone who's trusted him completely's been a fool. Over the years I've seen hundreds do it, over and over again. I never understood why. And *I* hold the record for doing it the longest. But at least in my own case I understand why. He's a villain through and through, but life around him is *exciting*.' "

"And how about you?" Clay said. "Do you put yourself in that group?"

"Of course," Whitman said. "Probably partly for the same reason as Julie. And I put Lionel, Dougie, Carl, and McGinnis in the box with us. We're not fools. We came in without illusions. We knew we were in his power. 'Under his orb and scepter,' as McGinnis says. We'd agreed to be, Lionel and me fresh out of college, as clients. Dougie, too—he didn't last long, only two years with the Cubs at short before he blew out his shoulder, but that was enough to tattoo him as one of Alec's serfs. Carl and McGinnis, a couple of sharp young lawyers, same deal. Faust'd been around, he would've seen it as a better bargain'n he made the first time—signed up with us, too."

"Faust," Clay said.

"Sure," Whitman said. "That's how he did it, old Alex. He may've lacked principles, but he didn't lack brains. He could size people up, figure out what they wanted most in the world and what they'd give to get it. Then in exchange for a six point five percent piece, he'd promise to get it for them. He wasn't as unreasonable as the devil. He didn't say the price of having their wildest dreams come true would be their immortal souls. He couldn't, really: For the kind of people his clients were, their idea of immortality— fame, celebrity status—was a major part of the package he was promising.

"And the way he looked at it, he already had his own piece of immortality, his stature in the field, his place in the pantheon. All he wanted from anybody else was a share of the loot he'd get for them. And don't let me mislead you here, all the mean things I'm saying about the guy, he *would* get you the loot.

"Because his sense of what they coveted was usually right—these young men, these *kids*, weren't exactly original thinkers. They generally accepted his offer. And he generally delivered *most* of what they could've reasonably expected from him when they signed up.

"Same with the five senior agents. Since I started with him, playing and then agenting, I've gotten almost everything he promised, and so have Doug, McGinnis, Carl, and Lionel." He smiled. "And just like his clients, none of us're wholly satisfied."

"Human nature, I suppose?" Clay said.

"Oh, probably," Whitman said. "The inevitable comparisons we all make. What we've had to do to get what we've got, what someone else had to do to get what he's got. You look hard enough, long enough, you're going to find someone who paid less and got more. Skipped Sunday school sometimes and didn't do as he was told, but still got more toys'n you did. It's inevitable, especially in a business built on cutthroat competition—people in it're competitive.

"Roger Clemens'll get thirty-one-plus million if he finishes out his four-year contract pitching every fourth or fifth day. Meaning he'll make almost eight mill a year for working seven-ninths—nobody really expects a pitcher to go nine innings anymore, though now and then he does—of forty, forty-two Toronto games a season. He'll be on the field and working about thirty-two percent as much as starting position players work.

"Gary Sheffield'll get over twice as much, sixty-eight million, his seven-year hitch with the Florida Marlins, or somebody. Assuming no injuries, suspensions, he projects to play about three times as many innings a year. Outfielders don't work as *hard* as pitchers do, don't use up as many calories. But in the American League, pitchers don't have to face the anxiety of standing up four or five times a game, sixty feet, six inches away from beefy guys like Roger Clemens or the human slingshot, Randy Johnson, throwing hundred-mile-an-hour fastballs. Rub the guy the wrong way, he may throw the damned thing at your *head.*

"So, whose deal's better? Either one'll tell you it's the other guy. And that his own fucking agent should've done better for him.

"Have I got as sweet a deal here with Alec as Doggie Collins has, top gun for Ruggles Brothers? Doggie makes a lot more money'n I do, probably fifty percent more. But Doggie has to work about twice as hard and long as I do. The Ruggles twins're over seventy years old. Think they've got enough money. So therefore they're slowing down some. Don't like the road anymore.

"Alex showed no sign he was starting to think that way, but he was eight or nine years younger. My thinking therefore up to now was that I didn't have to think about it. Whether I'd want to change my lifestyle for more money, time on the road. I got a bellyful of that during my playing days. I *like* being the house nigger here—which is what Alec actually called me once during a late-nighter years ago in Toronto. 'Term of endearment.' He was all liquored up, so like always, I took it in stride.

"Anyway, until today I figured there'd be time enough to face those issues when Alec created them, told me he's winding it down, packing it in. I doubted he ever would. And I never envied Doggie his job."

"Okay," Clay said, "let's talk about that. Using Pete's numbers, we calculated Mister Drouhin drew...Gary, what was that figure a year?"

"Seven point eight million, last," Bateman said immediately. "One point three in salary, six point five in profits. More'n Roger Clemens. Not as much as Gary Sheffield."

"And he couldn't hit or pitch," Clay said. "That sound right to you, Mister Whitman?"

"Oh, Alec could *pitch,* all right," Whitman said. "He didn't need a glove or ball; the game he played didn't draw the big crowds; but he could pitch you like nobody's business. That's how he pulled down all that money. But yeah, eight mill sounds about right. The guy had his faults but he worked hard and he did bring it in."

"Meaning you and the other senior agents didn't?" Clay said. "Putting in Sundays in the office—I'd call that working hard."

"So would I," Whitman said. "But you have to keep in mind here: rest of us all have other people in our lives. Carl and Lionel, McGinnis and I, all got wives and children. Dougie's the only one single. Well, divorced, twice, but he didn't have any children, either one his wives. But even though he's a workaholic like the rest of us, puts in the hours here, he does have a hobby competing for his time. His second wife said she was going to charge adultery and name Alex Drouhin Associates as co-respondent. But Dougie had a number of other 'friends' she could've named. Just like his first wife could've named *her.* He doesn't spend all *his* time in the office.

"But workaholics or not, *none* of us put in the kind of hours Alex did. He took the founding proprietor's full share, but he took the risks and spent the years to make this thing the lovely little gold mine that it is, and when he had it up and running he kept investing more sweat equity, year after year. He didn't let up a bit."

"Mister Whitman," Clay said, furrowing his brow, "how much did you make here last year?"

"Well, you mean in straight salary or deferred?" Whitman said.

"Both, if you don't mind," Clay said. "Although of

course all three of us in this room know you actually *do* mind—but be realistic. We're going to find out anyway."

"Well, by the time I got through bleeding salary into taxes," Whitman said.

"Your gross income, please, Mister Whitman," Clay said. "Not your net after taxes."

"Eight hundred and seventy-five thousand in salary," Whitman said, looking morose. "By the time the accountants got through taking every deduction they could think of and justify, the state had me for almost forty-six thousand and the feds'd gotten me for over three hundred and four K. I pay almost seven thousand dollars a week in state and federal taxes."

"Chin up, Mister Whitman," Clay said. "Among the many services you get for your contribution is prompt and diligent police work to solve serious crimes, such as first-degree murder, and bring their evil perpetrators speedily to justice. Eight seventy-five in gross taxable income. How much did you squirrel away for your golden years?"

"My partnership share last year was just under one point three," Whitman said.

"That would be just under one million, three hundred *thousand* dollars?" Clay said.

"That's correct," Whitman said.

"Making a total of what, Gary?" Clay said.

"Two point one seven five million, Boss," Bateman said at once.

"Certainly a handsome enough wage," Clay said. "Do I take it you were the top paid, next to Alex?"

"I'm a minority partner," Whitman said.

"And your interest, again?" Clay said.

"Twenty percent," Whitman said, "a one-fifth interest."

"Anyone else have one of those?" Clay said.

"No," Whitman said. "The way I acquired mine, it

wasn't a profit-sharing thing. I bought it from Alex when I retired from the Vikes. Once I'd learned the business, I found I really liked it. I thought I probably had a lot more aptitude for it'n I did for any of the alternatives. Broadcasting, maybe coaching, where I'd have to start all over at the bottom, work myself back up through the ranks. And I had no appetite at all for the travel and the hours either one of them requires. So the only question then was, am I going to go out on my own, or team up with Alex?

"We'd talked about the possibility of my joining him full-time when I finished playing. 'When you're finally ready to admit you're washed up.' But nothing concrete. Never'd gotten down to the real brass tacks, talked about, much less agreed on what my responsibilities'd be. What kind of compensation I could expect. So I put it to him, same way he'd trained me to put it to general managers and player personnel directors.

" 'As you know,' I said, 'I've got some capital. I've got confidence enough in my own abilities and the education that I got in college, grad school, and here, so I think if I start my own shop I can make a go of it.'

"He knew I wasn't joking. See, my father's a doctor. He likes *watching* football fine. Watching *me* play football beyond high school, that he wasn't keen on. He'd seen too many former athletes with bad wheels from old knee injuries. Bad backs from compressing their spines, crashing into other big guys. Getting buried under a couple tons of other men and their equipment. Slow nerve reactions, too many blows to the head. He had the money to send me to school.

"But the position I played, defensive back, you don't get piled on very often. If somebody gets hurt when a DB and a wide receiver collide, it's usually the guy who wants to catch the pass. Worst injuries I ever had were sprains and hamstrings I pulled on cold days at Green Bay and Buffalo. And I really did love to play.

"My dad realized that, but there was another thing. I had to get an education. The only way he'd let me play college football was if I also maintained at least a three-oh—that's a B—average while I was doing it.

"I respected my dad—and myself, just like I want my kids to respect me and their mother—because that's the only way that they'll respect themselves. I *studied* in college, graduated three-three, B-plus. 'Phi Beta fucking Kappa,' my teammates called it. When I finished my M.B.A. my thesis advisor told me I should go on for a doctorate in economics. I told him I was flattered but what I really wanted to do was make a lot of money, and I thought I knew a field where I could do that.

" 'So that's what I'm up against,' I told Alex. 'Do we join up and work together or do I fly the *coop?* Now you've got me all trained.' I knew he wouldn't feature me competing with him, using all his tricks, and I thought he had a valid claim. But I also thought I had a legitimate call on a piece of the action. More than just the off-season pay envelope I'd been getting. So the way we worked it out, we each did a separate audit of the business, on the understanding if his book value was lower than mine, that would determine my buy-in price. But if my estimate was higher than his, that would be the benchmark. Or else one of us would veto the deal and there'd be no buy-in.

"A guy named William Vickrey got the Nobel Prize in economics partly for dreaming up that bargaining system. Talk about an evil genius. The seller wants to get as much as he possibly can. But if he gives in to his normal temptation, to exaggerate its value, he's almost sure to find himself selling for less than he'd like to get, because the buyer's honest count will be higher.

"The reason the buyer's evaluation may well be an honest count, and higher, is because if the buyer gives in to *his* natural impulse, to understate book value, *his* appraisal will get thrown out and he'll have to pay the seller's higher price.

"Worked like a charm. We came in fourteen thousand dollars apart. Then we trashed the model and split the difference. He figured the shop was worth three million twenty thousand. My figure was three million ninety. I paid him six hundred and eleven thousand dollars, about a third of what was in my management account, and became a one-fifth owner."

"How much you figure that share's worth today?" Clay said.

"It's hard to put a value on a business like this," Whitman said. "So much of it's in intangibles, and depends on the individuals who're running it."

"Give it your best shot," Clay said.

"At the close of business Friday night," Whitman said. "I suppose a fair price for the agency would've been how much net profit you could've reasonably expected it to make in the next four years. That's about as far ahead as we feel able to predict anything in sports. Friday night that would have been around fifty-two million dollars, assuming Alex and I'd wanted to sell and could've found someone with that kind of money who wanted to buy it. Since I like what I do and can't imagine ever doing anything else, much less doing nothing, I wouldn't've wanted to sell, but my piece was probably worth around ten point four.

"Today, with Alex dead, it's certainly worth less. How much less I really don't know. Probably best that I don't. Might make me feel even worse'n I already do. Fortunately I don't have a pressing need for the money right now, and by the time this thing shakes out, we see where we're all headed, it may be worth ten mill again. Who knows? I still won't want to sell, can't imagine circumstances that'd make me change my mind.

"But they could come about, I know. My foresight's no better'n Alec's was. Last night when he dropped me off at my car in Concord, he certainly didn't imagine he'd be dead this morning. He was expecting an unpleasant discussion with Ginny Alter in Easton. Then to drive too fast up here and resume talking about Jean Claude Methodiste with Joe Corwin this afternoon. Smart Alec was a know-it-all, but he didn't know all of it. Maybe I don't, either."

"The other senior associates," Clay said. "Ballpark their earnings for us."

"Very little difference between one and the rest," Whitman said. "Six hundred, six-fifty K salary, buck and a quarter, buck and a half, maybe buck-seven-five deposited to consultant annuities kicking in when they reach sixty-five."

"A buck in this instance being a hundred thousand dollars," Clay said.

"Right," Whitman said.

"Juniors," Clay said.

"Barry and Maurice made about two hundred thousand a year," Whitman said. "In addition they both had pension plans that Alex funded for them, twenty-two-five a year. And they got a share of annual profits. This past year it came to about a third of base pay, little over seventy grand." He chuckled.

"Funny?" Clay said. "Seventy grand?"

"Hell no," Whitman said. "I just was thinking, Alex could be *such* a stinker. Barry used his bonus as the down payment on a three-bedroom condo in Cotuit. Front looks out on a golf course. Back deck's got a very nice view of Nantucket Sound. One of those gray-and-white counterfeit whaling villages, grow like weeds down there. He and Christine *love* golf. Barry's family never had the kind of money, meant you had a *beach house,* belonged to a *country club*. The kid was really pleased. He was *gushing,* thanking Alex for his great job.

" 'Jesus Christ,' Alex says, 'I know the guy who built that place. He's always after me, get our clients down there, tell the press how great his course is. Sat next to him one night at a Boston Boys'n Girls Club Banquet. He was drunker'n a *rat*. He's pathetic. He'd give his left ball to get a couple Bruins down there. Even *retired* Bruins. "I'm not *asking* them to come for the doughnut—I'll *pay* them to come. All's I ask's they pose for pictures I can use for the brochures. We got lots of money, pay them. What I paid to build that joint, what I sell those units for? There's more suckers inna world I ever dreamed of. *Lining* up to buy, prackly *trippin'* over 'em. I could buy *Paris,* if I wanted, knew what the fuck to do with it." '

"Barry was devastated."

"I know the type," Clay said sympathetically, "a real bastard. I hadda work with a guy like that once. Andrew. Andy was a real prick. Couldn't *stand* to see somebody else enjoying himself, taking a little pleasure in the fact he's alive and happy, maybe accomplished something made him feel pretty good about himself. Always hadda piss on it, spoil it. Retired now, down in Florida. He'll probably live forever, too, raining on parades. One of the women in the office, kind of a plain Jane, came in one Monday all excited, just can't wait to announce her boyfriend she'd been dating five or six years—she's no youngster—had finally asked her to marry him. Naturally she'd said yes. Andrew laughed at her. '*You?*' he says. '*You're* getting married? Tomorrow pigs'll fly.'

"The bastard that concerns us this afternoon, though, is

your bastard, who we now know for sure *isn't* going to live forever. He couldn't make it to Tuesday even though he had all that money, which now interests me a lot. Leaving aside what all his real estate and cars and so forth were worth—I'm sure it's a hell of a lot—what we have here in front of us, figuratively speaking, is a corpse who was worth eighty percent of fifty-two million while he was still up and about, somewhere in the very exclusive neighborhood of forty-two or forty-three million dollars."

"Assuming he could've liquidated it," Whitman said.

"Right you are," Clay said. "Assuming he could've sold it. But if he could've he didn't. So my question now becomes: Who gets it? Did he have a will, do you know?"

"Yes," Whitman said, "I was one of the three people who witnessed it. Didn't have it done in-house. He didn't want the hired help having any more information about him 'n they needed to do their jobs. Had it drawn up by Lorenzo Gabriella, guy he knew at Brown. Big-time, high-priced lawyer with a velvet voice and lovely manners at Rhine, Bachelder, and Arbors in a pretty tall building downtown. Alec asked me to join him 'for tea.' I thought he was joking, but I played along and sure enough, when we got there at four fifteen one afternoon, damned if they didn't serve us tea. Tiny little sandwiches, too. *Very* elegant.

"Alec looked it over—it was in a blue backer—and announced it was his last will and testament, 'sure to disappoint many on that sad distant day after *I've* been carried out, when Lorenzo carries out my wishes. Then those who pretended grief will really feel it.' Then he laughed, and signed it, and I signed and two secretaries in the Rhine office signed. Then Alec said, 'You understand, of course, FD, that no one witnessing a will's allowed to benefit under it. So you get *your* bad news today.'

"Actually the will named me a coexecutor with Lorenzo,

and I already knew that," Whitman said. "I said, 'Alex, the pleasure of your company's the greatest gift any one of us's could ever ask for.' "

"Beautiful," Clay said.

"You had to dust him off a little every so often or he'd dig in at the plate, take more liberties with you'n any self-respecting person should allow," Whitman said. "I learned that from Julie, early. He came in one morning in a fouler mood than usual. His car wouldn't start, battery was dead, and getting a mechanic out to his place in Wellesley to install a new one—he was still married to Bev then—'took a goddamned fucking hour.'

"Julie had an awful cold that day. She was miserable. Only reason she was in was because Alec and I'd been on a roll, going around the clock, closing one deal after another. She had a mountain of dictation to get out. That's another rule I'd learned from Alec: Never tell the client what the deal is on the phone. He'll want so much to believe you got him everything he wanted, which a wizard couldn't do, that that's what he will hear. Not what you are saying. And then when he doesn't *get* what his terms would've called for, and becomes dissatisfied, he's liable to sue you for the difference. For misleading him. Don't help him do it. Put it in writing every time. Make two copies for yourself. Enclose one of them and a return envelope with the original and mail it certified, return receipt. Make him countersign the copy and send it back to you. Keep it in a safe place, so that if he ever gets frisky on you, you'll have it to slap him down.

"Anyway, Julie didn't have enough sympathy to spare that day for Alec and his car trouble, so he snapped at her. 'What the *hell*'s the matter with you?'

" 'I've got a cold,' she said, and coughed. 'I feel like pure hell.'

" 'You look like it, too,' he said. 'You shouldn't be in here, giving it to us.'

" 'I hope not,' she said. 'I certainly don't want to give it to FD.'

" 'Or me,' he said.

" 'I didn't say that,' she said, and he pouted the rest of the day."

Clay and Bateman laughed. "Those Quakers don't play offense, but they play defense very well," Whitman said.

"Did he let you read the will?" Clay said.

"No," Whitman said, "but Gabriella gave him a copy to lock in his safe deposit box at the bank across the Square—Gabriella kept the original—and, of course, I have a key to that. So the next time I had something to put in or take out of the box, I took the opportunity to read it."

"And?" Clay said.

"I can't say I was pleased," Whitman said.

"Because he'd been telling the truth when he said you weren't going to get anything when he died?" Clay said.

"No," Whitman said. "He'd already taken care of me, outside the will. When he turned sixty he had a deed of trust made up. It transferred a quarter of his share—another twenty percent—of beneficial ownership in the agency to me. When he either died or became incapacitated. He called it his Twenty-fifth Amendment."

"Giving you forty percent of the company," Clay said.

"Right," Whitman said. "Making me the biggest, but not the *controlling,* shareholder. In the will he left the other sixty percent to a separate trust. Lorenzo's the trustee. The will directs him to have the business appraised immediately and sell Alec's share for sixty percent of the appraised value. Lorenzo's to use a third of the proceeds to buy a lifetime annuity for each of his daughters, the balance to be paid to their children—not their husbands—when they die. Another third's to be invested for Ronnie's benefit, any money left when he dies to go to anybody he wants. Last third's earmarked for Brown and various charities that I know Alec didn't give a real shit about, but'll look good in the paper." Whitman considered that. "I think he expected to hear his own eulogy, read his own obits. And enjoy both of them."

"Using your estimate," Clay said, "Friday afternoon each one of those shares would've brought about ten million dollars. Assuming the agency recovers financially after today's developments, each of the daughters'll have half a million a year coming in for life and their kids'll split ten million. Ronnie'll have about a million a year, and Brown and the charities'll divvy up about a million bucks a year. Forever and ever, amen."

"Right," Whitman said, "and that's what boggled my mind. The *ego* of the man. I was well aware he thought highly of himself, but this was incredible. He always trumpeted himself as indispensable, which you could tolerate as long's he brought the business in, but the will was proof he didn't think anything'd ever change that. No matter what happened to him, even death. The will assumed that when he died, the business'd be worth the same as it had been the instant *before* he died, when he would've told you himself he was the heart and soul of it. Mister Whole-Show believed the show would go on as before, *after* he stopped being in it. He assumed he'd survive his own death."

"You thought this'd create a problem for you," Clay said.

"Oh, you'd better believe it," Whitman said. "A problem I've now *got*. Assume his disappearance reduced the value of the firm by twenty-five percent. I have no idea what it'll turn out actually to be, especially since now we know his exit turned out to be a homicide, but use that as a marker.

Say today the joint's worth thirty-nine million. Sixty percent of that's twenty-three-nine. I haven't got it."

Bateman said: "Excuse me." Clay nodded. "Didn't the firm have key-man insurance on him?" Bateman said. "So that if he died suddenly, the policy'd pay enough to allow the firm to buy out his share and keep on going as before? Most outfits this size do."

Whitman looked gloomy. "For years we carried a twelve-million-dollar term-insurance policy on Alex, for that very purpose. Firm wasn't worth as much then. But the coverage was very expensive—premium was thirty or forty thousand dollars a year. And of course as Alex got older and the odds against him living through another year went up, the rate kept going up. So I dunno, six or eight years ago we decided it was just too much money. So we gave it up.

"Result is now I either figure out a way to raise almost twenty-four million, buy out the shares now in the trust, or somebody else does. And then does it. Once someone does—a big sports organization, shoemaker, Walt Disney—what I am is toast. Out on the street. The other four senior guys'd be fine—no new owner could run the joint without them. But I'm too closely identified with Alec. No new owner'd want me around."

"Yeah," Clay said, "you're in a very tight spot."

"You're telling me," Whitman said.

19

"*CUI BONO?*" CLAY SAID in his office late the next morning, the arch of his right foot jammed against the edge of
his desk. "Who benefits from this?"

"I don't think that helps us this time," Bateman said.
"The formula doesn't work on this one."

"Because too many people benefit," Clay said.

"Hell, *every*body," Bateman said. "I don't see anyone
close to him who isn't better off—most of them a *lot* better
off—as a result of him being dead. Happier, too."

"A lesson there for us all," Clay said. "Don't make it so
the people you annoy'd not only be more comfortable but
richer, too, you were to head west. They may figure it out,
take steps to ease matters along. This was murder for
profit. The natural crime-of-passion suspects—ex-wives,
and in his case, boyfriends—just don't pop to the surface,
way they normally do. The answering service tells us the
butch tennis player called in around seven A.M. with joyous
word Rhonda's rectal thermometer said she's ovulating, so
they're off to her date with the baster. Manhattan's wizard
baby doctor confirms. Therefore, scratch Ginny Alter's
meeting with Alex yesterday morning in Easton, and her
from any possible mention on the suspect list."

"The goalie's wife called the East Hampton cops Sunday

night from a motel and told them Jean Claude was bustin' up the house. She suspected when he finished with the saucers and the teacups, she was next," Bateman said. "The cops went there, found a couple windows broken, crockery all over the floor. No crime to destroy your own house, and he *is* a famous fella, so they took him to a pricey private hospital for 'exhaustion.' "

"Wears on a man," Clay said, "breaking windows and dishes. Makes the house a bit drafty, too. But still, if it draws the cops and they make a report, it isn't a bad alibi.

"Whitman wants us to think Drouhin's departure's dire news for him. Hasn't got twenty-four million to buy out the trust that Drouhin left most of the business. But Martigneau thinks the operation'll probably be worth just about as much next week as it was before Alex got shot in the head.

"Whitman said four years is the furthest you can project in the agency business. Probably based on the fact four years is generally the ceiling Drouhin put on player contracts."

"Meaning," Bateman said, "that for the next four years Whitman and everybody else who had a share of profits—and therefore knew what Alec's chunk was—had solid reason to believe *existing* contracts'd net the firm thirteen million bucks a year."

"Of which Alex would grab half," Clay said. He frowned and thought for a while.

"So I was definitely wrong," he said at last. "The shooter's motive couldn't have been money. Everybody who had money to gain if he died benefited if he died sooner more than later. If everybody's got the motive, that was not the motive."

"Six point five mill a year, over four years," Bateman said.

"Is twenty-*five* million dollars," Clay said. "*Now.* But

before he was dead, there was no assurance it'll be worth that a year from close of business last Friday. If Alec's still somewhat peculiar, late-in-life romance made the *National Enquirer* and caused a mass defection from the client roster, it wouldn't be. *But,* if someone took him out *before* that, if he bit the dust *before* any dirt got shoveled in public—"

"—the chances are a year from now, it probably will be," Bateman said.

"Any bank'll loan you face amount against guaranteed receivables at the going rate," Clay said. "John Roscommon taught me that years ago. And even without a down payment, and FD certainly could've made a big one, that'd be enough to buy control *now.* Which control Alec would *not*'ve sold, at least now, if he'd been rude enough to stay alive. But the way he set it up meant if he died, someone else'd get a deal. The motive was *timing.*"

"There's your *cui bono,*" Bateman said.

Clay snorted. "The beneficiaries all have good alibis. Clay went home for a late turkey dinner. Martigneau was flying back from New York. The other associates'll be bulletproof too. Same reason why Whitman didn't see any traffic on route Two on Sunday night: Everyone was home." He snorted. "I'll bet you the proverbial ham sandwich if we go up to Andover and question Whitman's next-door neighbors, they'll tell us they know *exactly* when he got home Sunday night: well after midnight. And he didn't go out again. And they will know this either because his car's got a loud muffler or he walked his barking dog past their house at one A.M.—woke them up so they looked out the window, and know it was him.

"I was wrong. I assumed something. *Damn.* Pete didn't call us 'cause he used to be State Police—he called us because he couldn't call the locals. He'd been in New York most of the night—had no *legit* way of knowing where Alec'd gone. Or that he'd gotten quite dead there. The guy had three residences in three different towns in Massachusetts. Plus another one in the Bahamas. He could've been in any one of them. Therefore Pete *couldn't* let the cops start asking themselves how he knew exactly where Drouhin was. Or how he could know that without also knowing he was dead. Exactly what they would've asked—what he *would've* made them do—if he'd called PD Easton.

"Yes," Clay said, "So it's clear enough who *had* Drouhin killed. It was at *least* Whitman and Martigneau. Likely the other four senior agents had a hand in it too, least as co-conspirators. The question's who they got to *do* it—actually pull the trigger."

"And the timing of it," Bateman said. "Why the shooter did it *now*. Where'd the urgency come from?"

"Well, for them there wasn't any *immediate* need," Clay said. "Just that nagging possibility that some balmy night Alec and Ronnie might show up at Symphony dressed up as Lucy Ricardo and Ethel Mertz. But that wasn't very likely, Pete and FD—plus whoever else was in on this little project with them—knew that. But the killer didn't. The killer believed disaster was imminent, and there was only one way to fend it off. 'Right now, tonight. He's getting ready to do something that'll *ruin everything*. So I have to stop him tonight.' "

"And that means the actual killer wasn't someone in the firm," Bateman said. "Because everyone in the firm who had something to gain if Drouhin died—"

"—would be an obvious suspect," Clay said.

"But also knew there wasn't any hurry," Bateman said. "So this was sort of elective surgery. The people who decided Alec had to go also decided things'd be better if he went now."

"So they convinced the shooter it was urgent," Clay said.

"Myrna's report says it was two forty-one-caliber shots to the head that fetched him. That is one, *big*, gun. No brass found on the floor makes me think it's a revolver. How 'bout a Dan Wesson six-shooter? The four-incher weighs three pounds. Novice'd want to use both hands to fire it. The powder burns and residue on the front edge of the desk indicate at least the first slug came out of the gun while the muzzle was resting on the edge."

"Someone who wasn't used to shooting guns and wanted to steady it," Bateman said.

"Someone who'd gotten the weapon, loaded, from someone who knew how to shoot, and had ready access to weapons. Someone who had some reason to believe that the sooner Alex Drouhin died, the better off everyone'd be."

"The Catanias woke up and answered the phone when Drouhin got home and checked in," Bateman said.

"But they didn't wake up and answer it when Ginny Alter called at seven yesterday morning, and they didn't answer it again when Julie called later on to tell Alec Tampa Bay was on the line. That's what led her to call Pete. Who then called us. So, two things: Why didn't the Catanias answer the phone again after Alex called them when he got home? And why didn't Julie call them on their line when she got no answer on his?" Clay said.

"Julie and the Catanias'll both say it was because his orders were they weren't supposed to answer his calls or go into his house while he was there. Until he called and said it was okay," Bateman said.

"In case he and Ronnie were having fun with salad oil on the kitchen floor or something," Clay said. "But the real reason was that the Catanias at least, and maybe Julie too, knew he was dead. And thought it might be better for everyone involved if the cops found the body, not them."

"They didn't answer his phone because they knew he was dead?" Bateman said.

"That'd be my guess," Clay said.

"Then the gun's in the pond," Bateman said.

"Maybe," Clay said. "Maybe it's in the underbrush along the road. But what I want to know even more'n where the gun is, is who put her up to this? Who actually convinced her not only that she had to do the dirty deed, but that she had no choice. My first nomination is Pete."

" 'Her'?" Bateman said.

"Angela," Clay said.

"Pete I can buy," Bateman said. "He'd be their go-to guy. After all, he's the one in the office with experience in murder. Up 'til now, far's we know, from the other side, but still, he ought to know the ropes. How to do someone in properly. But her?"

"*Her*," Clay said. "Angela's the one who pulled the trigger. Rigo doesn't have the balls to shoot a man in the face while he's looking at you, defenseless. She does."

Bateman shook his head. "I dunno," he said.

"I do," Clay said. "You get a feel for these things. Peter told her something. Convinced her she had no choice. At this point I don't know what it was, but if we play it right, she'll tell us."

"So what do we do now?" Bateman said.

"Come at it from the side," Clay said. "We find a way to *bother* everybody. Nose around the gate, I think. Make them think we buy the theory they've presented to us on a silver platter. Someone came to the house after Alex got home. He let them in and showed 'em into the study. They argued. The visitor or visitors'd come prepared for this. They shot him. Overturned a chair in their haste to get out, and that's why the gate's so important."

"You think?" Bateman said.

"Rigo said the gate was open when Julie called to tell them Pete'd called us—after Alex didn't answer the phone," Clay said.

"Making it look like the killer was in a hurry to get out, and forgot to close it," Bateman said.

"Right," Clay said. "The tape of the gate taken Sunday night and early Monday morning shows the gate opening and closing behind Alex, then opening again later on. But nothing comes or goes through it, and it doesn't close again, making it appear that Alex opened it to admit the killer-slash-killers well before they arrived, and then shut the tape off, to keep their identity secret, and no one turned the camera back on or closed the gate again after they left. To conceal the fact that the killer'd already been *in,* and'd *stayed* in," Clay said. "They opened the gate to confuse the dumb cops."

"Are the Catanias smart enough to think of that?" Bateman said.

"*She* might be," Clay said, "but Pete and FD most likely saved her the trouble. The whole thing was scripted for her, her and Rigo. My guess is FD, Dougie, Carl, McGinnis, and Lionel began to hatch this months ago. 'We've just gotta face it. He's not gonna *leave*. That's all there is to it. And if he stays, sooner or later, somethin's gonna blow up, and no one'll be able to fix it. We gotta get rid of him 'fore it happens.'

"Start with the fact that we know they were willing to do whatever they thought was necessary to keep the agency going. Some time ago they changed its orientation, *against what they knew to be Alex's wishes, without* his consent. They overrode him and went down-market to get volume. FD's explanation says it all. 'We had to, so we did.'

"Of course they would do that. That's what Alex'd taught 'em, his secret formula. Skirt NCAA rules about signing college players. Mislead recruits into thinking the fee for negotiating contracts covers all the other services, the high-priced financial pampering Alex and his boys're going to foist off on them when the big money starts rolling in. 'Whenever anyone asks you anything, lie automatically, 'til you're absolutely sure the truth might help you more. Bribe the police. Do whatever it takes.'

"Pete and FD both told us everyone in the place who knew about Ronnie was 'scared *shitless*' the word'd get out. FD at least was *very* concerned that one of the unions'd sanction Alex for his shenanigans, charging fees in excess of the rules. The Haggerty lawsuit we found on the desk showed he had good reason to be. If the unions'd been overlooking Alex's violations in the past, they weren't going to be able to much longer. And if FD was concerned, we can be sure Pete and the other four top guys're singing a worried song too."

"These were not the kind of people who left things to chance," Bateman said. "Remember how careful FD was to say yesterday that of course there'd be a memorial service, but they didn't know yet when or where it'd be?"

Clay grinned. "Because that's the only thing they hadn't planned," he said. "In fact they'd planned very carefully *not* to plan it, so nobody'd stumble on the reservations, start to wonder how the hell they'd had such foresight."

Bateman was delighted. He laughed and slapped his right hand on his desk. "*Damn*," he said, "this's fun."

"Uh huh," Clay said, "another good lad goes astray. This's not something you recover from, you know."

"Fine by me," Bateman said. "What do we do to prove what we know?"

"Introduce an element they didn't allow for," Clay said. "Create a commotion. Surprise was the advantage they had while they were planning to kill Alec. Nobody else knew what they were up to. Though hindsight says Alex probably should've. He'd already let the boys get away with mutiny on the issue of second- and third-level players. He also knew how they felt about him playing kissy-poo with Ronnie. And he knew they were very worried about the possibility of league sanctions.

"And plain common sense should've told him, no matter what they said, that they had to resent his taking half the profits. Should've occurred to him—as we now know it did to them—that if *he* went away, all the problems would, too. But it didn't, so they were free to scheme away. Thinking they could anticipate every move we'd make after the body was discovered.

"So far we've cooperated. Let 'em sit back and read lines to us they rehearsed a hundred times. Now let's upset the applecart. Today we go over the reports, the lab stuff. See what ballistics can give us. And make some arrangements, our own. To go down there tomorrow bright and early with about eighteen guys and all the goddamned heavy equipment we can possibly muster. Thrash around in the bushes; splash around inna pond. Create the biggest damned uproar we can. Sow the wind with the seeds of confusion. See if anyone gets rattled, reaping the whirlwind. Having to ad-lib for a change."

"Sounds good to me," Bateman said.

Clay picked up the phone and dialed the number for the Easton Police Department. "Chief Bertinelli," he said. "Frank Clay."

Bateman's face showed he was puzzled. Clay shook his head. "*Chick,*" he said, "glad I caught you. Listen, I think we're close to solving that little matter at the house on One-twenty-three." He paused. "Well, I am, too," he said, "but we both know these things're usually as much a matter of luck as they are insight." He paused again and chuckled.

"*Right,*" he said. "That's the way I've always felt, too. Take it any way I can get it. Look, what we're planning here is...well, we're thinking we'd like to fly the DA up to the property tomorrow in the State Police chopper. Have him tour the scene, then announce the arrests."

He paused again. "*Right,* that was *exactly* our thinking. *He's* the one who runs for office. We don't. But what I wanted to ask you was whether you could find it possible to go down there to Fall River in the morning and meet with him. Then fly with him in the chopper back up to the property, take part in the press conference, huh? I know he'd appreciate it—close ties with local law enforcement, really important with him." He listened.

"*Good,*" he said, "I'm glad to hear it. Never been in one of those things myself, either. Don't know's I'm all that eager to, either. But I'm glad you're game." He listened again. "Right, I'll coordinate it all from here. You'll be hearing from his office." He hung up.

"Didn't realize you and the chief were such pals," Bateman said.

"We weren't," Clay said. "But now we are, for life. And Chick'll be far, far away from us, come tomorrow morning when we want the stage, ourselves."

20

"WELL, YOU HAVE TO understand, Angela," Clay said, raising his voice so that Angela Catania three feet away at the front of the driveway of the house in Easton could hear him. "This's a *crime* scene. Your house, sure, to search that we'd either need a warrant or else arrest you in or near it and toss 'em spit subject to that. But I doubt what we're lookin' for's in there, so I don't think we'll needah do that."

He had a small black plug in his left ear; a black wire led around behind it and down his neck then down between the collar of his yellow shirt and the collar of his jacket. There was little wind and the pale sunlight seemed almost springlike, but Clay was taking no chances: This time he wore the trench coat, and a blue wool scally cap. She wore a green nylon windbreaker over a hooded gray sweatshirt and dark blue sweatpants.

There were seven two-tone blue State Police Chevrolet Caprice sedans, each with two antennas mounted on the roof and another centered on the trunk, parked along the southerly side of route 123. There were three more in the drive behind Clay's black Corvette. Angela's maroon Buick Regal sedan was pulled off the road beside Clay's car. The cruisers' V-8 engines idled blue smoke through the low-restriction dual exhausts, making the rumble that required Clay to speak loudly. The headlights and taillights and the red, white, and blue strobe lights on the roofs of the cruisers flashed continuously. The two-way radios gabbled static and garbled voices through the open windows at volume too high for comprehension of what was being said.

Troopers wearing high-cuffed gray work gloves, dark blue coveralls, and baseball caps used machetes and small, rackety gasoline-powered chainsaws to hack through the vines between the roadside and the chain-link razor-wire fence at the front of the property, yanking handfuls of severed tangled stalks out of the frozen ground and throwing them back over their shoulders.

A white Econoline van towing a fifteen-foot gray rigid inflatable boat approached from the east on route 123. There was a bar of blue and white strobe lights flashing on the roof. Blue mirror-image lettering on the front read STATE POLICE.

Clay led Angela by the elbow off the drive. He beckoned the van, waving it through and directing it down the drive. There was a large white, blue, and gold Massachusetts state seal painted on the side; under it was the legend: MASSACHUSETTS STATE POLICE DIVING. The man leaning out the window of the door on the passenger side had short black hair combed forward and a merry expression. "Alla way back," Clay shouted. "Down behind the house. You get there, turn right and follow the drive downah hill. Corporal Bateman's waiting. Show you where you oughta look." The man in the van gave thumbs up.

"Who're *they?*" she shouted, as the van proceeded down the drive. "Whadda they *want?*"

"Divers," Clay said. He turned away from her and

started east along the road, shouting to the men and women in the underbrush. "Any sign of anything?" In the near distance the concussive whupping-roaring sound of an approaching helicopter came from the south.

"Divers for *what?*" she shouted, following him, pain in her voice. When the blue and white State Police helicopter appeared over the tree line to the east, swinging south over the helipad at the rear of the property, she was startled, somehow unprepared for its arrival by the clatter of its approach. She swallowed and choked it out again. "Divers for *what?*"

He stopped, dropping his arms, turned and took two paces back, so that he was less than a foot and a half away from her. "Look," he said, pointing up at the helicopter. "That's the DA coming in now, get a firsthand look at the scene. We *know,* all right? They gave you up. They weren't here when you and Rigo did it, and they didn't dare to call you afterwards, so they don't know where you dumped the gun. But we're pretty sure you either threw it into the bushes or the pond. And when we find it, as we will, in one place or the other, we'll raise your prints off it, and that'll be the ball game."

"*My* prints? My fingerprints?" she said, stepping back. "I never touched no gun."

"Yes you did," Clay said calmly. "And when we recover that cannon, we'll raise your prints and prove it."

She stood still and stared at him. "You can't do that," she said. "After it's been in the water."

Clay nodded. "That's what we thought," he said, slumping and taking her by the left elbow. "Yes, we can."

She caught her breath. "Oh," she said.

"Yes," Clay said. "What exactly did Pete Martigneau tell you?"

"He called us Sunday night," she said.

"Monday morning?" Clay said.

"Monday morning," she said, nodding. "It was real late. After we went to bed. But before Mister Drouhin came in. Before Mister Drouhin called us."

"Monday morning," Clay said. "Why'd you pick up?"

"He called on our line," she said, dejected. "It doesn't have a bell like an ordinary phone. It's got a chime. Except for Mister Drouhin and Julie he's the only one who had the number. And our kids. They also have it."

"What'd he tell you?" Clay said, leading her toward his Corvette.

"He told me he'd found out Mister Drouhin'd decided to do what he'd talked about doing before. Which was to have some lawyer do something so we'd lose the house. He built for *us*. And the land it's on. He was going to get *rid* of us. Throw us out." She inhaled deeply, groaning and shaking her head.

He opened the passenger door and shifted his grip on her right arm to assist her. "Easier to get into these things if you sit down first on the seat and then swing your feet and legs in."

She did as she was told. As he shut the door she ran her left hand on the top of the dashboard and said, "I never been in one of these before, with two seats. All the ones that Mister Drouhin's always had, all these years we worked for him, I never sat in one before. I could've any time I wanted. Just go down the basement. Out in the garage. Wonder why I didn't."

Clay walked around the rear of the car to the driver's side, folding back the left lapel of his blazer to expose a black lavalier mike. "All units, all units," he said, "this's Clay. I'm bringing Mrs. Catania down to the main residence now, into the kitchen. I want Corporal Bateman to meet us at the rear of the house and join me while she

gives a statement. Divers: She says the gun's in the pond.
Suspend all operations at the front of the property. Troopers Ernst and Gagnon, take Mister Catania into custody
now. Cuff him and advise him of his rights. Put him in a
cruiser for the time being. Tell him he'll see his wife when
she's finished giving her statement."

He was silent as he started the Corvette, backed it
out onto the drive, and drove it across the plateau to the
knoll overlooking the slope to the big house. There was
another cruiser at the porte cochere, lights and engine off.
Behind the house the pond shone gray-blue in the sunlight
and the bare trees behind it were black against the vacant
sky.

She cleared her throat loudly, slightly startling him. "I've
often thought," she said, "so many times I've made this
drive, coming home from someplace where I'd gone by myself, without Rigo for a day, to be alone and think, and
pray, and seek to know God's will. How good He was to
us, to have given us so much. And yet we still lament and
cry out, for that which we do not have."

"Uh huh," Clay said.

"The children of Mammon," she said thoughtfully, "are
wiser in the ways of this world than are the children of the
Light. And thereof they pile up riches."

"So I've always heard," Clay said, taking the Corvette
down the slope toward the house.

"Therefore we are counseled, as the children of the Light,
in prudence to make friends for ourselves with the children
of wickedness, so that when we fail they may receive us
into everlasting dwellings. Luke, sixteen: nine." She hesitated, frowning.

"I do not understand this teaching. We have done that,
whilst we lived with Mister Drouhin, and among his
wicked friends, in their dwelling places. But these dwellings

are not everlasting. Nor was he. He was mortal. What the meaning of it is, I do not understand."

"No," Clay said, pulling up behind the house at the door next to the garage stalls in the basement. There was another cruiser parked there and a rail-thin male uniformed trooper about forty standing next to it.

The white van with the gray boat on the trailer behind it was parked down on the beach by the pond. Next to the sliding door open on the right side of the van, the man who had looked merry stood hooded in a black wet suit, a diving mask perched on his forehead, next to another man identically attired. Both of them were hunching their shoulders while troopers in blue coveralls put yellow tanks against their spines and made the red and yellow straps reachable for the divers to buckle against their torsos. Nicholson with two cameras on straps around his neck looked on. Bateman, back-to in a plain blue raincoat, his attaché case in his left hand, was speaking to the divers, gesturing with his right hand. They were nodding to him. He nodded back. Then Nicholson registered the Corvette and called Bateman's attention to it. Bateman turned and looked up toward the house. He waved his right hand to Clay, said something more to the divers, and began to trot up the slope.

"You are a man of this world, sir," she said, "and wise in its ways. Do you understand the teaching?"

"Can't say as I do," Clay said, shutting off the engine and opening his door. The thin trooper came to the Corvette and opened the passenger door. "Ma'am," he said, offering his left hand.

"Thank you," Angela said, grabbing it and pulling herself. "I told the lieutenant I was never in a car like this before. Even though I could've many times, in one of Mister Drouhin's. Any time I wanted. Maybe it was a good thing. If I'd ever done it while I was alone, or if Rigo'd been drinking, I might still be in it." She laughed, as she might have laughed to agree over supper that there indeed had been too much rain.

The trooper shut the car door behind her as Clay opened the rear door of the house. He followed her up the stairs into the hallway under the main staircase and from there into the kitchen. He heard Bateman hurrying up the cellar stairs after them, then shutting the door. She went placidly into the kitchen ahead of him, removing her windbreaker and folding it neatly before placing it over the chair where she had sat two mornings before. She pulled down the hood of the sweatshirt, then went around the table and took the chair where her husband had sat that day. She clasped her hands on the table and looked with placid expectancy at Clay, like a large and much older parochial schoolgirl confidently waiting to be tested on a subject she knew well.

Bateman put his attaché case on the table, removed his raincoat and folded it over the back of the chair to his left. He had a black plug in his left ear and a wire leading down inside the collar of his blue shirt. He had a lavalier mike clipped to his left lapel. He sat down and opened the case, taking out a new yellow pad and the minicassette recorder. He sat down in the same chair he had occupied two days before.

Clay removed his trench coat and folded it over Bateman's. He reached inside his blazer with his right hand and shut off his two-way radio. He took the earplug out and let it dangle from its cord over his shoulder. He went around the table and sat down in the same chair he had had that day. Bateman reached into his left inside jacket pocket and turned off his radio. He looked inquiringly at Clay. Clay nodded. Bateman turned on the tape recorder.

"For the record," Clay said, "this is an interview with

the same Mrs. Angela Catania with whom we conducted an interview recorded at this same table in this house two days ago relative to our investigation of the homicide of Mister Alexander Drouhin, the late owner. Present in addition to Mrs. Catania are Corporal Gary Bateman and myself, Detective Lieutenant Inspector Francis Clay. At the interview two days ago Mrs. Catania consented to the use of the recorder for the statement she and her husband, Arigo, then gave. I now ask her once again if she consents to its use at this time."

"No objection," she said, proud to have remembered the formula.

"At that time," Clay said, "I advised Mister and Mrs. Catania of their rights under the Constitution of the United States and they both said they understood those rights. So that there may be no misunderstanding, I now repeat that advice of rights. Mrs. Catania, you have an absolute right to remain silent. Do you understand this?"

"Yes," she said.

"If you say anything," Clay said, feeling the familiar chill he always felt when he recited the rights for real; it was as distinct as if someone had placed a cold hand on the back of his neck. He quivered. "If you say *anything,* it will be taken down and may be used as evidence against you in a trial in a court of law. Do you understand this?"

"Yes," she said.

"If you decide to waive your right to remain silent and answer any questions," Clay said, "you remain free to reassert your right to silence at any time, and refuse to answer any further questions. Do you understand this?"

"Yes," she said.

"You have a right to an attorney," he said. "Do you understand this?"

"Yes," she said.

"If you can't afford an attorney," Clay said, "the court will appoint one to represent you, without any charge to you. Do you understand this?"

"Yes," she said, nodding, smiling a little.

"Understanding all those rights," Clay said, "do you now agree to answer such questions as we may put to you? Understanding that you have a right to stop at any time?"

"Yes," she said.

"The form, Gary," Clay said.

Bateman removed an envelope from the bellows file set into the inside of the cover of the case and removed a sheaf of printed forms. He peeled off the top one and handed it to Clay. "Thanks," Clay said, spinning it around on the table to orient the document for Mrs. Catania. He pushed it across the surface in front of her, at the same time removing a ballpoint pen from his jacket and handing it to her. "This is a form stating the rights I have just recited to you. It includes a printed waiver of those rights. If you are still willing to answer our questions, please sign your name in the two places marked with an X. The first one acknowledges that you have been advised and understand your rights. The one near the bottom is your agreement to waive them."

She nodded once, firmly. "Okay," she said, and wrote her name twice, neatly, on the form. She put the pen down on top of it and pushed it back across the table to him.

"Thank you," Clay said. "Now Corporal Bateman and I will sign as witnesses." He signed and slid the form to Bateman. Bateman signed and returned the form to the attaché case.

"Very well," Clay said. "Did you shoot your employer, Alexander Drouhin, in the study of this house the night before last?"

"Yes," she said calmly.

"Was anyone with you besides Mister Drouhin when you shot him?" Clay said.

"My husband," she said. "My husband, Rigo. He didn't want to come with me when I said . . . when I said we had to. Do it. But I made him take off his pajamas and put all his clothes on, like I was doing, and we would go to see him."

"Him being Mister Drouhin," Clay said.

"Yes," she said.

"You were at your house when you had this conversation," Clay said.

"Yes," she said.

"What time would this have been?" Clay said.

"It was just past one in the morning," she said. "I know because I looked at the clock after I looked out the front window and saw the lights were still on in this house. So I knew he was still up. And I told Rigo, 'Hurry up. We got to do this tonight.' "

"After you were dressed, what did you do next?" Clay said.

"We come across the lawn and then the driveway," she said, "and we let ourself in by the back door downstairs that we just come in now, and Rigo went in the basement part and got the gun." She paused.

"I didn't know where it was. When Mister Martigneau brought it down to give it to us, I didn't even want to look at it. I said, 'No. Uh-*uh*. Don't want to see it. Not gonna take that thing.' Because, see, then I didn't really think that what he said was gonna happen, what Mister Drouhin would do to us, that he would ever do it. 'We been with him a long time. He depends on us.'

"But Mister Martigneau said that wasn't right. 'You're wrong. You're wrong,' he said, 'and you'll find out.' That yes he would too, do it. 'He said when the railroad comes through down here this land is going to be worth a lot of money, he's going to sell it right out from under you. And then where will you be? At your age and all.'

"That's what scared Rigo. He said to Mister Martigneau to give him the thing and he'd take care of it. 'I know a safe place for it where he'll never look, and if he does well, I'll just say someone must've left it there, in case they needed it.' "

She paused again and studied her knuckles, gnawing at her lower lip. She shook her head. "I know he was scared and all, but he never thought the time would come when we would ever have to use it. And then the other morning when Mister Martigneau called up, he still really didn't want to, but I said Mister Martigneau'd told me on the phone that once the lawyers started getting rid of us, that then if something happened to him, happened to Mister Drouhin, we'd be the natural suspects. 'Everyone'll think you did it. But if you do it now, then no one will ever know. They'll think it was somebody else.' And how to make it look as though someone'd come in and done it to him and then left."

"Mister Martigneau told you all this on the phone the morning before last?" Clay said.

"Yes," she said. "He told me it four times. I kept saying No and No, and he kept saying Yes, and telling me all over that we hadda do it *now*. The operator come on once and he had to put more money in, he talked to me so long, you know? The voice that comes on come on and said to put in some more money if you want to talk some more, and he put the money in and just kept pounding it on me. 'Mister Drouhin told his partner, Mister Whitman, told FD this very night that he'd decided, he was gonna do it, drive you off the property. Begin getting rid of you. Get you off the land.'

"I remember I was thinking 'Why's he in a pay phone when he's got one in his pocket?' We seen it every time he came here. Always had it with him. Always had to use it at least once while he was here. Someone didn't call him on it, he'd call someone else. Said he always had to be in touch. But I didn't ask him that."

"It was because he didn't want anyone to be able to find out he called you last night by tracing phone records," Clay said. "Well, making it a lot harder, at least. We would've had to back-check ever pay phone at Logan and JFK airports to find the one that he used, and then find a witness who could put him in it or near it at the appropriate time."

"Oh," she said.

"And so you came over here and let yourselves in," Clay said.

"And Rigo went and got the gun," she said. "He said he had it in the drawer underneath the middle one of the three TV banks in the security station. And his hands're shaking when he brought it out and I seen I had to be the one to do it. If it turned out we had to do it. So I took it away from him and put it inside my waist, these jogging pants I've got on now, and then we come up the stairs and when we come into the hall I yoo-hooed Mister Drouhin. But I knew he was in his study because that's where he always went when he was up late by himself here. And we went in there, and that was where he was. Sitting at his desk and reading something."

"Was he surprised to see you?" Clay said.

"I'll say," she said, looking grim. He said, 'My goodness, Angela, *way* past your bedtime. Isn't this pretty late for you?'

"And I said, 'Well, Mister Drouhin, that's what we come to find out. If it's pretty late for us. Do you mind if we sit down.' And he said no, he didn't mind, and so then we sat down. And Rigo was shaking. And I said...well, I just asked him if he was going to get rid of us. Take our house away from us and drive us off the place. And he said, 'My god, where would you get that idea?' Which was a way he had of dealing with you when you wanted to know something and he didn't want to tell you. Seen him do it many times.

"So I say to him, 'Mister Drouhin, please, you know? You got to be straight with us. We been with you a long time and we've always done, you know, our very best for you. Not saying that we're perfect, but we've kept the place up and things like you wanted done. And you always liked my cooking. And you've said so many times. But now, you know, we hear some things and they make us afraid. That you're talking to a lawyer, hiring him to get us out. And you have to tell us now, is that the truth or not?'

"And he lied to us," she said. Tears came to her eyes and she blinked them back. " 'No such thing,' he says to us. 'Give you my solemn word. I'd never want you out of here. Depend on you too much. Where you could ever get such an idea, it's a mystery to me.'

"And I said to him that was a lie. And he *denied* it. 'No,' he says, 'as God's my judge, that is completely true.'

"And then Rigo says, 'You lying *bastard*.' And he gets up on his feet and he was shaking like a leaf. And I am now afraid he'll have a *heart* attack. And then I won't have no husband, along with no place to live. And Mister Drouhin says to him, pleasant as could be, 'You call me that, you piece of shit? Maybe what your wife just said isn't such a bad idea.' And he smiled, that smile that you could always tell, when he's just got the better of someone. Pleased with himself, you know? He was *enjoying* it.

"And that's when I seen it was all true, what Mister Martigneau'd told us, and I got the gun out and I hadda use both hands like this," she held her hands out, the right clasped over the left, "and two fingers on the trigger, but I got it to go off."

"How many times did you shoot him?" Clay said.

She was unable to blink the tears back any longer. "Rigo said it was two," she said. She dabbed her cheeks with her fingertips and sniffled.

"And then you ran?" he said gently.

She nodded. "Uh huh," she said miserably. "I think I tipped over the chair. I couldn't look at him. I couldn't stay in that room. I couldn't wait to get out of there. I dropped the gun and just *ran,* as fast as I could, through the house and in the hall, and everything looked *just the same.*" Her voice was filled with wonder. "You know? Exactly the same. Like nothing'd really *changed,* and if I went back in there to his study, he'd still be sitting there and reading something, just like it did when we came in. And it'll never be, again."

"So your husband disposed of the gun?" Clay said.

She nodded. "I stopped once, at the doorway to the back, and I just stood there. And then I opened it and ran down the stairs and ran out in the yard and just stood there. It was cold, and moonlit. And then I hear Rigo come out behind me and I turn around and I could see he had the gun. It's in his right hand, and he shuts the door with his other hand and he walks down the lawn, like it was the most normal thing in the world, and when he gets to the pond he just throws that thing away out in the middle and I hear it splash. And then he comes back up the hill, and puts his arm around me. And then we went back up to our house. And that was how it was."

"You got all that, Gary?" Clay said. Bateman nodded.

"Okay," Clay said. "Now, Mrs. Catania, we're going to have some troopers come in and formally arrest you for the murder of Alexander Drouhin, and take you into custody. I mean it when I say we're sorry that we have to do this. Which I very seldom say to someone I'm arresting for murder—in fact, I never have before. But I mean it in this case because I think you were set up. And I'll make sure the DA knows my view on this."

"Thank you," she said. "I wouldn't have, you know?"

"No, I don't think you would've," Clay said. He reached across the table and patted her hand.

"Now Gary," he said, "call Trooper Gagnon and have her come in and go through the formalities with Mrs. Catania, and tell the DA he and the chief can call the press soon's we get the warrants and then give the word from Boston. Then get your coat on and tell Al Nicholson to round up a dozen other guys with six bluebirds and meet us at two hundred Clarendon. ASAP. Ten to arrest FD and the four senior associates, two to take custody from us of—"

Bateman grinned. "*Nooo,*" he said.

"On the contrary, *yes,*" Clay said. "I encourage the notion I have superior powers, but to ask me to forgo the pleasure of arresting personally that blowhard Martigneau would be a far greater sacrifice than I'm prepared to make, this side of the grass."

"MY GOD, *COPS* COPS AGAIN?" Martigneau said jovially, rising as Alice Medalie admitted Clay and Bateman. "What is it, Police Day or something? Already today we've had calls from a Boston cop who didn't bust Alec Sunday night for running a red light at sixty or so, wants box seats Opening Day, and a Lieutenant Pike out in Haymarket, wants the house box at Fenway for Patriots' Day. What game do you guys want to see?"

"Hey, we're through just watching you guys go through your paces." Clay said. "We came to invite you to our game, and we know it's gonna be good. You're under arrest: Murder One."